Wild Sapphire

Book Three in the Dream Traveller Series

T J Gristwood

Copyright © 2016 T J Gristwood

All rights reserved, including the right to reproduce this book, or portions thereof in any form. No part of this text may be reproduced, transmitted, downloaded, decompiled, reverse engineered, or stored, in any form or introduced into any information storage and retrieval system, in any form or by any means, whether electronic or mechanical without the express written permission of the author.

This is a work of fiction. Names and characters are the product of the author's imagination and any resemblance to actual persons, living or dead, is entirely coincidental.

The views expressed in this work are solely those of the author and do not necessarily reflect the views of the publisher, and the publisher hereby disclaims any responsibility for them.

ISBN: 978-1-326-82205-7

PublishNation
www.publishnation.co.uk

Dedication

This book is dedicated to my mum, Brenda, and my sister, Kaylor. You have both always encouraged me to follow my dreams. I thank you both from the bottom of my heart.

As always I would also like to thank all the amazing DJ's and musicians who have helped me write these books. Deep, Dark & Progressive I salute you!

Also by this author

Sleeping Sapphire

Waking Sapphire

Prologue

Mother Earth was dreaming. Her energy thrummed gently, deep within the core of her womb, and she sighed softly as she sent waves of beautiful, healing energy up and out towards the surface of her body. She could sense a change coming soon and it made her smile, a happy smile that she had not experienced for a very long time.

She had been sleeping for eons, and it had been a sleep filled with visions both wonderful and terrifying. Her body had been growing and evolving for thousands of years but had, sadly, been raped and pillaged of her magic and life essence over time ... But now the wheel was turning, and she sensed a new presence again ... a presence that could awaken the magic once more, and open the eyes of her children.

She waited patiently in her sleep, waited for the awakening to begin. She knew that it was all happening just as it should, just as the universe had planned it to ... in its own time, when her children would be ready to embrace her again and see her for who she truly was. The cause of this change was here again, walking on her with magic feet, which seemed to flit back and forth through the dimensions.

She remembered a time when the same magic had ignited her once before, and her children had remembered all that she was. She was happy that the time was once again upon them, that this special child she could remember from long, long ago walked once again on her tired body ... and could help her to awaken, so that she may flourish and become alive with magic like she had before.

It had been such a very long time, and Mother Earth had grown tired of waiting. She sighed, and felt her energy ripple in anticipation. Not long now. Not long to wait.

Chapter One

Sapphire stood perfectly still in the garden at Foxglove. All around her was quiet. There was not a sound or movement to distract her. With her eyes closed she pushed out with her senses. Her mind was travelling so that she may find her husband. She reached out into the woods and beyond but could not sense him, nor feel him nearby. He had left her angry, and without a word of goodbye.

On opening her eyes again, she shook her head slowly. Words could not describe just how pissed off she was with him right now. Fox, the man she loved and cherished with all her heart, was now on her shit list. It had been hours since he had stormed out of the cottage and left her standing with Charlie and Nathan – who right now, were on their way back to the hospital to check on Pearl.

Her magic glowed around her, pulsing with her anger. The sprites had settled back inside the cottage. Even they were afraid of her mood right now. This had been the first time Fox had left her without explanation, and she was bereft with sadness and anger at his foolishness. He had told her that he would remain by her side to protect her as her guardian, and that they would face whatever was thrown at them together. So much for that promise.

As she headed back inside the cottage she suddenly felt dead tired. Every bone in her body ached and her head thumped as if a drum was positioned at the back of her skull, promising to break through any second. She rubbed her forehead and went to the kitchen and did the only thing she could right now ... put the kettle on. She needed to think clearly and try to work out what to do next. With no one to turn to and no way of knowing where Fox was right now she had to rely on her own intuition and judgement as to which way to turn.

The one thing that she could not quite understand was that all sense of her connection with Fox seemed to have been severed, and she could no longer feel him. This, above all things, worried her the most. After everything they had been through together he seemed to have just vanished, disappeared off the radar, gone completely

AWOL ... and for the first time in a very long time Sapphire felt completely empty, lost without him. All that had come to pass was like a strange and unrealistic dream that she had wandered through. Nothing seemed real to her any more. None of it. The magic, the love she had experienced, the passion and lust ... it all seemed to have disappeared and to have been replaced by a void of nothing. If this is what it felt like to have your heart broken it sucked. Big time.

On autopilot Sapphire finished making herself a cup of tea – one of Pearl's strange herbal concoctions – and settled into the armchair by the fire in the tiny sitting room. She could sense the sprites in the corner, and could see the tiny flickers of their light in her peripheral vision as they hovered nearby. While sipping the tea she leant back slowly, feeling as if she had aged ten years in the last few hours.

She sighed heavily. How had it come to this? The seeds were still safely tucked inside her pocket within the magical pouch. They pulsed softly against her own magic, and gave her a sense of belonging for a moment. Even they seemed unreal now. Had all this been for nothing? The tea calmed her mind, and slowly she began to let go of her anger and her feeling of helplessness. After setting the teacup down beside her she leant back into the chair and closed her eyes again. She had never felt so tired in all her life.

"Fox, please come back to me. Please ... I cannot do this without you. Wherever you are ... please hear me and come back." She spoke the words softly, and a single tear slipped across her cheek as she did. Her head slowly fell to one side as Sapphire once more succumbed to a deep sleep. Her breathing was slow and soft as she began to fall once more into the world of dream travel, as only she – Sapphire Whittaker, dream traveller, and magical thirty-something – could do. Her life once more was completely and utterly turned upside down.

Sapphire was dreaming again. This time a sense of urgency pushed her through to the other world that she had become so familiar with over the last year, since she had learnt how to travel using this unique gift she possessed. Her mind watched from afar as she moved across time and space. Her body was relaxed and safe on the wings of magic as she raced to her destination. All the feelings that she had been holding just moments ago vanished with a calm acceptance that she was travelling to somewhere important.

Her body jolted slightly as her feet touched the ground. It was dark. The night air was cool and the sky clear, and scattered with stars that shone brightly above her. As she looked around she felt a sense of familiarity. Had she been here before, perhaps? On moving forward, she felt her long cloak brush softly against her legs, which sent shivers of anticipation up her calves into her limbs in a smooth, gentle caress. Around her everything was still. As she walked across the soft grass beneath her bare feet there was no sound, except the exhalation of her own breath, to establish exactly where she was.

Her eyes began to adjust to the dim light that surrounded her. She was on a hill that spanned out before her and gave her a view of a forest ahead that hung dark and silent in the distance. At the very top of the hill she could see a huge tree that stood charcoal-black against the skyline. It pulsed a soft, glowing green against the stark background. The life force of the tree seemed to recognise her, and she moved forward towards it with an eagerness that pulled in her stomach and urged her forward.

On reaching the tree she looked up in wonder at the greatness of its branches and the tiny lights that flittered between its branches and leaves. A pulsing within her chest pushed her to its trunk and she placed her hand against the cool bark, closing her eyes again as she connected with its energy. A bolt of light shot up from its roots and travelled down her arm into her body, making her sigh with a sense of relief at the pureness of its touch. She felt as if she had come home again. The power that coursed through her veins sang and tingled in excitement as it began to fill her with a new sense of purpose. Her mind filled with visions of happier times, moments that had filled her life so far with happiness and joy.

She could see Fox standing before her, his eyes dark with lust and love and his hair tied back, which gave the perfect frame to his beautiful features. A slight smile curved at the edge of his lips. God, he was glorious in every way. The image faltered, and was replaced by an animal that sat by her feet. It looked up at her with the same amber and black eyes that she knew so well to be her husband's. They glittered at her with an unearthly glow as the animal uncurled itself and stood before her. It was a fox, its coat a beautiful dark red that glistened like the golden leaves of an autumn day.

Sapphire, not understanding this vision before her, tipped her head to one side. The fox stretched lazily and then sat on its haunches, looking up at her with expectant eyes. Its tongue slipped out from between razor-sharp teeth and licked the fur around its muzzle. Sapphire bent down. Her eyes now narrowed and there was a frown on her face.

While sitting perfectly still the fox stared back up at her. Now its ears were flicking as if listening for danger. Its tongue licked again and she noticed that the fur was darker around its muzzle ... a darker red. Blood ... there was blood on its face. A gasp escaped her lips and she stepped back, feeling dizzy now. The vision before her made her feel frightened for a moment.

The fox stood up fully and yelped at her, a distinct cry that put the hairs up on the back of her neck. It shook its coat and then turned around. Its head moved slowly to take one last look in her direction before it took off at a run so fast it left sparks in its trail. Sapphire shook her head because she did not understand. Its eyes were so familiar ...the way they regarded her bore into her soul. It was as if she knew this creature. A fox ... her fox ... As her mind exploded at the idea of what this animal actually represented she moved and shifted once more. Her body shot off into space and took her breath away as it did.

Sapphire gasped for air as she landed again, this time in a place she knew well. She was in the castle on Shaka, in the powerful magician Conloach's room. A fire crackled in the corner of the room and the smell of incense filled her nostrils. Conloach was at his great table with his back to her and his head down as he pondered over various scrolls that were placed before him. Sapphire moved towards him hesitantly, not knowing if this was a vision or whether she was actually there. Conloach turned to face her just as she reached his side. His eyes grew wide and his expression changed to one of surprise.

"Sapphire, what are you doing here?" Sapphire felt giddy. Her body trembled slightly. She was so pleased to see him, a friendly face in the middle of the madness of her dream.

"Conloach, I had no idea I had travelled back to Shaka ... I need your help. Fox has gone ... I cannot find him." Her legs suddenly felt very weak and, without warning, she felt herself sag and begin to fall. Conloach caught her in a swift motion that was so quick she felt time had slipped for a second. One minute she was standing next to him, the next she was seated in his lap on the chair with her head against his chest. She could feel his heartbeat, steady and comforting, beneath her head, and his energy wrapping around her in a warm embrace.

"My child, do not fret. All is well. I will take care of you." Sapphire felt the tears that had come earlier threaten to reappear. It felt so good to be wrapped in his arms. She was so confused and empty inside without her man that this embrace felt like the next best thing. Conloach smoothed her hair from her face and, soothing her, whispered softly into her ear.

"I sensed a shift back on Earth but had no idea what had occurred ... Tell me what has happened, child." Sapphire closed her eyes and breathed in the familiar scent of patchouli and sandalwood that seemed to belong only to Fox and his father. It calmed her mind and soothed her soul.

"Fox was angry, Conloach. He left without a word and I'm afraid for him. I can't feel him anymore. Our connection has gone. Hecta has bound me to him, as you know, and I have no idea what to do. Pearl is trapped within his spell and I'm helpless to save her. Everything is a mess again. It's so unfair ... I just want to be free from all this." Conloach shifted slightly but still held her tightly. His energy hummed against her body, filling her with a sense of calm.

"Fox told me of the binding spell. I have been trying to find a way of breaking it, but Hecta has used very old magic. It is hard to undo, but I am sure I will find something soon to help you. As for Fox's disappearance ... he can only sever his connection with you if he shifts into his animal form, which is something he only does under extreme circumstances. I am assuming he is trying to track the gatekeeper.

"But do not worry, Sapphire. My son is strong and resilient. He will find a way to break the spell, of that I am sure." Sapphire lifted her head and stared up into the same eyes she had often looked into in the face of her beautiful husband.

"What do you mean by 'his animal form'?" Conloach sighed softly.

"Some of us have the ability to shift into the spirit of the animal we are connected to at birth. Fox has this ability, and his animal has all the means to track and find its prey. That is why you cannot feel him at the moment … he has become the fox that his name suggests."

Sapphire blinked at him. Her mind was swirling with the thought that her husband was a shape-shifter. The fox she had just seen must have been the man she loved. But the blood on its mouth told another story. Had he already found Hecta and harmed him? What if he was still pursuing him and could not turn back into the man she knew? She groaned and buried her head into the warmth of her father-in-law. This was all too much.

Conloach stroked the back of her head slowly.

"Sapphire, please do not worry. Fox is a strong warrior and, as clever as his animal spirit is, he will find a way and come back to you soon. Trust this, and trust your path. This has happened for a reason, as all things do that come to pass. I will connect with your witch and send her some help with healing until the spell can be broken. I suggest you go back to Earth and wait for him there. He will not find you here on Shaka if the last place he saw you was on your home planet."

Sapphire did not want to leave the safety of his arms, but knew he spoke the truth. Fox would expect her to be back on Earth, and waiting at Foxglove for him. The anger she had felt towards him had slowly diminished, and she knew that he had her best interests at heart. He loved her so much that he would risk his own life to set her free from Hecta's grip. Now her heart felt nothing but love, and a desperate need to hold him in her arms again. She wanted her husband back, safe and unharmed.

After pushing herself up slowly she stood once more. The connection she had with Conloach was still pulsing within her veins and filling her with new energy. He regarded her calmly and smiled.

"I am here whenever you need me, Sapphire, and I am always watching. Go home now, and I will reach out for Pearl to keep her safe within the spell she is bound to." Sapphire nodded slowly, and bent forward to place a chaste kiss on Conloach's cheek.

"Thank you, Conloach." Her body shook with emotion, and her mind flashed with sparks of light as she wavered and shifted once more. Without time to steady herself she was gone again, leaving Shaka and racing through the wormhole back to Earth.

Sapphire sat bolt upright in the chair she had been sitting on and gasped loudly as she landed back in Foxglove. Daylight filtered through the window, and she looked around her for any signs of life. She held her hand to her chest as she caught her breath. All was still and calm. Only the sprites remained in the cottage. They appeared before her and chattered excitedly at her return.

She leant back into the chair and sighed deeply. Conloach had reassured her that all would be well, but as she lifted her arm and gazed at the bracelet still clamped to her wrist she felt that this outcome was just a dream. Her husband was now wandering the land as a fox, and her friend was still unconscious in hospital. She had to do something or she would go crazy. After pushing herself up slowly she took a slow walk up the stairs towards the bathroom. Right now all she wanted to do was wallow in the tub, and that was exactly what she would do.

All the other mind-blowing stuff could wait.

Chapter Two

While holding two cups of coffee Nathan pushed the door to Pearl's room open with his hip and walked across to the bed, where Charlie remained seated beside the old lady. They had arrived back at the hospital and found Pearl in a new room, hooked up again to various drips and machines after the chaos of Fox and Sapphire's departure had died down. Police and hospital officials had taken a statement from Charlie, who had done a good job at bending the truth. They seemed to believe her story that some of the electrical equipment had blown for no apparent reason, and that Fox and Sapphire had played no part in shattering the windows.

Nathan had watched the police inspector look unconvincingly at Charlie as she had sniffed miserably through her tears of shock and upset to tell the story they had decided to spin. He knew they were unimpressed with her version of what had happened, and would no doubt be looking for a more logical reason for the devastation that had occurred in the room.

But for now everything had returned to some semblance of normal, and Pearl's condition had not changed. Charlie looked up at him with concern in her eyes.

"Any change?" he asked her softly as he handed her the coffee that had been heaped with sugar, just the way she liked it.

"None. She looks awful, Nat ... I wish we could do something – anything – to help, but after everything that has happened I have the feeling that this is way beyond us." Nathan pulled a chair across to sit beside her, and took a sip of his own coffee. He grimaced slightly at the bitterness of the cheap coffee.

"My head is still spinning, Charlie. I can't take this all in. Sapphire and Fox ... who would have thought any of this could be real? I mean ... Shit, man, what a headfuck." Charlie sighed and sipped her drink. Her face reflected Nathan's as she tasted the cheap caffeine fix.

"Nothing surprises me anymore, Nathan. In fact it all makes sense now. I've been thinking about everything that happened since Fox arrived on the scene, and I've remembered something that is pretty damn interesting." Nathan regarded her with interest.

"What?"

"The night at the festival when that guy attacked me ... It was him ... Hecta, the man who I made the jewellery for." Nathan shook his head, confused.

"Are you sure?" Charlie glanced at Pearl and back to him again.

"Yes, absolutely 100 per cent sure. He was chasing Saf even then, so this situation has been brewing for some time. God knows what's been going on for her in the past few months. This whole revelation of magic and the fact that Fox was not who we thought he was makes complete sense to me now. I know it sounds like something out of a Hollywood movie, but I believe Saf. I watched her change slowly over time before she left with Fox. Everything was changing. I think she was covering up a lot more than she was letting on. Pearl must be part of all this. She has always seemed eccentric, but now I believe she is like Saf and Fox. Something different, something special."

Nathan sighed as his brain tried to unscramble logic and reason from the fairy tale that was unfolding.

"Well, you are a lot more perceptive than me, gorgeous. I didn't have a clue what was going on." Charlie laughed softly, and placed the paper cup beside her on the bedside table before touching his hand with her own.

"My sweet Nathan, you are my rock. And I'm glad that you, for one, cannot shoot lightning bolts from your fingers or glow in the dark." While wrapping his fingers within her own Nathan lifted her hand to his lips and kissed her knuckles gently.

"I may not be magical, Charlie, but I am here for you in whatever way I can be. Saf and Pearl need us now – and Fox too, by the sounds of it. As strange and unreal as this all feels, I think we need to get our heads into a new place to deal with this crazy shit." Charlie smiled, grateful that her man seemed to be on board with all the new events shifting into place.

"Thank you, Nathan. Seriously, it's good to know. And yes, you are right. They need our help. Can you do me a favour and stay here with Pearl? I need to go back to Foxglove and make sure Saf is OK." He nodded and released her hand slowly.

"Anything you need, gorgeous." Charlie stood slowly to leave as a nurse carrying a clipboard entered the room and smiled at them.

"I just need to check her vitals again. Has there been any change since I left?" she asked. Charlie shook her head slowly.

"No, she's the same as when we arrived." Nathan glanced at Pearl as he watched her face for any new signs of life. The nurse fussed over Pearl, checking her pulse and the machine beside her. She frowned for a moment, then turned to Charlie with a smile.

"Well, her heart rate has gone up a little and she seems a lot more stable now, so there is actually some improvement. It seems that she is over the worse. She's a strong old thing, that's for sure." Charlie grinned, her face lighting up.

"That's wonderful news." Nathan smiled up at her.

"Go tell Saf the good news. She must be going out of her mind back at the cottage." Charlie grabbed her bag and took one last look at Pearl before she opened the door. She frowned and shook her head, thinking that she was now seeing things, as she had noticed a shimmer of light covering the old woman's body like a thin cloak of fairy dust that glowed softly against her skin.

She shook her head again as she left the room and hurried out of the hospital, eager to tell Sapphire that Pearl was starting to recover.

Chapter Three

Fox moved through the woods with the speed and agility his animal form gave him. His mind flashed with images of the landscape around him. His senses were heightened, so that the smells and sounds of the woodland creatures and plants overwhelmed him. Taking his animal form was something he never did unless he had to for several reasons. It was a risk, and it made him vulnerable. But in this form he could track faster and easier and he could move without detection by the gatekeeper – who, despite all the years of knowing Fox, was unaware of this particular gift he possessed. Of course Hecta knew that some of his people were shape-shifters, but this gift was not common and Fox only used this type of magic when he really needed to.

Although his body as a fox was familiar to him, and he slipped into its skin easily, he always found the sensation a little odd. The spirit of his fox was strong, and it would push thoughts and feelings into his mind that were purely animalistic. He often found himself attacking small animals and devouring them with relish before he had even realised what he had done. While in the form of the fox it was a pleasurable experience, but on returning into his natural form the images were somewhat disturbing. But it was a small price to pay for the many advantages it gave him.

He picked up a new scent that was undoubtedly the gatekeeper's – the scent of magic and darkness. It lingered in the air. His paws gripped the earth and his body was fluid and fast as he ran towards the gatekeeper. At last he had tracked him. At last he had found him. He was still on Earth, and he was close to Foxglove. In fact, Fox now realised that Hecta had been leading him on a wild goose chase, and he doubled back on himself towards the cottage. He had already travelled many miles across this strange landscape before he picked up the scent again.

Fox had feared he may have jumped through to another dimension again and he had lost him altogether, but no … the gatekeeper was greedy for his prize, and he had stayed here on Earth. Clever Hecta. But Fox now had the advantage. Hecta would not sense him coming in his animal form, and Fox could practically be on top of him before he would realise that he was coming. His muzzle lifted into a growl and his eyes flashed amber and black. He would not let him escape again, and this time he would deal with Hecta once and for all.

The bath water was deliciously hot, and sent soothing signals to Sapphire's exhausted body. She had filled the tub with scented oils of jasmine and rose and the smells wafted luxuriously into her mind, evoking wonderful memories of bathing with her gorgeous husband in the past. She trusted him, and knew that he would return to her when he could. There was absolutely nothing else she could do but wait for him.

After tipping her head back into the water she closed her eyes and rinsed her hair. The feeling of being submerged in water made her muscles relax just that little bit more. With her eyes closed she reached for the bath sponge that she had placed on the table beside her.

"Would you like me to wash your back, Sapphire?" The deep voice that had spoken to her did not belong to her husband. Sapphire opened her eyes with a jolt and sloshed water over the sides of the bathtub as she sat up abruptly. Her magic began to thrum loudly within her veins and the silver bracelets burnt hotly against her skin, causing shivers of discomfort and delight simultaneously to dance across her skin.

Hecta was standing next to the bathtub beside her. He wore an expression of amusement and arousal. His hands were clasped before his body, but she could see them trembling slightly. Her heart began to beat frantically within her chest, and her mind raced with thoughts of how the hell he had managed to walk into the room without her knowing.

"You look beautiful, Sapphire. Your skin is the most perfect colour." He paused, watching her with dark eyes that spoke of unthinkable things. "Flawless," he whispered as his pupils widened. Sapphire felt utterly speechless and totally vulnerable for a second. Her nakedness before him made her feel like a potential victim rather than the powerful dream traveller that she really was. Her hands flew to her breasts, which were raised slightly out of the water. Thankfully the rest of her was hidden by the bubbles from the scented oils.

"Get out of here, Hecta. Right now." He stepped closer to her and bent down slowly, so that his face was level to her own. His eyes skimmed her lazily, and he licked his lips.

"I don't think so, my lady. You are mine now."

Sapphire felt her body tremble at the gesture and it did so in confusion, because the bracelets were sending flickers of arousal down her arms into her breasts. She shook her head and removed her hands from her chest to grip the edges of the bathtub.

Hecta lost concentration for a moment. The flashing of her ample assets disarmed him for just a second. It was all she needed. While pushing her magic out from her very core Sapphire sat up and threw the water from the tub up and out in a force of power so strong that it hit him full strength in the face and made him fall backwards on to the floor. She pushed herself up to standing. Although totally naked she raised her arms above her head and filled herself with every ounce of magic she could. She drew on its power and forced the water from the bathtub so that it was now covering Hecta, who lay gasping for breath in a bubble-like pool of liquid.

From some dark, distant memory in the back of her mind she began to pull forth a spell, a binding spell of her own that took form in the words that she began to chant loudly as she looked at him with angry eyes.

Hecta opened his mouth and tried to gasp for air as she trapped him within the very water that had, just moments ago, been sitting in the bathtub. Over and over Sapphire repeated the words that tumbled from her mouth. She did not know where they came from or how she even knew them, but they created a binding prison within the water that Hecta was now trapped within. The bracelets on her wrists were burning intensely now, and the flickers of arousal had turned into white-hot pain.

Sapphire continued to chant, pressing the water closer and closer to Hecta and cutting off his oxygen supply. He struggled and fought hard against it, but to no avail. Her intense anger at what he had done to her and to Pearl added to the spell's strength.

She was drowning him, and by the expression on his face he damn well knew it.

Chapter Four

Charlie pulled up outside the gate of Foxglove and switched off the car ignition. It was dark, and God only knew what time it was, as hours had passed since she had left Sapphire at the cottage to return to the hospital. She could see lights inside the cottage and the glow of a fire in the lounge. She wondered absently if Fox had returned from his testosterone-driven quest to find and finish off the horrible Hecta.

While chuckling at her own sense of humour about all the strange, crazy events that had unfolded she headed towards the gate. Just as she reached to open the wooden gate she felt something brush against her legs and shoot past her.

"What the hell?" she said to herself. She watched the bushy tail of a rather large fox disappear as quickly as a lightning bolt across the garden. Transfixed by this weird encounter, Charlie watched open-mouthed as the door of the cottage flung open and the fox ran inside at full pelt and vanished as the door closed with a loud thud. Everything became eerily silent around her. The very air seemed to still itself and turn thicker. The hairs on the back of her neck began to rise, and she felt a tingling in her belly.

As she watched with wide eyes Charlie noticed the cottage start to change colour before her very eyes. It glowed a deep orange and the windows lit up brightly with flashes of white light, as if a thunderstorm was erupting inside the walls.

She stepped forward slowly, her mouth still open, as she continued to watch the display of lights flash inside the cottage. Charlie walked slowly up the path towards the front door with her heart beginning to thump loudly in her chest. Tentatively she reached out for the doorknob. Her hand was shaking slightly as she touched the copper handle. Just as she touched it a bolt of sharp white light erupted from inside with a piercing crack, which threw her to the floor and rumbled through the ground so loudly that the earth began to break beneath her body.

"Oh shit," Charlie whispered before her mind went completely blank.

Fox had hesitated for a moment before he shifted back into human form. After running swiftly up the crooked staircase he now stood with his tail swishing violently at the open door of the cottage's small bathroom. The vision of his beautiful, naked wife before him with her arms lifted to the heavens chanting some old, wild magic that even he did not know had caused him to stumble for a moment before taking action ... action that would be needed to stop Hecta from escaping the watery prison that Sapphire now held him within.

His body trembled and flickered before moving from fur and sinew to muscle and bone. The transformation process was always a little unnerving, even for him, but Sapphire seemed oblivious to her husband's incredible journey from fox to man as he stood in the doorway of the bathroom. Her sole focus was on the gatekeeper, who was struggling desperately now against the magic she had trapped him in. He was using every ounce of his anger and lust via the silver bracelets that circled her wrists. They burnt and sizzled against her skin, and the binding magic held within them was trying to resist her and pull her back into his spell.

Fox's mind spun as he tried to find some direction. His wife, although seemingly holding her own remarkably well, was wavering slightly under the pressure that Hecta was pushing on to her. Fox needed to help her somehow but his magic was weaker here on Earth, and he knew that at this moment he would need every single drop of his essence to help her destroy the gatekeeper.

After stepping fully into the room as naked as Sapphire was Fox began to chant his own spell, a spell that his father had taught him long ago. It was an amplifying spell used to increase the potency of any other magic that was being created, and it was often used when healing and mending objects that were in effect beyond repair and needed extra help in fixing.

Fox found that by reciting the old spell and focusing on the water he could help Sapphire push back against the now frantic Hecta. He was merely strengthening her magic with his own, linking in and sending whatever he could to help her crush Hecta.

Sapphire moved her eyes a fraction, as if she were now suddenly aware of his presence. Her pupils dilated and he saw her lips tremble, but this was the only indication that she could see or feel him. Fox remained steadfast, his own chant filling the room over and over as he amplified her spell.

The bubble-like pool of water Hecta that was trapped within was growing smaller around him. Each water molecule was being absorbed into the body of the gatekeeper. Fox could almost feel him drowning as the liquid filled his lungs and saturated his oxygen supply. Hecta's eyes grew wide with horror and surprise as he realised that Fox was now joining in with his obliteration. The bracelets began to fizz against Sapphire's flesh, and Fox was tempted to pull back and help her with the pain that must have been intense against her wrists. Just as he thought she could take no more they began to melt and disintegrate as if they were turned to liquid. Fox felt the binding spell start to break. As Hecta took his last breath he realised that the spell was at last being broken.

The sound of their combined voices chanting strongly within the cottage was creating wave after wave of such powerful magic that the whole cottage lit up with gold and silver lights. The floor shook and the walls trembled as, with one last word of wild magic, the gatekeeper was overwhelmed and the bracelets disappeared, releasing Sapphire from his grasp.

Fox felt his connection with her intensify once more and flood through his veins like sweet nectar. He moved forward closer to Hecta, who was now motionless on the floor. His eyes were closed, and his mouth was open like a fish that had given up the fight for breath now that it was on land and no longer able to breathe.

The bubble-like pool of water was gone, and had been completely absorbed by the gatekeeper. This had effectively drowned him and removed his magic and life force in one final blow. Fox nudged the body with his foot and nodded, satisfied that he was at last dead and gone.

Sapphire suddenly, without warning, crumpled and groaned. Fox managed to move at the speed of light to catch her before she hit the bottom of the bathtub and split her head open.

After lifting her gently out of the tub he carried her out of the room to the guest room across the hall and placed her on the bed. Her eyes were fluttering and her breathing was ragged.

"Fox ... Thank God you came back. Thank you." He kissed her softly and pulled the covers up over her wet, naked body.

"My beautiful Sapphire. You are safe now ... safe at last." She closed her eyes and allowed him to wrap his arms around her and whisper to her in his sweet lullaby language, which caressed her soul after such a traumatic event.

The vague thought that he was naked and why would this be entered her head briefly before she drifted into a form of sleep that she knew, this time, would be safe to visit.

Chapter Five

A soft breeze across her face brought Charlie out of her state of unconsciousness. She was aware of strong arms wrapped around her body and a warmth spreading through her limbs that tingled and shook her awake. As she opened her eyes she looked up into the face of Fox, who was carrying her into the cottage. He smiled down at her, his eyes flashing with sparks of gold that glittered like amber crystals in his handsome face.

"How are you feeling, Charlie?"

He spoke in a deep sing-song voice that made her tremble a little in his arms. Good God, the man was hot. Charlie blinked up at him. She smiled back and sighed before answering.

"As if I've been slapped across the head with a plank, Fox." He laughed and placed her in one of the armchairs, and unfolded his body like a graceful cat before standing back to inspect her. Seemingly satisfied that she was well, he nodded and looked up at the ceiling before returning his gaze to hers and saying,

"I will be back in a moment. Stay here."

Before she could reply he was gone. A shimmer of light was left where he once stood. Charlie shook her head, still finding it a little unnerving that he could disappear right in front of her eyes in such a manner. The cottage was quiet, but she sensed a new state of calmness that had been absent for so long. Something had changed, and it felt good to no longer hold the ball of anxiety in her chest that had taken lodging since Pearl's accident and Sapphire's trauma with the gatekeeper.

She wondered where Sapphire was, and what had caused the blinding light that had knocked her out cold. As she stretched her arms above her head she noted somewhat begrudgingly that her body felt heavy and achy, as if she had just survived a heavy workout at the gym. She needed to find out what was going on. Just as she began to push herself up out of the chair Fox returned with a cup of steaming liquid that he held out for her.

"Here, drink this. It will make you feel better ... Sapphire will be down in a moment." Charlie reached out for the cup. She was suddenly very thirsty.

"Is she OK? What's happened?" Fox smiled and crouched down so that he was eye level with her. He pushed the cup towards her gently so that she could steady her hand, which was still trembling slightly.

"Sapphire is fine. The binding spell is broken. Hecta is no more. All is well." Sipping the liquid, which tasted like honey and cinnamon, Charlie smiled.

"Well, thank God for that. I'm not sure I could take much more of all the stress you two were creating, Fox." He laughed again, and watched her with intense eyes. She felt the liquid fill her belly and warm her in a way that was both soothing and slightly strange at the same time. It was like turning on a tap that filled her with the most wonderful drug, which was healing her from the inside out.

"Hecta is gone?" He nodded slowly, a slight smile etched on his perfect lips.

"Yes. Gone." Charlie smiled lazily. The drink was making her feel as light as a feather. Her aching limbs were now loose and languid, and were making her slump back into the armchair. She felt good all over. She wondered if they could market this wonderful drink and return the world to a happy place once more.

As all tension slipped away Charlie smiled as Sapphire entered the room. Dressed in jeans and a T-shirt, she looked almost human again. Her eyes, however, were glowing bright blue and her hair sparkled like freshly spun threads of glitter.

"Saf, are you OK?" Sapphire came to her friend with a smile on her face. While crouching down beside her she took Charlie's hands into her own and squeezed them gently.

"Yes, honey. Hecta is no longer a problem." Fox was standing beside her dressed in black jeans and a fitted black jumper that showed all his muscles in all the right places. They looked like a pair of catalogue models. Charlie breathed a sigh of relief.

"Thank God ... Does that mean Pearl will be OK now as well? I should call Nathan and see if there has been any change. She had improved a little before I left. I was coming to tell you the news, but when I arrived here the cottage was lit up like a bonfire. What the hell happened?" Sapphire bit her lip and looked up at Fox, then back at Charlie.

"I drowned him in the water from the bathtub."

Charlie's eyes widened in shock.

"Holy crap ... where is he now?" Fox twitched slightly. "I have put him outside until I can find a place to bury him," he said somewhat sheepishly.

Charlie let go of Sapphire's hands and sat up a little in the chair. She was still feeling nicely fluid, but the thought of a dead body sitting outside the cottage was just a little unnerving.

"OK ... so I assume that could be a problem." Sapphire shook her head.

"No, it won't be, Charlie. No one here even knows he exists. He won't be missed. Fox will take him into the woods and bury him somewhere he won't be found. Everything will be OK. Trust me." Charlie nodded slowly.

"Fine. I trust you both, but we need to call Nathan and check on Pearl."

"Of course. That's our priority now, Charlie," Sapphire replied. Charlie noted that her friend looked much better, but her wrists were scarred with a deep red circle that was deep and angry. She reached across to touch her forearm gently.

"Is this from the bracelets?" Sapphire nodded, her face a mixture of emotion as she turned her wrists over to where the burn was deepest.

"It will heal. Don't worry ... Fox will help me."

Fox looked forlorn as he glanced at her wrists. He was obviously feeling some guilt at the fact that Sapphire had been hurt in the struggle to release the binding spell. Charlie was still having difficulty getting her head around the whole thing, but was just glad this nightmare was now over. Sapphire stood suddenly.

"Where is your phone, Charlie? I'll call Nathan. You rest, honey ... you look a little zapped."

Charlie laughed softly.

"Yeah, I feel zapped ... It's in my bag, but I'm not sure where that is. Fox brought me into the house." Fox disappeared and reappeared with the bag in his hand. Magic definitely had its benefits. Charlie grinned at him as he handed it to her, she had to admit it was pretty damned cool to watch him in action.

They left Charlie in the sitting room and returned to the kitchen. Sapphire put the kettle on while Fox stood silently behind her. She could feel the heat from his body radiating across to her and the magic flowing steadily between them again. It felt so good to have him back, so soothing and comforting. She had forgotten just how strong his magic was, and how strong their connection had been before Hecta had cut the tie.

As she placed the kettle on to the range he stepped closer to her and wrapped his arms around her waist, pulling her closer to his body. As he nestled his face into her neck he sighed deeply and spread his fingers out across her belly. Sapphire closed her eyes and allowed him to embrace her again.

"Sapphire, my beautiful wife ... I'm sorry you went through so much without me. I tried to track Hecta alone and finish him off, but as usual you beat me to the chase. My brave, wonderful woman."

He nuzzled into her neck, breathing in her scent, before placing soft kisses on her skin that sent tingles of delight across her clavicle and chest.

"I missed you," he mumbled as his tongue flicked into the shell of her ear. She squeezed her legs together tightly and placed her hands over his, holding him close as he continued to send sparks of arousal across her skin.

"Fox ... I missed you too. I have no idea how Hecta got into the cottage without me sensing him. But I was so angry ... He was just so smug. He dropped the ball just for a second, and then I had my chance." She paused as Fox slipped one of his hands slowly up under her T-shirt and ran his fingers across her belly.

"I have no idea where the spell came from that trapped him in the water. It just happened without me even trying. Thank God you came in time to help me."

Fox lifted his head and spun her around quickly so that she now faced him. His hands were no longer on her belly but holding her gently, on either side of her face. He stared at her intently, his eyes dark and filled with love and lust.

"The magic you used was old, wild magic. The only person I know who has knowledge of this is my father. He is connected to you now, my love, and I believe it was his doing." Sapphire gazed up at him, revelling in his presence once more. How beautiful he was … how good it felt to have him close once more.

"Then I have to thank him and you for both saving me." Fox tipped his head to one side. A smile crept on to his lips before he bent down to kiss her. The kiss was deep and filled with a passion she remembered so well. His hands moved to her back and pressed her closer. His legs were now either side of her body, capturing her completely. Her head tipped back, and with her hands now in his hair Sapphire returned the kiss with fervour. She felt their magic flare between them and fill her with a heat that burnt brightly within her chest.

"Aah, guys … we really need to call Nathan."

Sapphire pulled back and Fox sighed deeply as Charlie entered the kitchen.

"Seriously, you two, I can't leave you for two minutes without you getting lost in each other. Focus … focus," Charlie tutted.

Fox raised an eyebrow but smiled down at Sapphire, who laughed.

"OK, bossy. You call him, and I'll make tea."

Charlie shook her head, and grabbed her phone and disappeared again into the hallway. Fox continued to smile. His hands were still pressing her against him so that she could feel every defined line and muscle.

"I think we need to 'get lost in each other' much more, my love. It has been far too long."

Sapphire chuckled and pushed him away gently.

"Tea first, Fox."

Chapter Six

The three of them sat in the kitchen surrounded by glittering candles and drank tea. Charlie had called Nathan, and was pleased to inform them that Pearl had made a miraculous recovery and was now fully conscious again. The hospital wanted to keep her in for a few days just to check her vitals and help her regain her strength. Nathan was on his way over to pick up Charlie.

"So what happened to the fox I saw come crashing into the house earlier?" Charlie mumbled as she sipped her tea. Sapphire raised her eyebrow and looked across at her husband. His eyes drifted down to the table, a slight smile on his lips.

"What fox?" she responded. Charlie laughed.

"I saw it clear as day shoot straight past me into the cottage just before I passed out." Fox looked at her with wild eyes.

"I am sure the effects of Sapphire's magic were causing you to hallucinate, Charlie. There was no fox." She regarded him coolly.

"Mmmh, well, it looked pretty damn real to me." Sapphire tilted her head to one side and watched her husband, who remained cool and collected before her. She knew that Charlie had without a doubt seen him in his animal form ... but to explain that Fox was indeed a shape-shifter as well as magical would seriously blow her mind, on top of all the other knowledge they had already shared with her.

"Magic can do strange things, Charlie. It can make you see and feel things when you are in its presence that sometimes make no sense." Charlie narrowed her eyes at Sapphire and nodded slowly.

"Mmmh ... Sure, Saf. I'm still finding it hard to understand all this magical stuff, so whatever you say." Sapphire knew her friend wasn't buying what she had said, as usual, but was being polite enough to humour her.

A knock at the door brought them all out of the reverie they were in. Charlie jumped up surprisingly quickly, her face now animated.

"Nathan's here." She rushed out of the kitchen, leaving Sapphire and Fox alone.

Fox placed his hand over Sapphire's forearm and licked his bottom lip slowly.

"Thank you." Sapphire regarded him for a moment, watching his face for any underlying emotion.

"What for?"

"For covering the truth." Sapphire smiled and took his hand, clasping his fingers between her own gently.

"I think it is best that your little secret remains a secret, Fox." His eyes wandered again to the tablecloth. He looked somewhat uneasy.

"You know?" Sapphire lifted his hand to her lips and kissed his knuckles softly.

"Yes. Your father told me that you can shift into animal form. I saw him earlier. I travelled for a while when you left. I think I even saw you at one point during the journey, but I wasn't sure if it was a vision or if you actually visited me while I travelled."

Fox sighed and leant back in his chair just as Charlie reappeared with Nathan. His eyes told her that what she had seen had definitely been a vision of him as he wandered the land chasing Hecta in the form of his animal spirit.

"Hey, you two, how's it going? Good to see you back, Fox." Nathan looked tired but cheerful. He was wonderfully oblivious to what had happened at the cottage and the fact that a dead gatekeeper now lay in the garden.

Fox rose and walked towards him and reached out his arm in a gesture of welcome. Nathan pulled him into a bear hug, which took Fox by surprise, and thumped him on the back.

"It's really good to see you, man. Saf was crazy angry you left – and, to be honest, we were all worried – but Charlie tells me everything is OK now. The madman's gone?" Fox withdrew from the hug and smiled at him.

"Yes, gone. All is well again ... However ..." He paused for a moment, and looked back at Sapphire before returning his gaze to Nathan. "I may need some help in burying Hecta. He is heavier than he looks." Nathan paled momentarily, and looked understandably uncomfortable.

"Yeah ... sure ... right. Well, I'm sure I can help you with that." Fox nodded and stood a little straighter, and looked between the women before taking a step towards the hallway.

"No time like the present, then, Nathan. Shall we?"

The two men disappeared. Nathan kissed Charlie quickly on the forehead before leaving with a wobbly smile on his lips. He was quite clearly a little nervous about disposing of a dead body. Sapphire didn't blame him. It was just too weird to even think about, even for her. Charlie slumped back down into one of the chairs at the kitchen table and sighed deeply.

"God, I need to sleep, Saf. It's so late. This has, without a doubt, been the most severely weird and fucked-up few days I have ever had." Sapphire, despite the heaviness of the conversation, laughed loudly.

"Yes, it is, honey. I agree. I'm absolutely bushed." Charlie smiled wearily, and pushed a curl away from her face.

"So what next?"

Sapphire looked at her friend with a new sense of pride. She was taking this all pretty well, considering.

"After a good sleep, Charlie, I think we need a few days of normality, get Pearl settled back home, and then …" Charlie nodded.

"Yes, and then …"

Sapphire smiled softly.

"Fox and I will be going away." Charlie sat up straighter.

"But why so soon? You have only just got here." Sapphire sighed.

"I have to, Charlie. I came home for a reason. I have to do something, something very important, and it means that we have to leave again." Charlie pouted.

"Where are you going? Can Nathan and I come with you? We could do with a change of scenery for a while." Sapphire looked at her in consideration, thinking about her friend's proposal.

"To be honest, Charlie, I'm not exactly sure where we will be going … Well, I know where I need to start, and it's quite a long way away." Charlie's face brightened. She looked very interested now.

"And where is that exactly?" Sapphire smiled widely.

"Egypt."

Chapter Seven

Daylight filtered through the bedroom curtains in soft golden hues, causing Sapphire to stir from her sleep. She had slept hard and, thankfully, had stayed firmly put in Foxglove with her gorgeous husband wrapped around her. He was tangled around her now. His legs were pinning her to the bed and his arm was across her chest, pulling her close to his warm body. She smiled and stretched, which caused him to stir.

"Good morning my beautiful wife," he mumbled into her ear. He had returned to the cottage an hour after leaving with Nathan to dispose of Hecta. The location of Hecta's grave would be forever a secret to only him, as he had somehow removed the memory from Nathan when they had returned. He said it would be best that way.

Nathan had looked oddly stoned again, and Charlie had driven them back to their own cottage in the early hours of the morning. Charlie had not even asked why he was in such a state. She and Sapphire had discussed the trip to Egypt, and it had been decided that they would indeed come with them for a much-needed break. Sapphire had been surprised and happy to hear that Charlie had invested some of the money she had left her, and they had more than enough funds to take a holiday. They could make the travel arrangements and book the hotels easily in the next few days, before heading off to the sunshine. It was settled that they would all leave together as soon as the arrangements were made.

Sapphire felt comforted that her friends would be coming with them. Now that Hecta was gone they could travel safely, and might actually have some fun while she completed her mission.

"Good morning, Fox." Sapphire turned to face him, and found him smiling at her with a look of promise on his lips.

"How are you feeling today, my love?" He reached for her arm and lifted her wrist to inspect the burn marks, which were indeed now fading fast.

"I'm good. I feel fine." He nodded and kissed her hand softly, his eyes turning dark and needy.

"I want to make you feel even better before breakfast, my love." Sapphire sighed, and closed her eyes again as he pulled her even closer and kissed her with a passion that she felt in every part of her body from her head to her toes.

It was late in the afternoon before they were up and ready to leave the cottage again to visit Pearl. They had stayed in bed for a very long time before Sapphire had finally decided it was time to get up. Fox had tried his best to persuade her to stay naked for longer, and his tactics were certainly good enough to make her hesitate about leaving his arms more than once.

"I hope they actually let us back in the hospital, Fox," Sapphire said to him as they walked out of the cottage gate. The day was bright and crisp, with a freshness to the air that Sapphire felt in her lungs like a rude awakening. It felt good to feel so free again. She had not realised how much the binding spell had been dragging her energy down.

"Stop worrying, my love. They will let us in. I will cloak us if necessary." She regarded him for a moment. He also seemed full of life today. The dark cloud that had been hanging over his head had now been removed.

"I worry about you using your magic so much here, Fox." He raised a brow and chuckled.

"I feel stronger than ever, Sapphire. Without the gatekeeper to contend with I am the happiest I have been in a long time. My magic is strong. Stop worrying." He held her hand tightly and spun her around so that she was facing him suddenly, and wrapped her in his arms.

"Now close your eyes and think of Pearl. She will be so happy to see you, my love." Before Sapphire could argue the air began to fizz around them and her vision wavered. After closing her eyes she did as she was told, and seconds later they were standing next to Pearl's bed in the hospital. Fox stepped back from her and released her with a smug smile on his lips. Pearl was sleeping, her face now peaceful and delicately tinted with a healthy pink glow.

"Thank God," Sapphire said. She rushed to her friend's side and took the old woman's hand in her own. Happy tears began to form in her eyes as she sensed Pearl was no longer held in the dark prison Hecta had placed her in, and she was indeed well and very much alive.

By squeezing her hand gently Sapphire sent a pulse of magic into Pearl's fingers and watched tiny flickers of light begin to trace thin lines up her arm into her chest. Like a new frost spreading through her veins the silver lines of magic spread throughout Pearl's body, and her eyes began to flutter open. Pearl smiled and opened her eyes completely.

"Sapphire, my child, it is so good to see you again." Sapphire sobbed a cry of relief and leant forward to hug the woman, who responded with a gentle laugh. "Oh, my child, everything is OK now. No need for more tears. All is well."

Fox stood behind them, his hands clasped before him and a grin on his face. His magic was pulsing gently around him and reflecting his own happiness at the scene before him. Sapphire sat up, still holding Pearl's hand, and wiped away her tears. She was smiling now with joy.

"I thought I'd lost you, Pearl," she said. Pearl sighed and shook her head slowly.

"Oh, no, my child. It takes a lot more than that to get rid of such a stubborn old witch."

Sapphire looked back at Fox and smiled widely at him.

"Thank you." He looked confused for a second.

"For what, my love?" Sapphire smiled softly.

"For helping me save her, Fox. I could not have released the spell without you." Pearl cleared her throat and tried to push herself up in the bed.

"I thank you both. It was rather hard work floating around in that awful place where Hecta sent me, but I knew you were both trying to push through the darkness. I heard your voice, Sapphire, and of course I felt your magic on several occasions, Fox." She paused and looked at Fox with an expression of perplexity for a moment. "Or perhaps it was your father, Fox. You have such similar magic, but I am sure I felt his touch just before the spell was broken. It has been a very, very long time since I last connected with the great magician." Fox nodded slowly.

"We are all connected now, Pearl. Of that I am absolutely sure."

The door was suddenly opened by a nurse who walked into the room with a clipboard. She jumped as she realised there were other people in the room with her patient and gasped in surprise.

"I'm afraid no visitors are allowed in this room. Mrs Tanner is still under observation, and not well enough for guests." Fox stepped forward and flashed his best panties-dropping smile at her.

"I am sure you can give us just a few more minutes with our friend …" He paused and looked at her name tag and said, "Nurse Phillips." Her mouth opened as if to protest, but the slight quiver of her lips gave away her sudden change of demeanour.

Sapphire almost laughed out loud. The nurse had no chance of arguing with Fox when he was blasting her with his full megawatt charm. He stepped a little closer to her and tilted his head to one side after lifting his hand to take the clipboard from her now trembling hand.

"I will take that from you and leave it by the bed so that you can take your notes when you come back shortly, Nurse Phillips. Thank you for being so assiduous and checking on our friend. We won't be much longer." Sapphire watched poor Nurse Phillips turn a deep shade of red before shaking her head in mild confusion and turning to go back out the door. Fox shrugged and stepped back again.

"Now, where were we?"

Pearl listened with wide eyes that sparkled with interest as Sapphire told her what had happened to Hecta, and the reason she had returned to Earth with Fox.

"Where are these seeds now, Sapphire?" she asked. Her face lit up in awe after Sapphire had described to her how she had suddenly become the guardian of the strange seeds that until now still remained somewhat of a mystery to Sapphire and Fox. Sapphire tapped her pocket and said,

"I have them with me." Pearl sat up and raised her hand towards Sapphire while uncurling her fingers.

"I would very much like to see them," she said.

Sapphire looked at Fox, who nodded at her. After taking the pouch from her pocket she placed the enchanted packet into Pearl's hand and felt a sense of relief that Pearl was now holding the seeds. It seemed a heavy burden to be carrying, and even handing them over for just a moment took the load off. Pearl regarded the pouch. Her eyes wandered over the leather before she opened it, and she shook the seeds into her other hand. They glistened and shone innocently in the light like tiny diamonds. They were perfect in shape, each one shimmering with an azure blue like a tiny wren's egg.

Pearl sucked in her breath for a second and closed her eyes. Sapphire sensed her energy change as she scanned the items in her hand. On opening her eyes again Pearl closed her fingers around the seeds before placing them back into the pouch.

"Well, Sapphire, you have something truly amazing here. I can feel how powerful they are, but even I have no idea what they are actually for. The magic within them is strange and unearthly, but oddly familiar. They are definitely organic. They have their own living essence ... they are very special. I suggest you keep them very safe." She paused and, smiling, handed them back to Sapphire. "But of course I know you will do that, my child." Sapphire sighed and returned them to her pocket, where she felt them tingle and shiver against her own magic again.

"I know this sounds crazy, Pearl, but I think they need to be planted here on Earth at specific places. They need to take root, grow within the Earth, and help her recover her magic again." Pearl nodded, a look of contemplation on her face.

"Yes, yes, I think you are right. They are singing for their home again. Can you hear their song? It is very quiet, but if you listen closely you can just make out the tune they are whispering."

Sapphire frowned.

"I haven't heard any song, Pearl. Are you sure?" Pearl patted her hand gently.

"You will hear it in time, Sapphire. You just need to learn how to quieten that busy mind of yours." Fox chuckled from behind them.

"It is a skill that humans find difficult, wise woman. You know that." Sapphire shot him a look of disgust, making him laugh even more.

"No offence, my love." Sapphire snorted.

"None taken, my husband." Pearl clapped her hands in delight.

"Oh, my. You two are so funny. Of course ... I must congratulate you both on your marriage."

She held Sapphire's hand and lifted the sleeve of her jacket, and raised it up to look at the tattoo that ran in beautiful lines across her ring finger and up her arm. The scars from the bracelet Hecta had bound to her were still evident but fading by the hour. Pearl regarded the pattern with smiling eyes.

"So, pretty Sapphire, your magic is bound strongly now with your guardian." She looked across at Fox and frowned a little. "Take care of your precious wife on this journey, young Fox. Although she has grown in power immensely since I last saw her she is a delicate thing, and I don't want your hot-headedness causing her any more trouble. You hear me?" She scolded Fox like an old grandmother would before smiling again. Fox bowed his head solemnly.

"It is my reason for living, wise woman. Nothing else matters to me more than her safety." Sapphire watched the pair of them and rolled her eyes as they discussed her yet again as if she were a child ... a precious child, but a child nonetheless.

"Now, I think it would be best if you both leave me for a while before Nurse Phillips comes back and realises she has allowed you to stay longer than allowed. I am sure I will be home very soon." Sapphire blushed a little, and looked at Pearl with her eyes downcast.

"We stayed at Foxglove last night, Pearl. Would it be OK for us to stay until you come home? It means we have some space from Charlie and Nathan ... As much as I love them both its good to have some time alone." Pearl laughed.

"Oh, my dear child. You do not have to ask. My home is your home whenever you need it. You should know this by now. Enjoy the cottage until I return." Sapphire smiled again, her blush slowly disappearing. Fox moved to Pearl's other side, and he lowered his head slowly to kiss the old woman on the forehead.

"I thank you for your generosity, Pearl, and for making Sapphire happy again." Pearl actually looked a little flustered for a moment before batting him away coyly.

"No need for that, young man. Now off you go. I will see you again soon." They left the way they had come, on a sparkle of magic, and left a happy, smiling Pearl in her warm bed.

Before she closed her eyes again to take a nap Pearl thought about the seeds Sapphire had placed into her hand. Her body trembled as she recalled the power she had sensed within them, and the endless possibilities that may come from their appearance here on Earth. She knew instinctively that everything was about to change, and that this change would affect absolutely everyone there on the planet.

Chapter Eight

Sapphire and Fox had returned to an empty Foxglove. Empty from humans, that is. The sprites whizzed happily around Sapphire's head at her return. It seemed they already knew Pearl was fit and well again.

The day was coming to an end once more and Fox walked around the rooms, flicking his wrist and creating light as he went. Candles bloomed into life as he went, creating a soft amber hue against the walls. He bent down beside the fire and blew life into the wood, which whooshed as it came alive and sent flames up the chimney.

"Show-off," Sapphire chuckled as she watched him use his magic so casually. He turned his head slowly, his hair tumbling across his shoulders in dark waves that glistened with silver beads and a soft smile on his lips.

"Only for you, my love," he replied. She felt a sense of relief flood through her veins as she watched him uncurl to full height – relief that they were actually safe and untroubled for once. Or, at least, she hoped so. It seemed that her life had constantly been weighed down by a dark cloud lately, and she kept expecting the next rainstorm to arrive and soak her to the bone once more. Fox tipped his head to one side and took a step towards her as he searched her face for her thoughts.

"You look troubled again, Sapphire. What is bothering you?" As she leant against the door frame she shook her head slowly and looked at the floor.

"I keep thinking that something bad is going to happen again." He was suddenly standing in front of her, just a fraction from touching her. His uncanny ability to shift like a vampire at the speed of light made her jump. He leant forward slowly and pressed his forehead against her own, his warm breath caressing her skin and the smell of patchouli and sandalwood filling her nostrils.

"Nothing bad is going to happen now, Sapphire. Trust me. The danger has been removed. *You are safe.*" He spoke slowly and softly, and his voice was deep and warm. She felt it in her toes. His hands were on her arms and he squeezed them reassuringly, moving his head back once more so that he could kiss her softly on the top of her head. She wanted to believe him. Desperately.

"I know what will make that busy mind of yours stop racing." She glanced up at him beneath her lashes and her breath caught in her throat as she saw the change within his eyes. His own breath was hitched up a notch, and she sensed his body start to tighten. His muscles were moving slightly in a way that she instantly recognised. He had switched on the horny button.

She smiled shyly at him, pushed her hands under his shirt, and spread her fingers out across his back. The warmth of his skin tantalised her senses as she opened herself up for him. He smiled at her, and she nodded as their magic connected in a flare of sparkling silver light. His lips found her own and she allowed him to press against her, his tongue invading her mouth in slow, strong strokes that took control of her body in a way that she still found utterly amazing.

Her legs began to melt beneath her, and she found that he was absolutely right. All thoughts were now removed, apart from how wonderful this man could make her feel by the simplest touch and the slightest amount of pressure he exerted on to her now soft and pliable body. They fell into each other, pulling at their clothing so that it was quickly removed in a struggle of limbs that allowed them to make skin-on-skin contact.

Sapphire felt her body ignite beneath his touch. Her eyes were closed and her head was now thrown back against the wall as he slid down her body to remove her jeans. She had pulled his shirt open, and it hung at his wrists. His chest was now fully exposed and the top button of his trousers was undone. His hands slipped across her skin slowly, the heat from his palms making her tremble as his tongue found the top of her underwear and trailed across the cotton briefs she wore.

"You are so beautiful, Sapphire. So very beautiful," he whispered as he pulled her jeans completely down, so that she now stood against the wall in her underwear. He removed her boots slowly, one at a time, allowing her to step out of them. He stood up again quickly, with a rush of air that made her gasp as he took her into his arms and pulled her away from the wall so that she was flat against his chest. Her chest rose and fell quickly, and her heart was thumping wildly in her chest. Fox stared at her. His face was lit up by the candles that made his eyes shine brightly, the pupils wide and dark.

"Shall we dance, my love?" Sapphire raised an eyebrow and smiled at him, a little confused.

"Dance?" He slipped the shirt from his wrists and let it drop to the floor. He was still wearing his jeans, but the buttons were now undone to reveal his happy trail. He was commando, as usual, and the sight of the trail of dark hair leading the way to the promised area of pleasure sent a spike of arousal into her groin. He placed his hand against her back and his other hand at the nape of her neck, and pulled her against his now growing erection.

Their magic flared around them again, sending the sprites scattering from the room. Even they knew they were not invited to this particular party. He moved his groin very slowly, rolling his hips against her and swinging her to the side so that she dipped backwards in a move that would have impressed Justin Timberlake himself. Despite the flare of provocation that now surrounded them Sapphire laughed and allowed him to move her around the tiny living room in a slow dance that made her lose all tension from every single limb.

He kissed her neck, his lips opening so that he could suck her skin – gently at first, as his body continued to move to the silent music that he now created in the sway of his body. The suck turned into a slow bite, slow and hard, that made her eyes roll back into her head.

This is what he was good at: the art of seduction, the start of something dark and dangerous … a slow torture of her body that would begin with him peeling back her layers of bashfulness and expose the passion that lay beneath. And right now – with her man pressed against her, half undressed, standing in a candlelit room in her underwear – she felt like a goddess. All-powerful. Feminine, and foxy as hell.

He had that way, the way of a man who could tease you and please you until all inhibitions melted into the pot of sex that revealed the ultimate power within. Sapphire was more than ready to comply. After reaching down to his wonderful backside she grabbed and pushed back against him, a smile now on her lips as she squeezed the strong muscles beneath her fingers. He growled low in his throat and kissed her again like a man possessed, wanting to climb inside her and bask in the glow of her energy.

Sapphire felt him unclip her bra. It was slipped quickly and quietly to the floor. She sensed his fingers trail across her skin. His body was still moving against her, slowly rolling, moving with a grace and ease that fascinated her. Her legs were starting to shake a little, and he took this as his next cue to move them into a different position.

The dancing stopped and he swept her up into his arms ... her bare breasts were now pressed against his skin, her legs were hanging limply, and her head was feeling loose and fluid. While kissing her again, but softly now, he placed her down on the floor beside the fire. His eyes travelled across her skin, taking every inch of her in. She could see his mind devouring her body. His lip trembled slightly before he licked his top lip slowly.

"I am going to take care of you, my beautiful wife. Now and always. Never forget that." She watched his hair fall forward as he moved down her body and took one of her nipples into his mouth and sucked gently. She was gone. She had fallen into the depths of Fox and beyond.

Her eyelids flickered and her body shuddered as he pushed down her underwear and pushed one long, lean finger inside her, moving it slowly – tantalisingly – in and out, in and out, while his mouth created a small fire on her breast. While moaning without shame Sapphire gripped his back and held on as he began to dance in an altogether different way against her skin.

Oh, my God, this man was something else. Each and every one of her nerve endings was crying out to be touched ... and he complied, building her up and stoking the fire with fingers, mouth, and tongue. She called out his name and he murmured against her skin for her to hush as he continued to push her over the edge. Just as she thought she could take no more she felt him push his cock against the very edge of her opening. She hadn't even felt him remove his jeans.

She forced her eyes open again and gazed up into the face of the man she loved. He was so absolutely beautiful. His face was alive and handsome, and there was an expression of pure and utter lust etched on his features that made her push her hips up to meet him.

He smiled and entered her smoothly and slowly. The feeling was like it was every time he claimed her. Exquisite.

They made love on the floor with the fire burning beside them, and Sapphire knew that her husband was right. She was safe, she was loved, and all was well. They came together in a shower of gold and silver sparks that lit up the cottage like a Catherine wheel.

Another day was over, and finally her mind was free from worry.

Chapter Nine

The sound of the two men she loved the most laughing together made Sapphire smile a happy smile that filled her belly with a warm, fuzzy feeling.

Nathan and Fox were in the lounge of Charlie's cottage watching football, of all things, and doing man things, i.e. drinking beer and talking about stuff women really were not interested in. It still amazed Sapphire that Fox could adapt to such mundane human activities and fit into her life here back on Earth. She had even heard Fox calling out with Nathan when whatever team they were following had obviously lost a shot, or someone had committed a spectacular foul.

She was sitting in the kitchen with Charlie, looking at brochures of Nile cruises and hotels in Cairo. They had been drinking red wine and were now slightly tipsy, and were laughing themselves at the thought of lying out on a deck sipping cocktails in the sunshine while it was positively freezing there in England.

"This cruise company looks the best, Saf. I think we should go with them. I can book it online tonight, and we can get going within a week. If we fly to Cairo first and travel down to the river we can go sooner." Sapphire looked at the brochures and then across at the laptop they had on the kitchen table with other options open on the screen. It all seemed a bit crazy, even to her, that they would be taking off again so soon and on somewhat of a wild goose chase. She had no idea what she was actually doing, just a sense of where she needed to be. The wine bottle was empty, and she shook it over her glass and smiled at Charlie.

"Any more red, honey?" A loud cheer erupted from the living room again. Nathan's team had obviously scored. Charlie sashayed over to the wine rack and, laughing, pulled out another bottle.

"Who would have thought Fox would like football? Do they have football where he comes from?" Sapphire pulled a face.

"I doubt it. I hope he doesn't turn into some slob who just wants to sit on the couch at the weekends with his beer and footy." They both laughed, and Charlie stuck the wine bottle between her legs while she struggled to pull out the cork. She still had one of those highly lethal and completely impractical corkscrews that required brute force to remove the cork.

"Here, give me that, Charlie." Fox was suddenly standing next to her, appearing out of nowhere. She jumped with a squeal and almost dropped it on the floor.

"Fuck. You scared the shit out of me, Fox." He chuckled and took the bottle from her, and released the cork with a loud pop. Sapphire grinned at him. Her cheeks were a nice, rosy glow, and the sight of her very fuckable husband standing with an amused smile on his lips made her want to kiss him hard.

"You really need to act a little more human around my friends, Fox. I know they are both in on the secret now, but you will give Charlie a heart attack if you keep doing that." He slowly and expertly poured them both a glass of wine, and looked at her from under his dark lashes.

"Sorry. Apologies, Charlie. I came to get another beer for Nathan and me. I forgot to actually walk in." Charlie shook her head and plonked back down into her chair. She was definitely in a worse drunken state than Sapphire, which could have something to do with the effect of both her and Fox's magic being in the same room at the same time.

Sapphire wondered how Nathan was faring, sitting in such close proximity to Fox in the lounge. It was also interesting to her that she could drink so much more now without feeling totally off her skull. Perhaps her magic was making her more tolerant of the pleasures that you could indulge in on Earth. Now that was an interesting thought.

"We are going to book the flights tonight, Fox, so you and Saf need to think about buying some clothes for this trip." She paused, and looked up at Fox with slightly blurred eyes. "Or whatever it is that you do before a trip on your world. Oh, and you will need a passport."

Sapphire blinked. She hadn't even thought about that. She couldn't remember the last time she had been abroad, and wasn't even sure her passport was still valid or where the hell it was. Some of her personal belongings had survived the fire, but was that one of them?

Fox leant across Charlie to look at the laptop, which was filled with pictures of palm trees and pyramids.

"What is a passport?" Charlie groaned and took a sip of wine.

"Oh, Christ, this could be tricky." Sapphire shook her head.

"No, it won't. It will be fine, Charlie. We will sort it out. Book the cruise with flights to Cairo first. We need to leave sooner rather than later, as long as Nathan can get the time off." Charlie screwed up her nose then giggled.

"Actually, Nathan quit his job just before you guys both arrived. He hated his job. With the money Hecta paid me for the jewellery I made him we were sweet for a while, and we are both officially and temporarily unemployed." Sapphire laughed.

"Unemployed and about to head off with us on some mad adventure to God knows where."

Fox smiled across at his wife before heading to the fridge for more beer. Charlie lifted her wine glass in a salute.

"Here's to being unemployed and to 'God knows where'." Sapphire copied her, and they clinked glasses. Fox disappeared again, with two bottles of beer in his hand. Charlie leant forward, her hair falling in front of her face, and whispered, slurring slightly.

"Seriously, Saf, how are you and Fox going to get passports sorted that quickly?" Sapphire pushed her hair back from her eyes and smiled.

"Magic, Charlie. Magic."

Nathan's team won 2–0. He was well and truly happy, and just as drunk as Charlie was when Sapphire and Fox finally left for Foxglove. They left the two of them wrapped around each other on the sofa, cuddling and smooching as it approached midnight. It did not matter that it was the middle of the week. None of them had to get up for work any longer.

Sapphire held Fox by the hand as they walked back to Pearl's cottage. The night was clear and cold, and their breath misted the air around them as they headed down the path towards the woods.

"That was nice." Fox looked down at her and smiled.

"What, my love?"

"Spending time with my two best friends. It was nice that you spent time with Nathan, doing guy stuff. I love you for that. You blend in so well." He shrugged and squeezed her hand gently.

"Years of practice, Sapphire." She watched his face with interest.

"How many lives have you had to adapt to? How many worlds have you visited, Fox?" He smiled.

"It is hard to remember them all exactly, my love. But it is part of being a guardian. You learn to adapt to the habitat." She paused, pulling him to a stop. He looked at her with confusion for a second.

"Have you ever been married before, Fox?" He laughed and pulled her towards him into his arms, wrapping them around her waist. She looked up at him warily, suddenly not wanting the answer.

"No, Sapphire. I have never been married before. The role of a guardian is to observe and aid when needed. You changed all that, and you changed me for the better. I am no longer a guardian to any other than you, my beautiful wife, believe me. My time as a traveller with others is well and truly over." She nodded, satisfied, and reached up to kiss him tenderly before nuzzling her nose into his neck.

"Good. I can't bear the thought that you loved another before me." He squeezed her again and sighed.

"I never loved before you, Sapphire. You have changed my whole world. I am happy to become human for you." He released her and they continued their slow walk to the cottage.

"I would never ask you to become human for me, Fox. We will return to Shaka once this is done. I promise you that." He remained silent, but nodded. She felt a moment of doubt in his mind, but it passed as quickly as it had come. Sapphire knew at that moment that whatever she asked of him he would give it to her, whether it be that he remain here on Earth and lose his magic or return to his homeland and retain his magic forever. His destiny lay within her hands. She hoped that she could do the right thing for him. She loved him that much.

Pearl returned the next day to her warm and wonderful cottage. Fox pushed her through the front door with Charlie, Nathan, and Sapphire trailing behind, laughing and talking loudly. The sprites were ecstatic at her return. Sapphire was surprised that Charlie and Nathan seemed oblivious to the whizzing lights around their heads, but some things are best left unknown.

Pearl looked around the cottage with bright, alert eyes. She chuckled as Fox helped her up out of the wheelchair they had borrowed from the hospital to bring her home in.

"Well, this place certainly feels much better. The energy here is almost overpowering, to say the least." Sapphire blushed. She knew that between her and Fox and their regular activity the magic levels had most definitely been ramped up. Fox smiled lazily at Sapphire and winked. Charlie sighed as she caught the unspoken message between them and rolled her eyes.

"I can imagine, Pearl," she said. Sapphire put the kettle on and busied herself to avoid any further embarrassment.

"We are leaving again tomorrow, Pearl. I'm sorry we won't be able to help you settle back in properly." Pearl settled herself in the kitchen chair and smiled at them all.

"Oh, don't worry about me. I'm absolutely fine. I think I have had about as much excitement as I can cope with for a while. You need to go, I know you do. Just keep in touch and let me know how you are doing." Nathan, as usual, looked totally confused but nodded enthusiastically. Charlie began to gather cups and milk.

"Of course we will, Pearl. We should only be gone a couple of weeks. We might be back sooner." Fox stood in the doorway looking casually gorgeous as usual. The kitchen was far too small to accommodate them all at the same time.

"I will keep you informed, Pearl, and – of course – keep them all safe." Sapphire looked at him with a hint of disapproval.

"You won't have to play bodyguard this time, Fox." Charlie laughed.

"I kind of like the idea of our own personal bodyguard, Saf. Don't ruin the fun." Nathan looked a little put out.

"What about me, Charlie? I'm your bodyguard." She put down the milk jug and leant across to kiss him on the lips.

"Of course you are, sweetie." Fox watched them with amusement, his eyes twinkling mischievously.

"I could do with the help, Nathan. These two can be a handful." Pearl chuckled.

"I think you will have a wonderful time, ladies, with two such strong men to take care of you."

Charlie widened her eyes at Sapphire. If they had known what was about to happen then 'wonderful' would not be the word to describe it.

Chapter Ten

The next day they left via taxi to the airport. The fact that they were actually sitting together in a car for the first time seemed totally unreal to Sapphire. Fox had seemed as nonchalant as usual, and took the whole thing in his stride. Charlie chatted excitedly to them in the back of the taxi about the trip. Nathan was talking to the cab driver. The scene was normal, and extremely human. Fox held Sapphire's hand the entire time, and stroked her palm with his thumb in soft, soothing circles.

The boot was full with bags. Charlie had found it somewhat amusing that out of thin air clothes and passports had been produced for both Sapphire and Fox. Sapphire had no doubt that Fox had chosen her some special outfits for the trip, and she also worried a little that he was still using his magic at such a casual pace.

He seemed no different from her, but she knew that being on Earth was draining to him. He had wandered off into the woods for a while before they had left. He had not explained why, but on his return he had seemed renewed and full of energy. Perhaps he had found a place where he could recharge his energy. The thought pressed on her mind. She also wondered if he had been to check the site of Hecta's grave. This particular thought still caused her stomach to churn. It just seemed too easy that he was gone and they had nothing left to worry about.

They reached the airport and went through the motions of checking their bags in and going through security. She noticed with amusement that heads turned and people openly stared at Fox, and often at her, as they passed through the busy lines of people. It was unnerving and a little overwhelming that they were out in the open. She knew Fox was dampening down his magic to appear more human to the casual observer, but they looked so different from the average person and it brought them a lot of attention.

Charlie and Nathan seemed oblivious, but they were used to them now and were caught up in the buzz of the trip. They ate in one of the restaurants before their flight was ready to board and enjoyed a glass of wine. Sapphire started to relax a little and watched her two friends, happy that they were so excited about going away with her for a while.

Pearl had hugged them all with a tear in her eye when they left her. She had held Sapphire a little longer than the others, and whispered in her ear,

"Be safe, my child. I know the purpose of this trip will be very important, and you must remain vigilant. You can't be too careful, you know."

Sapphire had looked at her with a confused expression before realising that Pearl most likely knew more than she was letting on about the seeds. At this moment they were sitting in her jacket pocket and throbbing softly, as usual, against her body. She had started to hear a pattern within the pulsing energy of the seeds – a song, if you like, just as Pearl had said.

She had worried for a moment as she had passed through the metal detector at the airport that they would set the alarm bells ringing and cause a scene. But nothing had happened, and Fox had merely smiled his sexy smile at her when she stepped through. He had passed through security as if he had been invisible. She had noticed a slight shimmer around his body as he had stepped through. He had cloaked himself, and she wondered if he carried something on his person that he did not want the humans to find.

"That's our flight they are calling, guys. Let's go," Charlie announced with a smile. The dull voice relaying the flight announcements repeated the message that Flight 934 was now boarding for Cairo from Gate 5, and that all passengers should make their way to the said gate immediately. Fox smiled at her and reached for her hand again.

"Ready, beautiful?" As she threaded her fingers through his own and smiled back she squeezed his hand gently.

"Ready as I'll ever be."

Before long they were in their seats, strapped in, and ready to go. Charlie had gone all out and paid the extortionate fee for business class seats. Sapphire had never flown business class, and revelled in the extra legroom and fancy leather seating. Fox sat beside her, still holding her hand. His face remained calm, but she sensed he was a little nervous.

"You OK?" He nodded, and raised her hand so that he could kiss her knuckles.

"Mmmh … I'm fine," he mumbled.

"You look a little nervous." He looked across out of the window and raised a brow.

"It's my first time in a metal tube that takes me off the ground, my love. It's a little strange for me, that's all." She laughed and kissed him, a soft, closed-mouth kiss that pushed against his lips gently.

"You will enjoy it." He pulled her in for another kiss. He opened his mouth and ran his tongue across her lip, instigating a much deeper response.

"God, you two are at it again. The mile high club here we come," Charlie said. She was sitting across the aisle from them, grinning widely as they released each other after their little display. Fox chuckled.

"I am just enjoying my wife, Charlie." She laughed.

"As usual, Fox, you do it so well." They settled back into their plush leather seats, and Sapphire noticed Fox tighten his grip just a fraction as the engines roared and they took off from the tarmac and hurtled upwards into the sky.

They landed in Cairo on time. The flight had been smooth and the service had been wonderful. Sapphire had felt thoroughly spoilt and well rested.

The heat hit them with its full force as they left the plane. It was the middle of the day and the dry, stifling humidity sucked the air from her lungs. She wished she had worn something a little less heavy on the plane. Charlie looked glamorous and cool as she walked down the steps in leggings and a long floaty shirt with her heels clipping on the metal.

"Oh, my God, it's so hot," she giggled with glee. They walked with the rest of the crowd to the terminal, and went through the motions of passport control and baggage claim again. Once more Sapphire noticed that Fox seemed to slip through all the security as if he were not even there. After grabbing their bags they headed out of arrivals. A man looking like an advert for the Egyptian tourist board was standing with a sign that said *Daines* in black writing.

"That's our ride, guys," said Charlie. Their ride turned out to be a large black SUV with air conditioning and enough room in the back for a family of six. Charlie really had gone the extra mile. They watched the other tourists, who looked hot and flustered, fight with the local taxi companies. The noise around them was a mixture of horns blasting and people shouting in a strange, guttural language. It was chaos.

Sapphire was glad they could watch, distanced from the madness, from their air-conditioned box. With wide eyes she took in all the sights of the city as the driver took them at a crazy pace through the traffic. He seemed to know what he was doing as he weaved around the side streets, braking and speeding at a wild, erratic pace that made them bump around in the back, laughing.

Charlie thought the whole experience was extremely funny, and jumped up and down in her seat like a child. Fox remained silent, his eyes scanning the scenery as if he were already on bodyguard duty.

"God, I hope they have a good mini bar in the room. I'm dying for a drink." Nathan laughed, and kissed Charlie on the cheek.

"We just had wine on the plane, Charlie, you greedy girl." Before she could reply the driver slid them to an impressive stop outside a hotel that gleamed gold in the sunlight. Porters stood outside in white uniforms. They hurried like ants towards the SUV before they could even get out.

Sapphire was impressed. The Four Seasons hotel was like something out of a movie. Luxurious and opulent, it shone like a jewel in the sunshine.

The porters took their bags and they were ushered towards reception, where they were handed mint tea and cool towels – a five-star welcome for a five-star hotel. After checking in they headed up in the lift to the tenth floor. They had rooms next to each other, and Charlie chattered excitedly to Nathan as their keys slid across the keypad and the door opened to their room.

"See you downstairs in an hour, you two. We are going to freshen up." She winked at Sapphire, and pushed Nathan inside with a shove. Fox rolled his eyes but smiled. The porter opened their door and stepped into the room, and placed their bags on the rack beside the wardrobe.

The room was plush and huge. Fox flicked on the air conditioning and smiled at Sapphire.

"Please contact reception if there is anything else you need," the porter said in a smooth, silky voice with his eyes sparkling. Fox stepped forward and handed him a tip.

"Thank you. We will." The porter bowed at the waist and backed out of the room. As usual, Fox was staking his claim on her. She still found it funny, but was grateful for his protective nature towards her. After walking to the window she gasped and placed her hand against the glass.

"You can see the Pyramids from here, Fox. Look." He was suddenly behind her, his hands around her waist his face nuzzled into her neck.

"Mmmh ... the view is nice." She shrugged him off her neck and giggled.

"Look out the window, Fox, not at me." He kissed her neck softly, pulling her playfully against his chest.

"Yes, I know. I have seen it." She sighed deeply. It was an amazing sight, and she felt as if she had been there before. Well, actually, she had – with Fox, in her last dream. They had travelled here together, but it had been a different experience that time. Now they were travelling like regular humans doing human stuff.

"I can't believe we are actually here, Fox. This is really happening." He flattened his hands against her stomach and began to stroke her gently across her navel, his magic flaring against her skin.

"Yes, my love, we are here." He paused for a second before spinning her around so that she faced him. "Now what?" She bit her lip and looked up at him into those beautiful amber eyes that flashed at her playfully.

"To be honest, Fox, I have absolutely no idea." He smiled, his face lighting up.

"Well, until you do know let's take a shower and freshen up." He waggled his eyebrows suggestively. Sapphire laughed, and then let out a loud sigh. He had a one-track mind. Not that she minded. Not one damn bit.

Two hours later the four of them were seated by the pool in reclining chairs sipping a wonderful cool cocktail. Charlie was beaming. Dressed in a modest outfit suitable for the heat, she looked like a girl who was thoroughly at home in such luxury. Nathan looked relaxed and happy, wearing Ray Ban sunglasses that protected his baby blue eyes from the glaring sunshine. Charlie had definitely packed for him, and he too looked like a wealthy traveller dressed in linen trousers and a white shirt.

Sapphire was now much cooler under the sunshade. Her own attire was a fitted linen dress in cupcake pink. Fox lounged like a supermodel in white linen trousers and a loose mandarin-style shirt. His hair was tied back with a strip of black leather, and his beads glistened like diamonds in the sun. They were an impressive sight, and once again they had attracted more than one glance from the other guests at the hotel. Charlie leant forward and whispered to Sapphire,

"People are staring at us." Sapphire nodded.

"Mmmh ... it happens, Charlie. Get used to it." She giggled.

"I feel like a movie star. Oh, God, I'm glad we came." Fox sipped his beer. Drops of water slid lazily down the outside of the glass.

"You deserve the break, Charlie. We all do." Nathan nodded in agreement.

"For sure, man. After all the shit that's gone down recently this is a much-needed escape from reality." Sapphire stretched her legs out and wiggled her toes. It felt good to have some sunshine again. She really hoped to get a tan while they were here.

"Well, you two lap it up. Fox and I will be out for a while tomorrow. I need to go check out a few places before we head down the Nile on the cruise ship." Charlie nodded.

"Uh-huh ... sure. But you will be coming out with us tonight, won't you?" Fox waited for Sapphire's response, saying nothing.

"Yeah, definitely. We just need a little time on our own tomorrow." Seemingly satisfied with her response, Charlie slipped back down on to the lounger and threw her arms over her head.

"Good. Apparently there is an awesome restaurant with belly dancing not far from here, and I want to check it out." Fox blinked and looked at Nathan – who smiled apologetically, with a shrug.

"You gotta do it while you are here, Fox."

They spent the rest of the afternoon lounging by the pool after changing into swimwear and ordering more cocktails. Fox, saying he needed to get something, disappeared again shortly after they had ordered. Sapphire knew he was twitchy when sitting around. It was not in his nature to be still for long. Unless he was alone with her and they were in bed, of course.

Charlie splashed water at her playfully and laughed as Sapphire tried to escape from her.

"This was the best idea ever, Saf. I'm so glad we came." Sapphire floated on her back with her hair spilling out beside her. It glistened white and gold in the sunlight. She felt totally relaxed and at ease. The sun was warming her body nicely and she could almost feel the tension seeping out from her pores, where it was washed away by the cool water of the pool.

"Mmmh, it was a good idea. We all needed the break … but I'm here for another purpose, Charlie, and I will need to complete it before we go home." Charlie was propped against the side of the pool with her head back, her eyes closed, and her arms stretched out either side of her.

"And what purpose is that, honey?" Sapphire dropped her feet and swam over to her friend slowly before assuming the same position by leaning back against the side of the pool.

"I need to plant some seeds I have with me." Charlie opened her eyes and squinted at her frowning.

"Seeds?" She questioned.

"Yes, seeds, Charlie. Special seeds. They appeared to me in one of my dreams and I know that I have to place them in various places across the globe. This is the first place. The other places I'm not sure about as yet … although I have seen Fox and me travelling through America at some point in the future, so I guess we will be heading there soon." Charlie looked confused, but nodded.

"OK. Sounds weird, but OK." Sapphire smiled at her friend. Once more she accepted any strange piece of information that she chose to share with her. Both their lives had been turned upside down, and would forever be changed. She was a little relieved that Charlie had taken to this new way of life so well. It had certainly taken her longer to get her head around the complete and utter weirdness her own life had thrown at her since she had become a dream traveller.

A shadow loomed above them suddenly in the form of Nathan, who was holding two more cocktails and wearing a big smile.

"Buy one get one free, ladies!" he laughed.

Fox walked through the streets of Cairo, invisible to the local people who bustled about on their business. This place fascinated him, and he was enjoying being anonymous among the throng of people. Every corner produced new sights and sounds, which filled his senses with the smell of spices, the scent of incense, and the sound of people talking in such a strange, guttural language.

He smiled as he walked past a shop, where several men sat outside smoking from a large pipe that allowed them all to inhale the sweet-smelling herb that sat in the top. The water bubbled and hissed as they sucked in the air and breathed out with heavy-lidded, happy smiles. Fox could see that the herb they smoked was not just apple or cinnamon, and he chuckled that Charlie and Nathan would definitely be interested in such a place.

The energy here was vibrant and high. It shifted and spun around him, creating a kaleidoscope of colours that made him feel light as a feather. There was something very ancient about this place. He could sense it deep within his bones. The magic here had once been magnificent and powerful, but it was now a distant memory held within the bricks and sand beneath his feet. Its residual story, however, was still playing in a constant thrum against the people and buildings he walked between.

He knew that Sapphire had been drawn to this place because of its lost magic, and that the seeds had most likely called her here instinctively. As he walked down a side alley the sound of the street faded behind him and he let out a sigh. As energising and exciting as it was to experience this place it was good to step out of the mayhem for a moment.

The alleyway was cool, and sheltered by balconies that overhung from the tall buildings surrounding him. A few dogs were fighting over some scraps of food in a corner, and he noticed several large potted plants placed outside the doorways of places of residence.

As he walked silently up the alleyway he felt a shift within the air around him, as if he had stepped through a portal into another realm. His magic flared for a second, and his head swam momentarily. After shaking his head to clear the sensation he noticed a doorway at the end of the alleyway and a metal gate that was slightly ajar.

Just as he reached out to open it a man appeared on the other side and opened it wide for him to enter. He was old, with white hair and the darkest eyes and skin that Fox had ever seen on a human before. He was smiling at Fox as if he could see him as clear as day. He bowed slowly, and gestured for Fox to enter through the doorway.

Curious, but also on alert now, Fox smiled back and walked through into a courtyard that was filled with palm trees and other plants that were bursting with fruits and flowers. An oasis in the city.

The old man continued to smile at Fox, nodding his head slowly as if to an imaginary beat. He pointed to a stone bench beside a small water feature. The sound of trickling water filled the courtyard with a sense of tranquillity. Fox nodded and sat, and the old man sat down next to him.

"Welcome, friend. You are most welcome here." His voice was like parchment paper, rough and old but wise and warm. He reached out to touch Fox's hand, but hesitated for a moment before placing his palm on to the top of Fox's fingers. Fox felt the jolt of energy like the snap of a whip against his flesh. It scorched his skin before fading quickly. The old man smiled again as Fox withdrew his hand and prepared to stand up.

"I mean you no harm, magical man. Please stay a while. Are you thirsty?" Fox did not understand what was happening or who this man was. He had called him 'magical man'. Could he really see who he was? And how was that even possible for a human to see through his cloaking spell? He decided to play along with the old man. The situation was just too far from ordinary to ignore, and he seemed defenceless enough. He sensed no danger here, just a calm, peaceful energy that was soothing and, oddly, very familiar to him.

"Yes, I am thirsty," he replied. His new friend smiled even wider, and clapped his hands together twice. A young boy appeared from out of nowhere with a tray of drinks. He too smiled widely at Fox, and handed him one of the glasses without saying a word. Fox thanked him and took a sip. It was delicious. It was a cool peppermint sensation with a twist of lime, and the ice cubes clinked against the edge of the glass as he drank greedily.

The old man laughed and drank some of his own with the same enthusiasm, a fairly large amount dribbling down his chin as he did. As he placed the glass down on the floor Fox looked closely at the old man, and for the first time he really saw him. His aura was a deep purple and gold, and he actually had a halo of white surrounding his crown. This human was not entirely human after all.

"Who are you, old man?" he asked softly. The old man chuckled again. It was a sound of too many cigarettes smoked and a lifetime of stories to be told.

"The question is not who I am but what am I, young man. I think that is what you wish to ask me." Fox smiled at him. He knew now this was no coincidence. He had been pulled to this place, just as Sapphire had been driven to bring them to Egypt.

"You seem to know what I am," Fox said. The old man nodded eagerly. He touched Fox lightly again, but this time the energy was less ferocious and merely sparked against his skin.

"Yes, yes, magic surrounds you. I see through the veil you cover yourself with, young man. It has been such a long, long time that I had given up hope that you would come. But now you are here. Are you alone?" Fox was more than a little confused. What did this all mean?

"No, I am not alone. I am here with my wife, but she is resting at our hotel with friends."

The old man's eyes glistened with a keen interest at the news.

"And is she like you, my friend, made from magic?" Fox shook his head, laughing softly.

"No, old man. She is something else, something much more powerful than me." A look of surprise then exhilaration crossed the old man's face.

"Wonderful, wonderful. You must bring her to me. I have something for you both, but you must come together. Do you understand?" Fox smiled. On all his travels throughout his life this had to be one of the most interesting people he had ever met. Apart from his wife, of course.

"What is your name, old man?"

"Aziz. My name is Aziz. And you?" Fox raised his hand to shake the dark and age-worn hand of his new-found friend.

"Fox. I am Fox." Aziz shook his hand with a firm grip and beamed widely.

"Yes, yes, of course. Fox, it is a pleasure to meet you. I look forward to meeting your wife ... and she is?" Fox licked his bottom lip slowly and smiled his dark smile.

"Sapphire, like the crystal. She is a dream traveller." Aziz blinked and looked at him with perplexed eyes.

"This is something I do not know, magical Fox, but I am keen to see her. I was told that you would arrive, and now – at last – it seems you have. Come tomorrow and we can celebrate, and I will give you the gift that I have been keeping safe for you." Fox stood in a quick, fluid motion that sent his magic shimmering around him like a wave of heat. Aziz raised his hands in the prayer position and nodded his head as he smiled broadly.

"Goodbye for now, my friend." Fox looked around himself at the courtyard, and sensed the intensity of the energy here. He still had no idea exactly who or what this man was but he knew this interaction was the start of something special, something Sapphire would be very pleased to hear about. He could feel it in his magical bones.

"Tomorrow at noon, my friend. Bring your wife, and we shall celebrate. Yes?" Fox nodded and smiled.

"Tomorrow at noon, Aziz. I look forward to it."

Chapter Eleven

Fox returned to the hotel as night fell across the city like a cool sheet of silk. It had turned the air around him into something new. The city was now waking up to a different tune.

He walked up to their room to find Sapphire in the shower. She was singing to herself. It was a sound that made him happy, as it proved that at last his wife was at ease. He walked silently to the bathroom and stood in the doorway, watching her for a moment. The steam from the shower obscured her nakedness, but he could still see her perfect shape behind the screen. Her body moved with grace and a suppleness that made his stomach clench as she washed her hair.

"Sapphire, I am back." She spun around to face him, jumped, and dropped the bottle that she had held in her hand.

"Oh, Christ, Fox, you scared me." He stepped into the steamy bathroom and began to undress quickly. He wanted to join her and wash away the heaviness of the city. She watched him with wide, dark eyes as he opened the shower door and stepped inside. Her face was filled with anticipation as he reached down to kiss her, a soft, closed-mouth kiss. His hands, which were either side of her cheeks, held her gently in place.

She pressed her body – which was now being covered with hot water – against his, skin on skin. The sensation was more than pleasant. He released her and smiled, reached for the shampoo bottle, and turned her around again so that he could finish the task she had begun. He could feel her body tremble slightly at the closeness of his presence, but he remained focused and began to massage the shampoo into her scalp.

"I have some interesting news for you, my love." She leant back into his chest and moaned softly as his fingers worked up a lather.

"Mmmh, what is that?" He moved her under the stream of water and pulled his fingers through her long blonde hair, easing out the tangles and suds that were piled within the strands.

"I met an old man in the city. He has something for us, something that I think will help you on your quest. We are to meet him tomorrow at noon." She tipped her head back and opened her eyes, and looked up at him with a question on her face.

"Who is he?" Fox moved his hands to her waist and pulled her into his body, pressing his entire length against her own small form.

"I am not entirely sure right now, but I know he can help us and he is a friend." She pushed back against him and wriggled a little, feeling his body start to respond to her nakedness. While smiling at him she opened her mouth and allowed some of the water to fill it before letting it dribble back down her chin. The sight turned him on even more, and his erection grew rock-hard against her back.

"Sounds very interesting," she said. He spun her around and kissed her again, roughly this time, and caught her breath within his mouth. He could wash away the city in a moment. Right now he wanted to feel his wife wrapped around him. It seemed that taking a shower in this hotel was more than just a way of getting clean.

Sapphire dressed slowly after the shower with a large smile on her face. They had washed themselves squeaky clean after making love quickly and ferociously under the hot water, which had satisfied their need to connect again. She brushed out her hair and began to apply a little make-up, using black kohl eyeliner to emphasise her big blue eyes.

She watched Fox in the mirror behind her as he pulled up his trousers. He had changed into the more familiar waistcoat and fitted trouser ensemble she was used to him wearing, although the fabric was a dark blue cotton rather than the usual signature black leather he usually wore. He looked good enough to eat.

Her stomach rumbled, reminding her that she was indeed ready for food. They were due to meet with Charlie and Nathan in the reception in fifteen minutes so that they could go to the restaurant with the belly dancing that Charlie had mentioned earlier.

She piled her hair up on to the top of her head with some pins and pulled a few strands down around her face to finish the look. It looked messy, but chic at the same time. She had chosen a long dress that was a soft blue. It clung to her breasts, but flowed loosely down to her ankles like the robe of a Grecian goddess.

Fox looked up and caught her watching him in the mirror as he finished buttoning his waistcoat. He grinned at her mischievously. His eyes were still dark from their encounter in the shower.

"Are you ready, my love?" She applied some lip gloss and nodded. She was more than ready.

They took the lift down to reception with Fox holding her from behind, his head resting on her shoulder. She breathed in his scent. He was shower-clean, but with the soft undertones of his patchouli and sandalwood. She wondered if he naturally secreted the oils, as she had never once seen him apply anything to his skin.

As they stepped out of the lift they hit the bustle of people in the reception area and saw Charlie and Nathan chatting to one of the doormen. Nathan spotted them, and smiled and waved them over.

"Hey, you two, our taxi is waiting." Charlie was glowing. She had caught some sun that afternoon and was dressed in a long, flowing dress like Sapphire – although hers was in a bright red and was eye-catching and beautiful. She looked amazing.

"Come on, you two. We have been waiting for you guys. What took you so long?" Fox smiled lazily at them both, and Charlie laughed as they headed out to the black SUV that had brought them from the airport. This time the driver was accompanied by another man, who was dressed in a suit and who looked like a bodyguard. Charlie whispered into Sapphire's ear as they slid into their seats.

"Our protection for the night. The hotel provides him. Apparently it's not entirely safe for tourists around the city at night. Exciting, isn't it?" Sapphire raised an eyebrow.

"I doubt that we need security with Fox around, Charlie, but it's a nice gesture." Fox eyed the man suspiciously but said nothing.

The car ride was smoother than their journey from the airport had been. The traffic was heavy but they pulled up outside an impressive-looking building before it became a bore to be sitting in the car. Charlie chatted excitedly to them, telling them that the food here was meant to be exquisite and the entertainment was supposed to be the best in the city.

They were ushered through the door. Two sphinx-like statues sat on guard like pillars at either side of the entrance. The scent of jasmine filled Sapphire's nostrils as they walked through. The plants grew like ivy up the sides of the building, covering the stone with white blossoms. The restaurant was open-planned and led out at the back to a garden that gave a breath-taking view of the river and its lush banks. The tables were scattered around a beautiful interior that was in keeping with the Egyptian theme. Rich golds and purples coloured the fabrics and walls and swatches of material were draped around the edges, giving it a royal look.

The maître d' showed them to a table that stood at the back of the restaurant so that they had an excellent view of the gardens. Sapphire blinked at the low table with opulent cushions scattered around its edges. They were to sit on the floor. Charlie clapped her hands with glee.

"How cool is this!" Fox looked amused as Sapphire hesitated while looking down at her dress and back up again.

"I suggest you take your shoes off, my love. It may be easier to sit down without them."

They settled around the table. A gentle breeze coming off the river ran its fingers through her hair as Sapphire tucked her legs beside her. Fox sat cross-legged, looking very comfortable. Charlie fussed with her dress until it lay in a pool beside her long legs and trailed out like a vision of spilt blood. She looked like a vampire queen.

Sapphire watched the other customers around them survey their party with curiosity. They were also seated at floor level in places around the garden, and the glow of lanterns within the trees cast silver shadows on their faces. She noticed that most of the diners tonight were local, with a few foreign faces dotted in between. They must have stuck out like a sore thumb, but that was something she would have to get used to there.

"Where did you find this place, Charlie?" Sapphire asked. Charlie was still smiling like a happy cat.

"Online it's the best restaurant in Cairo. Stop worrying. We can afford it." Fox trailed a finger across her cheek, and leant in to kiss her neck softly.

"Enjoy, my love. You look beautiful." Sapphire sighed. As usual he had picked up on her nerves. She felt awkward, and a little out of her depth here. Charlie, in her usual style, ordered the food for them. The waiter was attentive and very helpful, and spoke in a deep, slow voice that made Sapphire wonder if all the men there were born to seduce.

Their drinks arrived first. Charlie had ordered gin and tonics for them, and a bottle of champagne to accompany the meal. Sapphire wondered just how expensive this place was, but dismissed the thought quickly. The food arrived shortly after. It consisted of an array of dishes that looked as good as they tasted: bowls of steaming meats, and couscous that filled the mouth with spices and heat.

Sapphire started to relax. This was indeed wonderful, and she was starting to feel her body loosen up as the drinks were consumed. They chatted among themselves, letting the atmosphere soak in. The champagne flowed freely, and the night air was filled with the chatter and bustle of happy people.

As the dishes were cleared and dessert arrived music began to play from the garden outside – a sultry, exotic beat that thrummed a heartbeat within Sapphire's body. The lights in the restaurant had dimmed slightly, and the energy switched once more to something else. The heat began to rise in Sapphire's body, and she noticed that Fox too had been affected by the change in tempo. His legs were now uncurled and he leant against her his shoulder, touching her bare skin. She felt his magic flare against her own and shiver softly down her spine.

The bag containing the seeds, which she carried with her everywhere she went, began to shimmer slightly. She pulled it to her and placed it under her dress. She did not want unwanted attention from a glowing bag of magical seeds to suddenly cause them any trouble.

As two women emerged from behind one of the palm trees Charlie and Nathan turned to watch the scene that was now unfolding before them in the garden. Dressed in folds of chiffon that shimmered in gold, orange, and red, they sparkled in the lights like ethereal beings. Belts of sequins glistened and shone on their hips as they moved like sparkling birds of paradise. Each movement they made in time to the music sent another ripple of flesh spiralling around and around.

It was fascinating to watch, and sexy as hell. Hair like ebony and skin like coffee gave them both a look of eastern beauty. Their eyes were lined with black kohl and their lips were ruby red. Sapphire watched them move across the garden. Their arms above their heads were swaying and moving like the head of a cobra, and their delicate fingers uncurled as they did.

Fox shifted beside Sapphire and moved his hand to her thigh, where he began to squeeze gently as he lifted her dress very slowly so that her calf and knee were now exposed. Her eyes questioned him as to his intention as he slipped his fingers under her knee and began to stroke very lightly at the sensitive skin underneath. The sensation was exquisite, warming her skin with his touch and the haze of magic that lightly touched her nerve endings like tiny electric shocks. As usual he knew what he was doing. His head was facing the dancers and his focus was on the show, but his thoughts and fingers were doing something else entirely.

Charlie and Nathan were oblivious, captured by the spell the dancers were weaving around the other diners. Sapphire closed her eyes briefly, catching her breath as Fox continued to stroke her skin lightly. His shoulder, which was still pressed against her, was hot and firm, and she could almost hear his breathing deepen as he played his game of seduction.

The dancers were close to them now, and Sapphire opened her eyes again to watch them. Fox removed his hand suddenly, making her jump a little at the loss of contact. He placed it further down her calf and slid down to her heel in a slow, fluid motion. Who would have thought that area of her body could be so sensitive? She fidgeted against his touch and he smiled, still watching the two women dancing. It seemed he had caught their eye and they headed directly for their table, weaving around the other diners seductively.

Charlie and Nathan gawped up at the dancers as they stood directly above them, swaying and jiggling their ample assets. One of the women winked at Fox and gestured for him to rise and join her. Charlie looked at Sapphire and raising her eyebrows. She gave her the 'Are you really going to let her do that?' look that Sapphire had seen her give many times before. She laughed and shook her head. She was not a jealous woman, and knew her man was well and truly hers. This would be interesting, and she was keen to see how Fox would react.

Fox looked at her for a second, his eyes dark and his expression flirtatious. She nodded at him, and he uncurled gracefully to his full height and took the dancer's hand in his own. Charlie almost choked on her champagne as the other dancer – taking her friend's lead – reached down for Nathan, who seemed a little less enthusiastic to join in the fun.

Sapphire leant back on her elbows and watched with amusement. This would definitely be interesting. Charlie, however, looked positively pissed off as Nathan clambered to his feet. People became caught up in the show and began to clap around them as the energy lifted around them.

Fox began to move with the dancer. He held her hand lightly, taking control as she hesitated for a second. Her eyes widened, as if she could sense that something was very different about this man. Her lips opened and she positively swooned as he took her waist, spinning her around and causing her silk scarves to fly out from her body and catch the air like a kite. With his eyes fixed on Sapphire he moved his hips into the back of the dancer and caught her other hand, spinning her around again. He danced like a wild stallion, dark and dangerous, and moving with her as if he had always known this dance. Watching him move with someone else in such a way made her body shiver. It was erotic, it was sexy, and it was turning her on. Just as he intended.

Nathan was doing well. He was also a good dancer and had some good moves, but all eyes were on Fox and his partner. The room was mesmerised, unaware that they were watching a show that was meant for one person only. His wife.

Sapphire smiled at him and sighed. Her body temperature was high and her magic sparkled around her. She was having a hard job controlling it. Fox, on the other hand, was having no trouble. He seemed to be enjoying himself immensely. He was such a tease. The poor belly dancer had no idea what she was dealing with, and her eyes grew wider as he swayed his hip into her back as she shimmied.

"Let her enjoy the ride," Sapphire thought. She knew it was just a bit of fun, and that the effect was aimed solely at her. The music continued, and the beat of the drums grew faster and louder and built up into a frenzy as other diners moved away from their tables and began to dance. The spell of the music and the dancing was weaving its magic around the restaurant like a flow of seductive water that trickled through each person into their bodies and into their soul.

Fox released the belly dancer in a graceful spin and stepped aside. His arm was now raised and his finger was crooked as he beckoned Sapphire to join him. She laughed again, and shook her head to free the fuzziness of the champagne that was now charging through her system.

She stood up slowly and reached for his hand. He grasped her firmly as he pulled her into his body and continued the dance. This time his eyes were blazing amber and black and flashing with sparks of gold as his magic unleashed itself for her. She felt it fizzle into her fingers and scatter in a pool around her feet.

He was cloaking the flare of magic between them but she could see – she could feel, she could smell – the scent of lust as it crashed around them. The restaurant had turned into a wild, erotic dancing frenzy that had been ignited by their hidden magical arousal.

Sapphire allowed him to sweep her off her feet and spin her around. She was caught up in the heat of the moment and closed her eyes again as he moved against her. His head bowed low against her neck as he whispered into her ear softly,

"I love you, my beautiful wife. Only you."

Sapphire was aware that they were now in the garden away from the other diners. Fox had led them away from the throng and they were alone and standing at the edge of the river. The cool breeze was sending shivers across her skin. She opened her eyes and smiled up at him as he held her close. His hands were behind her waist and his groin was pushing into her body. He was swaying slowly against her, a wry smile on his beautiful lips.

"Are you having a good time, Sapphire?" She nodded and smiled.

"Of course I am. With you as the entertainment how could I not be?" He chuckled and kissed her softly.

"We still have dessert to eat," he said. Sapphire sighed deeply.

"I don't think I could fit another thing into this dress, Fox." He kissed her again, pushing his tongue into her mouth and holding her neck so that he could position her at the right angle. She kissed him back, squeezing his buttocks tightly.

"Fuck dessert," she thought.

Charlie caught them kissing, and coughed loudly to get their attention.

"Come on, you two. Dessert is sitting in there, melting." She was laughing as she turned back into the restaurant. Sapphire felt as if she was floating. Fox draped his arm across her shoulder and led her back inside, his energy pulsing against her like a persistent reminder that he was the hottest man she had ever met. Ever.

The restaurant had returned to some resemblance of order again. The belly dancers were now talking to various diners, who were finishing their meal. Nathan looked flushed and had a big grin on his face. He had definitely enjoyed the show.

"What the hell happened? One minute they were dancing ... the next minute everyone was up, out of their seats. Did you two do something?" Charlie asked as she manoeuvred a piece of sweet pastry into her mouth. Fox smiled his sly smile.

"Maybe." Nathan was tucking into his plate of sweet delicacies. Sapphire just couldn't face another morsel. She was absolutely stuffed.

"We just can't take you anywhere without something crazy happening, can we?" Sapphire watched Charlie devour the pastry with envy. It looked delicious.

"It comes with the magical package, Charlie. Sorry." Nathan paused in his eating frenzy.

"Don't apologise, Saf. That was excellent fun." Charlie shot him a look.

"Mmmh ... a little too much fun for you, I think." He laughed and pulled her to him, kissing her on the cheek.

"Aah ... jealous baby."

Fox watched them with amusement. He took his fork and sliced a piece of the dessert, then lifted it to his lips slowly. Sapphire watched him take the pastry into his mouth and eat it as if it was a piece of her flesh. He smiled at her again. God, he was a bad, bad man.

After some strong black coffee they paid and left the restaurant – accompanied by their bodyguard, who Sapphire had not seen for the entire evening. He must have been good. Charlie and Nathan seemed as high as kites on the champagne and the energy of the evening.

She, on the other hand, felt exhausted. It had been a very long first day, and the jet lag was actually having an effect on her. By the time they reached the Four Seasons she was resting her head on Fox's shoulder and dozing against him.

"Shall I carry you up to bed, my love?" he whispered into her ear. Charlie and Nathan were already out of the SUV and, giggling and laughing, were heading into reception.

"No, I'm fine. Just tired." He nodded and helped her out while holding her against him with his arm wrapped around her waist.

"Goodnight, my friends. We will see you tomorrow for breakfast," he said to Charlie and Nathan as he directed Sapphire to the lift. They were heading out to the back patio, where hookah pipes and brandy beckoned.

"Goodnight, Saf. Goodnight, Fox … awesome night." Sapphire closed her eyes again and allowed Fox to lead the way.

She was aware of him undressing her and taking the pins out of her hair. He laid her on the cool cotton sheets of the enormous bed they had. He kissed her forehead and brushed her cheek softly.

"Sleep well, Sapphire." She felt her body melt into the mattress. Relaxed and happy, she allowed herself to drift into a deep and wonderful sleep.

Chapter Twelve

Fox watched Sapphire sleep for some time. He was wide awake, and his energy was high from the evening at the restaurant. She looked peaceful and happy in her sleep. Her face was relaxed and she looked younger than her years.

He needed to return to Shaka. It had been some time since he had connected with his home planet and the people he loved. While standing beside the bed he smoothed back a tendril of hair from her face, and kissed her softly on the cheek once more before standing back and tuning into his homeland. His body shimmered with magic before disappearing and leaving Sapphire alone in the room. He knew she was safe for now, and if she needed him he would know and would return immediately.

Sapphire stirred as if sensing his absence, but remained asleep. Her mind was floating on a cloud of delta waves and she started to dream. Her body remained in the soft, comfortable bed of the Four Seasons but her mind wandered. Far, far away.

A long bridge made from stone stretched out as far as she could see, its edges decorated with stone elephants and wolves. They remained completely still in the dark night that her dream took her to. She could see her dream-self walking along the bridge, moving slowly with a soft, graceful ease.

As she walked, the bridge ahead changed into a different scene. Several figures approached her, and she could see that they were men and women walking slowly in a line. Sapphire stopped to watch them, curious as to who they were and why they were there in her dream.

The woman at the front was cloaked in a long black robe. Her hair was white-blonde, and shone brightly like a full moon beneath the material that was draped over her head. As she came to a stop in front of Sapphire she lifted the cape from her head and revealed herself. Her blue eyes were sparkling brightly.

The Oracle stood before Sapphire, smiling her perfect smile. In her hands she held out a book, its pages open for Sapphire to see. On raising the book to eye level Sapphire could see a series of maps within the pages. A map of the world – of her home planet, Earth – sat before her. Shimmering against the paper were marks like tiny stars that glittered and shone at points across the globe.

Sapphire looked more closely and realised the stars were in fact trees. Silver, and bare from leaves, they sparkled brightly. This was a map of where she needed to plant her seeds: from Egypt to America to New Zealand and England. Other markers crossed the map, and Sapphire captured the information into her mind before the vision disappeared.

The Oracle smiled again and shut the book slowly. Her hair rose and fell around her face like feathers caught in the wind. Sapphire felt her body flicker and bend as the dream started to change. She was moving again, moving away from the bridge. She was now standing on the edge of a cliff looking out to sea. The moon was rising, a beautiful full moon that was tinged with a deep red. A blood moon.

Her head spun and she shifted again. This time she was standing in the woods that surrounded Foxglove, Pearl's cottage. The trees welcomed her and the animals called out into the night air.

Sapphire looked down and could see a large hole dug into the soft earth. The earth that had been dug out was piled high to one side. It looked as if someone had recently used some serious muscle to dig the oblong-shaped hole into the ground. Sapphire, momentarily confused, tipped her head to one side. It looked like a grave.

Realisation struck her in the stomach and she gasped and recoiled, and stepped away from the scene with horror. Her mind reeled and her body shook. The dream feeling was suddenly ominous and frightening. She fought against the urge to be sick and, gasping for air, clutched at her stomach. Her mind was spinning. What could this mean? Why was she seeing this? Just as her stomach rolled with the uncomfortable sensation of emptying her evening meal on to the ground beneath her feet she woke up.

Her eyes wide, Sapphire sat up in bed and gulped air back into her lungs. The room was dark and still. She could not sense Fox in the room, and she suddenly felt incredibly vulnerable. Her heart began to jump loudly in her chest. She reached for the bedside lamp and switched it on, illuminating the room in a soft glow of amber light.

"Fox ... Fox, where are you?" He appeared suddenly beside her, his face etched with worry.

"I am here, my love. I left for Shaka only for a short time, but sensed your fear. What happened?" She clutched the sheet to her chest and blinked back tears.

"I don't know ... I was dreaming again. I saw the Oracle. She showed me a map that would help me, and then I saw the woods at the back of Foxglove. There was a grave, Fox, a grave that had been dug up. It was empty. What does that mean?" He sat down beside her and took her into his arms, and held her against the warmth of his body and soothed her with his hands in her hair.

"I do not know, my love. Try not worry. I am sure all is well. I do not sense any danger. Shh, my love. All is well." Sapphire clung to him. The warmth of his body pressed against her, reassuring her that she was safe once more.

"I hope you are right, Fox, I really do." He kissed her softly on the top of her head.

"Go back to sleep, Sapphire, I will not leave you again. I needed to recharge my energy and see my father. I will stay with you while you sleep. Believe me, my love, no harm with come to you." Sapphire nodded, feeling her stomach begin to settle once more. The dream had been an omen. She could feel it in her bones. And it was not a good omen. That was for sure.

Sapphire woke the next morning with Fox wrapped around her. He was naked and hot against her skin and his arm was resting across her waist, pinning her to him. She sighed deeply. She had slept well on his return, with no more dreams to interrupt her, but the memory of what she had seen played heavily on her mind. The map was planted clearly in her subconscious and she knew where she needed to go, but for now they needed to find the first place to plant the seed in this strange and exotic land.

Fox had told her last night that he had met someone who could help them. She was eager to find out how. She shifted her weight and moved Fox gently away from his spooning position. He stirred and moaned as she lifted his hand from her waist. God, he was always so warm.

"Good morning, beautiful," he whispered as he stretched out his legs. Sapphire rolled over to face him and smiled. His hair was tangled across his face in dark tendrils, which covered his amazing eyes. She pushed them back slowly and watched him open them slowly as he blinked at the daylight that spilt into the room.

"Did you sleep well?" He pulled her back towards him and nestled his face into her neck.

"Yes, I did, my love. And you?" Sapphire yawned.

"Mmmh, yes. After you returned I did. Don't leave again without telling me. I was scared." He lifted his head and frowned.

"I am sorry, my love. I won't do that again. I would never frighten you on purpose." As she kissed him softly she sighed again.

"I know."

"Come on, let's get dressed. I'm starving." Fox laughed and threw back the sheet that was draped across them.

"As am I, Sapphire. But not for food." Sapphire smacked him playfully before escaping quickly to the bathroom.

"You have a one-track mind, husband."

They ate in the garden of the hotel surrounded by the palm trees and beautiful statues that were scattered throughout the flowerbeds and vegetation. The sun was beating down even at this time of day, and Sapphire was glad the umbrella above their table was giving them some shade.

"So you two are off on some secret adventure today, then?" Charlie was sipping her cup of thick black coffee. Her designer sunglasses gave her the look of someone who had a hangover. She most likely did.

"It's not a secret adventure, Charlie. I just need to spend some time alone with Fox today. We will be back later for dinner." Charlie nodded.

"Mmmh, sure. Nat and I will be going to see the Pyramids and do some sightseeing. The hotel has arranged us a guide. Should be interesting." Fox smiled.

"Enjoy, Charlie. The Pyramids are amazing." Nathan was piling more food on to his plate. He looked up at Fox with interest.

"Have you seen them before, Fox?" Fox nodded.

"Yes, but a very long time ago. They looked a little different then." Sapphire was surprised. She had no idea he had been there before.

"When did you come here?" He paused before answering.

"I travelled here once with another dream traveller, but only briefly. The land was alive with magic and mystery during the time of the Pharaohs." Nathan swallowed loudly.

"Wow." Now this was news to Sapphire. Of course she knew that Fox had accompanied her during her last dream to Egypt, but she wondered who the other dream traveller had been. It always made her a little edgy to realise she was not the first person Fox had played guardian to. It was the only time her jealous button was pushed. Fox lifted her hand and, sensing her emotion, kissed her knuckles.

"I was observing, my love, only observing. Remember, you are the first and last traveller that I will ever interact with." Charlie chuckled.

"And so she should be, Fox. My friend does not share." Sapphire smiled at her friend.

"It's OK, Charlie. I understand Fox more than you know. My brain just does a little human flip sometimes when I think about his past." Nathan shook his head.

"I still can't get my head around it, Saf. I'm not sure how you cope, to be honest." This time Fox laughed, which attracted the attention of some of the other guests.

"It takes time and practice, my friend, that is for sure."

Breakfast was finished and it was time to leave. Charlie hugged Sapphire before stepping into their transport for the day.

Fox stood waiting with his eyes alert and his energy high as he waited for Sapphire to say her goodbyes. He was keen to take her to see Aziz. After his brief visit to Shaka his father had told him that this man could possibly be a descendant from their planet, as only those with the magic of Shaka could see through his cloaking spell. Just as Pearl had once been part of their world it seemed that Aziz may have also walked the lands of his magical home.

He was also more than curious as to what the gift was that Aziz had for them both. His father was just as much in the dark as he was about that piece of information. He had been glad to see him and had briefly dropped into his home to see Kitten, who had been ecstatically happy to see him again. She had asked after Sapphire and when they would return home again.

Fox had no idea. In fact he had no idea where home really was any more. He would travel the dimensions with his wife until she needed to stop again. They had two places that were close to their hearts: Earth and Shaka. Both places held people who were dear to them and this alone caused them both some turmoil, as Fox knew that Sapphire loved her family and friends and that despite her magical undertones she would always be mostly human. He, on the other hand, was well and truly made from magic. They had connected in a way that until now had never been seen, and the fact that they had joined in marriage bound them together in more ways than one. But the future for them both was uncertain, and the task that his dream traveller wife was currently undertaking changed everything for both of them. Even his father was unable to help with that matter.

Fox led his wife in the direction he had taken the day before, through the maze of streets and the bustle of people. His body was alert, and he had switched on his cloaking spell so that they could weave their way through the humans without being detected. They attracted far too much attention when they were visible.

He had noticed that Sapphire's appearance had been changing daily. Her eyes were just that little bit more alive with the spark of magic, and the outer rim to her irises that defined his fellow people was growing wider and darker. The sapphire blue of her eyes glowed distinctly, and her hair was growing more and more like a sheet of white silk. She was even more stunning than he remembered her when they had first met. Her body was growing suppler, her muscles were growing stronger, and her body was becoming more curvaceous. The magic that coursed through her veins was changing her, and she was flourishing into a stronger creature ... stronger than even he had been, and Fox was pure magic. He was in awe of his wife, and his love for her was infinite. He would stand by her side whatever lay ahead of them now, forever protecting and supporting her. That was the one certainty that he had.

It did not take them long to arrive at the alleyway that Fox had found the day before. Sapphire stood at the Iron Gate and looked up at him. She too could feel the change in energy here, and her eyes grew wide with anticipation.

On cue the gate opened and Aziz stood, smiling widely. His face was alive with swirls of excitement that changed his aura into a moving pattern of gold and white. Fox returned his smile.

"Aziz, it is good to see you again. This is my wife, Sapphire. Sapphire ... Aziz." The old man opened the gate wider and bowed at the waist.

"Welcome, welcome. Come ... come inside, please." Sapphire held Fox's hand tightly. Her magic was skittering around her. It too seemed very excited to make contact with the old man. Fox walked through the gate first, still alert, and looking for any sign of danger. You could never be too careful. The courtyard was as calm and peaceful as before, and the trickling of water from a small fountain in the centre had created the perfect oasis.

"It is a pleasure to meet you, Sapphire. Your husband told me that you are a dream traveller. I am very interested to hear what this is." Sapphire smiled a little nervously at him as he led them through the courtyard into the building that was situated behind the array of potted plants and statues.

"Thank you, Aziz. To be honest I'm still discovering what it means myself, so I hope I don't disappoint you." He laughed at her response, and gestured for them to take a seat in the room they had entered. It was a simple room filled with row after row of bookshelves. The seating was a series of floor cushions scattered around a long, low table that seemed to be as ancient as the old man was.

Fox raised his eyebrows as Sapphire gave him a tired look. Sitting on the floor was obviously becoming a chore for her. They settled as comfortably as they could, and Sapphire took off her shoes again so that she could tuck her legs to one side. Fox watched the old man as he fussed around the room, moving objects around as if he were looking for something. He spoke in his own language to a person he could not see before sitting down opposite them with a small package that he had retrieved from one of the drawers in a large wooden cabinet that sat at the back of the room. The smell of incense, patchouli, and frankincense wafted around them. It made Fox feel as if he was back on Shaka. Aziz looked at them both expectantly, his eyes sparkling like a child full of mischief and something else Fox could not put his finger on. Was it envy?

"My friends, I have this gift for you both. It was given to me by my father and to him from his father. It has been passed down our family throughout the generations, with the same story that was told of two strangers who would arrive in our land. One male, one female, both would hold the old magic of our lands ... and the male would be named after a wild animal and he would be of light and shadow. I witnessed your shadow yesterday, my friend. The shield you wear around you when you wish to walk unobserved among us mortals without being detected. The light I see around you now.

"As for you, my dear Sapphire, I see something else ... something I have never seen, and I am keen to learn of this magic you hold within you. But this gift I have for you both is very precious, and I must make sure that you use it wisely."

Sapphire swallowed. Her mouth was suddenly dry and her hands were suddenly clammy, and the intense stare this strange man was giving her was making her nervous. Fox remained as calm as ever by her side but he sensed her unease and took her hand within his own, interlocking their fingers and sending a pulse of soothing light into her palm.

The door opened from the room beside them and a young boy entered with a tray of drinks. His smile was as big as Aziz's smile had been when they arrived. He placed the tray on the table and began to pour what looked like peppermint tea into coloured glasses for them.

"Thank you, Hassan. That will be all for now." Aziz was still smiling at them both as he reached for his glass. A whisper of steam lifted lazily from its edges as he sipped it slowly.

"Please, take some refreshment. You must be thirsty." Sapphire hesitated before following Fox's lead and taking her drink. She thought it odd that he would be serving them hot tea on a day that was blistering with heat outside. On taking a sip she found the tea to be wonderfully sweet and strong. The sensation of the cool peppermint and heat against her tongue was more than refreshing, however, and she was grateful for the distraction.

"Aziz, tell me ... When did your father tell you this story of our arrival?" Fox asked as he sipped his tea. The old man chuckled.

"I was a young man, full of adolescent thoughts, and believed the tale to be just a folk story – something to tell the young folk to remind them of times gone by. But my father was insistent that I keep this gift safe and never give up hope, for it was foretold by the masters of our race that you would return." He paused and then clapped his hands together with glee, making Sapphire jump with surprise. "And now you have."

Sapphire looked at the package that lay innocently on the table before them. She wondered what the hell it was.

"Can you tell us what this gift is, Aziz?" she asked. The old man nodded then shook his head, smiling at the same time.

"I have no idea, my dear, but I can tell you both that it is precious and powerful. It must not be used without conviction, and it must be used wisely and with caution." Sapphire mumbled under her breath,

"Well, that's a lot of help." Fox reached for the package.

"May I?" Aziz seemed positively animated now, and nodded with excitement.

"Yes, yes ... please open it." Sapphire watched as her husband unwrapped the package slowly. Her body was trembling, and the seeds that sat in her bag beside her were vibrating against her leg. She placed her hand on them like she would to a small child if she was chiding him or her about their behaviour. Fox removed the paper that surrounded the gift – which, when uncovered, turned out to be a small blue bottle filled with a translucent liquid. He lifted it higher, to eye level, so that he could inspect it.

A small gasp escaped Sapphire's lips as she watched the liquid inside turn into a swirl of pearlescent multi-coloured lights. It was alive and full of magic. The liquid spun and danced within the bottle like a small universe filled with a vast spectrum of stars and galaxies. It swirled and spun, sending shimmers of light out across the room.

Both of them, in unison, felt their magic ignite like a struck match, and suddenly the room was alight with bright white shards of crystal light. Like a prism that had been struck by the first beams of sunlight they shone and vibrated, sending lightning sparks out across the room.

Aziz let out a cry of delight and jumped to his feet. The young boy who had served them drinks was back in the room, his face a picture of disbelief and his arms above his head as he tried to capture the sparks that scattered across the walls and ceiling. Fox looked shocked for a moment, and almost dropped the bottle before regaining his composure and holding his hand over the bottle to dim the magic. Their magic withdrew and the room settled again into normality. Sapphire laughed.

"Well, that was different," she said. Aziz was standing and clapping his hands.

"Yes, yes, the magic has found you. How wonderful. At last I can pass this burden to you, my friends, for now the time has come for the magic to be returned to its rightful owners." Sapphire looked at Fox and shrugged. He took the bottle and placed it in his pocket, thus avoiding any more starbursts from combusting themselves suddenly in the middle of Cairo.

"Aziz, you must tell us everything you know about the magic within this bottle. Please ... We are as in the dark as you are at this moment." Fox looked serious. Sapphire realised that this was something even he was not sure of, and it troubled her.

"My friends, I have told you all I know. This gift was given to me by my father, and I was told to only pass it on to you when the time was right. I do not know what it does, only that its magic is strong and must be used with caution. But it has joined with you, as I was told, and now I am free." The young boy was now staring at them both with his mouth open, an expression of adulation on his face.

"Hassan, you may go now. That is all." Aziz pushed him out of the room, eager to have Sapphire and Fox to himself despite the young boy's curiosity.

"Sapphire, please tell me ... What is a dream traveller? I am keen to know." Sapphire shook her head. This was all a little too much for her now.

"Uh-uh ... no. I think you need to tell us something first." She took the bag of seeds from her handbag and placed them on the table before her.

"Have you ever seen anything like this before?" she asked. She emptied some of the seeds from the bag on to the wooden table and looked up at him expectantly. Aziz stood still, his body trembling slightly, his eyes wide. He bent down slowly and poked one of the seeds with his finger as if it were a wild animal about to bite him.

"By the gods, what have you here? My, my, my ... I have never in my life seen such magic. Where did you get these?" Sapphire looked at Fox, who raised a brow.

"I brought them back from a dream I had. I know that I need to plant them within the Earth and that they will help her to awaken, but what else they may be for I have no idea. I was hoping you might be able to help with that." The energy in the room had lifted again, and she noticed that Aziz was now sweating. Droplets had formed on his brow, and he looked almost pale.

"My dear, this is something else, something more powerful than I could ever imagine. My father did not tell me about this." Fox started to stand. The meeting, as far as he was concerned, was obviously coming to an end, and he was perhaps aware that things had changed again.

"Sapphire, it is time to go. Thank you, Aziz. I am sure that this gift you have given us will be of benefit to us, but for now we must take our leave." Aziz looked bereft.

"My friends, I did not mean to offend you. Please stay. No harm will come to you here." Sapphire was confused. Whey was Fox keen to suddenly leave? Had something happened that she was not aware of? Of course they had revealed their true colours to this stranger and just lit up his room like a bonfire display, but he had given them more magic. Surely it was OK to stay awhile, wasn't it? Fox took her hand and pulled her up. His energy had changed, and he was on a mission.

"We are leaving. Thank you again, old man. We may well see you again sometime." Sapphire stumbled as he led her out the door into the courtyard. She had only just managed to scramble the seeds back into the pouch and into her bag before he had dragged her out of the door. Aziz followed them, jumping from one foot to the other.

"My friends, please return whenever you are free. I am sorry if I offended you. May the gods protect you on your travels." Sapphire looked over her shoulder and smiled feebly at him as Fox pulled her forward out into the alleyway.

"Goodbye, Aziz. Thank you." She struggled to keep up with Fox, who strode forward like a man with a purpose as he pulled her out into the throng of people again on the side street. She pulled against him, urging him to stop for a moment.

"Fox. Stop. What the hell just happened? Why are we leaving?" He turned and faced her, his face grim.

"The magic he has just given to us was from a place far away, my love. It is dangerous and intoxicating. The old man would have been driven mad if we had stayed too long. We have just ignited a time bomb, my love, and we need to get away before it goes off."

Sapphire's head was spinning as they headed back to the hotel. Fox practically shoved her into the room and slammed the door shut behind them when they arrived. She was gasping for breath and slumped down into one of the chairs, grateful that the air conditioning was on full blast in the room.

"Fox ... Tell me, for the love of God, what is going on?" He took off his waistcoat and removed the bottle from his pocket. After heading into the bedroom he rummaged through his clothing and wrapped it inside a sarong that he had in his drawer and placed it inside. He then headed back into the main room, sat down opposite her, and pulled his hands over his face, sighing heavily.

"We have to keep the bottle away from the seeds for now, Sapphire. This I am sure of. The magic is too powerful to combine right now. I may need to speak to my father again and find out exactly what we have here. All I know is that my instinct was telling me to get the hell out of there after our magic flared so brightly. This must be contained, and we must make sure that the seeds are kept more safely. The time is not right for the two to connect. Not yet." Sapphire watched him with nervous eyes. This was all a little too weird. Suddenly their little trip was turning into something else.

"Fox, you are scaring me." He looked up at her and smiled thinly.

"You should be scared, my love. This magic is more powerful than you can imagine. We have been given something that our people have only ever dreamt of. It is the power of creation itself. With the combination of this essence and the magic of the seeds you hold anything is possible. Anything. No wonder Ebony was so keen to have you, my love. You are the key to this new creation. The key to new life. We must guard it well." Sapphire slumped back on to the chair.

"Holy shit," she said.

Chapter Thirteen

Pearl was feeling much better, like her old self again, and as it was such a lovely day she had decided to take a walk in the woods. She had wrapped herself up well in the warmth of her woollen coat and scarf. Although the sun was shining brightly the air was crisp and cold, and it made her breath appear in the air as white tendrils of smoke as she walked.

She carried a basket in her hand and was looking down at the ground for any herbs that may come in handy for her winter remedies. As she walked slowly along the pathway she smiled at the sound of birdsong, and felt the thrum of the earth beneath her feet. Sapphire and Fox had been gone a few days now, and she wondered how they were. She imagined them sunning themselves in the hot sunshine of Egypt and chuckled at the idea of Charlie and Nathan, excited at this new land they were visiting, behaving like two young children.

Before long she was standing at the tree where she had first met Sapphire, and she placed her basket on the ground. The tree had always been a good friend to her, restoring her energy and giving her many wonderful moments of meditation. She had often thought of the tree as a living portal to other lands, as her visions – when connecting to its energy – had taken her mind to places she had never seen in this lifetime.

As she placed her hand on the wizened trunk she felt its familiar burst of energy travel up her fingertips into her body. This time the tree felt different – stronger, somehow. She closed her eyes and connected with its throbbing pulse of magic, for that is what she could feel coming from the tree today – magic that was strong and pure. Something had changed, and she could feel the power of its new melody dance within her veins.

The air around her warmed slightly, and her mind wavered with a vision of a new land. A castle upon a hill stood proud and tall against a lush landscape filled with fields of corn and green grass.

Her mind was moving quickly with the vision, and her body trembled as she now found herself looking at a man within the walls of a castle. He was standing beside a table covered with scrolls and glass jars filled with herbs. She could imagine the smell of the incense that was burning on the table next to him … It was patchouli and sandalwood.

With a jolt of recognition her body shook as the man looked up directly at her and smiled. She knew this man, and she now understood what the magic was that was now coursing through the living veins of this tree. The portal to another world that she had indeed visited long, long ago was beginning to open. Conloach, the king and magician of Shaka, had seen her peeking through into his realm.

As she held her hand to her chest to steady her breath Pearl opened her eyes, smiled, and looked up at the vast canopy of branches above her. The leaves glistened in the sunlight, sparkling as if they were on fire. The tree stood magnificent and innocently beside her like a majestic giant, silent but wise.

Her body was still trembling, not from the cold but from the excitement of her new find. She could not wait to tell Sapphire on her return that this new magic was taking form within the planet, and on her very own doorstep. She spat into her hand and wiped the spittle on to the tree trunk in the age-old gesture of giving thanks for its exchange in energy before picking up her basket and continuing on her walk through the woods.

She hummed to herself an old Wiccan tune that her mother had taught her when she was a little girl. It told the tale of the turning of the tides and the power of the Earth, the Air, the Fire, and the Water, and was an old witch's chant that was almost forgotten in these modern times.

As she stopped to pick some mistletoe that was conveniently growing at a low level on an apple tree she wondered whether she should place some wards around the tree now that the portal was beginning to open. It would need to be protected now from any human who may stumble across it, so that they didn't end up with a surprise vision they were not ready for.

She continued to hum to herself with a smile on her lips as she nodded to herself. Yes, that is what she would do tomorrow. She would set new protection wards, and perhaps something a little stronger around the perimeter that would throw the average human off the path to the tree.

As she filled her basket with mistletoe she realised that she had walked a little further than usual, and that this part of the wood was not a place she usually visited. The landscape was dense here, and the air a little thicker and cooler. She sniffed the air like a dog for a second, sensing something else on the breeze apart from the earthy smell of woodland. Magic. She smelt magic.

She stepped forward and walked cautiously in the direction of the trail of magic. Her eyes widened as she found herself standing between two silver birch trees that stood like two pillars before her. The ground had been recently disturbed, despite the hard frost and the snow that had fallen recently. A pile of freshly dug earth had been placed beside a hole in the ground, which gaped at her like an open mouth.

She stepped forward with the smell of magic strong within her nostrils. While standing at the edge of the hole Pearl tipped her head to one side and looked at the depth of this cavity in the ground. It looked like a grave site, a grave that had been recently dug up ... and whatever had been inside was now missing.

Pearl felt a shiver run across the back of her neck, making all the hairs stand up on end. Something or someone had been there recently and had used magic to remove whatever had been buried there. Her mind was spinning at the awful thoughts that were now filling her head. Fox had said he had buried Hecta deep within the woods in a place that only he knew the location of. He had told her that no one else would ever find the burial place of the gatekeeper, and he had sealed it with magic to keep it safe.

Pearl stepped back. She suddenly wanted more than anything to be within the safety of her home again. The sun was still shining and the birds were still singing around her but she no longer felt as if this place was a sanctuary, as it had always been to her in the past. This was bad. Very bad. And she had to let Fox know the gatekeeper was no longer at rest within his magical grave.

While flicking through the magazine that had been sitting on the coffee table in their room Sapphire listened to the shower running in the bathroom. Fox had made her a sweet peppermint tea before heading into the adjoining bathroom to take a shower. He had reassured her that all would be well, and that she should rest for a while before Charlie and Nathan returned from their trip to the Pyramids that afternoon.

She felt jittery and unsettled after their meeting with Aziz. The seeds were safely tucked in her handbag and the essence was in the chest of drawers. Her eyes darted up from the magazine to the drawers, then back again. She sighed. She could not settle or relax one tiny bit. She felt as if she was hiding a haul of cocaine and that at any minute the police would come crashing in and arrest her for hiding an illegal substance.

She could hear the water running in the shower and, with a small smile on her lips, imagined Fox standing washing himself while naked. Perhaps she should join him. It might calm her spangled nerves. Her fingers stopped on a page within the magazine. She had stumbled upon an article that was promoting a trip to the Bahariya Oasis, which was apparently not far from Cairo. The article claimed it was a lush haven nestled within the desert and surrounded by black hills made from quartz.

Her attention was caught by the description of the temples and sites of interest, and she continued to read with excitement as she found that not only was this area home to ruins of the temple of Alexander the Great but to Bes … The god who protected against nightmares while sleeping and dreaming originated from this place.

Sapphire looked up from the magazine with her finger still placed on the page. Her body was tingling all over, and her magic was thrumming hotly in her veins. This was the place. This was where she needed to go. She jumped up from the seat and headed into the bathroom to find Fox standing naked, water dripping from his hair and a towel in his hand. He turned to face her, smiling, and giving her the best view she had seen yet on her trip.

"Did you want to use the shower, my love?" Momentarily distracted by his nakedness, she shook her head.

"No. Fox, I've found it, the place I need to go to for the first seed to be planted. Come look at this." He continued to smile at her while wrapping the towel around his middle and shaking his head so that droplets of water scattered around the room. Sapphire laughed as she tried to avoid a soaking. After grabbing his arm she pulled him back out into the bedroom. She stood over by the magazine with the pages open at the lush palm trees and the oasis of Bahariya. Fox cocked his head and frowned as he scanned the page.

"Well, it would make sense, Sapphire. Quartz amplifies and heals in great quantities, as this place suggests. It would certainly create something special." Sapphire was excited now, her eyes wide and dark blue.

"And Bes, the god of dream protection ... He is there, Fox. I know it's the right place. I can feel it in my bones. I've found it." Fox grabbed her and pulled her close, nuzzling her nose with his own and covering her in droplets of water.

"Well done, Sapphire. Well done."

As she took a sip of her cocktail Sapphire regarded Charlie from across the table, where they were currently enjoying their late supper.

"What time is our boat leaving tomorrow, Charlie?" Her friend was devouring a morsel of food with a look of delight on her face. She mumbled between chewing,

"About 3 p.m. We have to be at the dock at 2.30 p.m. to load our bags and get settled before we leave. Why?" Sapphire looked at Fox, who was tucking into his dinner with equal enthusiasm.

"Just wondered how much time we have before we leave," she said. Charlie watched her with curiosity.

"Do you have to be somewhere before we go?" Sapphire shook her head. Fox was now watching her with a glint in his eye and a smile on his lips.

"No, it's fine. I'm looking forward to the cruise." Nathan passed Charlie another dish and spooned some of the contents on to her plate.

"You should have come with us today, guys," Nathan said. "The Pyramids were awesome ... huge. Just seems crazy that people actually built them." Fox laughed and said,

"Maybe they didn't, Nathan." Charlie smiled.

"Something you want to tell us, Fox?" Fox, still smiling, wiped his mouth with a napkin slowly.

"Oh, no, Charlie. Some things are best left unsaid." Nathan stared at him, wide-eyed. "Aliens. I knew it. I bet it was aliens." They all laughed but Fox remained silent, a wry smile still etched upon his lips.

"Let's just say that the Ancient Egyptians were an interesting race of people, Nathan, and they had access to information that was, shall we say ... special." Charlie leant back in her chair, seemingly satisfied for now with her food intake.

"The mind boggles, Fox. I'm sure you could enlighten us with some very interesting stories regarding that." Fox placed the napkin beside his plate and placed his hand over Sapphire's, then squeezed her fingers gently.

"Another time, perhaps." Sapphire regarded her friends for a second. She was planning to take a trip out to the oasis that night when everyone else was sleeping, and wanted to make sure they had plenty of time the next day to gather their things before they had to leave. If all went well she would be able to carry out her plan and be back at the hotel without anyone else knowing what she was doing.

She would take Fox with her, of course. She needed him to help her with the essence, as he seemed to know something of its power. She hoped that she didn't start an earthquake or some other natural disaster by planting the seed and starting the ball rolling. Everything happening around her was falling into place but some of the pieces of the puzzle were still missing, and she was using pure instinct to carry out her task.

Fox looked at her with an intensity that she recognised as his way of questioning her motives. She smiled back at him and gave his hand a reassuring squeeze.

"Fox and I will get an early night and meet you at lunchtime if that's OK with you two. I fancy a lie-in tomorrow before we leave." Charlie raised an eyebrow.

"Yeah, sure. I know how much you enjoy your 'lie-ins' nowadays, Saf." Sapphire blushed.

They ordered dessert and finished their meal, laughing and chatting like comfortable friends who were enjoying their holiday. Sapphire knew that this evening would be the turning point for her and Fox, and although she was enjoying having her friends with her they did not need to know what was about to take place. They had already seen too much, and any more magical events may just blow their minds in a way that even she could not anticipate a human could comprehend.

Fox closed their bedroom door behind them and pulled Sapphire into his arms and hugged her tightly. They had said goodnight to Charlie and Nathan and were now alone again.
"So what's the plan, my beautiful wife? I am thinking we may be getting very little sleep tonight." Sapphire nestled her head into his warm chest and wrapped her hands around his waist. It felt so good to be within the safety of his arms.
"Mmmh ... I need to go tonight, Fox. I need you to help me with the essence." He kissed the top of her head and pulled back slightly so that he could look at her. She stared up at him, her eyes sparkling with flashes of white light.
"I am not sure we are ready for that yet, my love. I would rather consult my father first before we try to use the essence. It is dangerous and very powerful." Sapphire blinked slowly.
"Usually I would agree, Fox, but something tells me I need to do this now. Time is of the essence here. The seeds need to be planted, and I'm already aware of how many other places I need to travel to. This trip is just the start. After our cruise I need to plan the next part of the journey. I cannot waste any more time."
Fox sighed, still holding her tightly against him. His face looked troubled for a second, and his eyes were dark.
"If you feel that this is the best course of action then I trust your judgement, Sapphire."
As she reached up to kiss him softly on the lips she squeezed him before stepping back slowly.
"Can you take us there using your magic?" He smiled.
"Of course," he said.
They gathered the seeds and the essence. Sapphire placed the leather pouch inside her jacket and Fox tucked the essence inside his waistcoat. She noted with a wry smile that they balanced the two magical items – male and female, yin and yang – that were both needed to join together to create new life.
Her body trembled slightly as her magic flared momentarily when Fox took her by the hand, his face alive with a mixture of concern and excitement. She could feel his own magic tingle and shine within

her veins. He had stepped up a gear and pushed his magic outwards, making the room light up with flickers of gold and silver light as he focused on where they needed to go.

Sapphire pictured the oasis within her mind and thought of Bes, the god of dreams, and what they were about to face. The unknown. Fox licked his bottom lip. His hair was glistening like a halo around his head now. Strands of his hair were rising and falling as if a breeze was caressing him.

"Are you ready, Sapphire?" She nodded and gripped his hand tightly.

"Yes."

Chapter Fourteen

The desert air was cool and dry. The sky above them was as black as ebony, interspersed with a thousand tiny stars. Sapphire had seen many night skies on her travels, but this one was magnificent. She could see the belt of stars that could only be the Milky Way, and every star shone with an intensity that took her breath away.

They stood on a hill looking down on the Bahariya Oasis. Beneath her feet Sapphire could sense the energy of the quartz that was buried deep within the ground. Tiny lights blinked and shone from the dwellings around the oasis below. All was calm and still. It was beautiful. Fox released her hand and she looked up at him in the darkness. His features were shrouded by the black of the night. He shimmered slightly from the magic he had just used to transport them. He looked ethereal, like a god. He faced her slowly and smiled.

"Where now, my love?" Sapphire sighed. She actually had no idea, but her body was thrumming excitedly and she could feel the persistent buzz of the seeds in her pocket. They were close, of that she was sure. She closed her eyes for a second and pushed out with her magical senses. Her internal compass picked up the topography of the land before her. She felt a pulling within her chest that was urging her forward. She opened her eyes again on feeling a pulsing within her veins.

"This way," she said calmly.

Fox stood very still beside her. Only the slight whisper of his breathing on the air made her aware of his presence. She was focused on the place where she had taken them and now stood looking at the temple before her. The moon was but a slither in the sky, but it cast a silver ghostlike shadow across the ruins before them and made the stone look as if it was carved from glass rather than from the hard granite.

Sapphire could feel her whole body tingle all over from head to toe. The magic within her was moving fast around her veins, and she could see her fingers begin to light up with sparks of purple and white that sent flickers outwards like tinder from a fire.

"What is this place, Sapphire?" Fox did not move forward. She could sense his hesitation. There was something about these ruins that both of them could feel. Something different ... not quite magic, but magical nonetheless.

"I'm not entirely sure. But this is the place, Fox. I can feel it." She stepped forward towards the entrance of the temple. Two pillars marking the entrance leant precariously before her, and it looked as if one push would topple them over.

"Careful, Sapphire," Fox cautioned her.

Sapphire stepped through the archway with delicate steps and avoided touching anything around her. As she stepped over the threshold of the temple a shiver of magic ran up her spine and shot through the top of her head, making her gasp out loud.

It pulled her out of her body for a moment, and she was spinning suddenly in the night sky. She could hear Fox below calling her name, but the sensation was more than pleasant and she felt no fear. She closed her eyes and let her body drift through the magical wormhole, and filled her mind with a thousand pictures of days long gone by.

She could see the temple as it was in all its glory, a beautiful place filled with lush plants and colourful tapestries like a royal palace. This place had once been a great place of worship, and she could see visions of women dressed in white who were walking barefoot. They had long black hair and had dark kohl round their eyes.

At the centre of the temple was a pool of water with the most beautiful fountain Sapphire had ever seen. It seemed almost alive as it shimmered and shone in the sunlight. Peacocks wandered around the courtyard, their long tail feathers trailing across the stone flags. They too shone brightly in the sunlight, and the greens and blues of their feathers sparkled like gems in the light.

Sapphire could see a man sitting beside the fountain. His head was bowed as if he was praying. His hair was the colour of midnight and hung in curls around his head. As the vision intensified Sapphire gasped again as he looked straight up and smiled at her. He was covered in tattoos that glistened and sparkled with magic, and his eyes were the darkest brown she had ever seen. He lifted his hands towards her and blew into them, sending a shower of crystal dust towards her as he whispered,

"My gift to you, Sapphire, dream traveller. Use it wisely. Travel well, my child. Travel wisely, for this gift is coveted by many." She felt her body jolt again, and with a sharp twist inside her stomach she found herself back in the ruins and standing under the stars with Fox gripping her by the arms and his face alive with fear.

"Sapphire, where did you go? I was worried. Something happened when you stepped across into the ruins. The air rippled with power and you disappeared for a moment. I thought I had lost you again." He was breathing hard, and she could tell he was fighting back panic.

"I'm fine ... I'm fine. I travelled for a second, or it may have just been a vision. I'm not sure. But I saw this place as it was before, when it was used as a temple. There was a man sitting just over there by a fountain. He spoke to me." Fox looked at the space she was staring at. A pile of rocks showed nothing but the decay this place had fallen into.

"What did he say?" Sapphire looked into the magical eyes of her husband and sighed.

"He said I should travel safe and travel wise." She paused, suddenly aware that her jacket pocket now felt slightly heavier than before. "And that he had given me a gift." Fox frowned and shook his head.

"Who was he?" Sapphire smiled and reached into her pocket, to find a small pouch that was cool and smooth to the touch.

"It was Bes, god of dreams."

Fox stepped back and looked at her with concern.

"That is not possible, my love. The gods do not consort with us anymore. They are long gone from this world." Sapphire lifted the pouch out from her pocket and raised it up for him to see.

"But I saw him, Fox. He gave me this." Fox reached for the pouch and took it from her as if it was a bomb. After opening the pouch slowly he looked inside and then back at her while smiling slowly.

"A bag of dirt, my love?" Sapphire grabbed the pouch again and looked inside. It was indeed filled with what looked like dirt. It was damp, and smelt as if it had been freshly dug from rich soil.

"Well, that's what it looks like." Fox laughed.

"A precious gift indeed." She frowned at him and shook her head.

"Maybe it's something much more than just a bag of dirt, Fox. I will keep it just the same, thank you." He held his hands up in a gesture of submission.

"I mean no offence, my beautiful wife, but I sense no magic within its content." Sapphire, feeling a little silly, shoved the pouch back into her pocket. Surely this meant something, or was she finally going completely mad?

She walked away from him towards the pile of rubble that, in her vision, had once been the magnificent fountain. While standing with her hands on her hips she regarded the pile dubiously. It felt like the right place to start, but what if she was wrong? And what the hell was she supposed to do with a bag of dirt? Her head was spinning again, and it wasn't being helped by the constant zapping of magic that the seeds seemed to be emitting from her other pocket.

"Stop that," she snapped at them. They were obviously keen to get out of the pouch that Violet had made for her, like toddlers in a playpen who wanted to get out and play.

"I need to clear a space, Fox. Can you help me?" He was beside her before she could blink, and started to lift the rubble as if it weighed nothing. She watched him clear the area at the speed of three men. Show-off.

After standing back Fox eyed his handiwork. He had cleared the area into a rough circle with the rubble around the edge, so that it almost looked like the pool that once stood in its place.

Sapphire stepped inside and walked into the middle of the circle. The ground was hard, and she wondered how she was supposed to plant anything in this barren place and make it grow. Fox remained outside the perimeter of rubble with his hands behind his back as if he were waiting for something. Of course … He was waiting for her to do something, but what?

Sapphire looked at her husband. His features were outlined softly in the dark by his magic – which shimmered amber and gold, like his eyes. She remembered the first time she had met him, in her dream, when they had danced by the fire ... and then at the party, when he had kissed her in the garden.

So much had happened since then. So much had changed. She was not that person anymore. She was not Sapphire Whittaker, a thirty-something woman who had thought she was going crazy and who had no idea what was ahead of her. Now she was a certified dream traveller who possessed magic that no other had owned before. She had grown in so many ways, and now it was time to step up and be the person she was meant to be: a creator of new magic ...the instrument of change for the Earth that was sleeping beneath her feet and for the people on this planet.

It was time to make it happen, and she had to trust that she could do it. Half human or half magical ... it did not matter now. She had been given the chance to make a change, and the thought terrified her.

Fox stepped forward just slightly, his face etched with concern.

"You can do this, my love. I will hold the circle for you and keep you safe." She nodded and closed her eyes, grounding herself like Pearl had taught her ... It seemed like such a long time ago. She remembered what Pearl had told her about the magic of the plants of the life around her, and that everything had its own life force. She remembered Conloach telling her that the magic of Mother Earth had been lost and long forgotten. Was this the right thing to do? What would this change mean for her planet and her people, the people of Earth?

A fresh tingle of magic travelled from her feet up her legs into her body. It pulsed slowly and surely, filling her with a new surge of power. She could smell the scent of roses and honeysuckle and the air around her began to warm softly, like an English summer's day. Everything felt right.

Goddamn it. It was now or never.

"Throw me the essence, Fox." She opened her eyes and held out her hand. He tipped his head to one side, sighing deeply.

"Are you sure, Sapphire? The essence is very powerful, and I have no idea what it will actually do." Sapphire firmly pushed her hand out further, indicating he should comply.

"I know what it will do, Fox. Throw it to me ... please." He reached into his waistcoat and pulled out the bottle of essence. It glowed in the dark like phosphorous. He threw it across to her and stepped back while holding his arms out to his sides.

His magic flared suddenly, like a rush of fire. It swept around the circle, enclosing her in a protective bubble. He looked at her intensely before closing his eyes and whispering a haunting song in his sing-song language that began softly, like a witch's chant that would conjure great magic.

Sapphire placed the bottle of essence on the ground beside her. Still crouching, she removed the seeds from the pouch and tipped them into her hand. They glowed a soft blue and were humming gently, their own song strong within her ears like a heartbeat. She could feel the thump, thump, thump within her own body.

One of the seeds was glowing a little more brightly than the others. As she focused on the seed it changed colour and flickered into a dark green like the colour of lush grass. The smell of roses and honeysuckle grew stronger, and she knew that this was the one. Now the bag of dirt made sense to her. She could not break the ground here – it was much too hard – but the earth she had been given by Bes was fresh and fertile. Perfect.

As she scooped a small amount of the dirt from the other pouch and placed it on the floor she felt the ground begin to tremble. The sound of Fox chanting from outside the circle was almost deafening now, as if it was not just him working the protection spell. She did not want to break her focus, and sighed deeply once more before placing the other seeds back within the pouch.

While taking the green seed in her hand she pulled magic from within her core and outwards through her arms into the palm of her hand. She watched with wonder as the seed began to shine even brighter, a tiny network of silver flashes erupting within it like shards of lightning scattering across the horizon.

Sapphire placed the seed on top of the pile of earth and stepped back just a fraction. The seed continued to sparkle and flash. It shook slightly and sank a little into the pile of earth. The air around her was beginning to heat up, and a breeze now circled her like a tiny wind tunnel that lifted her hair around her face.

The magic swelled and augmented, growing and expanding. Her body was now a living conduit filling up with more and more power. She gasped as wave after wave crashed over her like an invisible ocean storm battering her with its angry swell. She was not even sure where it was coming from. It was all around her, above, and below, radiating outwards and inwards at the same time. It was like nothing she had ever experienced before, and she was suddenly unsure whether or not she should continue.

Was the world ready for such magic? Would her fellow humans be able to cope with such a change to their world? With her hand trembling, as if she was an addict on a comedown, she took the bottle of essence and held it before her while trying hard to remain standing against the wind that now spun within the circle.

The ground beneath her feet was hot now, and she could smell the leather of her sandals begin to smoulder. She had to finish this, and finish this quickly, before she burst into a ball of flames and turned to ash. After taking the essence she crouched down once more and removed the stopper on the bottle, and heard a snap like a branch breaking as she did so.

The essence was glowing so brightly now it felt as if an entire solar system may just break free and erupt before her. While closing her eyes and steadying her hand she took one big gulp of air before opening her eyes again and tipping the bottle very slowly so that a single drop fell and hit the seed. She replaced the stopper on to the bottle, placed it back into her pocket, and waited.

The strong magic continued to spin around her, and the wind was howling in her ears like a banshee. Then without warning everything slowed down. Time itself seemed to stop for a fraction. The seed seemed to sink further into the earth – and then, suddenly, it was gone. The howling of the wind stopped and seemed to pull inward, creating a vacuum that made her ears pop loudly.

Sapphire did not have a chance to stand up again, as the explosion of magic hit her full on in the chest – and she sprawled backwards and hit her head on the hard ground, which made her cry out in pain. The brightest flash of light she had ever seen cracked and roared above her head, and the ground trembled as if an earthquake had shifted the Richter scale off the charts. Her body was gripped with a pain so intense it made her shudder – and wild magic sped through her veins, making her body convulse against the ground. She closed her eyes and gripped the dry sand beneath her as she tried not to scream out.

"What have I done?" she thought before her mind went blank and she lost consciousness.

Roses and honeysuckle ... Sapphire could smell the scent strongly within her nostrils as if she were in a summer garden. Her eyes flickered open and her body threw another wave of pain throughout her limbs just for good measure, making her wince. Fox was holding her in his arms. His face was inches from her own, and his eyes were flashing dark gold and black. He frowned as if he too were in pain.

"Sapphire, my love," he whispered, as if afraid for her. She smiled at him wearily.

"Where am I?" He responded by kissing her hard. He was obviously thankful that she was alive and talking. His lips crushed against her own with a passion that made her whimper softly. After withdrawing slowly from her, the frown now gone, he smiled in relief. His face was oddly different, and his features were clearer and sharper. The magic around him flashed strongly, as if he had just plugged into a new energy source.

"We are still at the temple. Look ... look at what you have created, my beautiful woman." He lifted her up slowly, aware that she was still in pain. She felt as if someone had just run over her with a truck and then reversed back over her just for the fun of it. After blinking slowly and adjusting her position she found herself looking at something that just seemed entirely impossible.

The sky was no longer dark above her. A new day had dawned, and sunlight was beginning to rise gently over the horizon. A tree stood before her so unique in shape and size that she had no idea what it could be. It glistened green and silver, as if it was not quite there at all.

Crystal ... it looked as if it was made from crystal. Around the tree the ground was lush with green grass that had been scattered with wild flowers. A trail of ivy grew up the immense trunk of the magical tree ... and beside it a rosebush and a honeysuckle bush grew, vibrant and fragrant.

Fox helped her stand by holding her around the waist. Her legs felt like jelly, and her body throbbed uncomfortably. She felt utterly human and like utter crap.

"You created this, my love, with your magic and the power of the seed." He paused and looked down at her, still smiling. "Isn't it beautiful?" Sapphire looked back at the tree and nodded slowly.

"It certainly is," she replied. He held her closer and lifted her legs so that she now hung within his arms. Her head slipped to one side. "Now let's go home."

A young girl walked slowly along a corridor that flickered with orange light from the flames held in the metal sconces that glowed against the stone walls. She held a tray between her hands, and stepped quietly and steadily so that she did not spill the contents it held. Her long dark hair trailed down her back in silky curls that moved from side to side with the swing of her hips as she stepped towards the door at the end of the corridor.

She hesitated outside the closed door and adjusted the tray so that it balanced in one hand, which allowed her to free her other hand so that she could knock on the door before she entered. She hesitated before she knocked, and she could hear the low rumble of her master's voice on the other side of the wooden door frame. Another voice answered, and she stepped a little closer to see if she could hear what they were saying.

Her body trembled slightly as she placed her ear against the wood. If her master caught her eavesdropping she would be in big trouble. She could just make out the conversation. Some of the words dropped out as the voices rose and fell. Her master's voice was deep and thick with command, but it seemed the stranger was reluctant to give him the answers he craved.

"And what is it exactly you want me to do, Gabriel?" she heard the stranger ask.

"What you do best, necromancer. That is all," Gabriel answered. "Surely it is a simple task I ask of you, or is my coin not enough incentive?" She could sense the anger in her master's voice, and his impatience, and she became even more reluctant to knock on the door and disturb them even though he had instructed her to bring them food and wine.

"This task you ask of me is going to be almost impossible, Gabriel. Surely you can see that?"

Gabriel slammed his hand down on the table inside the room, which made her jump and spill some of the wine on to the tray.

"I need him alive, necromancer. This is your magical gift. Stop giving me excuses and start the process." She stepped back from the door and knocked timidly while waiting for her master to answer the knock.

"Enter," he shouted loudly. She pushed the door open with her hip and walked into the room, her eyes down turned in fear of him seeing the guilt in her expression.

"Put the tray on the table, girl, and leave us," he barked. She did as she was told, but took a quick glimpse at the stranger who stood on the other side of the table as she placed the tray down carefully. He was a tall, thin man with short, dark hair, which was curled tightly to his scalp. His face showed his displeasure and gave him a sour, unfriendly look that made him seem older than his years. He stared at her with distaste. His eyes were a strange bright green that glistened in the candlelight. His skin was a deathly white, and she could smell the oddest odour in the air. He smelt like something that had been decaying for a long time. He smelt like death.

She took one last look at her master. His handsome face was set like stone, which made her bite her bottom lip with nerves. His long blonde hair was tied back in a rope like braid to his waist. He was a beautiful man – tall and striking – with eyes that sparkled the lightest blue, like a crystal caught in sunlight.

The smallest smile graced his lips as he watched her retreat quickly from the room. It amused him that he terrified and aroused her at the same time. But he had always had that effect on women, and it gave him a great sense of power.

The necromancer grabbed the jug of wine and, his face dark with frustration, poured himself a glass.

"Your serving girl is sloppy, Gabriel. You should replace her." Gabriel looked at him with contempt.

"She has other uses," he snarled. After taking a glass for himself he too poured the wine into a glass and took a sip, then breathed out heavily and closed his eyes for a moment.

"I need Hecta alive, and I need this to happen quickly. He has information I need. I will find whatever you need to make this happen for you. Is that clear?" The necromancer nodded slowly.

"Yes, Gatekeeper, perfectly clear." Gabriel nodded with satisfaction. It had taken him a great deal of effort and magic to find Hecta and bring him back to Shaka after his disappearance. The fact that he had found him on Earth, and dead in a grave that had been dug only recently, had angered him greatly. Hecta was one of his most powerful gatekeepers, and his loss was something that grated on him sorely.

He had allowed Hecta the time, purely as an indulgence, to pursue a particular dream traveller who had taken his fancy. But the fact that this particular traveller had not only disappeared off his radar and killed his best gatekeeper in the process had now piqued his interest. He needed to know what Hecta had been doing while chasing her across the universe, and why she had been so interesting to a man who was, quite frankly, not interested in anything any longer.

Gabriel himself had been travelling for a long time a long way from home and had been told, on his return, of the battle between the queen, Ebony, and Conloach. As the master of all gatekeepers Gabriel had no interest in these petty squabbles, but for Hecta to be involved – and for him to now be dead at the hands of this new dream traveller – his interest had been ignited. He needed to find out exactly what Hecta had been playing with while he had been away.

Hecta's body lay cold in his basement, perfectly preserved but lifeless, without magic or breath. The necromancer he had acquired was his only hope of bringing him back, even if it were only briefly, to find out why the woman called Sapphire had turned him away from his usual path of gatekeeper.

He took another sip of wine and watched the man before him pile his plate with food. He disliked this man immensely, but he would have to keep him sweet to get what he wanted. After this disgusting man had finished filling his face he would find his serving girl and satisfy the other craving he had that was eating away at his body. It had been some time since he had lain with her, and the thought was easing his frustration at the situation he was now in. Gabriel was a man who did not take no for an answer. Ever.

Sapphire closed her eyes and pulled the pillow into her chest, curling her legs up into the foetal position. She needed to sleep. Her body was totally spent, and her mind was exhausted.

They had returned to the hotel and packed in time to meet Charlie and Nathan before they needed to board the cruise ship. The journey to the boat had been a hazy memory to her, with Fox literally carrying her and their luggage to their next destination. Charlie had been fussing over her, asking what was wrong, and was she sick. She felt sick, as if she was coming down with flu, and had mumbled something about not getting much sleep that night.

Fox had managed Charlie well and had taken control until they had found their room on the cruise ship, where he had put Sapphire to bed and stroked her hair while whispering to her in his beautiful language and kissing her on the cheek softly. She was aware of him in the room walking around quietly. It sounded as if he was unpacking for her. The thought made her smile as she drifted off to sleep.

She could hear the call to prayers outside on the riverbank and the sound of the engine as the boat began to cast off. They were leaving Cairo and heading down the Nile to Luxor, a journey that she could at least enjoy without the pressure of needing to complete part of her task. A vision of the crystal tree flickered into her mind as she drifted slowly into a comfortable sleep. It glittered and shone in the sunlight… beautiful.

Her mind stilled and all became silent. At last she could rest and recharge her energy, safe in the knowledge that everything was as it should be and the journey had at last begun.

Fox left his wife sleeping in their cabin and returned to the deck to find Charlie and Nathan. The daylight was fading, and the boat was moving at a slow pace downriver. The sensation of gliding across the water was soothing even to him, and he breathed in deeply as he walked across the deck to find Sapphire's friends.

They were sitting at the bar at the back of the boat, chatting and laughing with a handful of other travellers. Fox watched them for a moment while taking in the sights and sounds of the river as it passed by them leisurely. The bank of the Nile was certainly beautiful, lush, and green, a complete contrast to the busy city they were leaving behind.

He was troubled by the physical state Sapphire had slipped into after their experience at the oasis. It seemed that she had exhausted her source of magic, and it had left her frail and very human. He thought that he may need to return to Shaka and find a way of speeding up her healing process. Only his father and Willow would have the knowledge of how to do this.

As he approached the bar Charlie looked up and smiled widely. Some of the other guests also looked up to watch him as he walked towards them.

"Hey, Fox, come join us for a drink." He smiled at her amiably, noting that all eyes were now on him and the conversation had ceased. Even though he had dampened his magical glow it was apparent that he still stuck out somewhat in human company. One of the women in the group was watching him intensely, as if he were the dessert that she was looking forward to devouring after her cocktail. The thought made him smile even more. She could drool all she liked. He wasn't interested in the slightest. Nathan stood up to greet him, hugging him in a firm, manly bear hug.

"Is Saf OK?" he asked before sitting back on the bar stool. "She seems really tired." Fox nodded, aware that others were now listening to their conversation.

"She's fine, Nathan, just a little worn out ... maybe coming down with a cold. I've left her to sleep it off." Charlie, who was sipping her blue cocktail, looked concerned.

"If she needs any meds I have some aspirin in my case." Fox shook his head.

"Not to worry. I am sure a good sleep will be the best medicine. I'll leave her to rest until she is ready to come and join us." Nathan caught the bartender's attention.

"What will it be, Fox?"

"I'll have a beer, Nathan. Thank you." The bartender grabbed a cold bottle from the fridge behind him and placed a napkin on the bar with an ice-cold glass ready for the amber nectar. Fox waited for him to pour before taking the glass and raising it to his friends.

"To your good health, my friends." Charlie laughed and took a sip of her cocktail, which seemed to be disappearing fast.

"And to Saf's quick recovery." Fox hoped she was right, but the rest of the trip would thankfully be a much-needed break for them both after the events in Cairo. He wondered whether Aziz would have sensed the new magic that was now humming in the desert not so far away from him, and what this new addition to the planet would actually do to Mother Earth.

The essence had certainly played its part, but Fox was still concerned about the power of the magic it had created. He had seen magic created in this way before, but never on a place that did not already hold great power. If they continued to plant the seeds around the globe in the same way this planet would become something new altogether. He was not sure that the human race was ready for such change.

Sapphire was the only human he knew who could handle such wild magic. For that is what he had witnessed last night: wild magic that had been released into the ground and into the night air. He had held the circle as a way of protecting Sapphire from whatever she may have created, but had not expected it to be quite so magnificent. After the bolt of energy struck her and knocked her to the ground he had momentarily lost concentration and the shield he had created had weakened, sending shards of pure white light up into the sky. He was sure that people miles away would have seen something unexplainable lighting up the night that evening.

He was more than a little nervous that Sapphire's magic would have caught the notice of not only humans in the area but of other magical beings. Hecta was no more, but he knew that there were other gatekeepers out there scattered throughout the universe who were always watching for changes in the balance of things. He hoped the gatekeepers were busy elsewhere, and that they were oblivious to the shift in consciousness that was inevitably taking place now that the first seed had been planted.

The sun slid slowly below the horizon, casting a deep orange and red glow across the landscape. The sweet scent of incense and warm eastern air filled his nostrils and calmed his thoughts a little. They were safe for now, and that was all that mattered.

He was looking forward to spending some time with his wife without having to protect her from her own magic. The Oracle had warned him when they had first met that she was a woman with many gifts. He had just not anticipated how very unique and powerful they would be.

Chapter Fifteen

Sapphire awoke with a start. The room was dark, and she was disorientated for a moment. She had been dreaming of a man with beautiful ice blue eyes. His hair was the colour of white snow that sparkled like crystal in the sunlight. He had been smiling at her, and his face was handsome and strong. She had never seen him before, and wondered who he might be.

While moving slowly she lifted the sheet covering her and placed her feet on the floor. Her body still ached, and her head was thick and foggy. Damn it. She was definitely coming down with something. She could still feel the magic within her veins but it was like a trickle now, so weak it made her feel edgy and out of sorts. She had become so used to her magic in the past few months it now felt totally alien to her to be almost completely human again. It sucked.

Just as she stood up to find some clothes she felt the air shift beside her and Fox suddenly stood in front of her, his eyes glowing in the darkness.

"How are you feeling, my love?" Sapphire yawned and stretched her arms up over her head, hoping to release some of the tension in her back.

"Like shit, to be honest. What time is it?" He flicked his hand and the lights switched on in the cabin, illuminating the room with soft amber hues. It was the first time Sapphire had really looked at their new home. The bed was large and covered in soft pillows, and the furnishings were opulent and splashed with colours of purple, gold, and blue. She could see an en suite bathroom to the side of the bedroom and a balcony facing on to the water. The doors were open slightly, and a cool breeze flowed wonderfully inside. Charlie had certainly found them a beautiful cruise ship, and had gone all out on their lodgings again.

"Midnight. You have slept a long time. Are you hungry?" Sapphire nodded and shuffled across to the bathroom. She needed to pee badly.

"Mmmh, famished. Have you guys already eaten?" Fox watched her wander into the bathroom, appreciating her nakedness but alarmed at how pale she looked. Something was definitely wrong. Her magic was visibly weak, and more of it should have returned to her body after resting.

"I will get some food sent to the room for you." He could hear water running, and assumed she was taking a shower.

"That would be nice," he heard her shout from behind the door. He left quickly to find someone that could help with regards to some food. His head was spinning with thoughts of Sapphire's state of health.

When he returned with a tray laden with food he found her sitting on the bed with a towel wrapped around her head. She was dressed in a long, flowing sarong that was tied around her neck. He was relieved that she had some colour in her cheeks again, and her eyes were a little brighter. Her magic wavered around her in a weak colour of insipid green. It barely flickered, and made her aura look clearly unhealthy. This was not good. She smiled at him as he placed the tray on the coffee table and began to unload the food and wine he had managed to persuade one of the crew to find from the kitchen.

"Thank you," she whispered as he passed her a plate filled with fruit and cheese. After pouring them both a glass of wine he sat down beside her and regarded her for a moment before speaking.

"Your magic has been severely weakened, my love. I think it would be best for me to seek advice from my father and Willow as to how we can restore your strength after last night." Sapphire placed a date into her mouth and chewed slowly. It was sweet and soft and made her mouth water.

"I'm fine, Fox. Stop worrying." He shook his head, and lowered his eyes in exasperation. She could be so stubborn sometimes.

"You are not fine, Sapphire. I can see the change in your energy. If this is what happens every time you plant a seed on this planet it will eventually destroy you." She blinked at him while chewing slowly.

"Seriously, Fox, I feel as if I have a cold, nothing more. A few days in the sun will put me back on track. Stop stressing. Your worrying about me is spoiling the holiday." He frowned and took a sip of the wine. Sapphire took another date and bit into it, slowly licking her lips.

"Where are Charlie and Nathan?" she asked. Fox watched her eat. Her lips parted slowly and her tongue tested the fruit before she slipped it into her mouth. Just watching her eat caused his groin to ache – which was something he found totally frustrating, as she still had the ability to distract him even when he was trying to control a situation.

"They have gone to bed. Stop changing the subject." She smiled at him slyly, and again took a grape and plopped it in her mouth before crunching it loudly and letting some of the juice dribble down her chin.

"I'm not trying to change the subject. I'm just asking you a question." After placing the wine glass down he leant across the bed and slowly lifted his hand to her head. His face was inches from hers and he breathed in deeply, catching her scent and allowing it to fill his mind and travel through his body while filling his senses with her unique essence. She watched him take the towel in his hand and pull it gently so that it fell on to the bed and allowed her hair to tumble in damp tendrils across her shoulders.

"I am going to return to Shaka for a while, Sapphire, and ask my father and Willow if they can help with your healing. And then we can have the holiday you well deserve." Sapphire shook her head slowly, and closed her eyes for a second before opening them again and taking another morsel of food from the plate. Fox remained inches from her his eyes, watching her every move. His fingers were now combing through the hair close to her neck in slow, firm strokes. Her skin tingled in response to his touch, and her body switched into another mode. His magic flared against her in a soft glow of red and orange as his eyes began to darken with his arousal. She could feel it within her veins, and a slight shift in her energy began to pulse gently against her chest. His magic was feeding her own.

"Yes, husband." He chuckled softly, knowing full well that she was humouring him. She still felt it unnecessary for such action to take place on her behalf. He continued to brush out her hair with his fingers, and moved so that he could sit behind her while she ate silently.

The sensation of his hands in her hair was both soothing and sensuous at the same time. She was hungry, but the hunger was now changing into something else. Fox sensed her energy lift a little more as she allowed him to feed her with his own magic. It travelled down his fingertips into her scalp as he loosened the knots that had gathered along the length of her hair. She purred with approval as he began to massage her neck and shoulders, and he gently brushed her hair to one side so that he could touch her skin and send pulses of magic into her body.

"I know what you are doing, Fox," she said. She continued to eat, but took smaller morsels of food now as he distracted her with his finger work. He placed his mouth on the side of her neck and kissed her softly, sucking the delicate skin gently just below her ear. Tiny sparks of light flashed against her skin as his magic trailed down her chest and arms as he did.

"Mmmh, and what is that, my love?" he whispered.

"You are feeding me with you own magic, Fox. Stop it." He bit her again, a little harder this time, making her gasp and lean back against his chest. She was now paying no attention to the food, and her hands were clasping at the sheet on the bed.

"It is my magic. I will do with it as I please," he said. Fox moved the plate away from her and grasped her waist, then pushed his fingers down to the apex of her thighs. She moaned softly. Her head slipped further to one side, which allowed him access to her collar bone. The vein in her neck pulsed strongly as he dipped his tongue into the gentle dip that formed between her shoulder and chest.

"You need it. Not me," he whispered as she let out a soft whimper. His hands began to brush slowly up and down her thighs, moving across her stomach and up the sides of her body before trailing back down again.

The sarong she was wearing brushed against her skin like an irritating barrier as he pushed his magic into her flesh, sending wave after wave of soothing sexual release into her body. God, it felt good. She remembered what it had felt like the first time he had touched her … how her skin had flushed and trembled against him, how his magic had connected with her soul and opened her up like a flower to the sun. He had become so familiar to her in such a short time, and now it was like a long-forgotten balm healing her wounds from the inside out ... her magical man, who had given his magic to her freely and without inhibition from the very first time they had met. She loved him for it, loved him fiercely with a passion so strong it made her feel weak.

"Take it, Sapphire. Take it into your body, and stop fighting me for once. You cannot always be so strong and independent. I am your husband, your guardian, and your provider. Let me help you heal in the way I know best. And then let me heal you again with the help of my homeland and the people who love you there."

Sapphire let go, let him in, and allowed his magic to wash over her in a flood of sensation that filled every cell of her now overly sensitive body. He was right. She needed this, needed his help. His body felt hot against her now ... and the heat was growing as she closed her eyes and melted into him, feeling the strength of his arousal growing hard against her back. The room flickered with orange and red lights as his magic flared and poured outwards, sending shards of white sparks across the bed.

Without him even being inside her she could feel her body stretching out, reaching up like an elastic band that would snap at any moment. Every muscle within her legs, her back, and her arms relaxed and gave way to the probing magic that snaked across her body, licking and teasing her wounded soul.

She was aware of Fox shifting his position, and he was suddenly stretched out beside her on the bed with one hand on her stomach and the other propping up his head so that he could look at her. She jolted from the change of contact and, a little confused, opened her eyes. Her body was pulsing like a beacon in the night. It was as if he had suddenly pulled the plug from out of her electrical socket and left her teetering on the edge of release.

He smiled at her, his eyes glowing black and gold, his hair wild against his shoulders like a tangle of darkness intertwined with silver beads that glistened in contrast.

"Do you want some more, my love?" Sapphire sighed loudly and smiled. He was always the tease. The hand on her stomach began to heat up as he moved it slowly in a small circle against her navel. She placed her own hand against his to stop him, and bit her bottom lip to stop herself from squirming beneath his touch. She held him still, and watched his eyes for his reaction. He waited patiently for her next move.

"Yes ... yes, I want some more." He kissed her then, sliding over her body so that she was completely covered by his long, lean form. With his legs either side of her body the entire length of him pressed against her groin and stomach so that she could not move. His tongue invaded her mouth with strong, slow strokes, which made her groan against him as he pushed his magic into her body. It crashed against her, wave after wave, filling her up and pushing her further and further towards the edge of the cliff she had just been standing on.

She placed her hands into his hair and grasped on to him, allowing him to devour her, consume her, and complete her in a way that only he could do. She felt her magic grow stronger within her and ignite against his own. It grew like a heavy weight within her groin, pulling her down so that she lost all control. He knew exactly what he was doing. He was taking control of her energy and making her bend to his will.

And for the first time in a long time Sapphire was completely and utterly willing to let him do so. She forgot the reasoning behind it, forgot that on her world Fox could grow weak. She did not care, for this man loved her so much that he was willing to give it all to her so that she could feel like this ... so that she could feel like a supercharged meteor racing across the sky that would explode at any moment. And that is just what she did as he pushed one more time and forced her to climax in a way that she had never experienced with him before. Full body contact magic. Raw ... unbridled ... fucking ... cosmic.

Once he had released her mouth so that she could gasp for breath she felt him tear the sarong away from her now hot and sweaty body. He was kneeling above her after removing his shirt quickly. After throwing it to the floor he did the same with his trousers. The action was so fast it made her vision blur for a moment before she could register that he was now completely naked. Her body felt alive again, and her eyes cleared as if someone had just switched on the lights.

They were both naked, their skin glistening with a sheen of magic that shimmered like fairy dust against the dim light of the room. Fox paused for a moment, his breathing heavy and his magic vibrating against his body in streaks of gold and silver. Her eyes grew wide as he smiled at her with his lazy smile that spoke of so much more. He slid down her body slowly and entered her smoothly, making her cry out as he pushed deeper and deeper until she could take no more. He kissed her again, taking her head in his hands so that he could hold her in place.

Their bodies moved in time, completely in synch with each other as they climbed the mountain. Sapphire felt as if she could have died and gone to heaven. Perhaps she had. It would be a good way to go. But as they both reached the peak of the mountain and were lost in each other Sapphire knew that this was just the beginning and that she was most definitely the luckiest woman in the world.

Their magic connected and sparked pure white against the walls of the room, making the bed vibrate beneath them. She could feel Fox trembling above her as his body swelled with his need to release. She released her hands from his hair and grasped his buttocks tightly as he came inside her. His hips pressed roughly against her, pushing her over the edge. And she too climaxed long and hard, feeling the strength of her magic ignite again inside her. He fell against her, breathing heavily into her ear as his body finally gave way to the pleasure of the afterglow.

Well and truly sated, they both lay still on the bed enjoying the soft caress of their connection. The energy was returning to a gentle flicker against their skin. Sapphire sighed deeply, smiled, and turned her head to face Fox. His body slid to one side so that they lay facing each other. His arm lay heavily across her stomach and his leg pinned her own to the bed.

"Thank you," she said. He smiled at her, his eyes heavy-lidded and his hair tumbling across his cheek.

"You are most welcome, my love." Sapphire wondered absently whether they had woken up their neighbours with their noisy lovemaking. She had no doubt that the walls had been shaking along with the bed. The thought made her chuckle, and before long they were both laughing. Fox pulled her closer to his body and held her tight, placing soft kisses against her neck.

"I definitely feel better. I hope you do too, my beautiful wife." Sapphire laughed.

"I feel fabulous ... and very hungry again." Still grinning at her, he pushed himself up off the bed and walked to the bathroom. He looked over his shoulder as he switched on the light, and flicked his head towards the plate of unfinished food.

"Finish the food, Sapphire. I will take a shower and join you for some wine. My other appetite has been well and truly satisfied."

She heard the shower turn on and stretched out lazily on the bed. She reached for the food and began to eat again, her belly rumbling as she did. She felt amazing again. Her energy levels had lifted back up, and her body was glowing softly in the dim light. Happy days.

Chapter Sixteen

A gust of air blew gently across Conloach's face, making him look up from the scroll he was reading. He had been studying long into the night and had lost all track of time. He smiled broadly as his son walked towards him, his tall frame outlined by the glow of candlelight in the room.

"Greetings, Father. It is good to see you again." As he stood up to embrace him Conloach noticed a subtle change in his son's energy. Although he seemed healthy and strong his aura was tainted slightly with a strange green tint. His own energy, not recognising this new strain of magic, tingled in response. Fox held his father to him longer than necessary, and sighed deeply before stepping back.

"It is good to see you, Fox. Where is Sapphire?" Fox looked around the room absently, a faint smile on his lips, as if the sight of his father's chamber was a welcoming vision after his absence from Shaka.

"She is with her friends back on Earth. She is safe." Conloach motioned for him to sit. He was watching Fox intensely now. He knew that something was amiss, and could sense Fox pondering over the words that he obviously needed to say.

"What has happened? You do not seem quite yourself." Fox looked at his father and took in his strong powerful form, his keen eyes, and the surges of magic that surrounded him. Although he had not been away long, seeing his father before him made him realise just how different his own people were from Sapphire's species. He longed to return to Shaka with his wife and recharge in his own environment.

"Sapphire has planted the first of the seeds. We have travelled to a land on her planet that was once strong with magic. We were aided by a man there called Aziz. He knew of our arrival, and gave us an essence that strengthened the power within the seeds. I admit, Father, that I have seen nothing like this before. A tree made from crystal emerged from the joining of this magic.

"Sapphire has created something that is both amazing and frightening at the same time. It all but drained her of her own essence. It took much of my own power to restore her to health. I have come back to ask for your help and to see if Willow can provide some insight as to how I can heal her if this happens again when she plants the next seed." Conloach frowned.

"A tree made from crystal? Such a thing has not been created on our world before. In fact I have no knowledge of this. I will need to consult my library to see if I can find any useful information for you. I will ask Willow to come to me tomorrow and see if she can help. The tree of life is something we all have knowledge of through legend, of course, but I must admit that Sapphire's planet has never had such strong magic before." Fox looked down at his hands. The tattoo on his ring finger glowed faintly in the candlelight, indicating that his connection to Sapphire was still strong.

"I am afraid we have opened Pandora's box, Father, something that should perhaps have been left untouched. But Sapphire has been so set on this path that she seems unconcerned by how much the magic drained her on this occasion. I feel the darkness within the spell as well as the light. It still clings to her, and now to me."

Conloach flicked his hand, creating more light within the room and lifting the energy a little so that he could get a clearer look at his son. He did indeed look tainted.

"Mmmh, I see it." Fox closed his eyes for a second before opening them again and staring at his father intensely.

"Can you help me remove it? Should we continue on this path?" Conloach stood, reached out for his son, and placed his hand on his shoulder, sending a pulse of healing light into his body as he did so. Fox shuddered but remained seated, allowing his father to cleanse his energy. The smell of sulphur filled the air for a second and then disappeared. Conloach removed his hand and flicked it as if shaking off something nasty.

"All magic has a price, Fox. This magic is powerful. It uses both light and dark to create new life. You were not to know of its strength or purpose. I recommend extreme caution in the future." He stepped back and looked at his son as he scanned his aura for any remaining signs of the taint. It was gone. Fox was now a healthy shade of purple and gold, and his eyes were bright and strong once more. He smiled at him, letting out a sigh of relief.

"Thank you, Father." Conloach nodded.

"Bring Sapphire back with you next time, my son. I will cleanse her, but I cannot do this every time. This magic is powerful and dangerous. You will have to find a way to protect yourselves if you continue on this path."

Fox regarded him. He understood the seriousness of the situation they were now in. His instincts were yelling at him that Sapphire should not continue planting the seeds. Earth was not ready for this transformation, and his wife was not strong enough. The shift in consciousness she was eagerly anticipating would have to wait. Her safety was more important. He knew she would not be easily dissuaded, but seeing his father's concern had made up his mind. This new magic was unstable, and he had no idea what it had already shifted back on the planet his wife was so attached to.

Fox knew that he was back to the same problem he had found himself fighting with when he had first been given Sapphire as his new charge. She was human and he was not. He lived on a world made from magic. She did not. Although she had changed and grown within her power at incredible speed it was clearly a fine line between sanity and madness. He could feel a slight pushing within his skull, which indicated that he was indeed out of his depth. On sensing his confusion Conloach placed his hand on his shoulder again and squeezed gently.

"We always knew this path with Sapphire would be a difficult one, Fox. Everything is changing around us because of her very existence. The Oracle foretold these changes and the challenges it would bring you both." Fox shook his head slowly, his expression forlorn.

"I am totally out of my depth, Father. Nothing like this has ever happened before with any dream traveller. But she is my wife ... my love. I cannot put her through such danger, even if it seems that the goddess herself has chosen her for this task." He paused, lifting his hand to his hair and brushing it back from his face in frustration. "She will not be happy when I tell her the magic she is creating is a danger to herself and her planet." Conloach sat back down in his throne-like chair. He placed his hands on the wooden arms and stroking the wood lovingly.

"Who are we to say that this magic is a danger to her kind, Fox? We do not understand it, as it is not familiar to us. All magic has to be balanced, and there is often a price to pay for its power, but right now we do not know the outcome or the meaning behind it." Fox knew his father was right, but the path he was on with Sapphire was completely unknown and it troubled him deeply.

"Rest for a while here, my son. Stop thinking so hard. You need to accept that some things in this life are simply a journey to be taken without question … a learning that needs to be undertaken without resistance, as what we resist often persists." He hesitated before speaking again.

"Sapphire is something more than just a dream traveller. She is a hybrid of magic and flesh. A human with gifts that have never been seen before, she is linked to you, my son, in so many ways, but she is a strong individual who is just beginning to take her first steps into the world of power and magic. Perhaps her world – the world we have seen as weak and insignificant for so long – is also a hybrid of power that is awakening again." Fox looked at his father with fear in his eyes.

"That is what I am afraid of, Father."

A loud knock on the door made them both jump. Fox sprang up from his seat as if ready for battle. Conloach raised his hand in a gesture of reassurance.

"Enter." A young man entered the room, his face full of concern.

"My lord, I apologise for the lateness of my intrusion, but you have a visitor who insists on seeing you. He will not leave until he has spoken to you." Conloach raised a brow and looked from the young man to Fox with bewilderment.

"Very well, Raven. Send him in." Fox remained standing. The hairs were now standing up on the nape of his neck and he could feel the tingle of a new power snaking across his skin. An uneasy feeling of foreboding settled like a stone in the pit of his stomach.

Conloach stood, allowing his magic to unfold around them like a thick blanket of protection. He too could sense the power about to enter the room. Fox flexed his muscles in anticipation as a man entered the room. He was tall and broad, and long white hair flowed down his back in a thick braid. His eyes were of a piercing blue, and his lips were full and stretched into a wicked catlike grin. Conloach twitched slightly, but showed no other signs of emotion.

"Gabriel ... what a pleasant surprise." Fox watched the man step forward into the light. His magic swirled around him in a kaleidoscope of colours that was almost dizzying with intensity.

"It has been too long, Conloach. I am pleased to see you looking so well." Fox did not know this man, but could see he was of great importance and power. The sense of something threatening grew stronger within his bones. His gaze fell to Fox, and his smile grew wider.

"Ah, your son is here as well. How wonderful to meet you at last, Fox. I have heard much about you." Conloach stepped forward. Fox sensed his father's caution in his graceful movement.

"What do you want, Gabriel?" The stranger breathed in deeply and then let out a long self-satisfied sigh.

"To become better acquainted with your son and daughter-in-law, my king. Where is she, by the way? I do not see her by your son's side." Fox felt his magic flare angrily around him. On stepping forward he felt a brush of power push against him, warding him back.

"My wife is not your concern, stranger, and I feel your intrusion tonight to not be a welcome one." Conloach threw Fox a look of caution. He was obviously wary of this man. This was not good. Conloach was afraid of no man on his world.

Gabriel laughed.

"I think you are mistaken, young Fox, for you are her guardian and she is a dream traveller, and both of you are very much my concern." Fox looked at his father for guidance. He did not understand what was happening or who this man was. Conloach stepped forward again, just slightly pushing back against the shield this man had obviously created around himself.

"Gabriel, you need not trouble yourself with my son and his wife. They are causing no disruption within the balance. In fact I have no idea why you are here at all." Fox shook his head.

"Can one of you please tell me what is going on?" Gabriel looked directly at him, his eyes flashing sky blue.

"I am a long-standing acquaintance of your father's, Fox. I am surprised he has never spoken of me before. We go back a very long way." Fox looked at his father questioningly. Conloach sighed.

"Fox, this is Gabriel, master of all gatekeepers. Gabriel, this – as you quite obviously know – is my son, Fox." Fox, almost staggering, stepped back. The master of the gatekeepers stood before him in all his magnificence, a master of magic in his own right and the controller of his nemesis. Things had just turned from bad to worse in the blink of an eye.

Gabriel walked to the long table and seated himself down in one of the chairs, and folded his hands into his lap gracefully. Fox remained statue-still. Shock was travelling from his brain into his body.

"I need to ask you a few questions, Fox, if you could just humour me for a moment."

Conloach walked back to his chair and sat down. His energy was pulsing now. It was holding back the thick blanket of magic that seemed to surround the master gatekeeper. Fox shook his head, which broke the spell that seemed to be crushing his skull.

"What do you want to know?" Gabriel raised his hand and inspected his fingernails with an air of nonchalance.

"One of my gatekeepers has gone missing. One of my best gatekeepers. In fact, you may know of him – Hecta. His disappearance seems to have coincided with the birth of your new charge – who, it appears, is now also your wife. She has piqued my interest, and I would like to meet her and ask her if she has seen him recently." Fox searched his father's eyes for a clue of what he should say. Conloach regarded him with a blank expression.

"Why would she have anything to do with Hecta's disappearance?" Answering a question with a question was the only defence Fox could think of. He instinctively knew this master of magic could swat him like a fly if he so wished. Gabriel tutted.

"Now now, Fox, do not be so defensive. I mean her no harm, but I have heard through the whisperings of my people that Hecta had taken rather a fancy to your new wife – and, it seems, with good reason. She is an interesting traveller, I hear. I am very keen to see her for myself and find out what all the fuss is about." Fox remained silent, his mind racing at what action he should take. Gabriel looked slightly amused at his reaction.

"Bring her to me, Fox, sooner rather than later. I wish to ask her directly whether she has seen my best man recently." Conloach raised his hand as if to stop him speaking, but thought better of it.

"She is not able to travel at the moment, Gabriel. You may have to wait some time for such a meeting." Gabriel frowned.

"As you do not know me well enough to understand the seriousness of your insult, young guardian, I will let this comment go for now. You will bring her to me before the next moon rises or you will both feel the consequence of your ignorance." He stood up abruptly. While bowing at the waist to Conloach he looked at Fox one last time with contempt.

"Good evening to you both. I wish you a pleasant evening." And then he disappeared. Vanished. Just like that.

Sapphire leant against the railing on her forearms, watching the bank of the Nile move slowly before her like a movie playing on loop. The sun was high in the sky and the heat was intense, which made her squint even behind her sunglasses. Palm trees and long grass swayed gently in the breeze on the riverbank. It was such a lush scene of tranquillity, and it gave a picture of serene calm.

She felt far from calm. Her stomach was twisting and turning, and it had nothing to do with the lunch she had just consumed with Charlie and Nathan. Fox had not yet returned from his trip back to Shaka. She was starting to worry that something was wrong. He did not usually leave her for so long, and it was starting to make her feel twitchy. Charlie joined her at the rail and bumped her hip against her, making her jump.

"Hey, sweetie, you look as if you are miles away. Everything OK?" Sapphire faced her friend, who was smiling at her with a slight question to her expression. Her hair was tied up on the top of her head in a colourful scarf and her curls were lifting in the breeze. She wore a bright orange halter-neck dress that showed off the tan she was developing nicely.

Charlie looked fabulous, as she always did. But her question remained in the air, making Sapphire feel even more jumpy and slightly guilty, as both she and Nathan were still very much in the dark as to why she was really here.

"Yeah. Everything's OK, Charlie." Her friend eyed her suspiciously.

"Where's Fox?" Sapphire sighed and looked back at the river. She was watching a felucca in the distance dance on the soft waves of the water. A fisherman was throwing out his nets and making the sunlight reflect for a second on the nylon lines he threw out before him.

"He went home for a while. He should be back soon." Charlie shifted from one foot to the other. She tipped her head to one side and looked at Sapphire. Even with her large designer sunglasses hiding her eyes Sapphire could feel them boring into her and looking for a clue as to why she was being so quiet.

"You look better today. I was worried about you. Fox said you would be fine, that you had a cold. Is there something you aren't telling me, honey?" Sapphire knew this conversation could go one of many ways and she really wasn't up for any of them.

"Mmmh, I was feeling sick but I'm fine now. He had to go home just to recharge for a while." Charlie nodded as if understanding, but Sapphire knew her curious mind was spinning with other ideas.

"How does that work exactly?" Charlie asked. "Where is 'home'?" Sapphire stepped away from the rail. She knew Charlie wouldn't give up easily if she tried to smooth over some of the truths of Fox's disappearance.

"It's complicated." Charlie pouted a little but, after nodding, continued.

"Try me." Sapphire smiled back. Perhaps it was time, after all, for some real truths to be told.

"Let's get a drink at the bar and I will tell you, Charlie." Her friend grinned, obviously keen to be fed some gossip. Sapphire knew something had changed, and on Fox's return they would most likely need to disappear again. She could feel it in her bones. It wasn't fair keeping Charlie in the dark so much. Apart from the fact that Charlie was not stupid, telling so many lies was giving her another headache. They headed to the bar. Nathan was by the pool sunning himself. He too was turning a lovely shade of brown, and looked pretty damn hot in his trunks. His abs were glistening in the sunlight from the heavy dose of sunscreen that Charlie had most likely slathered on him earlier.

After finding two bar stools at the end of the bar Charlie ordered them a drink each, took off her sunglasses, and propped her head up in her hands as she looked across at her friend with wide, bright eyes. She was grinning widely now.

"You really hate this, don't you?" Sapphire sipped her gin and tonic, grimacing slightly at the sharp tang that hit the back of her throat. It was a strong one.

"What?"

"Telling me the truth about what's going on with you two: who he really is, why we are here, where you disappeared for six whole months ..." Sapphire laughed.

"No, I don't. It's just that some of the shit that has been happening to me, Charlie ... well, it's really just too crazy to explain without blowing your mind." Charlie chuckled. After taking her own G & T she spun the little plastic stirrer in her fingers absently.

"Saf, you are the best friend I have ever had. I always knew there was something different about you. I certainly knew there was something different about Fox. When you came home again with him out of the blue I knew things had changed drastically for you, but you don't have to carry the burden on your own, honey. Seriously, I can take it. I get it, I really do. Do you think I don't have enough imagination in myself to – just for a moment – believe that this reality we see before us is all there is out there? I see the weight on your shoulders. I see the changes in you. Just your physical appearance itself tells me something extraordinary has happened to you." She paused and took another sip of her drink.

Sapphire could feel her mouth opening slightly in awe. Her friend was more than just sharp: she was a sassy lady who could really see out of the box. Maybe it was all the drugs she had done in her lifetime. Maybe it was just intuition, but Charlie was telling her it was OK to share all the secrets. It was OK for her to offload some of the worry. Her stomach started to unravel a little, and she could feel her shoulders loosen just a little bit. God bless her friend.

"Yes, something extraordinary has happened to me, Charlie. And you are right. It is a heavy burden." Charlie sipped her G & T with a smile still playing on her lips.

"Tell me. Tell me what's going on, Saf, and share the burden. If it blows my mind, then so be it. I have the feeling it will just free me from this annoying voice in my head that keeps babbling on and on about life being something so much more than what I thought it was." Sapphire looked across at the other guests walking across the ship's deck who were talking, laughing, and having fun on their holiday. They were completely oblivious to what she was, where she had been, and how she had just recently started a chain reaction that could completely alter the world they lived on.

Charlie was right. If she didn't start sharing some of this headfuck with another human she might just go mad. Fox and Pearl didn't count. They were already vibrating at a different level, and knew so much more than she did. She took a deep breath and faced her friend again.

"OK, Charlie. If you are really sure you want to know … here goes."

They sat at the bar for over an hour. Charlie listened silently as Sapphire told her everything … the dreams, the travelling, her magic, and the transformation she had experienced when she had married Fox on that moonlit night back on Shaka. She told her of the beauty and the wonder of Shaka, of the people there, and how each person had their own amazing gifts of magic. She described Kit, and how sweet she had been to her when she had lost the child she was carrying.

Charlie watched her with tears filling her eyes as Sapphire told her of the visions she had experienced and how painful it had been to see Fox despair over the loss of his child. When she described the battle with Ebony and Hecta her face became still with shock. The only indication that she was actually registering what Sapphire was saying was the slight shaking of her head at the disbelief that her friend had been through so much. She touched the tattoo on Sapphire's finger and arm when she explained how it linked her for life with Fox, and she trembled slightly when Sapphire revealed the reason why they had travelled to Egypt, and at her description of the seeds, of the essence, and the of crystal tree that now grew in the oasis not so far away.

Charlie took it all, took it in a way that Sapphire could only describe as epically calm for a human who had just been told a tale so wild and so utterly spectacular that it could have been made up like a Hollywood movie. Even to her, as she spoke the words and retold her story, it seemed unbelievable. She had come so far, and in such a short space of time. Charlie leant back in the stool and blinked.

"Well, holy fuck and slap me with a stick. I think I need another drink – and maybe a big fat joint, after that revelation." Sapphire felt drained. Telling her story had left her spent.

"The first we can do ... the joint may be a little more difficult." They both laughed, and Charlie leant forward to brush Sapphire's cheek gently with her fingers.

"My dear, beautiful Saf ... I loved you before and I love you now, so much. I'm so sorry you have had to go through all this alone." Sapphire could feel tears burning her eyes. Her throat was tight with emotion. The magic within her pulsed with love for her friend.

"I haven't been alone, Charlie. Fox was with me the whole time, and you ... you were always with me." They were both silent for a moment. A special connection between them flickered in the air around them and joined them at last in the truth.

They say that the truth will set you free. Apparently it really did. Sapphire at last felt some of the heavy burden she had been carrying float away into the bright blue sky like a lost balloon carried on the wind. And, boy, did it feel good.

Nathan was suddenly by their side, looking at both of them with an expression of concern.

"You two OK?" Charlie faced her man and smiled widely, her pretty face lighting up in a way that Sapphire had not seen in a long time.

"Yeah ... yeah we are more than OK, gorgeous. Do you fancy a drink?" Nathan settled into the stool beside them and ordered a beer. Sapphire looked at him and studied him more closely. Nathan had always been such an easy-going guy – fun, and boyishly handsome in his own way. He was good for Charlie, and they had helped her so much it seemed only fair that he should also be let in on the secrets she had just spilt.

"Nat, Charlie may need to fill you in on some of the details as to why we are here later. I will let her explain in her own way when she is ready, but I just want you to know how much you mean to me and how amazing you have been since I came home. I am glad you are here with us." He smiled at her, his blue eyes twinkling with amusement.

"Sounds heavy, Saf, but I could see you two girls were having a heart-to-heart and knew it would probably have something to do with Fox disappearing again. Will he be back soon?" Charlie stroked his arm absently. She loved her man, that was clear to see, and it eased the burden for Sapphire a little that she had someone so wonderful to share her revelation with.

"I hope so." Nathan took her hand and squeezed it gently.

"Everything will be OK, Saf. Don't worry. Your man is a good one, and he loves you. That much is obvious. Relax for a while by the pool. I am sure he will be back before evening." Sapphire smiled, and linked her fingers within his own. His hand felt warm and soothing, which gave her comfort.

"Yeah ... some sun will do me good, I think."

They finished their drinks and headed back to the pool. Sapphire stripped down to her bikini. She watched Charlie and Nathan climb into the pool, and leant back in her lounger and closed her eyes. They would be arriving at the next port by nightfall. She just needed to trust that Fox was OK and would return soon. In the meantime she would try and catch some rays and top up her tan. Some vitamin D might just make her feel a little more energised. She noticed that even though Fox had fed her his magic she was still feeling slightly jaded. The thought troubled her, but she dismissed it quickly. No point worrying any more. She was on holiday, after all.

Fox did not return until late that evening. Sapphire had spent several hours by the pool sunning herself before returning to her cabin to shower and change. She was applying dark kohl to her eyes while sitting at the dressing table when he arrived. Suddenly he was standing behind her, which made her jump and draw a thick black line across her cheekbone. He laughed as she gave him an evil look before slipping his arms around her neck and kissing her on the top of her head.

"Where have you been? I was starting to worry," she grumbled. He pulled her towards his body, holding her close for a moment and enveloping her in the scent of sandalwood and patchouli.

"I am sorry, my love. I got caught up with some business that could not wait on Shaka." She watched him in the mirror and noted a slight furrow on his brow. He was worried. Not good.

"Mmmh, anything I should know about?" He let go of her and suddenly stepped back and swept his hand through his hair, a gesture she recognised that spoke of his unease and most likely some bad news he was about to give her. Crap.

"I have some good news and some bad news, Sapphire." She sighed. Double crap. He watched her as she continued to apply her make-up. She had arranged to meet Charlie and Nathan on deck in half an hour. They would be heading out for supper off the ship now that they had arrived at the next port. She had been looking forward to a chilled evening somewhere new on the bank of the Nile. Now she was not so sure that the evening would be a stress-free one after all.

"Give me the bad news first. Get it over with." His eyes darted around the room, anywhere but on her, which confirmed his worry.

"I need to take you back to Shaka with me tonight. You need to meet someone who has become interested in you." Now he had her attention.

"Who?" While licking his bottom lip he took a deep breath. His eyes were dark, the pupils dilating a little as he looked at her reflection in the mirror again.

"A man called Gabriel. He is the master of all gatekeepers." Sapphire dropped the lipstick she was holding. It clunked on the wood and rolled on to the floor.

"There is a master of gatekeepers?" Fox nodded slowly. His hands were on the back of her chair now. She could feel the warmth from them radiating into her spine in gentle waves of magic. He was trying to soothe her.

"Yes, there is. I have never met him before. In fact I was not even aware he existed until my return home today. My father has met him, but had never spoken of him. Apparently he is rarely seen, and is far too important to bother with the general duties of the gatekeepers. He leaves it up to them to sort out any problems." Sapphire watched him with wide eyes that blinked slowly as she processed this new piece of information.

"You mean me?" He lifted his right hand and brushed the hair away from her shoulder as he softly traced his fingers across her exposed skin.

"You are not a problem, Sapphire." She raised an eyebrow.

"Then why does he want to meet me?" Fox continued to stroke her skin slowly, sending shivers of magic into her nerve endings. He had certainly recharged from being on Shaka. He was positively glowing in the dark again.

"Hecta." Sapphire took a cotton bud and began to remove the line of kohl she had accidentally drawn on her cheek.

"Should I be worried?" He sighed and closed his eyes, as if contemplating the question. That in itself worried her.

"Maybe. I do not know this man but he knows us, and he knows Hecta is missing. It could be a problem, but at the moment he has no idea you killed him and that he is buried in the woods near Pearl's home. I will need to let her know that she may need to be careful when outside Foxglove. Gabriel may already be searching for him there." Sapphire finished with the cotton bud and dropped it into the bin beside her. Happy with her reflection, she started to brush out her hair.

"Well, he will have to wait until after dinner. We are going out with Charlie and Nathan. I need to get off this ship, Fox. I am starting to crave the feel of earth under my feet again." She watched him take the brush from her hand and start to work through the tangles. He loved to brush her hair.

"What was the good news?" she asked. He tugged her hair gently at the nape of her neck and smiled.

"I have brought back some herbs from Willow to help you heal. They will remove the taint the magic left behind when you planted the seed." She frowned.

"What taint?" He started to braid her hair slowly, his fingers nimble and quick, as he folded the white-blonde strands so that they fell heavily down her back.

"You cannot see it, my love, but it is there. My father helped remove it from me when I returned home. It is sapping your energy and your magic. Unfortunately it is a side effect of such wild old magic." Sapphire pulled a few strands of hair out of the braid and allowed them to frame her face. She watched him place his hands on her shoulders and lean down to rest his chin on the top of her head. His eyes flashed gold and black at her, and swirls of light were twisting within his irises. It was mesmerising.

"Is that why I've felt so odd today?" He smiled again, his face lighting up.

"Yes. Now stand up so that I can see you properly. I've missed you." She complied and laughed as he spun her around so that he could admire the long sundress she was wearing. "Beautiful," he said. He planted a kiss on her lips and hugged her briefly before releasing her and heading to the shower.

"How long do we have until we need to meet Charlie and Nathan?" he asked. She watched him strip as he went, discarding his shirt and trousers on the floor.

"In half an hour, so be quick." As she listened to the shower switch on she turned to the bed to see a cloth bag sitting on the covers. It was obviously Willow's bag of herbs.

"We will have to leave quickly after dinner, Sapphire," Fox shouted from inside the shower.

The thought of having to meet the master of all gatekeepers troubled her immensely. She had thought all her problems were behind her when Hecta had been disposed of. No such luck. As she shook off the feeling she opened the bag and looked inside. Her body trembled a little as the pouch opened. The herbs inside were fragrant and shining, as if they contained tiny crystals within the leaves. Perhaps they did.

To be honest, she was grateful that Fox now knew why she had been feeling so out of sorts. The seeds and the essence were safely tucked away in the wardrobe but their presence could be felt constantly against her skin now, like a subtle, tickling sensation whenever she thought about them. Creative magic, it seemed, came with a price.

Fox emerged from the en suite dressed for dinner in a linen suit in dark blue, with his white shirt crisp and bright against his waistcoat. He looked as edible as ever, and his hair was tied back with a black leather strip. Sapphire briefly thought about skipping dinner and staying there with her man before he took her hand and smiled.

"Later my, love. Later," he said with a smile as he read her thoughts.

They headed out to the ship's upper deck to meet Charlie and Nathan. Sapphire looked up at the stars scattered above them in the dark night sky. Charlie waved at them with a huge grin on her face as she noticed Fox beside her friend. Nathan greeted them both with a hug and slapped Fox on the back.

"Glad you could make dinner, my friend. We missed you today." Fox smiled at them both. "You certainly look rested." Charlie had a knowing glint in her eye. After all the information Sapphire had given her earlier she was now looking at the man before her with a totally new understanding. Fox, having picked up on her change of demeanour, cocked his head to one side.

"Something I should know?" he asked. Charlie tucked her arm into his and pulled him along with her to the gangplank so that they could disembark.

"Only that you look particularly handsome in that suit tonight, Fox." Fox looked behind at Sapphire and Nathan, who were following him and laughing. Sapphire winked at him and he sighed. Humans.

They ate in a restaurant that had been recommended by the manager on the cruise ship. The food was amazing and the setting luxurious. Sapphire was starting to get used to this way of life. She had never been one to revel in luxury but Egypt seemed to resonate opulence, and she was falling under its spell. It was such a beautiful place, with beautiful people. She would miss it when they had to finally return home. But as they ate, drank, and laughed she pushed the thought aside. They still had another week to enjoy, and apart from tonight's little trip back to Shaka she could continue soaking up the vibe.

She felt Fox watching her while she ate, his eyes rarely leaving her, which made her feel a little nervous. He smiled at her softly, reassuring her that all was well, when she caught his gaze. But she could feel it – sense it – in his actions as he poured her more wine and stroked her hand absently. He was hiding something from her, hiding his worry.

Charlie was laughing loudly at something Nathan had said, which pulled her back to the moment.

"Will you two be coming out with us tomorrow? We are visiting some of the temples and the market in Luxor." Sapphire nodded.

"Yes, of course. We'd love to, honey." Charlie dipped her finger into one of the sweet desserts that was now in front of her, and licked her lips.

"Good. You need to see some of the history of this place instead of working all the time." Fox smiled and raised his eyebrow.

"Working?" Charlie continued eating, making a face of delight as she swallowed the sweetmeat.

"Mmmh. Saf told us what you have been up to. It's time you both took a break." Fox looked at Sapphire in shock.

"It was time, Fox. They needed to know." He looked down at his hand. His fingers were interlocked with hers under the table, and their tattoos were glowing softly.

"Well, it seems I have underestimated you both, Charlie. To be privy to such a tale would make most people lose their minds." Charlie laughed.

"You should know by now, Fox, that we are not most people." He smiled again.

"Yes, I should." As Sapphire poured them all another glass of wine she laughed again.

"And you should also know that I lost my mind a long time ago, Fox."

Sapphire was actually feeling quite tipsy by the time they had finished dinner and returned to the boat, which sat dark and hulking against the shore. Feeling drunk was something she had not experienced for a while, and not at all since her return to Earth. Her magic was most definitely off. Fox had excused them from the after-dinner brandy at the bar and led Sapphire back to their cabin. He held her firmly around the waist as she stumbled slightly and giggled.

"A little drunk, my love?" He opened the door and guided her in. She kicked off her sandals and flopped on to the bed, her arms spread wide and her head to one side.

"Can't we visit Shaka tomorrow night, Fox? I want to play." He laughed, removed his suit jacket, and placed it on the back of the chair. His muscles strained against the waistcoat as he did. She watched him with hungry eyes.

"We can play on our return, Sapphire. Right now I need to give you some of the herbs and sober you up." She pouted at him. After reaching behind her head to loosen her braid she allowed her hair to fall freely around her shoulders in a cascade of waves. He watched her with amusement, then took the bag of herbs and a glass of water and began to mix them. She waited patiently and sighed deeply. The smell of rosemary and mint filled the air for a brief moment, and she felt her skin flush in anticipation of the potion he was making. On opening her eyes she found him leaning over her with the glass in his hand. It bubbled slightly and gave off a wisp of pink smoke.

"Drink up." She pushed herself up clumsily and took the glass from him with a pretend frown.

"Bossy," she said, slurring slightly. He steadied the glass in her hand as she gulped the contents down. She felt her magic fizz furiously against her skin, and the sensation made her head spin even more than it already was from the alcohol. She was aware of Fox gripping her arms to steady her, and whispering words in his language that seemed to heighten the effect of the herbs – which was spreading through her limbs in a warm and wonderful rush of light.

Her head began to clear, and she opened her eyes and looked at the room before her with new senses. Fox grinned at her. He released his grip and moved back from the bed. His aura glowed around him in gold and purple.

She hadn't realised how much the taint had stripped her of her magic. She could now see him clearly. His magic throbbed around him, adding to the overall effect he had on her spangled nerves.

"That's better," he laughed. Sapphire sat up and shook her head, feeling as if she had just dropped one of Charlie's little white bundles of joy.

"Oh, my God, I feel amazing. What was in that stuff?" Fox reached forward to help her off the bed.

"Probably best you don't know, my love. Are you ready to leave now?" As she held his warm hands within her own she tipped her head back to look up at him. His eyes were glinting against the flare of her magic.

"Yes and no." He kissed her softly on the lips, igniting her horny button briefly before he withdrew.

"That's good enough," he said. Before she had the chance to close her eyes again he had wrapped his arms around her and sent a jolt of magic into her solar plexus that pushed them through the wormhole and out into space and time. As she gasped for breath Sapphire felt her mind struggle to remain in control as they travelled back to Shaka away from Egypt and the cruise ship, away from her two friends who were sitting drinking brandy on the deck.

The last thought that passed through her mind before she felt her feet touch the ground again was,

"I hope this doesn't take too long. I am as horny as hell."

Chapter Seventeen

Sapphire looked around her at the familiar surroundings of Conloach's chamber. Daylight filtered through the high windows, showering the room with tiny motes of dust that sparkled in the light. She stepped back from Fox and took a deep breath. The energy in the room was high and she was aware of the great man himself, even though she could not see him. Fox released her hands and smiled. A warm, deep voice jolted her back into the moment.

"It is good to see you again, Sapphire. I trust you are well." She turned around to find Conloach standing behind her dressed in his purple robe, with his black leather trousers peeking out from beneath the edges of the cloak. He seemed to glow in the sunlight with his magic strong and fierce around him. She had almost forgotten just how powerful he was. She smiled and stepped forward, kissing him on the cheek she felt the softness of his skin against her lips. Their magic sparked against each other for a second before she withdrew.

"I am very well, thank you, Conloach." His eyes swirled with patterns of gold, and slight creases formed at their edges as he smiled at her.

"I am pleased to hear that. Fox has told me much of your travels recently back on Earth, and I have to confess I have been a little worried for you." Sapphire looked back at Fox, who was now standing beside the great table and pouring them both a drink. His face gave nothing away.

"I'm fine. Nothing has happened that could not be dealt with. Oh, and thank you for the herbs." He moved his hand in a gesture of indifference.

"You are welcome, although Willow is the one you should probably thank. She has more knowledge about removing such taints from wild magic." Feeling as if she was in trouble again, Sapphire felt a blush grow across her cheeks. As usual, they were keeping her safe and clearing up her mess. Some things never changed.

"I had no idea that the combination of the seeds and the essence would cause problems, Conloach." He laughed and took the goblet Fox handed him.

"Yes, Sapphire ... no idea what you were actually dealing with and how powerful it is." He paused and took a sip of the wine. "But that is not really the problem right now, my dear."

Fox handed her a drink. She shook her head, suddenly feeling nervous. The last thing she needed right now was another alcohol-induced fuzz. It was obvious she was in trouble again. Damn it. Fox had totally played this visit down, but now she could sense – practically feel – the seriousness of the meeting she was about to attend imminently. It pissed her off, but she refused to let either of them know. Sometimes the mere fact that she was still part human seemed to make them think she was stupid.

"Fox told me about Gabriel. That's why I'm here, isn't it?" Conloach walked to the table, pulled out a chair, and gestured for her to sit. She did, and looked at Fox for some hint of what would happen next. He smiled at her, but she sensed his apprehension. There it was again: the look of worry. Now she was really starting to get twitchy, and even more pissed off. She did not like it when he treated her like a child. If he thought she needed protecting after everything they had been through together he was delusional.

"Yes, that is why you are here. He has requested this meeting with you – and, to be perfectly honest, Sapphire – it could be a problem." Fox remained silent, and sipped his wine. Right now she could punch him for letting her return so unprepared.

"Why is he a problem? He knows nothing about me, or what happened to Hecta." Conloach closed his eyes for a second, as if he was counting to ten after his child had said something stupid or rude.

"Gabriel is a very powerful magician as well as the master of gatekeepers, and not someone you should underestimate. It is likely that he has known of your existence for as long as we have, and that Hecta's disappearance is high on his priority list. He is unfortunately very dangerous to you, daughter."

Sapphire blinked her big blue eyes at him and bit her bottom lip while she digested this new piece of information. The fact that he had called her 'daughter' had stunned her a little, and the added bonus that someone else could have been spying on her for the whole time she had been stumbling through this crazy world of magic just added to the whizzing sensation that was now making her head spin.

Fox placed his goblet back on to the table and tentatively reached for her hand. She knew he could sense her growing frustration with both of them.

"Sapphire, there are still many things you need to learn about our world and the people who live here. Even I was not aware of Gabriel's existence." His eyes darted to his father briefly, and Sapphire noted with amusement that he also seemed a little pissed off at Conloach that this new threat had been kept a secret from them both until now. She allowed him to take her fingers to his lips and kiss them gently, which sent a soft wave of his magic into her fingertips. As usual he was trying to soothe her with his seductiveness. Well, this time it just wouldn't be enough. As she pulled her hand back she frowned at him.

"OK. So now we have established that this Gabriel is a big problem to me, and that by the sounds of it I am likely to get my arse kicked again if we don't figure something out. Can you please both stop pussyfooting around and tell me if there is anything else I need to know?" Both men stared at her, their mouths open slightly. She loved the fact that she could still surprise them – but, then again, she was not from their world, and she sure as hell knew that the women of Shaka did not speak back to their men. It was actually quite liberating. Fox coughed back a laugh and shook his head while a small smile appeared on his lips. Conloach frowned. After taking his goblet from the table and turning his back to them both he strode to the fireplace and leant against it. He was probably counting to ten again.

"I will need to shield you when he arrives, Sapphire. I do not want him seeing the extent of your magic or knowing anything about your recent activities with the seeds back on Earth. The very fact that you now have the power to create new magic on another world puts you in danger. Ebony wanted this magic from you, and so could he. The unfortunate death of Hecta just adds to our problems when dealing with Gabriel. He will not forgive you for that. I know him well enough to anticipate his retaliation for such an act." He turned around to face her.

"To be completely honest, and without pussyfooting around – whatever that means, Sapphire – you are in the worst kind of danger that you could imagine. Gabriel is not someone you want to make an enemy of, and I was hoping that this day would never come for either of you. In all the years that I have ruled and that Fox has acted as guardian to the dream travellers who have existed Gabriel has never shown any interest in any other traveller.

"His excuse of finding Hecta is just a smokescreen. I have no doubt whatsoever, Sapphire, that he knows there is something unique and different about you. You are part human, after all, and that in itself has piqued his interest, as it did Hecta's." Sapphire could feel her body shaking now. She did not know if it was from the fear that was starting to spread like an infectious disease throughout her veins or sheer frustration that she was again being threatened. Damn it, she was looking forward to the rest of her holiday. The burden of being given the seeds and the essence had been heavy enough without this added bonus. Fox twitched beside her. He was clearly uncomfortable with how this conversation was turning out.

"Fine. Someone else wants to steal my magic again and turn me into a corpse. Well, that's just wonderful," Sapphire spat out. Conloach laughed, and his face lit up as he did. Sapphire could not see what was so funny.

"My love, no one is going to hurt you. Not while I am breathing. You know that," Fox said. He brushed his fingers across her cheek as his eyes flashed at her. He was also pissed off, and she could feel the anger bubbling beneath his touch. His magic was flickering around him now in flashes of red.

"Both of you calm down ... I have enough power to shield you, Sapphire. Gabriel will be none the wiser, as long as you remain calm throughout the meeting and tell him nothing that could alert him to what has really happened to his gatekeeper." Sapphire sighed.

"Oh, no problem. You want me to lie my arse off and act the complete innocent, then, do you?" Fox laughed, and bent down so that he could kiss her softly on the lips.

"You are so beautiful when you are angry, my love." She allowed a small smile to grace her lips.

"Flattery will get you everywhere, Fox," she said. Conloach shook his head in frustration.

"Gabriel will be here very soon. I need you both to get some kind of story together as to when you last saw Hecta and what you have been doing recently." He paused and pinched the bridge of his nose in exasperation. "Try to at least make it believable." Fox nodded and looked at Sapphire with an intenseness that she knew meant business.

"Tell him that you have not seen Hecta since the battle with Ebony, Sapphire. He disappeared then, and you have not seen him since. We have been with your friends on Earth ... on holiday." She stared up at him with an expression of disbelief.

"Really? Is that all you can think of?" He shrugged his shoulders. Clearly that was the best he could come up with. She pushed herself up from the chair, her legs feeling a little wobbly.

"I will think of something. It's me he is interested in. I will come up with a story. Don't worry." Conloach raised his eyebrows. He clearly doubted that she would be able to give Gabriel something convincing.

Sod them both. She was stronger than she looked, and being female gave her the natural ability to lie through her teeth. Conloach walked towards her, and looked down at her with what she felt was a little sadness in his eyes.

"The shield will protect you, Sapphire, and hide your magic. But it will not hold for long, so we need to keep this meeting short." She nodded as he reached for her. His hands, heavy and warm, landed on her shoulders.

He closed his eyes, and she watched with fascination as his magic flared around him in a thick purple aura that enveloped her like a cloud of smoke. The sensation was totally overwhelming and made her whole body convulse. Her eyes even slipped to the back of her head for a second. It felt as if she was rushing through a vast vortex of vibrant colour, and it was the best and the worst ride she had ever been on.

The sound of someone moaning filled her ears, and she realised the sound was coming from her own lips. It felt so intense that her toes were literally curling in her boots. Her whole body was shaking now, and her veins were fizzing with the magic that he was pumping in and around her. It was utterly disturbing and completely intoxicating at the same time. She felt as if she was being turned inside out, and the pulse of her magic was spinning in all directions and moving in and out of her body.

The heaviness of his hands on her shoulders suddenly disappeared, and she reeled backwards. Fox caught her before she actually fell back and hit the floor. Fox was saying her name, but all that she was really aware of was a ringing in her ears. Gradually her vision cleared, and she blinked back tears that threatened to fill her eyes.

"Sapphire, my love, are you OK?" With his hands around her waist to steady her Fox lifted her back to standing. She shook her head to remove the irritating buzzing.

"Holy shit, Conloach, you could have warned me. That was freaky." Conloach regarded her coolly, his eyes still flashing with the remnants of his magic.

"I apologise, Sapphire. Shielding in this way is somewhat intense." Fox was looking at her as if she had suddenly grown two heads.

"Intense is not the word I would have used. I feel as if I'm not in my body." Fox was staring now, his face a picture of concern.

"Actually, my love, you aren't." Now she was confused.

"I have removed your essence for a while, Sapphire ... borrowed it, if you like. That way Gabriel will not be able to sense how strong you really are." She shook her head. The buzzing had reduced to a slightly less aggressive ringing now, but she definitely felt odd.

"I have absolutely no idea what you are talking about, Conloach. And, quite frankly, I don't want to know. Let's just get this over with."

Sapphire sat in the heavy wooden chair with her hands in her lap. She clasped them together tightly as she tried to stop them shaking. They felt clammy and hot. She could have sworn that sweat was starting to bead on her forehead. She felt really, really odd.

Fox stood behind her with his hands on her shoulders. He was pumping his magic into her, but it was if she was observing the whole thing rather than experiencing it. The shield Conloach had effectively thrown around her felt like a thin film of invisible silk that touched her skin like a summer's breeze. Conloach stood to their right. She was intensely aware of him, and could feel him breathing in and out as if she was breathing at the same time as him. If he had indeed borrowed her essence she was effectively in two places at once right now. What a headfuck.

A heavy knock at the door made her jump and Fox gripped her shoulders a little more tightly, which sent another pulse of soothing magic into her body. This time she felt it like the slow drip of honey into her limbs, which made her giggle. Shit. She felt as if she was drunk or high, or both.

"Hold it together, Sapphire, for fuck's sake," she whispered to herself in her head.

A young man entered. He was dark-haired, and quite clearly nervous. Sapphire recognised him immediately from the day at the market with Kit.

"Master Conloach, you have a visitor. He has told me that you are expecting him." Conloach nodded his head slowly.

"Thank you, Raven. You may send him in." Sapphire sensed Fox flex the muscles in his arms. If she hadn't been utterly terrified it would have turned her on.

Without a sound a man dressed in a long white coat that swept to the floor entered the room. His hair, which was as white as snow, was tied back in a thick braid that trailed almost down as far. Sapphire felt her eyes widen with astonishment as she looked into his ice blue eyes, which immediately met her own with a knowing smile. She knew this man. She had seen him before in one of her dreams. Oh shit.

"Welcome, Gabriel. Would you care for a drink?" Conloach gestured to the wine standing on the table. Gabriel removed his gaze from Sapphire and regarded Conloach coolly.

"No, thank you, Conloach. I am pleased to see you have brought Sapphire to me. Well done." Sapphire immediately disliked this man. His arrogance slid from his body like a snake – a poisonous one, at that.

"Yes, she is here as you requested." Fox remained completely still behind her with his hands still holding her shoulders and his energy pulsing strongly into her body. He was in full attack mode. She could almost sense the muscles flexing and twisting with his urge to sweep them both away from this room and away from this man. Gabriel stepped towards her, his hand outstretched as if to take her own.

"It is a pleasure to meet you at last, Sapphire. You are indeed as fascinating as I was told."

Without even thinking she raised her hand as he leant forward to clasp it. She had not even intended to let him touch her. She felt the shield push back slightly against her skin as his fingers touched her. He was so close to her body now that it made her gasp softly.

His head moved to one side and the smile grew wider on his lips. He grasped her hand tightly and closed his eyes, breathing in heavily as if he were actually breathing in her scent. The action gave her the creeps. The shield flexed back out as he withdrew. His eyes were flashing with tiny white orbs that looked like snowflakes ... amazing. She was lost for a second within them, and felt herself slip a little further down into the chair.

Fox held her upright and gripped her even harder, which brought her back into the room again.

"I am glad that you chose to come back to Shaka to meet me, Sapphire. I have some questions for you." She nodded slowly, as if she had turned into a puppet. She was aware of Conloach, who was watching her with intense eyes, beside her. She felt oddly detached and shook her head slowly, in a desperate attempt to hold herself together.

"And you are ...?" He laughed with a deep, almost disturbing tone, which made her shiver.

"Of course ... how impolite of me. I am Gabriel, master of the gatekeepers." She suppressed a giggle.

"Pleasure to meet you." Was she slurring her words? He pursed his lips before smiling again. He was actually very good-looking when he smiled, which was even more unnerving to her.

"Now that we have finished with the introductions I would like you to tell me where my gatekeeper Hecta is. I believe you were the last person to see him before he just ... disappeared." He flicked his fingers into the air as he said the last word slowly and dripping with sarcasm. Sapphire paused before answering, acutely aware that the atmosphere in the room was thick with nervous anticipation. It practically pulsed like a frightened heartbeat.

"I have absolutely no idea. The last time I saw him he rudely interrupted me while I was taking a bath." She felt Fox shudder behind her. His whole body actually shook in total shock at what she had just said. Gabriel threw his head back and laughed.

"Well, I must apologise on behalf of my man. Such a thing is gross bad manners. In such circumstances a lady's privacy is most important." He paused, and licked his lips as if he were about to pounce on her and eat her alive. "I must say I am slightly envious at the thought of such a meeting." Fox gripped her shoulders even tighter. She could feel the waves of anger practically crashing off him now. He said nothing.

"Well, to be honest, I thought it was rather rude myself, and told him to get the fuck out of my house."

Conloach stepped forward. Gabriel raised his hand to stop him from coming any closer. His eyes were flashing even more brightly blue. The snowflakes within them had now turned into a snowstorm.

"Oh, fuckity fuck. Now I've done it," Sapphire thought to herself.

"And what was his response?" Sapphire could feel sweat forming between her breasts now. The shield was pressing to her so tightly it was crushing her and making it hard to breathe.

"He left, and I haven't seen him since. Which, quite frankly, is a relief. I am sure you know that Hecta and I have never really seen eye to eye."

He dropped his arm, allowing Conloach to move again – which he did, but only an inch towards them. The heat in the room had gone up so much that Sapphire felt as if a fire had started at the base of her spine and was travelling upwards towards her head. Gabriel crouched down to her level and looked her straight in the eye with his arms resting on his knees. The magic surrounding him was so bright it made her squint.

"I see. Well, I will have to continue my search for him, then … which is rather a problem, as I really do hate losing my men with no trace." His eyes flicked from her own to rest at her breasts. She held her breath as he scanned her slowly. His gaze rested on the obsidian necklace that nestled between them. She watched his expression change to something that resembled confusion and excitement, and it then clicked back quickly to stony and cold. He reached forward to touch it, his fingers shaking a little as he did. What the fuck?

"Where did you get this?" Sapphire was momentarily shaken. Why would he be interested in her necklace?

"A friend gave it to me," she answered defensively. His eyes darted back to hers. For a second she saw something inside them that revealed something else of the man before her. A vulnerability.

"What friend?" Fox was clearly distressed. His fingers were biting into her shoulders so hard now she could hardly keep still.

"A woman on Earth called Pearl. She is a very good friend of mine." Gabriel was suddenly standing again. The action was so fast it was like a blur. Perhaps he was part vampire too. He turned his head to one side with his expression shifting from exhilaration to pure disbelief. Conloach looked completely confused.

"She is still alive?" Gabriel all but whispered. Sapphire felt the thick, heavy sensation of foreboding fill her limbs. This was not good. Not good at all.

"Do you know her?" He sighed heavily, shook his head, and suddenly regained his composure, the arrogant man once more.

"Perhaps." The air shifted slightly, Sapphire could feel the shield start to waver a little. The crushing sensation was loosening. She looked at Conloach, who raised a brow. They needed to move this along, and quickly.

"Well, it was very nice to meet you, Gabriel. I hope you find Hecta soon. And, if you do, please tell him that the next time he wants to pop up in my world he needs to give me some notice, so that I can at least have some clothes on." Gabriel laughed and clapped his hands together with glee.

"Oh, my beautiful lady. It really has been a pleasure to meet you. I had forgotten just how amusing humans could be." He turned to Conloach and narrowed his eyes.

"You will keep me informed if you hear anything, won't you, Conloach?" Conloach bowed slightly.

"Of course, my lord." For the first time during the entire meeting Gabriel turned his gaze to Fox.

"Keep her safe, guardian. She is a rare find. You are a lucky man." He stepped back and smiled once more at Sapphire, an intense smile that she could feel probing into her very soul. "Until we meet again, Sapphire ... travel well, travel safe. Blessed be." And then he disappeared. Just like that.

"What the hell was that all about?" Sapphire blurted angrily. Conloach looked at her, his expression perplexed.

"I have no idea why he would even question you about the necklace or about Pearl. It is a mystery to me, I am afraid, but I think you should ask her when you see her next whether she has any knowledge of Gabriel." Fox had released his grip on her shoulders, and was now standing beside her and looking at her with concern in his eyes.

"The shield did its job well, Father, but I don't think for one minute he actually believed Sapphire's story that Hecta just left the house when she told him to." Conloach stepped towards her and gestured for her to stand.

"No, neither do I. Sapphire, I need to remove the last trace of the shield and return your magic to you. Are you ready?" She stood up slowly and took a deep breath.

"Ready as I'll ever be." The process of removing the shield and returning her essence was as intense as before, but this time she was prepared. The sensation of her magic returning to her body was like a cool shower of fresh autumn rain after the heat that had filled her body while Gabriel had been in the room. As she opened her eyes again after Conloach had removed his hands from her shoulders she shuddered a little.

"He gave me the creeps. Are all the gatekeepers so intimidating?" Fox took her hand and threaded his fingers through her own.

"Their magic is strong but different from ours, my love. Gabriel is the most powerful of them all, and he knows it – hence the ability to intimidate you – but I feel we have at least brought ourselves a little more time before the truth is revealed." Conloach nodded.

"You will both need to be extra vigilant from now on. I fear that Gabriel will be keeping a close eye on you, Sapphire." She nodded, sighing loudly.

"That's what I thought. I've seen his face before in one of my dreams, so I think he may have already been watching me. I'm worried about his connection to Pearl. I need to talk to her about it, but that won't be possible until we return to Earth. I have to get back to Charlie and Nathan first."

Conloach walked to the table and began to pour himself some wine. She didn't blame him. She felt as if she needed a stiff drink herself. There was something about Gabriel that was completely unnerving. It was if he had known all along that she was lying, and he was just testing her. His magic was powerful, and she had felt it touch her soul when he had gripped her hand. It was intoxicating and dangerous, like nothing she had felt before. Fox held her hand. After pulling her into his arms he held her to his body for a moment, breathing in her scent.

"He will not harm you, my love. Do not fear him." She allowed the heat of his body to calm her. His chest was firm and comforting against her head.

"I don't doubt that, Fox – but he is just another thing in our lives to worry about, a shadow lurking in the background. I really hoped that after Hecta's removal from my life things would settle down." Conloach laughed, a deep rumble in his chest.

"Because of the nature of what you are, Sapphire, life for you will unfortunately never be that straightforward." She frowned at him.

"Mmmh ... Thanks, Conloach, for the vote of confidence. I think I'll push that thought to the back of my mind for now." Fox released her slowly.

"We will return to Earth, Sapphire ... spend the rest of our time with your friends and relax a little. My father will keep an eye on things here and contact me if anything changes." Conloach sipped his wine, and the colour in his face slowly returned. Sapphire realised that even the great magician had been shaken by the gatekeeper's visit.

"Fox has told me of the changes already taking place on Earth from the joining of the seeds and the essence, Sapphire. You must be careful if you feel that this task is still yours to finish. I am still concerned with the outcome of this change on your planet. The magic is strong, and I do not know how it will affect your people or their Mother." Sapphire stared at him.

"You don't think I should continue planting the seeds?" His eyes flashed at her.

"I cannot give that judgement, Sapphire – this is your journey – but I will consult the Oracle on your behalf to see if she has any insight to where this may lead for you all." She watched him, and felt the weight of her burden on her shoulders once more.

Why did everything have to be so damn difficult? She had really believed that this was the right path, that she could help lift the energy back on Earth and enlighten her fellow humans. Now she wasn't so sure. A slow trickle of doubt filled her mind. The seeds and the essence were back in Egypt, floating along the Nile with Charlie and Nathan. She felt the urge to return to them immediately now that Gabriel was on the scene. Fuck it. Nothing was simple any more.

"Before we go home I will check on the oasis again to see what has happened since the crystal tree appeared. I think that would be the best course of action before we move forward, Sapphire," Fox said. She nodded in agreement. She had the uneasy feeling that already the presence of the tree could be giving out signals to Gabriel and the other gatekeepers.

"Let's go back, Fox. I want to make sure that Charlie and Nathan are OK." The beads in his hair glistened in the sunlight as he nodded. After pulling her into his arms again he looked across at his father one last time before he sent the familiar pulse of magic through her body to transport them.

"I will see you again soon, Father. Thank you for your help. Blessed be." They left Shaka on a powerful wave of magic, with Sapphire feeling as if she was being swept away on a sea of uncertainty again. It weighed heavily on her heart.

They arrived back on the cruise ship in the early hours of the morning. All was quiet, and the water was lapping gently against the hull of the ship like a gentle lullaby. The air was deliciously warm, with the subtle undertones of exotic spices that lingered against the breeze. Sapphire blinked up at her husband. His silhouette glistened in the darkness from the remnants of his magic.

She felt her body shiver slightly after the joining of their energy. Fox always initiated the travelling, but she also powered the force behind it. Her brain was whizzing with all the new information she had gained on returning to Shaka. She felt as if she had taken a line of speed, and was flying high in the sky. She definitely needed to calm down.

"We should return to our room, Sapphire. It is late, and everyone is sleeping." Her eyes adjusted to the darkness, and she could now see his eyes more clearly. They flashed at her with tiny gold sparks, which reflected his still slightly agitated mood.

"I need to ground, Fox. I'm totally wired ... not ready for sleep at all." He smiled at her, showing her his perfect white teeth.

"We don't need to sleep." She felt her body tremble at his response. She had been twitchy when they had left earlier but, with the arrival of Gabriel, sex had been the last thing on her mind. Until now.

"Can we go somewhere else? I feel like being in the open. The cabin is too cramped." His expression changed to one of amusement.

"You just love the outdoors, don't you, my love?" She felt a blush spread up her neck.

"It's beautiful out here. Surely we can find a private spot somewhere on the bank, can't we?" His deep chuckle made her smile.

"For you, my beautiful wife, I shall find us the perfect place." He closed his eyes for a second and breathed in deeply. She watched his eyelids fluttering as if he were reaching out with his mind to scan the topography. While taking her hand he raised it to his lips and planted a soft kiss on her palm.

"Let's go." Without warning he literally whisked her off her feet into his arms and transported them back off the ship to a place that was more secluded and beautiful than she could ever have imagined.

Her eyes readjusted again to take in the scene before her. They were standing on the bank of the Nile under a huge palm tree surrounded by soft grass and wild flowers. The scent of the flowers filled her head with pure, aphrodisiac sensations and made her limbs feel immediately pliable. She could see the ship in the distance. The soft lights on the decking were catching against the dark water like fireflies.

Fox placed her feet back on the ground and grinned at her as he stepped back and lifted his arms into the air, which sent a spark of magic across the ground. She gasped with joy as the grass lit up with tiny candles that flickered inside coloured glass holders. They formed a circle around a pile of plush cushions and blankets. He had even managed to manifest a low table with wine and glasses. It was certainly handy being married to a man who could create whatever he liked whenever he felt like it. Damn handy, indeed.

A half-moon teased the shadows from above them, which made the leaves of the palm tree seem longer and bigger than they actually were. The breeze rustled the grass and sent another shiver up her spine. After taking her hand he guided her to the blankets and helped her to sit. She stretched out her legs and sighed happily, looking up at the stars that twinkled like jewels in the inky blackness.

"You really are the perfect husband, Fox." He laughed and poured them both some wine.

"I aim to please," he replied. She took the glass and sipped slowly, enjoying the heady, oaky taste as it slipped down her throat. Her mind was still busy, but just being here with him back on Earth in this wonderful place was already starting to slow down the chatter. He watched her silently as his fingers stroked the glass. She could feel his energy start to rise and swell around them, and her body responded with goosebumps that travelled up her arms and across her chest.

"You really have nothing to fear, my love. I will take care of you. All will be well, I promise you." She smiled at him, desperately wanting to believe what he had said.

"The reality feels somewhat different, Fox. I want to believe you – I really do – but things have changed again for all of us, Pearl included. I wish I could just switch my brain off for a moment and feel some peace." He took the wine glass from her hand and shifted his body so that he could lie closer to her, with his arm propping up his head and his hair falling across his shoulder.

"I will help you switch off that busy mind of yours, my love." He paused and trailed his fingers across her forearm, which sent another shiver of magic across her skin. "Now close your eyes and just breathe. No other action or thought is required."

He leant down to kiss her throat and began to flick his tongue across her sensitive skin. As he did she felt her body slip slowly back against the ground, deeper and deeper, until her muscles began to unwind. He mumbled to her sweet words in his own language as he kissed her, words that flickered across her senses and heightened the sensations he elicited as his tongue traced her earlobe. His hands travelled across her body, stroking and squeezing and gently removing her clothing as he travelled down towards her waist.

She gasped as he pushed his hand inside her underwear and pressed the heel of his hand against her. His lips had moved to her breasts, where each one was given a flick and a lick of his tongue until her nipples stood erect and her body arched up towards him. His hand moved against her, and his fingers were now probing her where she felt the warmth of his energy connect with her own and open her up like a flower. She was hot and wet by the time he slipped his fingers inside her, and began to move them gently with the sway of her hips.

She whispered his name, panting against the waves of desire that were now flowing freely through her veins and igniting each nerve ending like a bolt of electricity. His mouth replaced his fingers and she threw her head back and gripped the soft cushions beside her as he filled her with the warmth of his tongue.

Her mind finally let go of all the mental chatter that had been crashing through her brain like an unwanted visitor earlier. The glow of magic surrounding them flickered behind her eyelids as she moved her hands to his head and gripped his hair. His mission to release her from her troubles was making her body spasm beneath him. He made her climax with tongue and fingers, gripping on to her as she cried out into the night. For now she had found some peace, and for now she could switch off reality.

Fox removed his own clothing quickly and efficiently. Before she could even think straight he was inside her again, moving his hips against her, filling her with his own desire, and bringing them both back up again to the top of the mountain. Sapphire held her husband tightly as he washed away the fear and uncertainty in the only way he knew how. And, boy, did it feel good.

The next day arrived bright and clear. They had breakfast with Charlie and Nathan on the deck, and laughed and chatted about the day ahead. Sapphire felt slightly more relaxed and enjoyed the company of her friends, who were excited about visiting the temples at Luxor. Fox watched her silently throughout breakfast with a slight smile on his lips. The night before had been like a dream for Sapphire, and it had certainly grounded them both after the difficult meeting with Gabriel. She had decided it was best not to tell Charlie about the new threat hanging over them. She had given her too much information already.

They left the cruise ship together and headed out to the temples, ready for a day of sightseeing. Sapphire desperately wanted to relax for the remaining part of the holiday, but was itching to return home so that she could see Pearl and find out if her witchy godmother had indeed encountered the master of gatekeepers at some point during her long life.

They wandered through the mystical temples, taking in the sights and sounds of this wonderfully exotic and historical place. Fox filled them in with some interesting historical facts of his own as they walked through the great columns and statues. It seemed that his knowledge of her world extended back through history. He only gave them teasing titbits of information, which made them all raise their eyebrows. It seemed that he had visited Earth on several occasions before he had been given the task of protecting Sapphire.

She watched him as he walked like a graceful big cat and wondered just how much she really knew this man. How could she ever know someone completely who had lived so many lives before her? But for now it was a comfort that he was hers, and that his life was now connected to her path only.

They returned to the ship as the sun began to slip down beneath the horizon, casting a blaze of orange and red across the landscape.

"Why don't you have a shower and change before dinner, Sapphire? I will return to the oasis and check the crystal tree. I won't be long," Fox whispered to her as they walked back on to the ship's deck. Charlie and Nathan were ahead of them, holding hands and laughing, oblivious to their conversation. Sapphire nodded and clutched his hand tightly. She did not want him to leave her side, but knew that it was necessary.

"Don't be long. You know I worry." His lips found hers, briefly reassuring her.

"I promise I will be back before dinner, my love." He released her hand and stepped back into the shadow of the ship's upper decking. She watched him move silently away from her smiling before he disappeared in a shimmer of light. Charlie turned around as if sensing the shift in energy.

"Where's Fox gone, Saf?" After stepping forward to catch up with them she tucked her arm into the crook of her friend's arm and hugged her to her body.

"He won't be long. He has gone back to the oasis ... just needs to check some things out. I'm heading for a shower. The heat was intense today. I feel like a wilted flower." Charlie laughed.

"Yeah, you smell like one too, honey," Charlie said. Sapphire slapped her forearm playfully.

"Hey thanks a lot."

They parted company and Sapphire returned to her cabin, swinging her bag beside her as she did. She had bought some jewellery and spices from the market outside one of the temples and wanted to unload them before stepping into a cool shower. She did indeed feel like a sweating mess.

As she opened the door to her cabin she sighed in relief at the cool air conditioning that hit her body. She placed her bag on the bed and began to strip off her clothes before heading towards the shower. Fresh towels had been placed in pretty flower shapes on the bathroom cabinet. Once she had switched on the water she loosened her hair from the pins she had placed in it earlier.

Her eyes caught a twinkle of light that glistened on top of one of the towels, and she hesitated for a second as she opened the shower door. She frowned slightly as she stepped towards the bundle. A ring lay on top of the white cotton and beside it a small card was placed, with her name written on it in handwriting she did not recognise. With slightly shaking hands she undid the envelope while looking at the ring, which glistened in the overhead lights. It was a pretty flower shape, and its petals sparkled like crystal rainbows. While opening the card she stood naked, trembling slightly. The sound of the water from the shower behind her was filling her head with white noise. The card read,

Please pass this gift to Pearl when you see her again, Sapphire. Tell her it is from an admirer. Travel safe. Travel well. She dropped the card to the floor. Her hand was resting on her chest, which now rose and fell quickly. He had been here in their room. Gabriel had been here. Suddenly nothing felt safe at all.

"Sapphire …" She spun around, almost slipping on the tiles as she did. Fox stood behind her with a concerned expression on his face.

"Fuck! You scared me." He reached for her and wrapped her into his arms. Her body was still trembling slightly.

"I felt something was wrong, and came back as quickly as I could. What has happened?" Sapphire pressed her head against Fox's chest and tried to calm her breathing. Her heart was beating so fast in her chest it felt as if it would jump out of her throat at any second. Fox stroked her hair gently, enveloping her in his magic and sending soothing waves across her skin.

"Gabriel left something in our room for Pearl. I just found it before I stepped into the shower." He reached for a towel and flicked it open with one hand so that he could hold her while he covered her naked body. She was shivering from fear rather than cold. Steam from the hot shower had filled the room, making everything misty and wet.

"What did he leave?" he asked. Her head moved slightly, indicating the cabinet.

"Over there," she said. She felt him move so that he could take a closer look. His arms were still wrapped around her and trying to calm her body, which still moved involuntarily against him.

"How do you know it is for Pearl?" Fox asked. Sapphire pushed her hands against his chest and moved him back for a second. Then she looked up into his eyes, which scanned her face with trepidation.

"There is a note with it. It says that I should give it to Pearl and that it is from an admirer, but I know it's from him, Fox. After the way he reacted to the necklace it has to be him." Fox released her and bent down to pick up the note she had dropped to the floor. His eyes moved across the note, the blackness of his pupils growing larger as he read it.

"Strange," he said. Sapphire hugged herself as she tried to stop her body from shaking.

"No shit. It's damn weird, Fox. I cannot for the life of me think how he would know Pearl, and why he is now asking me to give her a gift from him ... plus the fact that he has been here is freaking me out." Fox nodded slowly.

"He is playing with us, Sapphire, that is all. It is their way. They like to play games." She shook her head.

"Not with me, he doesn't. It's not right. I don't like it." He looked at her, his eyes flashing with a hint of anger.

"Neither do, I, Sapphire, but there is very little we can do about it right now. We have to play the game, carry on as normal." He paused and reached into his pocket to pull out a small bundle of cloth, which he held out before him.

"I managed to retrieve this from the tree before returning. It is blossoming already. They are the most beautiful flowers you have ever seen. And there is something else you should know." Her fingers reached out hesitantly to touch the bundle.

"Do I really want to know?" His eyes lowered to the mystery item briefly before returning to hers. "The tree is cloaked. No one but those with magic can see it at present, which means it is actually hidden from the rest of your world ..."

He hesitated, then opened the cloth to reveal a flower so small and intricate in detail it took her breath away. Like a perfect crystal snowflake shaped into delicate petals that glistened in the light it was utterly mesmerising.

"Which, believe me, Sapphire, is probably for the best. I have never seen such strong magic from a living thing. It practically blinded me when I stepped through the cloaking shield." She touched the flower tentatively. A spark of magic connected with her own as she did and travelled up her arm, giving her a rush of energy that almost took her head off. She stepped back, stunned.

"Holy crap," she said. He recovered the flower and put it back into his pocket.

"Exactly," he said in agreement. After taking the ring and the note Fox brushed his fingertips across her cheek softly. "Take your shower, my love. I will take care of these."

He kissed her quickly on the forehead before leaving the room and closing the door behind him. She stood completely still as she held the towel around herself. The rush of energy she had felt when she had touched the flower had felt very familiar to her. In fact she could remember exactly when she had felt it before. It was the same intense feeling that she had experienced when she had taken the little bundle of drug joy that Charlie had given her at the party and at the festival ... the same buzz of wonderful, intoxicating energy that had opened her chakras and blasted her into hyperspace.

Oh, my God. Had she just created the first magical drug tree? What had she done? Her head was spinning again. The water from the shower, which was still rushing against the glass behind her, brought her back to reality. As she shook her head in bewilderment Sapphire let her towel drop to the floor and stepped inside the shower cubicle. While tipping her head back and allowing the water to cascade across her face she smiled, holding back an inappropriate giggle.

"At least Charlie will be pleased," she thought.

Chapter Eighteen

The necromancer stood back from the low table before him and wiped his brow. The air was thick around him, like a blanket of stagnant smoke that clung to every item within the room. It covered him with the cloying sweetness that he was accustomed to ... The smell of death.

The body lying on the table was well preserved within the chilled room in the basement of the house Gabriel had given him to work in. He was almost finished. The magic he had used to bring this person back to life had been incredibly difficult to obtain, and had pushed him to the very limits of his skill and knowledge. But this had been a very special person, one filled with his own unique magic. Such a person was always difficult to reanimate. But not impossible.

Gabriel had doubled his fee when he had complained that to bring back a gatekeeper was to break every rule within the magical boundaries. Such magic was of course illegal within this world, but his master had seemed unconcerned with such petty worries. He, on the other hand, was looking forward to leaving this place as soon as the task was done.

After placing one last herb within the cauldron beside the body he began to chant, low and deep, closing his eyes so that he could focus on the magic. He knew that Gabriel would be here as soon as Hecta stepped back across the veil into his body again. He did not know how long the spell would last. It was different for each person he worked on. Some would remain attached to their body for only a few minutes; others would linger for several months. It was entirely dependent on the strength of the individual's magic and the sheer determination of their soul to reattach itself.

As a necromancer he had performed this ritual many times, and for many different reasons. He still had no idea why Gabriel wanted Hecta alive again. He had explained the consequences of bringing back the dead, and how it could destroy a soul or turn it completely insane. That was the chance you took when bending the rules of life and death. Everything came at a price.

Gabriel had asked that he do his best not to spoil Hecta during the process. He had made it perfectly clear what the consequences would be for him if he did.

The necromancer's chant became stronger and louder. The air around him started swirling into a thick dark smog, which covered Hecta's body like a spectral figure trying to take form. As he felt the energy within the room lift higher and higher his chant became faster and his body shook with the effort of finding Hecta's soul, which was somewhere out there in the ether. His magic pushed and probed and his mind stretched out as he called to Hecta to return to his physical body, to reconnect and reanimate within this room.

He felt another wave of magic enter the room as he felt the first whisper of Hecta's energy flash through his mind. Gabriel was there. While trying to remain focused on the job he continued to chant, to call to Hecta's soul, and to persuade him to return to the world of the living.

It was never an easy task to recall the dead. They were effectively in a place that no one would want to return from. A place of eternal peace. Well, most of them were, anyway. Gabriel joined him in the chant, expanding the magic so that it pressed against the walls of the room and saturated the very air he was breathing. The magic was intensified tenfold, causing the necromancer to falter for a second as his head spun.

He placed his hands on Hecta's body and pulled hard on the heavy cord that had once connected his soul to his body, and which was about to reunite one to the other. He could feel Hecta struggle a little against his magic, but something changed as Gabriel continued to chant with him. He felt the gatekeeper shift slightly, as if hearing his master again ignited some memory within him of the life he once had.

It was well known that once the veil was crossed the memories of one's previous life often left – and thus enabled a new life to exist, if the soul chose to reincarnate. This would give the soul a clean slate and a new set of challenges to live and learn. The necromancer sensed that Hecta had indeed lived a very full life in his previous position, and that Gabriel was reminding him of this as he pulled him back.

The necromancer focused hard on the task at hand, and on the final, delicate stage of reapplying the soul to the body without damaging it. He pressed his hands against the body's chest and pushed with all his might to reconnect them. The room flared brightly with dark magic that smelt of sulphur and fire as Hecta's soul travelled briefly through his body and into its own.

The necromancer shuddered as he released his hands from the body and stepped back, gasping for air. The body before him shimmered a luminescent gold in the darkness as the soul reattached itself and flickered under the pressure of such a strong reanimation. He waited with bated breath for the body to respond. Hecta's eyelids flickered and his hand twitched. The necromancer sighed with relief. The first step had been completed. Now he would have to wait and see if the mind had accepted such a difficult transition. Some did not.

Gabriel stepped out of the shadows, his eyes bright with anticipation. Hecta's body trembled slightly and his skin turned from ghastly white to a healthy pink. Like the sun rising from above the horizon he was reborn. He opened his eyes and blinked. His head turned slowly to the side, revealing dark, coffee-coloured irises that swirled with flashes of red and gold. He smiled a dark, almost sadistic smile, which made the necromancer step back further.

"Master ... you found me." Gabriel reached out and took his hand within his own. His magic flared, bright and iridescent, around him.

"Yes, my child. I have found you, and now that I have you will need to help me with something I know you will enjoy immensely." He helped him sit, and pulled him up slowly like a mother would to help her sickly child. "But first you must rest. I know this journey must have been hard for you and I will reward you for your obedience, Hecta. For you have always been the best servant to me, and your loyalty will be well rewarded."

Gabriel looked at the necromancer with a slight smile on his lips.

"You have done well, necromancer. Now you may leave, and do not speak to a single living soul of this task you have completed for me. If I find that you have I will track you down and destroy you." He paused, narrowing his eyes. "And there will be no peace for you within the eternal realm if I do. You can count on that."

The necromancer bowed and said nothing. He needed no further reason to leave, and he knew Gabriel had the magic and the intent to make his death a most unpleasant one if he did break his word. He left with his money and did not look back.

Sapphire lifted her head from Fox's shoulder, opened her eyes, and yawned. She had slept during the entire taxi journey home. They had spent the remaining part of the week in Egypt enjoying the cruise and relaxing in the sunshine. None of them had wanted to leave. Charlie, especially, who wanted the bubble of happiness to continue, had clung to every last moment. She had also slept in the taxi with her head against the window. Nathan was seated in the front, talking to the driver as they made their way towards her cottage.

It had been a real shock to step off the plane earlier that night into the cold air of England once more. Only the heat radiating from Fox beside Sapphire was stopping her body from shaking.

"We are here, my love," Fox whispered as he removed his arm from around her shoulder so that she could sit up. He looked as fresh as a daisy, with his eyes glowing softly in the dark and a slight smile on his lips. She wondered how he managed to always look so good. His magic was holding up well, considering all the use it had been getting recently.

The taxi pulled up outside Charlie's little cottage with the engine still running as Nathan sorted out the fare.

"Charlie, sweetie ... We are home." Her friend stirred beside her and moaned softly.

"I want to go back. It's fucking freezing here," she grumbled. Fox laughed as he opened the door. He uncurled his long, lean form so that he was standing beside the taxi with his hand reaching in for Sapphire. Charlie scratched her head and looked a little confused.

"I can't believe we are home already. I must have fallen asleep," she said. Nathan was opening her door.

"Come on, sleepy. I need the front door key so I can take the bags in." She pouted at him, clearly not happy that they were back in the UK and about to enter a cold house.

"OK, OK ... keep your hair on," she snapped.

Sapphire stepped out and looked up at the night sky. Clear and brightly lit with stars, it stared back at her, amused. God, it was cold. Her breath left her lips in white wisps of mist, which made her feel even colder. She felt as if she was dreaming again, and that she would wake up any minute on Egyptian cotton sheets in the beautiful room they had had on the cruise ship. No such luck. They were back in good old Blighty, and it was time to regroup.

Fox helped Nathan with the bags, and the girls dashed inside as soon as Charlie had found the key and headed for the lounge so that they could light a fire. Charlie was jumping from one foot to the other.

"Fuck ... It's so cold, Saf. I need to get the heating on. I can't believe I forgot to set the timer." Nathan placed the last bags in the hallway. He too looked a little weary. The journey home had been a long one.

"I'll put the kettle on," he said with a yawn.

Fox stood in the doorway with his hands above his head, holding on to the frame. Sapphire admired the view for a second. His muscles flexed against his shirt, making her heart rate spike. He smiled at her and lifted his eyebrow.

"Can I help you get a little warmer, ladies?" Charlie was swearing at the firelighters, which were disintegrating in her hands as she fumbled with the box while trying to get a fire going. She looked up at him standing in the doorway and sighed.

"Yes, fucking please, Fox. That would be much appreciated." He laughed as he crossed the room and moved Charlie to one side. While flicking his hand at the fire he ignited the small pile of kindling, which had most likely been sitting there for the last two weeks – and, amused by this, nodded his head.

"There you go, Charlie. Now you can relax." She frowned at him, reached for the wood, and threw on a few logs.

"Funny, Fox. Very funny."

Sapphire brushed her hand up his arm as she passed him. She needed to unpack and make sure her vanity case had not been touched. She had packed the seeds, the essence, and the crystal flower inside her make-up bag after sealing them all up within a plastic pouch and then folding them inside a sarong. Fox had told her not to worry, and that no one would see them when they went through the airport. She trusted him, but could not wait to actually get them out and put them somewhere safe ... although 'safe' would probably mean travelling to Antarctica and burying them under a mountain. Fox watched her silently as she bounded up the stairs to her old room, carrying the vanity case with her. He knew she needed the reassurance that everything was as it should be.

Sapphire unzipped her vanity case and began to unpack the contents. Her room was icy cold, and she shivered as she did. Her fingers trembled as she placed the items on her bed and began to check that everything was there. The seeds glowed a soft blue within their pouch. The essence was silent, for once, in its bottle, and the bag of dirt was also still, thankfully, intact.

She did not unwrap the crystal flower. She could feel the flow of its energy through the fabric it was packed inside. It would need a protective pouch like the one the seeds had if she was going to travel around with it. Just touching it made her body feel slightly floaty. There was no way she was letting anyone else touch it, especially not Charlie or Nathan. They would probably be blasted into hyperspace and never return.

As she unpacked the last remaining items from the vanity case she found another sarong, and hesitated before letting it unravel on the bed. Fox had packed the ring and the note for Pearl in the sarong as well. It sat innocently on her bedcover, glistening like a forbidden fruit.

"Touch me," it said. She remembered the bracelets that Charlie had made for Hecta and shivered. The ring did not hold any magic that she could feel, and certainly not a binding spell like before, but she was nervous of this gift and wrapped the ring and the note back up again. After taking all the precious items to her sock drawer she shoved them inside and shut it quickly. She would deal with that tomorrow.

"Saf, tea's ready," Nathan yelled up the stairs. After heading out into the hallway Sapphire clicked on the heating, turning it up to high before she ran back down the stairs. They were home and they were safe. That was all that mattered right now. A cup of tea in the kitchen with her friends and her husband were an added bonus.

Sapphire huddled under her duvet, dressed in flannel PJs. She felt Fox slip into the bed beside her and pull her into his warm body. She shivered, despite the heat from his naked body that pulsed against her steadily.

"Sleep now, Sapphire. I will rest for a while, then return to Shaka with the crystal flower. I want to show it to my father and see what he thinks," he mumbled into her hair, and kissed her softly.

"It's in my sock drawer. I didn't want to touch it again. Can you ask Violet to make another pouch for it?" He hugged her closer, pressing his fingers against her stomach and making her squirm.

"Of course, my love. Stop worrying." She was exhausted. The journey home had certainly taken it out of her, and she needed to sleep. The last thing she remembered before drifting off was Fox stroking her gently and whispering to her in his sing-song language. She really must learn what he was saying to her at some point in the future.

Sapphire was dreaming again. She felt her body lift into the soft, languid world of dream travel. Everything around her was turning into something much more smooth and silky.

Her eyes fluttered open and she found herself standing outside a house surrounded by woodland. It looked oddly familiar to her. Daylight filtered through the tree canopy above her and cast golden shards across the grass, which glistened as if it was covered in morning dew. Her bare feet confirmed the fact that the grass was wet and it was dawn in this dream world.

She walked towards the house as she wondered whether this was real or a vision. Lately her dreams had often been a mixture of both, and her body trembled a little in anticipation of what would unfold. Fox was nowhere to be seen and she assumed he was back on Shaka, but knew that he would arrive if she needed him.

As she approached the door of the house it opened wide and a young woman stepped out. She had long chestnut-coloured hair that sparkled with gold highlights in the sunlight. She was a classic beauty, with strong features and sparkling hazel eyes. She too looked oddly familiar. She walked towards Sapphire but did not acknowledge her, and stepped past her on nimble feet that took her to one of the flower beds nearby. This was a vision, then.

She bent down and began to pick some of the flowers that Sapphire realised were in fact different kinds of herbs, and were similar to the ones that Pearl grew in her garden at Foxglove. The young woman began to sing to herself, a sweet song that was almost a whisper on the air. Her voice was clear and in tune. Sapphire tipped her head to one side. Even this woman's voice sounded familiar. She felt a jolt of recognition fill her head as the woman continued to sing. This was Pearl ... Pearl as a young woman, but in a different world.

Sapphire stepped forward slightly to take a closer look. Her heart was thumping loudly in her chest. As she moved closer a man suddenly appeared beside her. His approach had been so silent that she had not even seen him leave the house. His hair was the colour of white snow, and it trailed around his shoulders and down past his waist like the most magnificent stallion's mane. It shone with silver strands that caught the light and reflected back at her with magical sparks. His eyes were the brightest pale blue she had ever seen, and they lit up as he reached the younger version of Pearl.

She turned to him, and smiled a smile full of love. She stood up and reached for him, and he pulled her into his arms and kissed her firmly on the lips. Sapphire felt as if she was a voyeur watching something very private and very intimate. She felt extremely uncomfortable watching such an immensely touching moment between two people who had no idea she was there.

The man slowly released Pearl and held her at arm's length. His eyes were glowing with powerful magic, which took form in the shape of tiny snowflakes. Sapphire gasped and stepped back as his eyes lifted from Pearl and looked straight at her. He smiled lazily and cocked his head to one side. He looked straight into her soul and whispered into her mind,

"Hello, Sapphire."

She stumbled back away from the scene and gasped out loud. It was Gabriel. Gabriel was Pearl's lover in a previous life, and he knew she had seen him and the vision of their happiness. Her mind spun at the possibilities this new piece of knowledge gave her. Did Pearl even know that she had been with this man? Not just a man, but the master of all gatekeepers. Had he projected this imagine into her mind? The young Pearl looked so happy as she stared up at him with adoration: happy, and in love.

Sapphire felt her body shake and her dream state shift again. She was travelling back through the wormhole quickly now, which made her eyes roll back into her head. With a jolt and shower of white light she landed back on her bed at Charlie's cottage. It was dark in the room, and she was alone. Fox was indeed back on Shaka, and Charlie and Nathan were still sleeping in the room across the hall. Still dressed in her PJs, she shivered once more. How could this be? What did it mean for Pearl? Her heart thumped and her mind swam.

There was only one way to find out. And the person who was most likely to know was also sleeping in her little cottage not so far away, completely oblivious to the truth that Sapphire had just learnt.

Chapter Nineteen

Fox leant against the door frame, watching Violet at work. Her hands were moving so fast they were like a blur as she created the magical pouch that would help keep the crystal flower safe. His body was restless, and his mind was swimming with the possibilities that this new creation could have for not just the people on Earth but for his own kind.

His father had looked at the flower with curiosity and awe as he held it in his palm earlier that night. His face had lit up briefly with a white light that had consumed his body like a meteor shower as the flower had touched his magic. He confirmed to Fox that this was indeed something simply so powerful that it could either destroy or illuminate any life that it touched. Fox knew at that point that Sapphire's task was more dangerous than they had originally anticipated. Such magic could cause serious implications in the balance of all life. It would change the connection between many worlds and the consciousness of the people who came into contact with it. It was such a beautiful, innocent object that could harness so much change.

He shivered a little at the thought. They would need to discover just what effect the crystal tree with its new fruit would do to the human race and to Mother Earth herself. Violet looked up at him and smiled. The pouch was completed, and she held it up for him to see.

"It is done, my lord. Is there anything else I can help you with?" He looked into her beautiful purple eyes and smiled back.

"No, Violet, you have done well. Thank you." She hesitated for a moment, her eyes searching his and probing for more information.

"What will the pouch hold, my lord?" He pushed away from the door frame, walked towards her, and slowly took the pouch from her hand. Its magic flared against him. Powerful. Protective. Perfect.

"Something that needs to be kept very safe, Violet. Something I am not sure any of us are ready for yet." She blinked wise eyes at him.

"Then feel safe in the knowledge that the magic I have sewn into this pouch will keep it safe, and protect the person carrying it from the contents." He placed the pouch into his pocket and handed her a bag of gold coins, which clinked solidly on the wooden table as he placed them down.

"As always, Violet, your work is worth its weight in gold." She nodded her head slowly, took the bag of coins, and slipped them into a drawer beside her.

"It is a pleasure to work for you, Master Fox. Please send my love and blessings to Sapphire. I hope to see her again soon." Fox sighed. He knew it would be some time before his wife could return to Shaka and resume any form of normality. His head buzzed slightly with the uneasy feeling that they would never have a normal life, a life where they could live in peace with children running around barefoot in his garden. The vision burnt fiercely in his chest, he wanted it so badly. He hoped that she did too, but where would they ever feel completely settled? His home was Shaka, a world formed from magic. Her world was so far removed from his that it seemed an impossible option.

It all boiled down to one thing and one thing only. Whatever Sapphire wanted he would give her. He was completely at her mercy. Wherever she went he would follow. His love for her was that strong. All-consuming, like a drug coursing through his veins, she was the hypnotic pull that held him like a moth to a flame. But for now he would return to her Earth and they would continue with the journey with her seeds, if that was her wish.

As he left Violet and stood outside her home in the warm, dark night of his home planet he felt a deep sense of loss. His wife was a dream traveller, and she possessed such strong magic that she would never truly be his to control or own. She had a fierce independence and a strong will that sometimes made him feel weak around her. The fact that she had no idea just how powerful she really was made it all the more bittersweet. He had been utterly exhausted from using his magic back on Earth, and it had taken his father some time to recharge him that evening.

He had been hiding the fact well from his beautiful wife that Earth did indeed sap him dry. He hated lying to her, and he had been using his magic so casually in front of her during his stay so that she could sense nothing was amiss. She was the only reason he could function back on Earth now. Her connection to him fed his magic, and all that he did was reflect it back to her when she needed the reassurance. She was the powerful one. She was the prize that everyone wanted. And he knew Gabriel wanted her. Whether it was just for the power she possessed or her beauty, as Hecta had, he did not know.

But he felt it like a cold hand pressing against the back of his neck, gripping tighter and tighter. He knew that Gabriel would be coming for her, and that he was not strong enough to protect her when this happened. As he held the crystal flower in his hand and looked up at the sky above him Fox felt the wave of unfamiliar, intoxicating, and almost alien magic flood his veins like a smooth slide of silk across his skin. It swept across his body and touched him in places that he had forgotten existed – a sensual, delightful whisper of all the things it could give him if he chose to take it.

He licked his lips and closed his eyes for a moment as he allowed the magic to wash over him. It was seductive and playful, and made his body tingle and swim in a soft caress of wanting. This was a new type of magic. A drug, even to him. Dangerous, and utterly amazing.

He knew that if Sapphire continued to plant more of the seeds and create more trees that blossomed such powerful magic they would all be in serious trouble. He knew that the human race was nowhere near ready for such a prize. They were, after all, a race powered by the all-consuming need to have more. More power, more sensation, more materialism, more lust … more of anything that they could touch, smell, and taste. It was the nature of them.

This little flower would be like a new kind of heroin to their system. It might set their minds free, but it might also destroy them, because humans also liked to control anything that might just give them more power or money. They had been given free will, just like his own people had, but he had watched them fight and rage against each other for things of much less significance for thousands of years.

It terrified him that with such a precious gift given to them they would annihilate it and destroy their planet, and then all the things Sapphire held dear to her would perish. The process had already begun with the crystal tree back in Egypt. The only positive thing was that the tree was cloaked at present, so that no human could actually find it. But how long would that last?

After opening his eyes again and shaking himself to regain his clarity he slipped the flower into the pouch, where it instantly became silent. The magic that had coursed through his body subsided, leaving him feeling slightly bereft. Something that felt that good had to be bad. Bad, bad, bad. He needed to get back to Sapphire and talk some sense into her. He knew that now. This could not happen. It would destroy them all. He reached out with his mind and clasped on to the strong light that linked him to Sapphire, and swept himself through the wormhole to reach her again.

She was waiting for him in the kitchen with a cup of tea wrapped inside her hands as if she were clinging to it for comfort. Her eyes sparkled brilliant blue as she saw him reappear before her and her lips curled up into the smile that he knew so well – a beautiful smile filled with love. She looked so utterly ravishing sitting in her nightclothes, with her hair a tangled white-blonde mess around her shoulders. He could never tire of looking at her.

"I was starting to worry. You were gone all night." He glanced at the clock that sat on the wall behind her. It was 7 a.m. He moved quickly to her side and bent down to kiss her on the lips. Her mouth was warm and soft like a peach, ripe and ready to eat. She released the cup and took his head into her hands, wrapping her fingers into his hair to deepen the kiss. She tasted like spiced cherry tea.

He felt his body respond to her magic, her warmth, and the love that she gave to him in that kiss. His tongue probed gently and opened her mouth so that she could let him in, let him kiss her harder and stronger. Any worry that she may have just had melted as he kissed her, lifting her from the seat and wrapping his arms around her tiny waist as he did. She was the most perfect thing to him. Her body was like a precious object to be worshipped and hungered for. It still shocked him to think that she was his, that she had given herself to him in every way possible – and without any doubt in her mind that he could keep her safe and always protect her.

She trembled slightly against his body as he tipped her head to a better angle so that he could move his lips to her throat. Her pulse quickened beneath his tongue as he slid it slowly and deliberately up to her earlobe, where he caught it between his teeth and sucked it slowly. She whimpered slightly and clutched his hair at the roots, making his groin clench hungrily. He released her soft flesh from his teeth, with his breath coming hard and fast against her hair.

"You waste time and energy worrying, my beautiful Sapphire," he said. He could tell that she had been holding all the tension in her body like a coiled spring until he returned. His energy was also pent-up and frustrated. He could almost feel the energy from the crystal flower in the pouch filling his veins again and urging him forward to take her here and now on the kitchen table.

"I always worry when you are not by my side, Fox. I can't help it." He pulled back slightly so that he could look at her again. Her eyes were soft and dark, and filled with lust.

"I am here now, Sapphire," he said to reassure her. She pushed her body against him. Even through her flannel pyjamas he could feel the warmth of her body like a heatwave against his skin. Fuck it. He flicked his hand behind him and shut the kitchen door, and added a wave of magic to keep it shut just in case Charlie or Nathan stumbled in.

He claimed her lips again and began to unbutton her pyjama top. She responded by tipping her head back so that he could remove it from her shoulders and leave her naked from the waist up. He panted softly, with his eyes devouring her breasts. While staring at him with her mouth slightly open she traced her finger across his lips, making his cock twitch excitedly. She smiled and reached across to the teacup and moved it from the table on to the counter. As she stretched across he watched her breasts lift high as she moved. God, they were utterly mesmerising – so full and beautiful for such a tiny frame.

As she looked back at him she pushed herself up on to the table, and leant back and smiled at him with an almost cocky look on her face. She was no longer the shy Sapphire. He loved it when she released her inner goddess. He was still fully dressed, but as he slid her pyjama bottoms down her legs and threw them across the floor he knew it would not be long before he too was completely naked.

"I missed you," he whispered as his eyes wandered across her flat stomach and rested on the perfect triangle that led to her most intimate of places ... a place that pleasure could be obtained in such a way it could blow your mind. She nodded slowly and raised her hands above her head so that she could grip the table.

"Show me how much," she said.

He growled low in his throat and began to rip his clothes off, kicking his boots off as he removed his trousers. He was rock-hard and so turned on it hurt. She lay on the table and looked up at him with the face of an angel. His thoughts were far from pure, and all he felt as he pulled her waist towards him and his cock entered her in a slow, precise slide was that he had to fuck away all the doubt and confusion that had been clouding his mind just moments before he had entered the room.

She was surprisingly wet already, and her body opened up for him as if he had just spoken the magical words 'open sesame' and she had been the doorway to his heaven. He pushed inside her slowly, inch by inch, until he could go no further, and watched her face change as he did. Her pupils were huge, dark, and dilated, and they made her eyes look seductively sexy. Her lips were open into the shape of a perfect O. Lust, fierce and strong, filled his body, and he began to move in a way that pushed her further up the table despite the way she clung fiercely to the edge.

While holding her waist he pulled her back towards him, claiming her and keeping her still as she began to move beneath him. Her hips came up as he thrust into her. His head spun and his blood rushed down south, making his legs feel momentarily weak. She groaned and whimpered his name over and over as he fucked her on the kitchen table. The tiles beneath it gave off a complaining screech as he literally moved the table a few inches across the floor.

Their magic began to flare brightly around them, scattering like white fire throughout the room. They lit up like two orbs burning fiercely, getting hotter and hotter until he thought the table would actually catch fire. His need to come burnt red-hot in his groin, making him harder inside her – but he held back, gritting his teeth and waiting for her to find her own release before he could give in to the desire that pushed against him like a tornado.

He reached for her left breast with one hand and took her nipple between his fingers. He squeezed it gently, which created an electric current that he could see as a flicker of red light travel down to her pussy. That did it. She came undone beneath him. Her body was shaking and bucking, and her legs were wrapped around him now and holding him inside her. There was no other place he would rather be. As he watched her glow with the release of her orgasm he let go, and allowed his own release to consume him. He let out a cry of relief as he came hard ... so hard it almost took the top of his head off.

Sapphire lay spent beneath him her head to one side. Her hair was an even more untidy mess around her, like a beautiful halo of shining light. She actually glowed. Her magic flickered against his skin, teasing him with tiny aftershocks. He panted, trying to slow his breathing as he slowly withdrew from her. His legs felt incredibly weak. Fuck, that was good.

Someone banged loudly on the kitchen door.

"For God's sake, you two ... Is nowhere sacred from your fucking? I want to make a cup of tea," Charlie shouted from the other side of the door. Sapphire slapped her hand to her mouth as she tried to stifle the laugh she wanted to release. Fox shrugged, smiling his 'I really don't give a fuck' smile. He bent down to retrieve his clothes, and he pulled his trousers back on and threw Sapphire her pyjama bottoms.

"We will bring some tea out for you, Charlie. Two sugars, isn't it?" Fox shouted back. Sapphire was blushing dark red now, and pulling her clothes on frantically. Charlie did not reply. She had obviously retreated back to her bedroom. Fox did not know what was funnier, the fact that he now had to make tea for her or that she had heard them fucking like animals in her kitchen. Humans ... no sense of humour.

After knocking lightly on Charlie's bedroom door Sapphire stood outside holding two cups of tea in her hand. While trying not to drop them or burn herself as she waited she tried to calm the blush that was spread across her chest and face. She was horrified and mildly amused that Charlie had heard them in the kitchen. Fox was taking a shower. She could hear the water beating down on him in the bathroom. He had kissed her hard before leaving her to make the tea, and whispered in her ear that they needed to talk when she was ready.

"Come in," Charlie shouted. Opening the door carefully Sapphire walked into the bedroom with her head down.

"Here's your tea," she said. Charlie was sitting up in bed with her arms crossed in front of her chest. Nathan was still under the covers – oblivious, as usual, to what was going on.

"Oh, for God's sake, Saf. You can look at me, you know. It's not as if I haven't heard you and Fox shagging before." Sapphire placed the cups on the bedside table and raised her eyes to look at her friend, who now had an amused smile on her lips.

"I'm sorry, Charlie. We just got carried away. He had been away all night and had just returned." Charlie took the tea and nudged Nathan with her elbow as she did.

"Nathan, tea's here." She sniggered and grinned at Sapphire.

"Well, I hope you at least wiped the kitchen table afterwards." Nathan mumbled something sleepily and turned over. Charlie laughed softly.

"Honey, with a man as fine as yours I don't blame you. I was only teasing you." Sapphire sat on the edge of the bed and felt the weight of her embarrassment lift a fraction.

"Thank God you are so understanding. Anyone else would evict us," she said, with a slight smile on her lips. While taking a sip of the tea Charlie smiled at her.

"Don't be daft. It's fun having you two around." Nathan stretched and moaned again as he woke up. Sapphire watched him push himself up and reveal strong pec muscles that could almost rival her husband's.

"Morning, Saf. How are you guys feeling today?" Nathan asked. Charlie snorted.

"They are feeling just fine, honey, that's for sure." Sapphire fidgeted on the bed and felt the blush begin to return.

"So what's your plan for the day, hon?" Charlie asked her. Sapphire regarded her as she wondered what she should tell her about her most recent discovery.

"I need to visit Pearl ... give you two some time alone, I think." Charlie smiled.

"OK. Perhaps we can make good use of the kitchen table while you are out." Nathan blinked at them both reaching for his tea.

"Did I miss something?" Sapphire laughed.

"No, Nat. Nothing of importance, anyway. We will see you later, OK?" Charlie grinned.

"Yeah. See you later."

Fox was drying himself with a towel in her room with his back to her. His hair dripped droplets of water down on to his shoulders. She watched his muscles flex as he moved the towel across his waist. He was so deliciously gorgeous. No wonder she had let him fuck her on the kitchen table. He turned his head and smiled at her as she closed the bedroom door behind her.

"Is Charlie still mad?" She smiled and walked across to her wardrobe to find some clean clothes. She also needed to take a shower before visiting Pearl. Evidence of their earlier activity was still a sticky, wet mess between her legs.

"No, she's fine. She was just teasing us. Thankfully my friend has no shame, and does not give a shit that you just fucked me on her kitchen table." He laughed and bent over to use the towel to dry his hair. He rubbed it enthusiastically for a few minutes before standing up straight and flicking it back behind him. His eyes sparkled.

"The perfect friend, then." As he grabbed some jeans, a T-shirt, and a thick jumper, she watched him tie his hair back with a leather strap.

"Perfect in many ways. Not in others, but she is my best friend and I love her just the same."

Fox began to pull on his trousers. She noticed that he was back to his leather gear again. Sexy as hell. He pulled a thick black jumper over his head, which made him look like a rock star once more. She sighed before heading for the shower. Would this man ever cease to make her weak at the knees?

"We need to visit Pearl today, Fox. I won't be long in the shower," she called to him as she left the room. He had said he wanted to talk to her, but it could wait. She needed to find out whether Pearl remembered anything of her previous life and to give her the gift Gabriel had left. It may just trigger a memory. The thought troubled her more than she cared to admit.

The door to Foxglove opened quickly and revealed a beaming Pearl, who looked very much refreshed and healed after their absence.

"Welcome home, Sapphire ... Fox. Come in, come in." She stood back to let them into the cottage, which was invitingly warm and cosy after the chill of the winter air outside. Fox followed Sapphire into the kitchen, where Pearl began to busy herself with making tea.

"Was your trip successful, Sapphire? You certainly look well, both of you. The sun has obviously done you good." Sapphire pulled out a chair and sat down, feeling a little uncomfortable down below. She could still feel the pounding Fox had given her earlier.

He smiled at her from the doorway. He was leaning against it casually, as he always did, and his eyes were shining. Pearl did not notice the post-sex buzz of energy between them – or, if she did, she was polite enough not to comment. After placing cups on the table she began to pour them some of her herbal tea. The smell of apple and mint filled the air, making Sapphire feel as if she was truly home again.

"It was, Pearl, but the result is a little overwhelming." Pearl regarded her with bright eyes.

"I sensed a shift in energy while you were away. Something has changed, and I gather it is from your little seeds." Fox stepped into the kitchen.

"Sapphire has created something we have never seen before, Pearl. A new kind of magic, in the form of a crystal tree. By combining the seeds with an essence that we were given by a man in Cairo she has created something of a miracle." He paused and looked at Sapphire, who regarded him silently.

"I fear that this is far too powerful for your humankind to experience right now," he added. Sapphire frowned.

"What did your father tell you about the flower?" she asked. Pearl took her tea and sipped it, her face a picture of concentration.

"Well, that does sound interesting. Tell me more." Fox pulled out the chair next to his wife and sat down. She was staring at him with those big blue eyes as if confused at his words.

"Sapphire is manifesting magic so strong now that even my father is concerned it will cause destruction rather than a healing for your world." He looked at Sapphire and took her hand and held it gently on the table. "The flowers blossoming from this tree are like an intoxicating drug even to my kind, Sapphire. It is dangerous to unleash such a thing on your people. They are not ready."

Pearl placed her cup back down and looked at them both. Her hands were now in her lap, as if she were about to scold them.

"Do not be too quick to judge the human race and their ability to evolve, Fox. You may think that what Sapphire has created is too dangerous for our kind, but I feel inclined to disagree on this occasion. I have felt the energy of our Mother become restless and impatient. She has been waiting for this change for a long time, and I think Sapphire is more than capable of overseeing this transformation. Your love for her creates your own fears that it will somehow destroy her. But you must remember, Fox, that we all exist for different reasons. Sapphire has her own path to walk, as well as the one she has chosen with you." She paused and watched Fox intensely.

"You will do well to remember that, guardian," she added. Sapphire felt him grip her hand a little more tightly. Pearl's words had obviously hit a nerve, but he said nothing. She felt a little awkward, and the kitchen suddenly seemed very small around them.

"I would like you to look at one of the flowers Fox retrieved from the tree, Pearl, before we make any more decisions. To be honest, I'm a little scared of what I have created. And, although every instinct tells me that this is the right path for me and it will help our planet, there is also this little niggle in my mind that it could be way too powerful and just make everyone go mad." Pearl laughed, which broke the uncomfortable atmosphere that had slipped into the room.

"I am sure it can't be that bad, Sapphire. Of course I will have a look for you." Sapphire paused. She looked at Fox, and then back at Pearl again, with nervous eyes.

"There is something else. I have a gift for you, and I need you to tell me if it means anything to you." She reached into her bag and pulled out the ring that Gabriel had left in her room on the cruise ship. Fox watched her slide it across the table to Pearl – who remained, at that point, impassive.

"It is beautiful, Sapphire. Did you buy this for me in Egypt? There really was no need to buy me a gift."

Sapphire watched her reach out for the ring that sat innocently on the table. Next to her she could feel Fox's energy change slightly. He was also anticipating some sort of reaction when Pearl touched the ring that may not be pleasant.

"No. It was a gift left for you from an admirer." Pearl touched the ring and shivered slightly, as if something had indeed touched a nerve and made her flinch. Magic uncurled from the ring like a tiny seedling emerging from the earth. It was the most beautiful thing Sapphire had ever seen. Pink and blue, it settled around the ring like a mist hovering in the air. It smelt of lavender and roses. Pearl gasped. Her hand recoiled as if the ring had bitten her. But the look on her face was one of pure delight, as if she was looking at something that she had lost and found again as if by accident.

"Pearl, are you OK?" Sapphire asked. Pearl remained still. She was staring at the ring as the magic wavered around it and gave off the most intoxicating scent. Fox stood quickly. He grabbed one of Pearl's lacy napkins and threw it over the ring. The air suddenly changed back to the smell of herbal tea and normality.

"Oh my," Pearl whispered. "It is so beautiful ... so very beautiful." Fox rested his hand on her shoulder and sent a pulse of grounding magic into her frail body. Sapphire watched her snap out of the spell that had captured her when she had touched the ring.

"Who gave this to you, Sapphire?" Pearl blinked as her focus returned. Fox looked across at her with worry on his face. His hand was still on her shoulder, but Pearl seemed to be unaware that he was even standing beside her.

"Well, I was hoping you might have known when you touched it, but obviously the memory is buried deep," Sapphire replied. Fox now looked confused. They both stared at her and waited. Sapphire sighed.

"I had a dream last night when you returned to Shaka, Fox. Well, it was a vision, actually. Sometimes that happens when I dream ... And, anyway, I saw Pearl as a young woman. She was standing outside a house not unlike Foxglove, actually. And then suddenly Gabriel appeared, and well—" She paused, suddenly uncomfortable at retelling her vision, which had clearly been so intimate.

"It was pretty obvious that you and he – Gabriel, that is – were in a relationship at some time, and from what I saw it was in another life on another world." Fox shook his head.

"What?" Pearl looked utterly confused. "Who is Gabriel?"

Sapphire looked at the ring hidden under the lacy napkin. She knew that something would happen when Pearl touched it, just knew it. But Pearl seemed to have no knowledge of Gabriel – which was actually quite comforting, as there was just something a little too weird about the master of gatekeepers that made Sapphire edgy.

"He is the master of all gatekeepers, and I met him while we were away. It's a long story. But he seems to know you very well, Pearl. He recognised the obsidian necklace you gave me as yours. To be perfectly honest, it was all a little weird. And then I had the vision. He looked straight at me and said 'Hello'." Fox lifted his hand from Pearl's shoulder and pushed it through his hair and shook his head again. He was clearly distressed.

"You tell me now, Sapphire. This is important. He is reaching into your subconscious, showing you something that at the moment we do not really understand. You must tell me if he comes to you again. He is dangerous. Do you understand?" Sapphire glared at him.

"I didn't feel threatened by him, Fox. You are overreacting, as usual." Pearl reached out for the ring again, but Fox removed it quickly from the table and put it in his pocket.

"I think it would be best if we kept this safe, Pearl. I did not like the way it made you react when you touched it." She looked disgruntled, but nodded.

"I have no recollection of him, Sapphire. None whatsoever. I know that I have lived many lives before, and sometimes the memory of those lives filters through when I am making remedies or feeling the magic around me. My mother told me that I was special and gifted. It was always the same. Even as a child I would sense and feel things that others could not. But she guided me through the confusion of being so different and raised me to understand that my knowledge had been passed through me from my previous incarnations and from the generations before me. My mother was a very powerful witch in her own right." Fox was pacing the kitchen floor now. It made Sapphire nervous.

"He is very powerful and very dangerous, Pearl. Even I was unaware of him until recently. I fear that now the connection has been made back to you via Sapphire you could in fact be at risk again." Sapphire took her tea and sipped it. She needed something to calm her now spangled nerves.

"Don't scare her, Fox." He looked at her, his eyes swirling with flashes of gold and black.

"She should be scared, Sapphire, and so should you. This man is not like Hecta or the other gatekeepers. His magic is all-consuming. It is as strong, if not stronger, than my father's. There is no telling what he will do next." Pearl sighed heavily.

"Oh dear ... that reminds me. I was walking in the woods the other day and I found what looked like an open grave. Did you by any chance dispose of Hecta out there, Fox?" He whirled around so quickly it made Sapphire's head spin for a second.

"Yes, I did." He said something that sounded like a cuss in his own language, and his body shook a little with what looked like anger. "This changes everything. If Gabriel has found Hecta and taken him back to Shaka then we really are in deep shit." Sapphire wanted to laugh out loud. Hearing her husband swear in such a human-like way was just too funny. He walked over to the kitchen door frame and grabbed it above his head with his back to them as if trying to calm himself down.

"Fox, please sit down. Let's work this out together. Please."

Pearl was drinking her tea again. Despite the way the conversation was going she seemed completely calm, God bless her. He turned around, his face a picture of concern.

"We need to take the seeds, the essence, and the flower back to Shaka, Sapphire, and hide them. I wanted to talk this through with you, but with Gabriel sniffing around it is just too dangerous to carry on as you wanted. We cannot risk it." Pearl regarded him coolly.

"Sit down, Fox." He did reluctantly. Sapphire reached for his hand and squeezed it tightly.

"I want you to show Pearl the flower first, Fox," Sapphire said. "She needs to see it, to feel its magic. I want to know if she has the same reaction as we do to its magic." He nodded slowly and reached into his waistcoat to retrieve the pouch tucked safely inside. Pearl chuckled.

"You are like a magpie, Sapphire, that keeps bringing home new gifts. How will I ever keep up with you?" Fox frowned again, but handed the pouch across the table to her. Pearl held it for a moment before opening the pouch and letting the crystal flower drop into her hand. She closed her eyes and sighed deeply. Sapphire watched as the energy of the flower slipped across her body and enveloped her softly. Its magic was totally different from that of the ring. Almost like a bubble of light that was so gentle and alluring, it seemed to sing a gentle siren's call that lingered in the air.

She felt Fox move beside her. His body suddenly grew hotter and his energy reacted to the magic as if he was coming up on a Class A drug. Sapphire suddenly felt as if she was watching everything from another room. Her body was fluid and supple. The magic of the flower was affecting them all in different ways. Pearl's face was one of pure contentment and of being totally at peace. Fox was radiating sexual energy so strong it made her head swim. Sapphire was feeling as if she had just stepped into a pool of pure white light that made everything around her crystal clear and as sharp as a diamond.

Pearl opened her eyes again and smiled. She placed the flower back into the pouch and fastened the tie around it, effectively sealing off the potency of its magic once more. Fox let go of her hand, which he had been gripping so very tightly, and let out a sigh of relief. Sapphire felt her energy reconnect with her body and ground once more. She had been flying like a kite. It was amazing.

"Well, I must say, Sapphire, that was really something else. So peaceful and calming. I felt as if I was cocooned in a warm, soft place with the most amazing sensations running throughout my body. It was almost like being back in the womb ... so very safe and wonderful." Fox reached for his tea and took a huge gulp, as if he needed to steady his nerves.

"Thank the gods. It clearly has a different effect on each person who touches it." Sapphire looked at him as the smile returned to her lips. She knew he had been in a totally different place from Pearl, and the evidence was bulging against his leather trousers. He watched her eyes flick from his waist and back up again as he shifted in his seat.

"It is not amusing, Sapphire. Anything could happen to the people who come in contact with this new magic, which would make it even more unstable and potent." She placed her hand in his lap under the table and squeezed his erection, which made him bite his bottom lip hard.

"Stop stressing. This is actually a good thing. Now that we have seen Pearl's reaction to the magic we know that it is not all doom and gloom. In fact I think it could probably do a great deal of good for a lot of people." She lowered her voice. "Especially those with low libido." Pearl smiled. She had missed Sapphire's last comment.

"I think you should follow your instinct with this, Sapphire. It is truly a gift and could change many things, but in some ways I also think Fox is right in being cautious," Pearl concluded. She clasped her hands together and shook her head, as if to break the spell fully. After standing up she smoothed down her skirt and smiled at them both.

"Well, I think I have definitely had enough magic for one day, and need to process all this new information with a walk in the garden. Would you care to join me?" Fox shook his head. His erection was still prominent beneath Sapphire's hand.

"We will join you shortly, Pearl. I would like to finish my tea." Pearl raised her eyebrows, a little perplexed, but continued to smile.

"Very well. I will see you shortly." As she left the room Sapphire laughed out loud and released her grip on Fox's groin. He had the grace to smile at her.

"You are a wicked wicked woman," he groaned deeply. She leant in to kiss him, brushing her lips on his neck and nuzzling him gently.

"Mmmh ... that's why you love me," she said. He took her hand and kissed her knuckles.

"You go out with Pearl. She may wish to speak to you alone, my love. I need a moment."

She laughed, then stood up and left him in the kitchen to 'finish his tea'.

While she stood beside the silver birch, with her back to Sapphire, Pearl looked like a woman much younger than her years. Sapphire could see how Pearl could have been such a strong and beautiful woman in her previous lives, and in this life as a young woman. She turned to face her as she walked up to the tree.

"Are you OK, Pearl? The magic from the flower is very strong." Pearl held a piece of lavender in her hand. Despite the cold weather and the time of year it was a herb that endured all. She looked thoughtful as she crushed the flower in her fingers.

"Of course. I have never felt better." She paused and looked at Sapphire with what looked like trepidation. "But I am a little concerned about Gabriel. If your vision is true, Sapphire, and I have lived a life with this man before, it could really change things between us." Sapphire reached out for her hand. She took it within her own and grasped it gently.

"Nothing will change our friendship, Pearl. You are like a mother to me, and I will protect you in any way I can. You know that." Pearl smiled, her eyes wrinkling at the corners. They were a beautiful hazel colour, something Sapphire had never really noticed before until now ... they were the same colour as she had seen in her vision.

"I hope that it will not come to that, my dear. It is such a shame that you cannot move on with your life in the way you had hoped with Fox. It seems that your path is a little more challenging than we originally thought." Sapphire released her hand, but placed her arm around Pearl and huddled against her in the cold air.

"Mmmh ... There was me thinking when I left here for Shaka that we could set up home and live like normal magical people in a world full of fairies." Pearl chuckled.

"You don't need to go to Shaka to live with fairies, Sapphire. You know that." While leaning her head into Pearl she sighed.

"There are many things I know now, Pearl, that a year ago would have seemed utterly inconceivable. How life changes so quickly." Pearl turned her head slightly to look at her.

"Do not be sad, Sapphire. Your path is one of amazing lessons and adventures. To be a dream traveller is to be open to such change and embrace it for what it is." Sapphire hugged her tighter.

"And what is that exactly, Pearl?" Pearl looked at her as if the answer was as clear as day and she was slightly stupid.

"Why, it is the path to enlightenment, my dear ... enlightenment and happiness, if you are lucky."

Sapphire felt Fox step out of the cottage. He had clearly recovered from the effect of the crystal flower.

"I need all the luck I can get at the moment, Pearl, that's for sure."

Fox stood silently behind them, but she sensed he wanted them to return home. He had other things to discuss with her. She released Pearl. Then she kissed her cool cheek and stepped back, smiling as she did.

"We will visit again soon, Pearl, but in the meantime please promise me you will strengthen the wards around your garden. And if you need anything let us know." Pearl dropped the lavender to the floor and smiled back.

"I will be fine, Sapphire. Don't you worry about me." She looked at Fox. "Be gentle with her, Fox. Sometimes your crashing through every situation like a mad bull causes your wife stress." He nodded solemnly, a slight smile on his lips.

"As you wish, Pearl. Your guidance is always gratefully received." Sapphire took his hand and they left through the little wooden gate with the birds singing around them.

The day was moving on, and despite the temperature being so low the sun was out and the sky was a beautiful clear blue. They walked home hand in hand, saying nothing. Both of them were absorbed in their own thoughts after their visit to Pearl. Sapphire could sense Fox was totally against her planting any more of the seeds. He wanted to dissuade her from continuing this journey, but something told her it may not be that easy. She wanted to do something normal for once – take a day off from magic and the problems it created.

"Let's go out for lunch, Fox, somewhere nice. I think we both could do with some time out." He looked at her with those beautiful eyes that stripped her bare every time he looked at her.

"Whatever you want, my love," he replied.

Chapter Twenty

They walked into the village and ended up having lunch at The Swan pub. The irony of the visit was not missed by Sapphire as she ordered them two pints and a hot meal. It had been many months before when she had sat in this pub with Charlie and Nathan before heading down the yellow brick road to Simon's party. That had been the first night she had really made contact with her husband – the magical man who now sat with her by the fire, nursing a pint of beer.

How life had changed for them both after that night. He was leaning back in the leather chair with the air of a man who had not a care in the world. His legs crossed at the ankles and his eyes were sparkling in the dim light of the fire that burnt beside them. He watched her intensely as she sipped her beer. She knew that this was all an act, and that he was actually twitching like a horse covered in flies in the summer under that cool exterior.

"So what did you want to talk to me about?" There were few other patrons in the pub at that time of the day. She did not even know what day of the week it was, but clearly it was not the weekend. She had lowered her voice slightly. She was acutely aware that anyone close by would be listening to their conversation, as all eyes had been on them since they had arrived.

"This is probably not the best time to discuss it, Sapphire. Let's enjoy our food and relax for a while." She twisted a piece of her hair in her fingers while watching him sip his beer.

"Is that because it could turn into an argument?" He raised an eyebrow and smiled at her, with his lips just twitching with amusement.

"Perhaps." The young girl from behind the bar was suddenly standing beside Sapphire with a tray of food. She was blushing furiously. Her eyes were flicking from Fox to the tray in quick succession.

"One order of sausage and mash, and a ham, egg, and chips for you."

Sapphire smiled at her and watched the girl unload the plates. She was waiting for her to indicate whose plate belonged where. Fox regarded her coolly.

"Mine's the sausage and mash. Thank you," she said as she helped the girl, whose hands were suddenly shaking a little. Fox seemed completely oblivious to the effect he was having on the young girl. His eyes barely registered her presence. She scampered off, but not before one last glance was given in his direction. Sapphire sighed. Would it always be like this with him around? He was a constant woman magnet. Fox leant forward and looked at the food warily.

"I assume I will like this, won't I?" She laughed and pushed his plate towards him.

"I picked you the easiest thing on the menu, Fox. It's not unlike your food back home. Try it. You will like it, for sure." He placed the beer on the table and picked up his knife and fork.

"The beer is good." He was trying to change the subject.

"You really don't have to make small talk about the food and drink, Fox. Just tell me what you are thinking, and what's really bothering you about all this." He began to eat. His face indicated that she had indeed picked the right meal for him. After swallowing a piece of ham he placed his knife and fork down and looked directly at her. His eyes were dark and intense.

"The magic is too powerful for your people, Sapphire. I really think it would be wise to take a step back from this task you seem so set on fulfilling, despite Pearl's reassurance that you are all ready to take a leap into the unknown. I have watched your people for a very long time and I see things a little more differently. The way that the flower affects even me is unnerving. If it was unleashed on to humankind it would cause nothing but confusion and possibly, in time, create severe problems within the structure of your race." She looked at him with a piece of mash stuck to her fork.

"Seriously, Fox, you really are something else." He tipped his head to one side and frowned.

She could not believe how biased he was being towards her fellow humans. She knew they were simple creatures compared to the magical beings he lived with on Shaka – and yes, deep down she knew that humans were usually greedy, power-seeking, not particularly nice dog-eat-dog inhabitants of a planet they were slowly destroying. But ... they were also capable of the most amazing, wonderful, creative, loving, and beautiful things. They could join together in unison and help one another in times of need, be tender and kind, and give sweetly and honestly to a stranger if such an occasion should arise. They were a mixture of the extremes: the good and the bad. A perfect balance of light and dark.

She had seen this many times over in her life already, and especially since she had discovered her new talent and opened her mind to the exciting possibilities that her fellow people could someday perhaps be liked those on Shaka ... people who lived in a new vibration, a new wave of magic, and who might live full lives that were happy and in harmony.

Fox blinked his beautiful eyes at her. She could feel his energy swirling around him in waves of mixed emotion.

"I am giving you my honest opinion, Sapphire." She realised that yes, he was giving her his honest opinion, and she saw something else that until this point she had never truly seen within him: his complete and utter indifference towards humankind. It made her feel quite suddenly very sad. Although they were joined completely in every way possible – by blood, by magic and by a bond so strong with love it made her head swim – she was human and he was not. Well, she was part human, and that part she still desperately clung to. As if he saw the thoughts clambering through her head he reached across the table and took her hand squeezing it gently.

"Do not be angry with me, Sapphire. Believe me, I wish more than anything that your people could experience this magic and revel in it to their delight and benefit." He paused and waited for her reaction. She remained silent as she tried to digest not just her food but her thoughts.

"But I truly feel afraid for your people if this magic was just plucked from each tree and used without guidance and insight," he added. He let go of her hand, sat back in his chair, and grabbed his pint. Fuck it. They were going to have the argument he was trying to avoid. They would just have to agree to disagree. In fact, as he looked at her warily now, she had an idea brewing in her head. She started to eat again – slowly, taking her time. He did the same. Silence hung around them as the fire crackled quietly beside them.

"I'm not angry with you, Fox. Far from it. You have been honest with me, and I am thankful for that. For once you are not hiding your true feelings from me. But for now we will just have to see things a little differently and you will have to trust me for once." He nodded his head, obviously keen not to let the conversation get heated in this quiet, comfy environment.

"As you wish, my love." They ate their lunch in silence, with a strange energy shifting between them. For the first time in a long time Sapphire knew that she had to prove to him that she was strong enough to see this through, and if it meant proving to him that her fellow humans were capable of stepping up to the mark she would do just that. She knew just the person she would begin her little experiment with, and that it could take some careful planning on her part.

They returned to Charlie's little cottage early in the evening after they had finished another two pints of beer and avoided talking any more about magic, seeds, or the impending fate of humankind. The sky was dark above them and the air was growing colder again, with the promise of rain. Charlie, looking a little drowsy, opened the door. She was clearly suffering from jet lag or just the heaviness of being back in the winter darkness again.

"Hey, you two, good day?" Fox said nothing and headed to the kitchen after smiling weakly at her as he went. Charlie raised her eyebrows at Sapphire. "That good, eh? What's up?" Sapphire shook her head and pulled off her boots.

"We need to talk and without the boys around. Can you arrange something with Nathan ... get Fox out of the house for a while?" Charlie, clearly curious, nodded.

"Sure. He's in the lounge. I'll go and speak to him."

Sapphire could hear Fox in the kitchen. He was making tea, a human habit he had picked up that made her smile. She stood in the doorway watching him take the cups out of the cupboard with his back to her.

"You OK?" she asked. He turned to face her with his hands gripping the counter behind him.

"Of course. Do you want some tea?" As she walked towards him she felt her body sigh with the heaviness his energy was giving off in waves that felt thick with unease. She placed her hands on his chest and looked up into his eyes.

"Stop worrying. We will be OK." He let out a slow, soft sigh and touched his forehead to her own.

"I know," he said. She felt a new presence behind them, and looked around to see Nathan standing at the door looking a little awkward.

"Fox, I'm going over to Simon's for a game of poker soon. Do you fancy coming with me? Some guy time might be good for us both." Fox released the counter and pulled Sapphire into his body while wrapping his strong arms around her and resting his chin on her head.

"I have no idea what poker is. But sure ... it sounds good. I think Sapphire could do with some time out after our holiday." He held her tightly, and she felt the power of his muscles clenching around her. He did not want to let her go, and certainly did not want to go out tonight without her. But he was doing what he knew she wanted him to do, and for that she was thankful.

"Cool. I'll go and get changed. We can leave in, say, ten minutes." Fox looked down at her. He was watching her with cool, dark eyes.

"I'm doing this for you, you know," he said. She smiled up at him and reached up on tiptoes to kiss him on the nose.

"It will be good for you. Don't cheat with the poker. The guys won't like it." He laughed and released her as the kettle pinged off.

"I will have my tea later when I return, beautiful wife."

Now for the tricky part.

"Leave the flower in my room, Fox. You shouldn't carry it around with you at the moment. After everything we have talked about I think it would be best to keep it hidden until we go back to Shaka." He stared at her, a picture of confusion on his face. She really didn't want him seeing through her little plan.

"OK. Are we planning to go home again soon?" Sapphire worried her bottom lip before she spoke.

"Yes. I want to go back and see Kit again for a while. It's cold here, and I think you need some time there before we do anything else." She watched his eyes light up.

Gotcha.

Fox nodded, and kissed her softly on the mouth before heading upstairs. She watched his broad shoulders leave the kitchen before slumping back against the counter again. She did want to return to Shaka with him, but that was just a distraction. What she really needed was him out of the house and the flower here with her and Charlie. Her little experiment depended entirely on her friend's willingness to jump into the unknown for her. She hoped that Charlie would be up for the task, and that she wasn't about to fuck things up completely.

Sapphire pulled a bottle of red wine from the rack and began to uncork it. The two men had just left, and the door had thumped loudly behind them as they had exited. Nathan was chattering to Fox about the simple rules of poker. Her husband had looked at her with amused eyes as he left, after blowing her a kiss. The lounge was warm and cosy and there was a fire burning in the grate as she walked in to find Charlie curled up on the sofa, her legs tucked up beneath her. She held the wine bottle and two glasses in her hands and smiled broadly.

"Right let's have a drink and a chat." Charlie turned off the TV that was playing on mute in the background. She reached for the stereo remote and clicked it on, and smiled as the soft beat of some ambient chill tune filled the room. Charlie reached for her wine glass and smiled slyly at her.

"Right. What's this all about, girlfriend?" After filling their glasses Sapphire sat down beside her and looked at her friend with a twist in her gut. Should she really ask her friend to do this for her?

"Remember the tree I told you about in Egypt, Charlie?" Charlie took a slug of the wine and nodded her head.

"Yeah. What's happened with it?" While pouring herself a glass Sapphire took a deep breath.

"The tree has blossomed, Charlie, and the flowers it has produced are like a new kind of magic – a drug, if you like, that seems to affect everyone who touches it differently." She paused and took a sip of the oaky red wine. "I want to see how it affects you." Charlie regarded her silently, a sly smile spreading across her lips.

"Cool. Is it trippy?" Sapphire laughed. Her friend's willingness to take the leap was so free and easy. She had always been the more reckless of the two, and was unafraid to try something that may just alter her mindset in a new and wonderful way.

"It's a risk, Charlie. You would be the first real human to try this, and I have absolutely no idea what will happen." Charlie nodded, and her face lit up with excitement.

"It's obviously important to you," she said. Sapphire looked at her friend and felt a stab of guilt. What if the magic of the flower did tip her friend over the edge and into a sea of oblivion? She suddenly felt as if this was all wrong.

"It is, but I want you to understand that it is very powerful – and although I have seen its effect on Pearl, Fox, and me, I cannot be sure what it will actually do to you." Charlie's face flickered with fear for a second before she grinned mischievously.

"Fuck it. I'll do it for you, Saf. To infinity and beyond ... I'm up for it." Sapphire nodded.

It was now or never. She suddenly realised she was shaking a little, and nerves and excitement were racing through her veins. She knew Fox would be angry with her for carrying out this little experiment without him by her side, but this was her thing – her mission – and she wanted to do it on her own. After leaving Charlie in the sitting room with her glass of wine she went up to her bedroom and rummaged through her sock drawer to find the pouch that held the crystal flower. The seeds, the essence, and the bag of dirt she had been given back in Egypt were all there sitting like naughty children among her socks and tights. After grabbing the new pouch Violet had made to contain the flower she headed back down the stairs with her heart fluttering in her chest. She could feel the energy thrumming against her hand as she held it. The power held within was almost radiating with its own eagerness to be consumed and held by another hand.

Charlie looked at her as she entered the room. She had drunk half the glass of wine. Perhaps she was a little nervous under all her bravado. While settling down next to her on the sofa Sapphire held the pouch out in her hand and regarded her friend seriously.

"I will ground you and keep you safe, Charlie. Don't worry." Her friend licked her lips and eyed the pouch with inquisitiveness. Her eyes flicked back up to Sapphire's and she took a deep breath.

"I trust you, Saf. Let's do this." After unwrapping the cord that was tied around the opening to the pouch Sapphire tipped the crystal flower into her hand. It landed softly in her palm and twinkled up at her like a beautiful gem. Innocent, but guilty at the same time. She could hear the music playing on the stereo in the background, but a new song entered her ears as the flower glittered in her hand – the sweet song of magic. Sapphire could feel its pulse within her body, a steady rhythm that tickled her skin in a soft caress. Charlie stared at the flower with wide eyes.

"It's beautiful, Saf. Like a tiny, beautiful snowflake." Sapphire sensed her energy change. Charlie was as mesmerised by this object as she was.

"Yes, it is. Take it in your hand and just allow it to connect with you. I will be watching you to make sure nothing bad happens." She hoped this was true. She had absolutely no idea what it would do to Charlie. Pearl was full of her own magic, as was Fox, and this would be the first time someone completely human had touched it. Charlie licked her bottom lip and worried it with hesitation just for a second before she took the flower in her hand and held it within her palm. Sapphire held her breath as she watched Charlie and anticipated the flow of magic that had unfolded when Pearl had taken the flower earlier that day.

Charlie closed her eyes and remained as still as a statue. Nothing happened. Sapphire waited. Her body was trembling slightly. Charlie opened one eye and looked at her while smiling.

"Can't feel a thing, honey." She laughed, opened both eyes, and held the flower out in front of Sapphire. "Perhaps I'm supposed to bomb it." Sapphire gasped.

"God, no, Charlie. I don't think that would be a good idea." Charlie grinned like a naughty schoolgirl. Without warning she snapped one of the petals off the flower, and popped it in her mouth and swallowed it before Sapphire could stop her.

"Charlie, no!" Charlie put the remaining parts of the flower down on to the couch, reached for her wine glass, and took a slug.

"Chill, honey. It will be fine. Let's see whether anything happens now." They waited. The ambient chill music in the background played softly. Its beat created a new sense of calm that seemed to grow louder as the minutes ticked by. Sapphire could not believe what her friend had just done. Her mind was tilting on the edge of panic. Charlie, on the other hand, seemed quite content. She watched Charlie's expression and aura for any change. Charlie smiled at her. They were face to face and both looking into each other's eyes with the expression of someone waiting for a bomb to drop.

And then it did. Sapphire felt it in her solar plexus. The energy hit her hard as Charlie's face changed so suddenly it was if a bright light had been switched on inside her head and was glowing from the inside out. Her eyes became softer and her muscles relaxed. Her aura changed into a light purple colour with swirls of pink and gold. Her hair began to glow and her body began to relax. Her shoulders dropped and she looked totally at peace.

Sapphire watched in amazement as Charlie almost lifted off the couch. Her energy fizzled and wavered around her as if she was somehow reconnecting with something that had been buried so deeply inside her it had been lost until now. Sapphire tried hard not to panic. This was something she had not expected. It was as if Charlie had suddenly become a magical being surrounded by swirls of strong magic, which seemed to dance and sway within her aura.

Her eyes were now closed and she remained as still as a person would within a deep meditation, but a smile began to uncurl on her lips. She looked utterly beautiful. Her face was transformed and her body was glowing an unearthly deep purple that made her look like an alien fairy. Sapphire could hear the deep beat of the magic within her own veins, a steady flow of sensual wonderful power that made her own magic begin to flare brightly.

She watched Charlie with awe as she shone and sparkled within the new magic that surrounded her. They were joined together by the beat of the music in the room and the magic that swirled around them. It was beautiful, wild, and intoxicating, a perfect magical connection binding them together. Sapphire was not sure whether she should touch her friend and pull her back or close her eyes and join in with the journey.

Without warning Fox suddenly appeared in the room beside Charlie, his face wild and panicky. He had obviously sensed the shift in energy around them and transported himself back. Sapphire held up her hand to stop him from coming any closer. His eyes glowed dark amber and black and his body was alive with tension. He looked as if he was ready to devour her or Charlie or both of them at once.

"What have you done, Sapphire?" he growled.

Suddenly Charlie opened her eyes and the magic stopped. Just like that it dissipated, as if the cork had been put back into the genie's bottle and he had been swept back inside. Charlie stared at Sapphire. Her pupils were so black and huge they looked as if she had just been taken on a journey so far away that it had made her brain pop. Her voice was almost a whisper as she spoke.

"Oh, my God. How long have I been gone?" Sapphire let out a sigh of relief. Fox stepped forward to look at Charlie more closely.

"You've been here the whole time, honey. You were held in the magic just a matter of minutes." Charlie shook her head. Her body was still soft and languid, and she was smiling as if she had just had the best orgasm in the world.

"No, that can't be possible. I was gone hours. It felt like hours. Oh, God, Sapphire, it was wonderful ... amazing ... I can't describe it. It was awesome." Tears had formed in her eyes, and she was now crying. They fell across her cheeks silently like raindrops. As she took Charlie's hands within her own Sapphire beamed.

"That good, huh?" Charlie continued to shake her head in disbelief.

"Saf, oh Saf, you cannot even to begin to imagine what I saw, where I went. You have to believe me when I tell you I feel as if I have been to heaven and back. I saw so many different images and people, people who looked like they were angels. But they were blue – blue angels." She laughed and hiccupped suddenly, her hair falling across her face. Fox stared at her. His body was now resuming its normal stance and the energy was stilling around him.

"I've seen angels for the first time in my life. Holy fuckin' shit. That was some seriously trippy shit." She said still smiling as if she was indeed on a trip. They all stared at each other for a moment. Sapphire looked up at Fox with a slightly guilty expression.

"Don't be mad at me, Fox. I just wanted to try just this once, to see what would happen." He sagged, visibly relieved that Charlie had survived the trip.

"Well, now you know," he mumbled, with a slightly grumpy tone to his voice. Charlie jumped up suddenly, and spun around the room as if she was on speed.

"That was so fucking incredible, Saf. You have to let Nathan have a go. He would absolutely love it." Fox raised an eyebrow and looked at Sapphire with his hands now on his hips.

"That is exactly what I was afraid would happen. It is intoxicating, Sapphire, utterly consuming. Now the whole world will want it, and that's when the trouble will start." Charlie was dancing and swaying now. Her face was alive and the tears were still running down her face. She giggled as if she was drunk.

"Don't be a spoilsport, Fox. It's awesome. You should try it." He regarded her coolly.

"That's the problem, Charlie. I have."

Sapphire watched her friend spin around the lounge as if she was in fact on drugs. It was amusing and horrifying at the same time. She had done this. She had created the flower and actively encouraged her friend to take the leap, and now she was spinning around like a crazy person on acid in her own living room.

Fox grabbed Charlie by the waist and held her to his body. His magic pulsed around them both. Charlie looked up into his eyes with an expression of glee before he grounded her and her body slumped against him.

"I think we should put her to bed, Sapphire. She has definitely had enough magic for one night." Charlie giggled. She looked slightly less manic, but still off her head.

"Are you going to put me to bed, Fox? Oh, God, please take me to bed." Sapphire could not believe what a mess she had created. This was not safe. Charlie was a giggling tangle in his arms. Fox picked her up like a child and held her against him so that she could not escape. He gave Sapphire one last look of exasperation before heading up the stairs.

"Saf, Saf, Fox is putting me to bed. Don't tell Nathan. He will be mad," Sapphire heard her giggle as Fox carried her up the stairs. She put her head in her hands and leant forward. Although she was feeling terribly guilty for subjecting Charlie to such an ordeal she also felt incredibly satisfied that Charlie had experienced something so wonderful. When her friend returned to the real world she would find out exactly what had happened to her and where she had been and what she had seen.

Could this be just a mind-altering drug? Or was it a change in consciousness, after all? She was baffled by the fact that they were all reacting to the flower so differently. And why had it only taken effect when Charlie had eaten it? Just by touching the flower Pearl, Fox, and she had felt its magic. Was it due to the difference in their energy? It had to be. There was so much she did not know, so much she needed to do before she could truly bestow this gift on her fellow humans. Just thinking about it gave her a headache.

Fox reappeared in the lounge with his eyes flashing at her in a mixture of anger and agitation. She was in trouble. Again.

"I had to literally knock her out before she stopped gabbling like a mad woman, Sapphire. She was totally sky-high on the flower's magic. God knows how long it would last in someone's system if we were not around to control it." She grabbed her wine glass and took a healthy sip. She really didn't need another Fox lecture.

"Did you just leave Nathan at Simon's house without saying goodbye?" He blinked at her, not understanding the question.

"Of course not. I told him I needed to leave as soon as I felt the shift in energy coming from the house. He looked as if he already knew you were both up to no good, anyway." She could feel him trying to control his temper, and suddenly it seemed extremely funny. She started to laugh. He cocked his head to one side as if he could not believe she was laughing at him.

"What's so funny, Sapphire?" She was really finding it hard to control her laughter now. She was on the verge of hysteria.

"Fox, for once in your life please just look at the funny side of it. Charlie is OK. Nothing bad has happened. In fact this was the best way to find out exactly how the magic would affect another human. Now we know exactly what it does, and we can adapt accordingly." He stifled a smile. His body was rigid and his muscles were tense, but she could sense he was also starting to see the humour of what had just happened.

"What you just did was highly irresponsible, very dangerous, and could have gone horribly wrong. I should put you over my knee and spank you hard, Sapphire." She laughed harder, and narrowed her eyes at him.

"Ooh ... promises, promises," she retorted. Without warning he leapt at her and grabbed her from the sofa, sweeping her up into his arms and over his shoulder. She was crying with laughter now as he strode out of the room with her. Her head was dangling behind him and her hair was almost touching the floor. He smacked her hard on the backside, making her squeal.

"Put me down, Fox," she shouted at him as she laughed. He opened the back door and took her outside into the garden and deposited her on the grass. It was cold outside, and the air hit her like a brick wall and brought her back to her senses. His breathing was erratic. Hers was now short and quick as she tried to recover. She lay beneath him as he knelt above her with his body pinning her to the ground. He was still clearly angry and agitated and, it seemed, somewhat turned on all at the same time. He pushed his groin into her waist, and she felt the evidence of this hot and hard against her.

"I am very cross with you, Sapphire. You took a big risk with Charlie tonight and exposed us both to the magic of the flower again – something which, at present, causes me some discomfort." His eyes were heated and she could sense the waves of mixed anger and arousal crashing off him. While biting her lower lip she tried to calm her breathing. It was funny to see him so affected by the power of the crystal tree, but it was also disturbing that it made him so filled with testosterone. Anger and sex were the two things this particular hormone created, and at this precise moment he had both in abundance.

"I really am sorry, Fox. I know it was a risk, but no harm has been done. Please calm down." By wiggling beneath him she managed to free her hand and pushed it against his chest, sending slow flickers of her own magic into him. His body relaxed slightly and his lips parted a fraction.

"I feel as if I should fuck you right now on the wet grass, Sapphire, just to teach you a lesson and make me feel better." She sucked in a breath and pushed more of her energy into him as she tried to soothe the animal inside him that was uncurling like a predator.

"Let's go to my bedroom and you can do what you want to me Fox, not here," she whimpered softly.

He kissed her without warning. His lips were warm and his tongue pushed inside her mouth in a command that said he was in control. After letting out another soft whimper she went limp beneath him and let him kiss her harder. She really did not want to get caught by Nathan on the back lawn being devoured by her husband – or by the neighbours for that matter, and she hoped that at any minute he would regain his senses and take her back inside.

He released her mouth suddenly and lifted her from the grass in one quick movement, which took her breath away. Before she could even register what was happening they were in her bedroom. The door slammed behind them, making the frame rattle. He threw her on to the bed and smiled at her. She could see that his face was changing. The anger was leaving but he needed to have some release, and she knew that it was up to her to help him.

He stepped towards her and began to pull off her clothes. He was breathing hard now, and his body radiated heat. After helping him remove his own clothing in a tangle of limbs they were quickly naked and Sapphire, caught up now in the heat of the moment, was panting loudly. He pushed her up to the top of the bed, and her head crushed against the pillows. He looked at her one more time. His eyes were wild, and there was a strange smile on his lips. It said,

"I am going to fuck you hard," and then he travelled further down south and began to devour her with his very talented tongue, making her head thump back and her eyes tip to the ceiling.

"Oh, my God," she whispered as he pushed her body up and up to the place she knew so well from his clever touch and lick. When she felt like she could take no more he flipped her over and slammed into her, rock-hard and almost painfully. She cried out as he fucked her and tipped her over the edge. They lit up the room with their magic, which was roaring in her ears.

He called out her name as he came quickly. It was like hot silk, pouring through her veins in a climax that made the bed shake and the walls vibrate. A picture fell off the wall and crashed loudly on the floor, which broke the glass. She fell into the pillows like a rag doll, her body utterly spent despite the fact that she had only teetered on the edge of her own release and not actually fallen off the precipice. He fell down beside her and laid his hand across her back, then put his mouth to her ear.

"That is how dangerous this magic can be, Sapphire. Look at what it does to me." She rolled over slowly and looked into his eyes. They were soft again, sated, and full of love, but with an edge of sadness. She knew he was scared, scared of how this magic affected him and whether it would do the same to others. But in her heart she knew that it was just reflecting the very sexual man that he was, and the heat of his passion. She would teach him how to control it and teach him not to be afraid. He pulled her close and kissed her again, tenderly this time, with a slow soft push of his tongue – a tongue that caressed her mouth now, but which moments ago had bruised her with its fierceness.

"I love you, Fox," she whispered between his kisses. He pulled back and looked at her with eyes that glowed amber and black.

"Now I will make love to you, Sapphire, and you will find your own release." And he did just that.

The morning arrived, cold and a little overcast. Sapphire turned in bed to face her husband, who was sleeping soundly beside her. In his sleep he looked younger and almost innocent, and the dark lashes on his eyes rested against his skin like flecks of black ink. His breathing was deep and comfortable and his hair tumbled across his shoulders and on to his arms like a mane. As always, the sight of him made her stomach quiver. He was just so damn beautiful.

Without waking him she slid out of bed and made her way to the bathroom. It was early, and the house was quiet. Nathan had returned late that night. Sapphire had heard his footsteps coming up the stairs as she had drifted in and out of sleep after Fox had made love to her.

Sapphire wondered how Charlie would be feeling today. She had not dreamt that night, and she felt fully rested and ready to take on the world. She stepped into the shower after taking a pee and allowed the water to wash over her and wash away the scent of her man. It was always a bittersweet thing to do, as she loved the way his smell of patchouli and sandalwood clung to her body after they had been together.

Today she would do some research and see what she could find on the Internet regarding the way Charlie had reacted to the flower. Perhaps there were similar drugs already here on Earth that had the same effect, and the flower was merely a reflection of that but in a magical form. As she wrapped her hair in a towel and dried herself she felt amazingly calm and full of clarity.

The experiment had worked in more ways than one. She was beginning to understand now what she had created, albeit in a sketchy kind of way. The flower seemed to bring out your innermost thoughts and the very essence of who you were, although Charlie's reaction had been so very strong – and almost a journey of some kind that Sapphire did not fully understand at the moment.

She also knew that she had to return to Shaka with Fox for a while before continuing her task. There were things that needed to be done there. And she had the feeling Gabriel was watching her, and she needed the safety of Conloach and his magic before she could make her next move. She also wanted to find out what had happened to Hecta's body. This was the only troubling thought she had that day. Hecta was dead and that was the end of it. If Gabriel had found the body and somehow returned it to Shaka then so be it.

She went back to the bedroom and, trying not to wake her husband, dressed quietly in a jumper and sweatpants. He stirred as she left the room but seemed to be sleeping deeply, and she was grateful he was. She did not want to wake him just yet. She headed down to the kitchen, flicked on the kettle, and heaped a spoonful of coffee into a mug. Her old laptop had been ruined in the fire, but Charlie had a brand-new one in her office at the back of the cottage and she intended to make full use of it before anyone woke up. She poured the hot water into her mug, stirred it, poured in some milk, and watched the spoon swirl the contents. She wondered absently as she left the kitchen whether she would find anything useful.

An hour later Sapphire's head was spinning. She had found that the Internet was full of information about drugs. Every type of mind-altering substance was listed. Some were chemically produced, with long names that she could not even pronounce, and others came straight from Mother Nature herself. It was fascinating that throughout history humans had been on the search for all kinds of substances that could expand their minds or just allow them to escape reality.

The site she had found most interesting talked about a brew of a particular vine and plant extract called ayahuasca that, when ingested, produced a spiritual awakening and purging of the body.

The local shamans of the areas it came from believed this created great healing. She researched the many references to DMT, the main psychedelic ingredient in the plants that caused this reaction. It was mind-blowing. Literally.

Most of the drugs she found were listed as Class A, due to the fact that they contained a high risk to the user and had high penalties for anyone found using them or selling them. It seemed like a sordid world of power, control, and greed. She wondered why her fellow humans wanted to take such risks (although she remembered that she had in fact done just that in the past). She also wondered why it created so much controversy between the two camps in the world: those against such use, and those who championed the benefits of some of the drugs she was researching.

There was way too much information for her to really make up her own mind either way. But the one thing that she did feel struck true, after all the research she had done that morning, was that nature provided an abundance of mind-altering substances but humans could not stop themselves from tampering with them. They always seemed to want to make them more powerful, trippier ... more, more, more. This was what Fox had been trying to warn her of: the need for humans to control and prosper from their need to jump off the edge.

The door to the office opened and Fox stepped inside. He was holding another two cups of coffee, and smiled at her warmly.

"What are you doing, my love?" He handed her one of the cups and touched her cheek gently as he looked over her shoulder at the screen, which was open on the page about the chemical constituents of DMT.

"Research," she replied. As he sipped his drink he stroked her hair softly, from the crown of her head down to her neck, as if she was a cat.

"Mmmh, found anything interesting?" While looking up at him she noticed that his eyes were still a little heavy from sleep. She realised that he would not understand any of what she had found. His world was already full of mind-altering drugs but it was normal to them, and was called magic.

"Lots of stuff, actually, and it has helped. But you don't need to worry about it. Did you sleep well?" He knew she was giving him the brush-off, but let it slide.

"I did. Very well, in fact. Charlie and Nathan are still sleeping. I could feel you nearby when I woke up, but did not expect to find you in here." She closed down the page she was looking at and turned to face him.

"I just needed to spend some time alone checking some stuff out. This place is so familiar to me, and it's been nice to sit out here for a while." He released his hand from her hair and leant back against Charlie's workbench.

"I will leave you for a while then, Sapphire." She reached out for his hand.

"No, it's OK. I'm done now. I'll make us all some breakfast." He nodded and sipped his coffee while watching her with dark eyes. She did not want to admit to him just yet that he had probably been right all along, and her wonderful crystal tree could be more dangerous than she had thought.

They walked back into the cottage together. Sapphire noted that the sky was heavy with thick cloud now, and hinted at rain or even snow. It was cold. She wished it was summer again, and knew that a return to Shaka would bring back some of the wonderful sunshine for her and Fox that they had experienced in Egypt. It was a shame that Charlie and Nathan could not join them.

Fox sat at the kitchen table and watched her gather eggs, bacon, and tomatoes to make them breakfast.

"I want to go back to Shaka, Fox. I need to speak to your father again, and I have missed Kit." He raised an eyebrow.

"Of course. Whenever you are ready." Charlie appeared at the doorway as Sapphire placed the frying pan on the hob.

"You're leaving again so soon?" she asked. Sapphire had not heard her come down the stairs, and suddenly felt guilty. She knew Charlie would not want her to leave.

"Just for a little while, honey. I have to go back with Fox. Don't worry. I won't disappear forever." Her friend sat down opposite Fox. She was wrapped up in her dressing gown with the hood pulled up over her head.

"How are you feeling today? Did you sleep OK?" Sapphire asked her as she placed strips of bacon in the pan.

"I feel fine. I slept like a log. Can't remember how I got there, though. Did we drink that whole bottle of wine last night?" Fox looked at her in surprise. Sapphire glanced at him before answering.

"No, honey. You ate some of the crystal flower and went on a mad one before Fox had to put you to bed." Charlie yawned and turned to face her with a look of confusion on her face.

"What are you talking about?" Fox leant back in his chair and stroked his chin. His eyes were sparkling with amusement.

"Don't you remember, Charlie? I asked if you would help me find out what the magic of the flower would do to someone completely human. You bombed it and went on some kind of psychedelic flipout." Charlie's mouth opened slightly.

"No, I don't remember. We were having a glass of wine in the lounge, then I woke up with Nathan snoring next to me. I thought we had overdone it and I'd passed out." She paused. "I kinda remember dancing round the living room and seeing Fox, but that's it." Fox looked at her and smiled slyly.

"Probably just as well, Charlie," he said. Sapphire frowned as she flipped the bacon. Well, that was just bloody wonderful. Charlie did not remember a thing about the little experiment, which meant it was totally useless and not some door to enlightenment at all. Crap.

"Oh," was the only response she could think of.

"Are you making breakfast for everyone? I'm starving." Charlie yawned again. She looked as if she had smoked a big fat one.

"Yeah, I am. Go and wake up Nathan. I'll make you both some coffee." Charlie hugged herself tightly, smiled, and left the table. She shuffled back up the stairs like a zombie. Sapphire looked at Fox, who looked rather pleased with himself.

"Well, that's just shit," she said. He laughed.

"I think it is for the best, Sapphire. If Charlie cannot remember the experience it is for a reason. I am actually relieved that she has not come down the stairs glowing like a lantern this morning. Perhaps the magic is a temporary thing, which is forgotten quickly by the human brain."

She was not impressed. Talk about raining on her parade. She really had thought this was a big thing, and that she was helping her fellow humans. Now it seemed as if it had all been a waste of time.

"Do not look so sad, my love. You have not failed in your task. You were not given any guidance or clue as to what you were meant to do with this magic or what it would create. Some things take time to evolve." She sniffed.

"Do you mean that humans are not capable of receiving my magic yet?" He laughed.

"Maybe it is just Charlie who is not ready." She looked up at the ceiling thoughtfully.

Maybe he was right. None of this made much sense to her any more, and she really needed some time out from thinking about it. Charlie and Nathan reappeared, with Nathan looking decidedly more awake than his lady.

"Hey, you two ... everything OK after last night?" Sapphire felt herself blush. She was not sure what he was referring to. Was it Fox's sudden disappearance from poker night, their sex session, or Charlie's weird stoned-like behaviour? Fox smiled at him.

"All is well, my friend. Apologies for my sudden absence last night, but the girls needed me." Nathan nodded and plonked himself down on one of the chairs.

"Yeah, what did you do to her last night, Saf? She was snoring like a pig when I came in ... and my girl can drink." Charlie punched him on the arm.

"Hey, be nice," Charlie said. Sapphire flipped the kettle on again and tried to control her blush.

"No, it wasn't like that, Nathan. I asked Charlie to try something for me, but it turns out it was a little too strong and she can't remember a thing this morning." He looked at her with wide eyes.

"Sounds very confusing," he said. Fox laughed and said,

"Not as confusing as poker." Sapphire finished making them breakfast and decided it would be best not to probe Charlie any further regarding the incident. Maybe in time her memory of the journey she had experienced would come back. Or maybe it wouldn't. She did not know which scenario was less troubling.

They spent the rest of the day chilling out at the cottage. It seemed that Charlie was still a little the worse for wear after her forgotten experience. Rain had decided to fall heavily after lunch, which made them all hunker down in the lounge to watch a film. Sapphire snuggled into the warmth of her husband as they watched the movie. It was a comfortable feeling, being with her friends and the man she loved in such a familiar and easy scene. But she knew that she needed to get back to Shaka and to speak to Conloach again regarding her bundles of magic, which still sat in her sock drawer upstairs. Maybe he could give her some enlightenment about how Charlie had reacted, and why she had no memory of the event.

She was also feeling a little out of sorts. Her own magic was feeling strange within her body, and she wondered if she needed to return for a recharge. Fox always seemed better when he returned to his homeland.

After the film had finished she made them all tea and toasted sandwiches. She was putting off the inevitable, and could sense Fox watching her cautiously as she cut the sandwiches up in the kitchen.

"Do you want to leave tonight, Sapphire?" he asked. As she placed the sandwiches on a plate she looked at him with sad eyes.

"Yes, and I feel bad leaving Charlie so soon, but I need to talk to your father." He helped her place the mugs of tea on to a tray and nodded.

"And there is something else bothering you, Sapphire. Tell me." While pausing before she spoke she scanned his expression, which told her he knew more than he was letting on.

"I feel odd. I think I need to recharge my energy back on Shaka. I think being here is having the same effect on me now as it does to you." He brushed his fingertips across her cheek.

"You are more magic than human now, my love. Earth's energy does not sustain us the way that Shaka does. It will always be so." She knew he was right, and that he had possibly been hiding how drained he had been in the last few weeks that they had been here.

"It makes me sad to think that I will not be able to stay here for very long any more. This is my home, Fox, and I wanted to live here happily ever after with you. But I know that's not possible any more." He pulled her into his chest and hugged her tightly.

"We have two homes now, Sapphire. You will always be able to come here. It is the nature of your magic. Like me, you can travel to both worlds. But the process is exhausting at times, and you must find a way to balance it. We will find a way. Do not worry so much about the how and the why. It is what it is." She pulled back from his embrace and stared up at him with sorrow in her eyes.

"We don't have a real home here, Fox. We are just visitors to either Charlie or Pearl. My home is back on Shaka with you in your beautiful house. I'm not kidding myself any more. Too much has changed within me for it to be any other way." He sighed.

"You are aggrieved at having to let go of your Earth, Sapphire. It is a normal reaction. I had to go through the same thing a long time ago when I became a guardian. I knew then I would never be able to truly settle like my other people ... stay in one place and live a normal life." He smiled at her softly. "But the sacrifice has been worth it now that I have you." As she reached up to kiss him she allowed the comfort of his strong arms around her to make her feel safe again. He was right. Their worlds would never be simple, straightforward, or normal ever again. But they had each other, and that was all that mattered. She knew that returning to Shaka would help them both, and by doing so she could soothe some of the uneasiness that was creeping into her mind.

They would have one last normal night with her friends, and then return to the world of magic that she now knew was quickly becoming her true home.

Chapter Twenty-One

Hecta sat at the heavy wooden table and looked at the food placed in front of him. He felt nothing. He had been reborn but his body felt strange and cumbersome, and his mind was a thick, heavy sludge of mixed memories and insouciance.

Gabriel had allowed him time to readjust, and had been unusually kind to him in the past few days. It meant nothing to him, this body, and this place felt all strange and unfamiliar. The first spark of life that he had felt when the necromancer had pulled back his essence and replaced it within the shell of his body was long gone. He had initially had stronger memories of who he had once been and why he had existed. He had been a gatekeeper – and a powerful one, at that. He had been destroyed by a person far more powerful and sent to the afterlife due to his own weakness and stupidity.

She had done this to him. She had taken away his rational thinking and his strong commitment to keeping the gateways safe and balanced. His memories of Sapphire were a mixture of need, anger, and frustration. She had captivated him with her beauty and her magic. In the end it had been his downfall. At first he had been excited at the thought of capturing Sapphire with the help of Ebony ... until he had realised the priestess had meant to kill her and take her magic for herself. Until Sapphire had destroyed Ebony he had been trapped and – for the first time in his existence – had been a puppet to someone else.

Gabriel had always been in the background, overseeing the gatekeepers and allowing them the freedom to carry out their job of keeping the balance. Like a spider's web woven with intricate designs he had danced around the universe in the same way as the guardians had for thousands of years. They were linked together with the same purpose: to watch, to protect, and to balance the magic that had allowed them all to exist for so long. Now it all seemed like a dream, and he did not know why he had been pulled back again into the world he had left.

The door to the chamber he was in opened and Gabriel walked in, surrounded by a swirl of strong magic. His eyes lifted slowly to his master.

"Are you not hungry, my friend?" Hecta wanted to laugh out loud. Food did not seem relevant any more. His body was not even really alive, just suspended in animation and waiting to wither and die again. He felt it in his bones like a death sentence waiting to be carried out.

"No, my lord. The action itself seems irrelevant now." Gabriel walked to him and sat beside him in one of the heavy chairs.

"Then do not worry yourself with such trivial things. You are here for another purpose, Hecta, and I will not force you to act in a way that does not feel right to you any longer." Hecta felt a flare of anger swell in his chest. His master had no other use of him than that of a dog to be used for his own amusement and bidding.

"Tell me why I am here, then, master. I feel nothing but discord within my mind since returning to you." Gabriel smiled. His eyes were swirling with a mini snowstorm.

"I know you are angry and upset that I have brought you back, Hecta, but you must understand that I need information from you that is very important, and I have a task for you that will help us find peace once more." Hecta looked at him blankly.

"What could I possibly know that would be of any use to you, my lord? You are the all-seeing, all-powerful being of our world. There is nothing you do not know already." Gabriel laughed.

"Ah, but you are wrong on this account, my friend. There are many things I do not have knowledge of, and you are of more importance than you think." His face was cold and hard as he looked into Hecta's eyes. "Your time on Earth with the dream traveller and your connection to her are vitally important to me. I need to know everything that happened when she first came into her power. You will tell me everything about her and who she is connected to, so that I may decide what to do next." Hecta shrugged.

"My memories are confusing, my lord, but I will tell you everything I know." Gabriel leant forward slightly.

"Tell me first of the witch on her world who helped her. You have seen her and interacted with her before, haven't you?" Hecta pushed the plate of food away and reached for the tankard of wine beside it. He was at least thirsty.

"Her name is Pearl. She was the first contact Sapphire had who could help her understand her transition into magic. She is old, but strong for a human. Her magic has been passed through her from generations back. I believe she may have been one of us many lifetimes ago as she has much knowledge of our magic, and the wards surrounding her home are strong. It was no coincidence that Sapphire found her. They have formed a close bond." He paused and sipped the wine.

"She was hard to dispose of. My efforts to send her into the afterlife failed, due to Sapphire's magic being so strong. I tried to bind Sapphire to me and to send the witch into the darkness ... a mistake I regret on my part." Gabriel's nostrils flared for a moment as anger rose within him.

"You will not touch her again, Hecta. She is of importance to me. You should have reported her presence when you first found her back on Earth. I shall forgive you this time for making such a mistake, but do not displease me again on this matter." Hecta nodded. He had no idea why the old witch would be of any importance to such a powerful master of magic.

"I will do as you ask of me, my lord." Gabriel leant back in the chair and nodded, and placed his fingers together in the shape of a steeple close to his lips. His eyes flashed again.

"Now tell me everything you remember, Hecta. Leave nothing out. Tell me about all the events, the people, and the places you visited with her, and how her magic felt to you. Tell me now."

Hecta sighed. This would be a long night.

Returning to Shaka was like a breath of fresh air to Sapphire's body and mind. It was daytime when they returned, and the garden surrounding Fox's home was filled with fragrant flowers. The grass was thick and lush beneath her feet.

They had said goodnight to Charlie and Nathan before travelling back on a trail of magic to Fox's homeland, and to find herself suddenly standing on the lawn outside his home again took Sapphire's breath away. The wave of magic they had used to transport themselves was still clinging to her skin and making her shiver, despite the warmth of the air around them. Fox held her within his arms as he always did when they travelled. His body radiated heat and the heady scent of patchouli and sandalwood.

She could feel the grass, soft and silky against her bare feet. It always amazed her that her clothing would adapt to wherever she may end up after such a journey down the magical wormhole. It was as if the magic would bend and shape to take into consideration each place she visited on her travels. It was pretty damn convenient, to be honest.

Fox was wearing his signature leather waistcoat and trousers. She was now dressed in a long, fitted dress that was cool against her skin. He released her slowly and smiled at her as he stepped back. His eyes travelled across her body in approval.

"Nice dress," he commented. She laughed and shrugged.

"I'm not sure how that happens, but I'm grateful for it."

A loud squeal made them both turn around quickly – to find Kit running towards them, her face lit up with excitement.

"You are back," she said with a huge smile on her face. Fox smiled as she flung herself at Sapphire and wrapped her arms around her, hugging her tightly.

"It's so good to see you again. I have missed you." Sapphire squeezed her back, warmed by the young girl's obvious fondness for her.

"I missed you too, Kit. Are you OK?" Kit stepped back quickly, suddenly aware that she was behaving in an overly familiar way with her master's wife. She smiled at Fox and dropped a quick curtsey.

"I am well, Sapphire. My lord, it is good to see you too." He smiled at her.

"That is obvious, Kit. I'm glad you are well. I assume you have taken good care of everything in our absence." She looked down at the grass shyly.

"Yes, yes, my lord. Everything has been taken care of. Your father is also well, and Bear has been to visit recently. He is keen to see you again, as it has been some time since your last visit." Sapphire frowned.

"How long, Kit?" Kit looked at her smiling sweetly.

"Two moon phases have passed since your last visit, my lady." Fox took her hand and squeezed it gently.

"Time passes differently between our worlds, Sapphire. Do not forget that, and do not worry now we are back. We can relax for a while and recharge our energy." She sighed and shook her head. The whole thing about time bending was still unfamiliar to her, and really messed with her head. She placed her hand on his chest, and her eyes grew wide for a second.

"Do you still have the seeds and the flower?" He released her hand and patted his chest.

"They are all in my pocket, Sapphire, safe and sound." Kit stared at them both.

"You have brought the seeds back to Shaka? I thought you were leaving them on your Earth, weren't you?" A light breeze tickled Sapphire's cheek and made her snap back into the reality of where she was. Another planet, another dimension … with a bag full of magic, that she needed some help with.

"I was, Kit, but things have changed. Let's go inside and catch up. Hopefully you have something for us to eat. All this travelling has made me hungry." Kit nodded enthusiastically.

"Of course. Come, come … I have so much to tell you." Fox raised an eyebrow and smiled. His amusement filled his eyes and made them sparkle brightly in the sunlight.

Sapphire felt a swell of happiness fill her chest. It was good to be back again. She could feel the magic filling her body as she walked across the lawn. It uncurled gracefully around her like a familiar friend touching her senses and making her feel alive. Once more she wished more than anything that her friends could experience the rush and wickedly sensual delight of literally walking on magic.

She followed Kit and Fox back into the house that was now as familiar to her as Foxglove and Charlie's little cottage were. This was her home, and she was glad to be part of it again. She had not realised how much she had missed the energy here on Shaka, and how grateful she was that it began to heal the weariness that had been dragging her down in the last few days.

Kit fed them both and chatted excitedly about the recent events on Shaka since their departure. It seemed that the people of Calafia had been busy harvesting a new crop and celebrating the abundance of this world with a festival of their own. Kit told them, with a slight blush to her cheeks, that she had met a young man at the harvest festival and that he had been visiting her recently.

Fox questioned her about this young man with the concern of a father. His eyes were alert and bright as she relayed to him that his name was Falcon and that his family lived nearby on one of the farms. Sapphire listened with a smile on her lips as the young girl recalled fondly his latest visit to court her when they had ridden out, accompanied by Bear, to the waterfall and had had a picnic. She still found the system of dating here on Shaka somewhat ancient and old-fashioned, but it was sweet and innocent – and rather humbling, compared to the system on Earth. Fox eventually seemed satisfied that this young man was worthy of her attention and told Kit that he was welcome to visit her at his home, as long as she was chaperoned.

After they had eaten Kit did her usual disappearing act and left them alone in the sitting room. The last glimpse of sunlight cast slithers of gold light across the wooden floor, which gave the room a warm, soothing glow.

Sapphire felt relaxed and at ease. Her energy had lifted considerably, even in the short time they had been back. Her eyes were adjusting to the shift in magic again and she could see everything with her new magical senses, like a newly born vampire making everything glow eerily as dusk began to fall.

Fox pulled her into his arms and draped her across his legs as he sat down on the couch. After sighing heavily she leant back on to the cushions and allowed him to cradle her like a child while his fingers traced patterns across the skin on her arms.

"You seem happier, my love," he said. She closed her eyes and, revelling in his touch, she purred with approval.

"Mmmh, I do feel better already. I hadn't realised how out of sorts I was feeling until we returned." She paused, opened her eyes again, and stared up at him while watching his expression thoughtfully.

"It must have been awful for you when we first met. Travelling to Earth and back again to be with me all those times must have left you shattered." He smiled and continued to stroke her softly, which sent sparks of silver light across her now sensitive skin.

"It wasn't so bad. You were worth it." His face seemed relaxed, and his eyes sparkled with flashes of gold against the dark rings that outlined his irises. She could never tire of looking into his eyes. They were utterly mesmerising.

"Still, I appreciate it more now. Thank you." He laughed softly and squeezed her against him.

"We are similar creatures now, my love. You will understand more as time goes by what it means to be made from magic ... the gifts it gives us, and the sacrifices we must make to balance its power."

His touch was starting to trigger other responses within her body now, and she bit her lip as she tried to rein in the pulses of arousal that were beginning to flow through her veins.

"It feels like bloody hard work sometimes," she said. He laughed again and leant down to kiss her. She accepted the kiss gratefully, closing her eyes again and letting her body melt against him as his tongue pushed softly against her own. He moaned softly into her mouth before releasing her.

"That's not the only thing that is hard right now," he said. Sapphire smiled up at him. It seemed that the return to Shaka had awakened their magic in more ways than one.

"Let's go to bed, Fox." He nodded, and lifted her up so quickly that she squealed in delight as he threw her over his shoulder and headed upstairs to their bedroom.

Fox awoke with a start. The room around him was dark and heady with the scent of the flowers from the garden outside. The temperature on Shaka was hot for this time of year, and he was covered in a fine film of sweat. The sheet that had once been draped across his body was now scrunched at the base of the bed frame. He could hear Sapphire breathing softly beside him. She had fallen asleep quickly after they had made love earlier that evening.

He stared at the canopy above him, which glowed an eerie white in the darkness as he lay on his back with his arms above his head. After stretching his body out against the soft sheets he breathed in deeply and filled his lungs with the magical air around him. He had no idea why he was now wide awake. He too had fallen into a deep sleep after he had made love to Sapphire.

A smile slipped on to his lips as he remembered the feel of her body beneath him and how her legs had wrapped around him as he had pushed deep inside her. He turned on to his side to face her, and opened up his senses to allow his magic to press against her and to check if she was travelling in her sleep. He could just see the outline of her features in the darkness. The faint glow of her own magic glittered against her skin in a soft violet colour. It shimmered and danced with a life of its own. She was so very beautiful when she slept. Her lips were parted slightly, and her dark eyelashes fanned out against her cheeks. Her naked body shone like a pearl, translucent and flawless in the moonlight. She was totally perfect.

He sensed that she was indeed dreaming, and the slight flutter of her eyelids indicated that she was travelling far and fast. He concentrated harder to probe into her dream and connect with her as she travelled on the ethereal plane. As he did his body jolted suddenly as if he had hit a brick wall. His muscles tensed with the shock of the impact. Sapphire moaned softly, and her body began to twitch. Her energy shifted, and the magic surrounding her began to glow more brightly. Fox sat up quickly and reached for the candle beside him.

"Light," he said and the candle flickered to life, illuminating them both in the darkness. He gasped as he touched Sapphire. Her body was icy cold and her lips were turning a slight shade of blue. He grasped her arm and shook her gently to wake her.

"Sapphire ... Wake up, my love." She did not respond, and he pulled her towards him. Her body was like a lead weight as he gathered her within his arms. She literally felt like an ice cube. His heart began to race a little as he pushed his magic outwards further and tried to connect to her while she travelled. This was not safe, and was not something he had ever encountered before when he had connected with a dream traveller. It was as if she was suspended in another time, and wherever she was he was not able to reach her.

"Sapphire ... wake up." He shook her harder and pushed his energy into her body to warm her up. She groaned. Her head was lolling awkwardly to one side. Her magic had changed colour now to a silver blue, and was beginning to pulse strongly. Flashes of luminous silver threads under her skin were making the room light up like lightning against a stormy sky.

Without warning a bolt of white light erupted from above the bed and shot down into Sapphire's body, making her shake within his arms. He was temporarily blinded by the intensity of the energy that surrounded them. A low, deep moan filled his ears as he clung desperately to his wife. The air around them crackled and spat with shards of power, which singed Fox's arms as he held Sapphire against him. Her body was still ice-cold and the conflict of extreme heat and the ice-cold temperature of her body caused steam to rise from their bodies, which sizzled against the air.

Fox felt his own magic falter and shake at the shock of such strange magic. His mind was reeling with panic. In his head he could see Sapphire running through a landscape of snow and ice, her white-blonde hair flying behind her like a beautiful flag. She was running so fast that her image was just a blur within his mind. He closed his eyes and clung to her with all his strength as the white bolt of light above them continued to pour powerful, undiluted magic into her body. In his mind he pictured Conloach, and he called out to him loud and strong,

"Father, come to me now." The room was filling with steam and the sound of electricity sparking against the floor deafened him as he held on to his wife. On opening his eyes again he saw his father appear beside the bed, his face alive with concern. He raised his arms above his head as he pulled his own power into the room.

Fox watched with horror as his father threw his magic at them both and forced Fox away from Sapphire so that he crashed against the wall. His head hit the floor with a bolt of power so strong it knocked him unconscious for a second. The sound of his father chanting filled his ears as Fox shook his head and brought himself back to reality. After pushing himself up from the floor he stood quickly, and watched with confusion as Conloach surrounded Sapphire's body with a protective bubble which contained the magic that poured into her from the heavens above.

"Father, what are you doing?" he shouted loudly. Conloach slowly lowered his arms and stared at Sapphire before moving across to his son.

"A new strain of magic is being downloaded into her body, Fox. You must not touch her until the transition is completed." Fox shook his head in frustration.

"No! Stop it, Father. Stop it now. She is in trouble. Help her." Conloach regarded him coolly.

"She is fine, my son. Do not worry. She is safe, believe me." Before Fox could react to his father's confusing statement the energy from above her body disappeared and the room became dark once more, except for the candle he had lit just moments before. The sound of his heavy breathing filled the air, and the charge of new magic clung to his naked body like morning dew. The bubble of magic that Conloach had created around Sapphire's body shimmered and broke, and she moaned softly. Her body was shaking now as she curled up into a ball. Fox flung himself at her.

"Sapphire ... By the gods, my love, please wake up," he pleaded, his voice rough with emotion. Conloach grabbed the sheet that was lying at the bottom of the bed and wrapped it around her naked body. Fox held her within his arms again and rocked her back and forth. His hair was falling across her face as he cradled her against him.

"Sapphire ... Sapphire, please wake up." His voice was deep and low, his words desperate. Conloach frowned, but remained silent as he watched his son hold his wife tightly to his body.

"She will wake soon, my son. Give her some space." Fox looked up at him with dark eyes.

"How can you be so calm, Father? What the hell just happened?" Conloach sighed. He walked across the bedroom, grabbed Fox's leather trousers, and threw them at him.

"Get dressed, Fox. Stop panicking and focus. She will need you when she wakes up again."

Sapphire moaned softly as she regained consciousness. Her head felt as if she had been hit by a sledgehammer, and her muscles were sore and heavy. She tried to open her eyes, but an invisible bat took a swift strike at the back of her skull and made her cry out and decide to keep them closed. She felt the strong arms wrapped around her rocking her gently.

"Be still, my love. It's OK. Everything is OK now."

Fox. Fox was holding her and she was OK. Alive and OK. Her body relaxed just a fraction. Her mind was starting to awaken again, and the pain within her head gradually began to ease slightly. After taking a deep breath, which rattled in her throat, she tried to open her eyes again. By squinting against the dim light in the room she eventually managed to prise open her eyelids.

Fuck. Everything hurt. Where the hell had she just been, and what had just happened to her? Fox was staring at her as if she had grown two heads. His expression was one of acute concern and fear.

"Thank the gods, Sapphire. You scared the hell out of me." She smiled a crooked smile.

"Well, hello to you too." He laughed, and his expression quickly changed to one of relief. She was wrapped in a sheet, but that was all. Her body was shivering against his warm chest.

"Where did you go, my love?" As she pushed herself shakily away from him she noticed Conloach standing beside the bed they were sitting on. He regarded her with a blank expression, and his magic was pulsing steadily, a dark purple and gold, in the dim light.

"Hello, Conloach," Sapphire said. Conloach dipped his head slowly, and a small smile slipped on to his lips.

"Sapphire, it is good to see you again." Fox kissed her softly on the forehead. His relief was palpable. She sensed her nakedness under the sheet, and knew that Conloach had quite possibly seen quite a lot of her that evening.

"Mmmh, I guess Fox called you at some point tonight. It seems things got out of hand while I travelled this evening." He chuckled in response.

"Just a little, daughter. You have been gifted, it seems, with a new strain of magic on your travels tonight, and scared my son somewhat." Fox hugged her tightly to his chest. She noticed he was wearing his leather trousers and nothing else. Her mind whirled with the possibilities of what they had witnessed. She had experienced something that was at that moment unexplainable. She needed a stiff drink or a very strong joint. Or both. Then she remembered where she was, and sighed in disappointment as she realised that would not be possible. It sucked, being both human and magical at the same time. Big time.

"I need some water, Fox. Can you get me something, and maybe a chaser of something a bit stronger?" He nodded, and kissed her again before releasing her so that she could rest back against the pillows.

"Of course, my love. Whatever you need." He slipped off the bed and moved quickly out of the room with supernatural speed: her beautiful and sexy magical vampire.

She pulled the sheet closely to her body and looked across at Conloach warily.

"What did you see?" He raised a brow and moved to the chest at the end of the bed.

He took out a blanket and placed it over her body, obviously concerned that she was still cold despite the heat of the night air. From the way her nipples were pointing directly outwards she knew she most definitely was.

"A download of magic that was more powerful than anything I have ever seen, Sapphire. You were held safely within your dream while it saturated your body. Fox was lucky to only receive minor burns during the process." She shivered and pulled the blanket up under her chin.

"I'm sorry. I didn't mean to hurt him, and had no idea that was going to happen. I was dreaming and found myself in a place I have never been to before, but which was strangely familiar."

Conloach sat on the bed beside her. Fox reappeared with the water and a tumbler of dark liquid. She hoped it would warm her up. She was still freezing. He held the water to her lips, and helped her take a few sips before swapping it for the tumbler.

"It is like your whiskey, my love. Drink." She moaned softly with thanks as she sipped the warm liquid. Hot and fiery, it slipped into her belly and immediately warmed her throat and stomach.

"Thank you." He smiled softly in response. His eyes were dark with concern.

"Tell us what happened, Sapphire," he said gently.

As she sipped the fiery drink slowly Sapphire gathered her wits and tried to recall the dream she had just experienced. Fox and Conloach waited patiently for her to recover while watching her with curious eyes.

"I found myself in a strange, barren landscape full of snow and ice. Nothing else except the wind blowing in my face and the bitter cold surrounded me. I was virtually naked except for a thin slip dress. I knew that I was freezing, but felt totally numb to it." She took another sip of the drink. Just thinking about how cold it had been in that strange world made her shiver again.

"I was trying to work out why I was there and get my bearings when I felt something behind me. The snow started to fall heavily, and I couldn't see anything. It was like a white-out. Everything was eerily quiet except for the wind. Some of my dreams in the past have been pretty scary, and this one came top of the list. I wanted to get the hell out of there, and started to run." Fox watched her with his eyes flashing with concern.

"I saw you briefly, Sapphire. You were running at incredible speed, but that can happen sometimes in a dream state. Your magic changes and your abilities increase. I could not join you. Something was holding me back here in Shaka." Conloach looked up at the ceiling as if for inspiration.

"Some events are meant for the individual only, my son. It is rare that a guardian cannot join their charge but, when the magic is so strong and intended for one person only, forces beyond our knowing take control of the dream state. I have only seen this once before." Sapphire blinked at him and shook her head slowly.

"What do you mean?" Conloach looked at her with intense eyes.

"Only the most powerful of our kind can download new strains of magic in such a way." Fox turned to him and frowned.

"How do you know this, Father?" Conloach smiled softly.

"Because it happened to me once." A small O shape appeared on Sapphire's lips.

"No shit," she whispered, looking shell-shocked. Conloach walked across the bedroom towards the balcony where the sun was beginning to rise once more. It cast a deep orange streak across the horizon. It was going to be another hot day.

"Tell me more, Sapphire. What happened next?" Fox asked her.

"I felt as if something horrible was going to happen, and I just couldn't get away quickly enough – although, weirdly, I could feel a new presence in my dream. I think it was the Oracle." Fox's eyes opened wider. Sapphire looked apologetic and shrugged her shoulders.

"Sometimes she comes to me in my dreams. I was just starting to panic when I found myself in a cave. It was like the crystal caves you and I visited – the cave with the different chambers. But this cave was so vast and so beautiful. Everything was so clear, and it sang to me like the most amazing choir of voices." She looked confused for a moment as she tried to find the right words to describe her experience.

"It was like heaven. I felt so emotional, and my whole body was humming with power. The crystals were clear quartz, I think ... amazing. Anyway, I was trying to hold myself upright. The pressure from the voices and the energy around me almost knocked me to the floor when suddenly everything went completely quiet and still, and I found myself floating – literally floating – in a sea of green grass. I know that doesn't make any sense at all. How could I be floating in grass? But, to be honest, a lot of my dreams don't make any sense.

"And then I heard a voice as clear as a bell that said ..." She paused and lowered her voice dramatically.

"It said, 'Now you are ready, Sapphire'." She shrugged, clearly confused, before taking another sip of the drink. Fox sighed and looked across at his father for any clues as to what had happened. Conloach smiled.

"You have nothing to fear, Sapphire. The download of power you received has completed your transition into the next phase of your energy shift. You have been reborn, if you like." She sighed.

"I don't feel reborn. I feel like shit." He laughed.

"The process is somewhat exhausting, but you will feel much better after some rest." He looked at Fox. "I will leave you both now, my son. But contact me if you need me." Fox nodded and watched his father disappear before his eyes.

He turned to Sapphire, took the drink from her, and placed it on the table beside them. She watched him move across the bed, and was grateful for his warmth as he pulled her once more into his arms.

"I thought I had lost you again, my love. You have this uncanny ability to scare the hell out of me." She sniffed and snuggled her head into his neck as she breathed in his scent and felt the softness of his hair against her cheek.

"Sorry. I didn't ask for this, Fox. It scared me too. I'm exhausted from all this travelling and magic." She felt his fingers in her hair, stroking her gently and trying to soothe her. "I thought coming back to Shaka would be a rest for us both, not another challenge." He kissed her softly on the forehead.

"Unfortunately, Sapphire, it seems that your life will always be a challenge." She turned her head up to him, wrapped her hands around his neck, and pulled him down to her lips, then kissed him in response to his words of truth. She wanted to lose herself in her husband again and wipe away the memory of being chased in a barren snow-filled landscape. The sound of the angelic choir in the crystal cave still rang in her ears and made her skin ripple with goosebumps.

Her body felt heavy and uncomfortable, but she could also feel a new layer of magic riding in her veins. It trembled in her belly and skittered across her palms like an excited animal waiting to be let out of its cage. Fox responded to her kiss and pushed the blanket away from her shoulder, eager to help her remove the memory of the dream with something much more familiar.

"I love you, Fox," she mumbled between his kisses, as he pulled her closer and pushed the dream away from her mind.

Hecta stood silently in the shadows of the huge tree at the end of Fox's land. He had been watching and waiting for movement within the house and was now rewarded for his patience, as he saw Fox leave the house alone and head to the stables. The task Gabriel had given him would be easy, considering that both Sapphire and Fox thought he was dead and buried in the ground back on Earth.

After telling his master all the events that had led to his death back on Earth he had thought that Gabriel would leave him to rest for a while before any further action would be required of him. But no. Gabriel had then told him that he was to go to the house Sapphire now lived in with Fox immediately and wait for her return to Shaka, as it seemed that her travelling between the dimensions had been frequent of late. Gabriel had been keeping an eye on her and Fox and knew that they had recently visited Earth, and the shift in energy there indicated a change that she had made herself on that plane during this visit.

He was to observe her carefully and search the house, if necessary, for any signs that she was hiding something valuable. For that is what Gabriel had sensed when he had met her with Conloach and Fox for the first time not so long ago. She would not suspect it would be Hecta snooping around, and that would give him the element of surprise.

Hecta felt a sense of conflict within his mind. Despite the fact that he was no longer really alive, a trace of his humanity made him feel oddly sorry for her. She had been pursued by Ebony when she had been alive, and was now being hunted like a prize animal by his master. It seemed that everyone wanted a piece of her powerful magic, and that this threat would continue for her while she still held it within her body.

Despite the fact that she had in fact ended his long life and sent his soul across the veil to the other world, he felt very little anger now towards her. His initial return to his body had evoked many emotions regarding the dream traveller, but as the time slipped by he felt fewer and fewer of these. This was not his business any more and he wanted to return to the calm world he had been sent to, where he could feel only a sense of peace again. But he knew that Gabriel had the power to stop his soul from returning to such a place again, and that was the only reason why he now stood in the shadows waiting for his moment to get closer to Sapphire again.

He did not know how long Fox would be away from her or where he was going, but as he watched him canter off into the sunset towards Calafia he knew that he had better be quick if he was to gain any useful information for Gabriel. He had waited all night and day for this moment. After pushing himself away from the tree he walked slowly across the lawn with the hood of his cloak pulled low over his face and his feet silent on the grass. He sensed no other person in the house except Sapphire, and he could feel her energy burning brightly in the front of the house. She was possibly in the kitchen area, where he had observed the young serving girl moving around earlier that day.

He used the talisman Gabriel had given him earlier to create a protective shield around himself, and chanted softly under his breath as he approached the house. The arrival of dusk created a welcome relief to the heat of the day, and the fading light now disguised him nicely as he crouched down below the window. He would take a peek inside before he broke in and had a look around.

As he stood up slowly, so that he could just see into the window, he felt a wave of magic hit him in the chest. It almost knocked him off his feet, but he remained steadfast and watched with wide eyes as Sapphire moved around what was in fact the kitchen. She was wearing a short summer dress that skimmed her hips and fanned out as she moved, showing off her curves to perfection. Her hair was loose around her shoulders and trailed down her back, shimmering in the many candles lit around the room.

Seeing her again in the flesh made him feel a flicker of excitement. She was a sensuous creature, and the new wave of magic around her accentuated this tenfold. He remained low near the window so that she would not see him, but suddenly she stopped what she was doing and looked directly out of the window as if she had in fact sensed his presence. Perhaps she had. Despite the protective shield that now surrounded him maybe her magic had become so strong since he had last seen her that her sixth sense was able to detect him crouched down by the window.

He held his breath and slipped back along the wall, so that if she did look outside she would not be able to find him. As he crept silently around the house he looked up at the balcony above him and scanned the wall to see how easy it would be for him to climb up inside. His magic had almost disappeared when he had returned to his body, and it was only Gabriel's use of the necromancer that had enabled him to even function. He could no longer transport himself inside the building just by thought and will, as he had been able to do so easily before.

He frowned and reached out to touch the brickwork before him. After pulling himself up by gripping on to the trellis that was arranged below the balcony he began to climb up slowly, and cursed silently as he caught his hand on a rose thorn that had tangled itself in his cloak as he climbed. With one last burst of energy he landed on the balcony as silently as he could and crouched down low again in case Sapphire had heard him.

He waited for a few seconds before pushing the balcony door open and stepping inside the room. A large bed sat against the wall. It was surrounded by a canopy with white curtains that draped around the edges, giving it privacy from the rest of the room. The furnishings were sparse but cut from wood with exquisite design and craftsmanship.

He realised he was standing in their bedroom, and a sudden wave of frustration hit him hard in the chest again. She could have been his once, but Fox had claimed her, and he could smell and almost taste the joining of their energies in this room now. It made his chest clench in what felt like anger.

Damn. This whole experience was vastly unpleasant for him, and he cursed Gabriel for bringing him back from the dead. He did not want to be reminded of his failures or faults, and he certainly did not want to see the result of Sapphire and Fox's happiness and joining of power. For that was what was all around him now as he moved through the room, silently looking for anything of interest.

Their combined magic hung in the air, thick and heavy and full of lust. It made him feel slightly nauseous. A chest of drawers to the side of the bed caught his eye. A mirror and a vase of fresh flowers were placed on top. A brush and pots of lotion were also scattered across the smooth wooden surface, indicating that Sapphire used this area.

He paused before touching the handle of one of the drawers. All was quiet in the rooms below. He assumed that Sapphire was now eating or resting in the kitchen, and he nodded to himself. He felt safe to continue.

On opening the top drawer he found various pieces of clothing and underwear and a pouch made from leather tucked below them. Touching the items made his skin feel strange. Ripples of some lost memory tried to surface, but were replaced with pain as his fingertips brushed the pouch. He jumped back and held his hand protectively to his body. He cursed again and shook his head as he tried to release himself from the pain that had hit him when he had touched the innocent-looking item. It was protected by a strong spell, and was obviously of some importance to Sapphire. Unfortunately, without his old magic to aid him, he would be unable to investigate further, and Gabriel would have to retrieve this object himself if he wanted it.

He rummaged through several of the other drawers before he noticed that his finger was bleeding. The rose thorn earlier had obviously cut him and he had not realised, because he had little sense in his body any more. The blood was a dark red, almost black, and it oozed lazily from the cut on his finger. After wiping it on his cloak he sighed deeply. He would have to return another time and continue his search. While sucking on the offending cut he was about to step out on to the balcony again when he felt a shift in the energy by the doorway. As he turned around he saw Sapphire standing just outside the door staring at him, her face ashen.

"Hecta?" she whispered as if she had indeed just seen a ghost. He remained still for a moment. His mind was whirling with a mixture of panic and excitement.

"Sapphire," he said softly back to her before turning around and leaping off the balcony into the garden. The pressure of his recently resurrected heart beating hard in his chest made him run fast across the grounds as he headed for the cover of the tree again. He needed to disappear, and disappear fast, before she could realise that he had actually been real and not just a vision or a ghost returned to haunt her.

He hoped that his master would not be angry with him but, more than that, he hoped to see and speak to Sapphire again. The magic that had surrounded her as she stood in the doorway was unlike anything he had ever seen before. Powerful, intoxicating, and utterly beautiful. It made him want to be alive again. To be really alive, not just sitting in transit inside a shell that he could no longer really connect with. He felt the first glimmer of a smile slip on to his lips, and the thought that he had to see her again – and soon – was pounding in his head.

As she held the door frame to steady herself Sapphire stared into the bedroom and out at the balcony where she thought she had just seen Hecta standing and staring at her. The sound of his voice as he had said her name echoed in her ears. Like a whisper on a gentle breeze, it had been spoken with such sadness and was empty of all emotion.

She shivered. Her breathing was a little fast, and her heart fluttered against her ribs like a butterfly trapped in a room trying to escape. She was seeing things. It couldn't have been him. It wasn't real. Hecta was dead. She had killed him, and Fox had buried his body. She had not even felt his presence. No other magic but her own permeated the air around her, and the only reason she had gone upstairs was to run a bath before Fox returned from visiting Bear.

She had heard no noise coming from the bedroom. She had to be seeing things. That was the only explanation. Either that, or Hecta was now haunting her for all the things she had done to him before she had finally killed him. Maybe this new strain of magic now thrumming in her veins was doing weird things to her mind as well as to her body, which since this morning had been throbbing wildly.

Fox had been fascinated to notice her aura constantly changing colour every few hours throughout the day. He had also told her that he was finding it even harder to keep his hands off her now, as she was radiating sexual energy like an animal in heat. Just what she needed ... not. They had sex all the time as it was and, as much as she enjoyed Fox's attention, her body could only take so much.

She still felt very human despite the power radiating off her in uncontrollable flashes that made her skin light up as if she had neon bulbs in her veins. Fox had told her it would settle eventually and that she should rest for a while, as he needed to see Bear and catch up with any changes in his kingdom that needed his attention.

After letting go of the door frame she walked into the bedroom and into the adjoining bathroom to run the bath. The balcony doors were open, and the night air lifted the canopy around their bed gently. The smell of the wild flowers in the garden filled her senses and calmed her a little after the fright of seeing Hecta. She bent down to turn the water on for her bath, and as she knelt beside the edge she placed her fingers under the water and watched the clear liquid cascade against her skin. Everything was heightened again. It felt as if she was high, and her lips parted slightly with a sigh as the warmth of the water caressed her skin.

"Oh, God, I am so in trouble again," she said out loud as her body vibrated and flashed a light pink colour. "I just want to be normal," she mumbled. "Fat chance of that."

As soon as she realised she was talking out loud to herself she shook her head, and left the bath to run after tipping some rose oil into the flow of the water. After stripping out of her dress she went back into the bedroom, and padded across to the chest of drawers where she kept her clothes to look for something she could tie her hair up with. She frowned as she noticed one of the drawers was slightly ajar and that a dark smudge on the wood, which she had not seen before, had appeared suddenly.

She touched the spot tentatively and drew her fingers back as they connected with the thick, black-looking liquid. Her skin began to tingle, and the obsidian necklace that she happened to be wearing again that evening throbbed against her chest. She held her fingers up closer to her face and inspected the offending liquid, and turned her finger into the light to get a better look. It looked oddly like blood. But it couldn't be blood, could it? While shaking her head and turning quickly back to the bathroom she hurried to the sink and turned on the tap, wanting nothing more than to wash off the sticky black substance. Her stomach was doing strange flips, and the obsidian was dancing with heat against her skin.

"Not again … seriously … when is life going to give me a break?" she mumbled as she rubbed her hands together with soap to remove the stain. It clung stubbornly to her fingers before literally sliding off down the plughole. As soon as it did her body calmed down, and the necklace returned to a cooler temperature once more.

Her bath was half full, and she could not wait to slip in it and relax. Returning to Shaka was suddenly full of surprises that, quite frankly, she could have done without. She left the water to run and she removed her underwear, not bothering to find a hair tie, and slid down into the warm water. She was still feeling a little cold despite the heat of the day and the water that enveloped her. She hoped that this new strain of magic would settle soon, and that her temperature would return to normal.

She would ask Fox to check the chest of drawers and see what he thought when he returned home from visiting Bear. She felt as if she was losing her mind again. It wouldn't be the first time. It was actually nice to be alone for a change, and as the water rose slowly around her she leant back in the bathtub and closed her eyes.

For the hundredth time that day she recounted her dream and tried to decipher exactly what it meant and how this new magic that thrummed in her veins would help her finish the task she had been given. The ice-cold landscape and the crystal cave had felt very familiar to her, but why? The seeds had been given to her in a previous dream, the essence had been given to her back on Earth, and the dirt to plant them in had been given to her by the god of dreams in Egypt. It was as if she were being given tiny pieces of a huge puzzle that the universe expected her to complete all on her own. Her head hurt just thinking about it.

She had returned to Shaka to talk to Conloach about Charlie and her reaction to the crystal flower she had brought back from Egypt. Tomorrow she would go to Calafia and speak with him. She would also find Willow and ask her if she had any potions that would ease the stiffness in her muscles that had not let up since the magic had entered her body last night.

But right now she wanted to switch off her mind and relax her body as much as she could in spite of the bolts of power pulsing at random times throughout her system. As she slipped further into the hot water she tipped her head back and allowed her hair to float around her shoulders. With her eyes still closed she breathed a sigh of relief as, finally, her muscles began to let go.

She hoped Fox would be gone for at least another hour before returning. She really needed some time out.

Chapter Twenty-Two

Sweat dripped down Fox's face and off the end of his nose and splashed on the stone floor below him as, using the bar above his head, he pulled himself up once more.

"Fifty ... fifty-one ... are you sure you are not going soft, my friend? Your ability to do pull-ups is looking as if it is causing you some trouble this evening." Bear laughed as he watched Fox struggle with the effort of the workout he was spotting for him.

After dropping to the floor Fox wiped his forehead and grinned at his friend. They had been working out in the barn to the side of Bear's house for the last hour. It was equipped with various items that could be used to push the body to the extreme. It was similar to Fox's armoury, and it too contained various weapons to practise with along the walls. Fox was stripped down to his waist, and his body glistened with the evidence of his efforts. His abdominal muscles bunched hard as he began to carry on with his workout, and he pushed himself up with his arms and ignored Bear's teasing.

"You are just jealous, old friend. It has been some time since we worked out together, and I doubt if you could even lift that bulk of yours off the floor for more than ten sets." Bear laughed again and walked across to a punchbag that hung from the ceiling. He began to throw his fist into the leather, which made the chain shake perilously as he pounded it. He too was stripped to the waist, and his huge muscles rippled as he worked the bag.

"It is good to spend time with you again, Fox," he said, panting as he threw a jab into the bag causing dust to fall from the ceiling in protest. While jumping up again Fox shook the sweat out of his hair and sent it across the floor in a spray of droplets.

"Yes, my friend, it has been too long since we have enjoyed each other's company." He smiled as he watched the warrior before him spin around and give the punchbag a kick so hard it made him step back in fear the ceiling would collapse around them. "Seeing you do that also reminds me not to piss you off, my friend." Bear stopped his pounding and turned around to grin at Fox, who was looking at the wall of weapons.

"Ah, my temper is much more in check nowadays. Thanks to the barmaid – and her regular workouts – my testosterone is much more stable." Fox lifted an axe from the wall and began spinning it around his head, flexing his muscles again in a deadly dance.

"Whereas mine is abnormally high and causing me some discomfort ..." Bear laughed.

"Your wife is not fulfilling your needs, Fox? I seriously doubt that ... What has changed?" Fox nodded for him to choose a weapon. He was full of adrenalin, and the workout had made his blood fizz in his veins. It felt good.

"She fulfils every need I have, Bear, but her magic is overpowering – even more so now. She has, just last night, downloaded a new strain of it that is pushing all my buttons. I came here tonight to get away from her for a while until it settles. Both of us needed a break from each other, I think." Bear chuckled as he grabbed another axe and swung it around his head.

"Much has changed for you both, Fox. I can see that in you tonight, but I have no doubt you will both soon regain your balance." He grinned devilishly and crouched a little into a defensive stance. "In the meantime feel free to release your frustration on me with your axe, old friend."

Fox smiled and stepped forward to attack. They clashed together with their muscles straining. The air was filled with static energy and the mixed scent of sweat and testosterone. Fox was enjoying this time with his oldest friend doing the things they had done so many times in the past. Since he had been given the task of guarding Sapphire his life had been turned upside down in so many ways, but this felt familiar and safe to him and he welcomed the distraction. He knew that Sapphire was safe at home, and that if she needed him she would call to him.

The new magic that had been downloaded into her body was more overpowering than anything he had ever seen or felt before. His father had said that he too in the past had experienced such a thing, and it made Fox wonder how long it had taken Conloach to stabilise it. Sapphire was an extraordinary being: human, but filled with magic. The fact that she was also a dream traveller made her unique and precious, something Fox was more than aware of lately.

Frequently, of late, he had felt almost out of his depth when around her. She kept him on his toes in more ways than one, and even though the Oracle had warned him of this he still found the pressure of being her guardian a challenge at the best of times. However, his love for his wife inspired him to be the best he could possibly be, and this workout with Bear was just what he needed. He made a mental note to do just this on a more regular basis so that he could remain physically as strong as he could, and keep the edge of the warrior finely tuned so that he could protect Sapphire in their future together.

Fox was distracted by his thoughts and Bear narrowly missed his head with his axe, which quickly brought him back to the moment and the weapon he held in his hands. Bear laughed loudly as Fox regained his stance and counter-attacked, blocking him with a loud crack as the handle of both axes crashed together. With their faces close together Fox stared into the fierce eyes of his friend, and pushed with all his might against the huge bulk of muscle before him. Although straining with the effort Fox felt his feet begin to slide back on the stone tiles. With his arms trembling he laughed out loud.

"Yield ... I yield, my friend." Bear released his hold and dropped his axe. He was panting hard. Fox did the same and they stood for a moment, both breathing hard after the fight. Bear shook his head and chuckled with a depth to his tone that made him sound like his namesake.

"I think that is enough for tonight, my friend. Let's retire with some well-earned ale. My housekeeper has left out some cold meats in the kitchen, if you are hungry ..." Fox nodded and smiled.

"That sounds like a wonderful idea. I'm done." After placing the weapons back on to the wall Bear thumped Fox on the back before draping his arm around his shoulders as they headed back to his house.

"We should do this more often, Fox. You have boosted my ego tremendously with your failure to beat me tonight. Thank you." Fox laughed.

"And you have helped work off my frustration," he replied.

They headed across to the house, which was lit up cheerily with flames that burnt brightly in the sconces on the walls. Bear's home was as rugged as he was. Made from heavy stone and wood, it was much smaller than Fox's grand house but equally as comfortable. On entering the house Bear threw him a towel so that he could wipe himself down before they ate. Fox, who was by now dressed in his waistcoat again, watched his friend gather food and drink for them both on to the kitchen table. Bear glistened with sweat in the candlelight. His long hair, damp and dark, curled around his shoulders.

After sitting down heavily Fox took the ale Bear passed him and, grateful for the hydration, swallowed the contents of the tankard in long, deep gulps. Bear slid him a plate of meat and bread before he began to devour his own tankard of ale and food. They sat eating and drinking in comfortable silence for a while.

Fox was feeling more relaxed than he had in a very long time. He had not realised how tightly wound up he had been, despite the frequent sex with Sapphire. Men definitely needed two ways to release their testosterone: a good fight, and a good fuck. Both gave satisfying results, and a calmness that usually resulted in a brief time of equilibrium. Fox had also meditated regularly in the past, which also helped, but he had found that almost impossible lately with so much happening in his life with Sapphire. Bear watched him with amusement.

"Your mind is busy tonight, my friend. I can almost hear the cogs whirling in your brain." Fox smiled at him.

"You know me well, Bear. I was just thinking how much I needed that, and how good I now feel. There's nothing like a good fight with a trusted friend to put you back into balance." Bear, sploshing some of the liquid over the edges as he did, refilled their tankards.

"I am always here for you, Fox. You know that. As a listening ear, or as a partner to fight with." Fox nodded.

"And I am grateful for that, my friend." They continued to eat. Bear consumed double the amount Fox did, but there was nothing unusual about that. Fox leant back in his chair and sipped his ale while closing his eyes for a moment.

"Sapphire has created something quite amazing back on her home planet, Bear. It is a tree made from crystal which has produced flowers so unique and strong with magic that I fear for her homeland and its people." Bear looked at him with curiosity.

"And this has been the reason for your long absence?" Fox nodded and opened his eyes again.

"Being guardian to Sapphire has turned into something I had never anticipated. The journey with her is like nothing I have ever experienced, and is changing daily. Thoughts of us ever being able to lead a normal life together are now just a pipe dream." He paused and looked down into his tankard for a second.

"She was with child before we were married, but lost it." Bear stopped eating and wiped his mouth with the back of his hand.

"I am sorry to hear that, Fox, but I have no doubt that she will give you many children in the future. I have no doubt she is the most fertile of females." Fox smiled.

"Yes. Yes, she is. But I sense a reluctance within her to have a family soon. She is still coming to terms with her abilities and the changes in her life. It has been a lot for her to deal with in such a short space of time." He ran his finger around the rim of the tankard absently. "As a human it is a wonder she has not lost her mind with all the things she has had to accept and embrace in her new life." Bear stroked his beard slowly and watched Fox with a new intensity.

"She is not only a dream traveller, Fox. She is clearly a creator of new life. I can see the energy around her shifting and spinning constantly. Her body is a vessel for a new kind of magic that none of us have seen before. It is no surprise to me that she has created such an amazing thing on her home planet." Fox blinked with surprise.

"You see this in her?" Bear nodded, his expression one of amusement.

"Of course, Fox. She has blossomed since I first met her. I believe she will change many things on both our planets. The likes of Ebony and Hecta would not have been so interested in her if she had been your average magical creature." Fox took another sip of ale.

"She has also gained the interest of someone else very dangerous lately, my friend." Bear frowned.

"Who?" As he sighed deeply Fox ran a hand through his hair.

"Gabriel, the master of all gatekeepers, someone my father had not previously told me even existed. We met for the first time before our last trip back to Earth. I fear he is also keen to learn more of

Sapphire's newly acquired magic, and he does not know even half of what has been happening lately. We have managed to keep him at a distance so far, but I doubt that will be possible now that she has increased her power again. I am waiting for him to turn up at my doorstep unannounced." Bear nodded slowly.

"I am happy to stand guard for you, Fox, if you feel threatened. Wolf can be made available if needed. You know that we are here for you both." Fox smiled weakly.

"I would not ask that of you. You have done enough. The battle with the queen and Ebony cost enough lives – and to be honest, Bear, I believe Sapphire has enough power now to protect all of us if it came to that." Bear smiled.

"Ah, now I understand your dilemma a little more, Fox. Your wife is the one who can protect you, and not the other way around." Fox shrugged.

"As always, Bear, you see straight through me. Yes, I believe that if push came to shove my wife could kick all our arses." They both laughed. Fox found the honesty of their conversation refreshing. At least someone understood how he felt. Frankly he was a little intimidated by the strength of Sapphire's magic, even if at the moment she had no idea how to use it or knew just how powerful it really was. After taking one last gulp of ale he stood up and smiled at his friend.

"Thank you for tonight, Bear. I am grateful for your company and for your honest friendship." Bear regarded him from across the table. His face was still red from the workout in the barn. He smiled and raised his tankard.

"It is always here for you, Fox. I look forward to the next time."

Fox nodded and turned to leave the house. The night air was starting to cool, and the stars were bright in the dark sky above him. As he looked up at the thousands scattered across the vast space he wondered absently which one he would visit next with his wife on her travels. He closed his eyes briefly and visualised his home and her face smiling at him on his return. After pulling himself up on to Midnight he stroked the thick neck of his horse and spoke to him softly in his own language before kicking his heels into his flanks and heading back to Sapphire so that he could bathe and climb into bed beside her, thankful that his ardour from earlier was now silent and peaceful.

The house was dark except for a flicker of candlelight in his bedchamber when he arrived back home. After stepping quietly through the house upstairs to the bathroom to avoid waking Sapphire he quickly stripped out of his clothes and began running a bath. The room was hot and steamy, and held evidence that Sapphire had already bathed earlier that night. He had not realised how much time had passed since he had left her to visit Bear. He sensed that she was indeed sleeping and he moved quickly after gathering a towel and some bath oils so that he could wash off the sweat clinging to his body from his workout earlier. He wanted to join her in the bed as fast as he could. The urge to be close to her again was strong within his body.

As the tub began to fill with water he moved to the doorway once more to check on her. She was facing away from him. Her body was half covered by the bed sheet and her magic was pulsing softly in the darkness in a steady glow of pink and violet. The realisation that her aura was at last stabilising made his body relax a little more. The flashes of white light that had been skittering across her veins were no longer apparent and her energy now seemed calm and serene, thank the gods. He wasn't sure how much more he could handle of the strong energy that she had been radiating earlier that day.

His testosterone levels were now nicely sedated, and he wanted nothing more than to hold his wife in his arms without his cock standing to attention like an eager adolescent who could not control his own body. He smiled at the thought and returned to the bathroom, and lit another candle before slipping into the hot water. As he let out a sigh of contentment he tipped his head back and allowed his body to fully submerge under the hot water. As he resurfaced seconds later he was aware that he was no longer alone in the room. Sapphire stood in the doorway, wrapped in the bed sheet. Her body was leaning against the door frame and her face was in shadow. She scratched her head and yawned loudly.

"I wondered when you would come home," she said. He smiled as he ran his fingers through his wet hair and then placed his arms along the back of the bathtub.

"I tried not to wake you, my love. Go back to bed. I will join you shortly." She pushed herself away from the door frame and walked towards him with the sheet trailing behind her. Her face became illuminated as she stepped into the candlelight and Fox sighed at the sight of her beautiful eyes, which glistened deep violet and blue in the soft glow. She smiled back sleepily with her hair ruffled and wild across her shoulders. She was the most gorgeous thing he had ever seen right at that moment – like a goddess emerging from the dark, all curves and cascading hair. His cock twitched under the water. He cursed the Gods for his continued weakness and reaction to the sight of her standing before him.

"OK, but don't be too long, Fox. I need you wrapped around me so that I can fall asleep again." As he looked from her and back down to his unruly member he laughed softly.

"You are killing me, Sapphire." She tilted her head to one side, clearly not understanding his current problem. He grabbed the soap and began to wash quickly. He wanted to get clean and out of the water as quickly as possible now.

"OK ... I have no idea what that means ... I'll see you in a sec," she said. Fox groaned as he watched her shapely arse disappear from the room again. Just when he thought he had things under control she had totally confused him again. He closed his eyes and counted to ten, then he finished washing and thought of something that would trick his body into submission. He wanted nothing more than to jump straight out of the water and into the soft curves of his wife, but he was doing his best to give her some space and time to readjust to the new magic flowing through her veins.

After stepping out of the bathtub he grabbed the towel and gave his body the fiercest rub-down he could withstand while willing his cock to stand down. Eventually it seemed to get the message, and he sucked in a lungful of air and blew it back out again so that he could calm his spangled nerves. He strode quickly into the bedroom and literally dived under the sheet and pulled Sapphire close to him, gritting his teeth as he felt her skin connect with his own and create a sparkle of light that flickered across them both.

"Mmmh," she moaned softly as she snuggled up against him. "You smell good. Did you have a good night with Bear?" Fox wrapped his arm around her waist and shifted his body so that his groin was not pushed completely against her warm derriere.

"Yes. It served the purpose I needed, and it was good to catch up with him." Sapphire sighed. Sleep was obviously enveloping her again quickly now that she was within the safety of his arms.

"Good. I love you, Fox," she mumbled. Fox held her waist gently, and tried desperately to keep a little distance now as his body responded to hers. This was getting to be a joke. Within minutes he could hear her breathing change to a soft, even pattern. Her chest rose and fell gently as she slipped into a deeper sleep state. Fox shifted again. His eyes were wide open and his body was on full alert. There was no damn way he could sleep now, with her soft curves pressing against him and her new magic teasing his skin with flickering licks of fire that ignited him in goosebumps.

He moved away slowly from the heat of her skin. He then turned over on to his back and stared up at the ceiling while willing his body to calm the fuck down. He smiled at his internal struggle while watching the curtain lift and fall softly around the bed as the night air captured the material in the light breeze. His body was literally pulsing next to hers ... but he could feel something else that made him frown just for a moment.

A new energy within the room seemed to permeate in the air. This was something that he had not sensed when he had first come home. He had always had an overly acute sense of smell, something that his shape-shifting ability had blessed him with over the years, and now it seemed to be on full alert. He lifted his head from the pillow and he sat up quietly in the dark while looking around the room with his magical eyes, which pushed his senses out further to find the source of this strange energy.

He could smell it now ... it was something that he had smelt many times in his life, and it made his nose crinkle in distaste. It was the faint but distinct smell of death.

He slipped away from his wife and off the bed as quietly as possible and padded naked across the room with his nostrils flaring as he tried to pick up the exact location of the scent. His pupils widened and his body thrummed with power as he headed towards the dresser beside the wall. In the dim light he could see that one of the drawers was slightly ajar and several items of clothing were hanging out untidily from the inside.

Sapphire had a habit of leaving things this way when she had finished dressing. Charlie had warned him of her messy habits, and he smiled as he headed to the drawer to close it. Just as he reached out to push it back to its flush position the smell grew stronger, and he stopped short as his hand touched the wood. A slight smudge of dark liquid caught his eye, and the cloying smell of something that had been dead for some time caught in the back of his throat.

Blood. There was blood on the drawer, and it did not belong to him or Sapphire. In fact it did not belong to anything alive at all. This blood was a creation of something unnatural, something that had been formed from magic – and not from the good kind. His mind flashed with a myriad of possibilities as to how and why this was in his bedroom and on Sapphire's underwear drawer. As he looked back at her sleeping soundly in the bed he shook his head in confusion. She had not mentioned anything untoward when she had greeted him tonight.

He headed to the bathroom, picked up a washcloth, ran it under the tap, then wrung it out before moving back to the chest of drawers. As he washed off the offending liquid he sensed the darkness of the magic mixed within the blood and shivered as it tried to connect to his own energy.

He held the offending item out and away from his body, and swiftly left the bedroom to head down the stairs and remove it from the house. He stood in the garden completely naked and looked around to find a suitable place to deposit it. The cool night air finally slapped his body out of the lustful spell he had been under from touching Sapphire, and he chuckled softly that this strange item had at least successfully removed his erection.

As he placed the cloth under one of the large stones in his garden he returned to the house and wondered what his father would make of it. There was definitely something odd about this, and an uneasy feeling tickled the nape of his neck as he made his way back up the stairs. He was now fully awake, and thoughts of rest were unfortunately far from his mind.

Sapphire was still sleeping peacefully as he dressed. He would take another ride on Midnight and blow some of the frustration away in the night air. As he pulled up his leather trousers and slipped a shirt over his head he hoped that whatever was now sitting under a rock in his garden turned out to be of no consequence at all and was not another unknown threat against his wife. After taking one last look at a sleeping Sapphire he kissed her softly on the head and took off to the stables once more. It was going to be a very frustrating night indeed.

Hecta watched his adversary canter off into the night on his black stallion. A smile uncurled on his lips, and he licked them like a cat about to devour its milk. He had returned to Gabriel earlier that evening and told him of the events that had occurred. As he waited for his master's wrath at the slip-up with Sapphire he had been surprised that it had not come as Gabriel had processed news of the item in her drawer. Gabriel's icy blue eyes had grown wide and filled with flickers of snow shapes, as if an excitement within him had been ignited when Hecta had described the leather pouch that had been surrounded by a protection spell.

Hecta knew that Gabriel would, without a doubt, make his move very soon and discover what this protected package contained. It was out of his hands now. Gabriel had become agitated, however, when Hecta had told him that he had injured his hand when climbing up the trellis. As Gabriel used his powerful magic to heal Hecta's flesh he told him that he was to be more careful, as the body he now owned could not withstand the normal scratches or injuries that his magical body had once coped with easily.

Hecta had slipped away from his master without being noticed shortly after being dismissed. He wanted to see Sapphire again, no, he needed to see her again. The intensity of the need burned within him. It was if his empty mind had been reignited, and a slow burn of his old self was now simmering under the surface like a caged lion. Sapphire's presence and the magic that flared around her had begun something within this cold shell – a reawakening and a reanimation of a new kind.

He was waking up. He could feel it fizzing in his veins as he walked closer to the house. He was drawn to her like a moth to a flame. The need to feel alive once more was great within his chest, and his heart seemed to beat a little faster – as if it was actually really alive instead of a dead thing that was held together only by magic.

He was feeling bold as he walked up to the front door and reached for the handle. It opened without even a glimmer of wards or protection. The smile grew wider on his lips. Her guardian was growing careless. His arrogance that any threat from him had been removed on Earth had caused him to leave without protecting the house.

As he walked into the hallway his newly awakened heart fluttered excitedly. He could feel her upstairs, sense her presence as if she was a glowing fire in a cold, dark forest pulling him up the stairway like a man starved of heat and warmth.

He turned to the right at the top of the stairs and headed to the bedroom he knew she was currently sleeping in. After opening the door he stood silently watching her. The room was aglow with her magic. It filled the air with the scent of roses and jasmine. It was totally intoxicating, and like a pure, undiluted drug to his system.

He walked across the tiled floor and sucked in a breath as the sight of her uncovered body filled his mind with a thousand thoughts, all of them impure. Her hair cascaded in white-blonde locks across her shoulders and down her back, leaving her chest bare. Her eyes were closed and her lips were parted slightly. He watched, fascinated, as her chest rose and fell gently. She was so utterly mesmerising, beautiful, and lush in the dim light of the night. He desperately wanted to touch her, but his fingers shook as he reached out with his hand and he bit his lip as he tried not to make a sound.

As he leant forward her magic suddenly flared out and touched him, causing him to cry out in shock. Her eyes flew open and she sat bolt upright in the bed. Shards of silver light spread across her skin, and she looked at him with absolute confusion and fear.

He stumbled backwards and knocked into a low table, causing the candlestick and glass that had been sitting on it to crash to the floor. Her mouth opened and closed like a fish that was out of water. Hecta felt a wave of her magic slam into his chest, and he moaned loudly as it filled his body with heat that burnt so fiercely it travelled outwards into his arms and legs and made him shake like a rag doll.

Sapphire grabbed the sheet and pulled it up to her chest so that she was no longer naked before him. She remained in the bed and just stared at him in utter shock. His eyes rolled into the back of his head, and he felt the heat of her magic explode within his brain. It snaked its way between the synapses and switched on the dead grey matter that had, only moments ago, been functioning purely from the magic of necromancy. He slumped to the floor, and felt the crushing sensation of white-hot pain envelop him and course through his body as he screamed out.

His whole life flashed before his eyes once more as if he were slipping away across the veil, just as he had back on Earth. But this time, before he lost consciousness, he felt something else. Something he had never felt before. He felt the caress of pure, unconditional love, so strong and intense it tore through the pain and left him floating silently on a cloud of bliss-filled contentment. She had given him back his life, reawakened him, and achieved something completely impossible. He had been reborn and his magic had been reinstated. Only this time it was different. Completely different.

Chapter Twenty-Three

Sapphire jumped out of the bed and stood over the inert body of Hecta.

"No, no, no ... this is not possible," she gasped. Her voice was breaking with ripples of terror as she stepped back from Hecta, and her mind was whirling like a spinning top.

Hecta was alive. He was here on Shaka at her feet, living and breathing. This could not be real. She must be dreaming. She could feel the power radiating from her body and the new magic within her burning strongly in her veins. It cast itself over the room with flickers of white and gold light that filled up the entire space.

Her breathing was erratic as she tentatively moved her leg and kicked his body to see if he was in fact real. His leg moved and his head lolled to one side at the kick. She jumped back with fright and screamed as the realisation that this was in fact real and not a dream at all hit her full on in the chest. Her scream echoed off the walls and shattered the magic being cast out from her body. The shards of white light that had been skittering across her skin ceased and everything went dark. There was just the sound of her heavy breathing filling the room which, just moments ago, had been her sanctuary.

Where the hell was Fox? Sapphire stepped away from Hecta, who remained completely out of it on the floor, and searched frantically for something to wear. Just as she found a robe Fox came crashing through the bedroom door. His eyes were wide and his body was on full alert.

"Sapphire, what the hell has happened?" She practically ran to him, threw herself into his arms, and buried her head into his chest. Tears began to fall steadily from her now. She could not stop them.

"Hecta ... Hecta is here. He's alive ... Well, I think he's alive. He's over there on the floor by the bed." Fox gripped her arms tightly.

"What?" He stared at her, his eyes wide and dark with confusion. Sapphire clung to him, not wanting to turn around and face what seemed to be a nightmare unfolding before her.

"I woke up and found him standing over me. My magic was going crazy. In fact I think I saw him earlier tonight, but thought I was imagining things. He can't be real. I killed him, Fox. How can this be real?" Fox removed her from his body and gently prised her fingers from his arms.

"Go downstairs, Sapphire. Do not come back up." She looked up at him and nodded. Fear was etched clearly across her face. After taking one last quick look back over her shoulder at the dark heap on the floor she fled from the room and disappeared.

Fox stepped forward. He had grabbed one of his daggers as he had entered the house. After hearing Sapphire scream he had transported himself back to the house immediately, leaving Midnight to find his own way home. He always kept weapons in the house as a habit, and they were strategically placed in various hiding places that Sapphire was not even aware of.

His body was trembling with adrenalin and pure rage because, if what Sapphire had told him was real, Hecta had somehow been resurrected and was now unconscious on his bedroom floor. Holy mother of the gods. How? While keeping the dagger in front of him and moving in a defensive position – he was ready for anything – he moved towards the body on the floor.

When he looked down he could clearly see that this man was indeed Hecta. His eyes were closed and his head was to one side. His chest rose and fell gently as if he were actually sleeping. Magic surrounded him, a dark green aura that glowed and was softly interwoven with flashes of gold. It looked nothing like the old energy the gatekeeper had exuded when Fox had previously encountered him. Before it had always been dark, red, and clearly angry. This aura was calm and serene; the colour of a healthy heart chakra, almost glowing with love. Fox shook his head and bent down to get a closer inspection.

"Motherfucker," Fox whispered. A cold fury began to fill his body. This man, his nemesis, had tricked them all again. Somehow he had not only risen from the dead but had been brought back to Shaka. And now he had brazenly approached his wife and been zapped by her new magic, which had created a new life within his body. This new magic now pulsed within Hecta's veins, and he had achieved this without his or his wife's consent.

He grabbed Hecta roughly by the legs and began to pull him across the floor and away from the bed. He took his dagger, cut off a piece of the gatekeeper's cloak, and made a makeshift rope to tie both Hecta's feet together. He repeated this with Hecta's hands, and he bound him tightly in case he woke up and decided to get feisty. There was no way he would allow this disgusting creature to harm his wife ever again.

He would kill him right now if he could, but first he needed to find out exactly how Hecta had been brought back to Shaka – and, indeed, how he had been brought back to life. As he threw the heavy weight of the unconscious Hecta over his shoulder to take him down to his armoury and restrain him until he could call Wolf and Bear he had the awful realisation that he knew the answer to both those questions ... Gabriel.

Sapphire was sitting in the lounge with her legs tucked up underneath her and a blanket around her shoulders as she watched Fox stride out of the house with Hecta slumped over his shoulder. He did not even stop to see where she was. She jumped back up and ran to the door and watched him disappear behind the house to the armoury.

"Fox, please be careful," she shouted at his retreating figure. She worried her bottom lip as she held the blanket around her shoulders. She felt suddenly cold despite the balmy night air. It must be the early hours of the morning now, and she felt utterly spent and confused. How could Hecta be alive after all this time? It made no sense to her whatsoever. And what had happened to him after her magic had connected to him? He had flipped around like a dying fish on the floor, totally zapped, for what seemed like a very long time. How had she done that?

She headed back upstairs and ran to her drawers and searched for the pouch that held the seeds. They sat, innocently buzzing, in among her underwear.

She grabbed the pouch and, breathing erratically, held it to her chest. Thank God they were still safe. Is that what he had been doing? Snooping around looking for the seeds? Did he even know they existed? She felt as if her head would explode any second.

"Sapphire, my love, are you OK?" Sapphire jumped out of her skin when she felt Fox standing immediately behind her. He too was breathing heavily. He pulled her into his arms and held her against him, and squeezed her tightly.

"I'm OK … I'm fine … I just don't understand what's happening." Fox kissed her on the top of her hair and breathed in her scent. His body was trembling slightly.

"He will not harm you, my love. He is bound tightly, and I have put a protection spell around him to stop him from breaking free until Wolf and Bear get here. I have called them. They won't be long." Sapphire looked up into his eyes, which flashed amber and black wildly.

"Will you bring Conloach here?" Fox blinked.

"Yes, in the morning, once we have woken the fucker up and questioned him for a while. I don't want my father here to see that. Or you, my love. I want you to go back to bed. I will bring Kit here to watch over you while we deal with Hecta." Sapphire felt new tears sting against her eyes. Her throat felt tight, and her heart was thumping like a bass drum.

"Please be careful, Fox. I have no idea what happened between us when my magic connected with him. He could be very dangerous when he wakes up." Fox practically growled.

"He will not harm you, Sapphire. Ever again." After kissing her on the lips firmly one last time he pulled back from her. He said nothing more, but stared at her with an intensity that almost scared her.

"Fox … Please be careful." He nodded, then turned quickly and left the room so fast it made her hair blow upwards in the backdraught.

Bear stood with his feet wide apart as his hand stroked his beard. A frown was etched on his brow as he stared at Hecta, who was bound to the chair before him.

"By the gods, Fox, how could this be?" Fox paced the floor with agitation and heat radiating from him. His eyes were flicking up from the floor to Hecta and down again as his mind processed the night's events. Wolf stood beside Bear with his face impassive and the darkness of his skin glistening in the light of the torches that had been lit around the armoury.

"At this precise moment, my friend, I have absolutely no idea." He paused and scowled at Hecta. "But once I have woken him up I will damn well find out." Wolf stepped forward and crouched down so that he was eye level with the gatekeeper. His eyes scanned the man before him, and his hand reached slowly for the blade that was strapped to his thigh.

"We should kill him, Fox ... dispose of him now once and for all, in the way we know best, and end this madness." Fox shook his head.

"No. I need to question him and find out how this happened." Bear watched his friend tremble with anger and realised that the situation could get out of control if Wolf had his way.

"Wake him up, Fox. I will get him to talk." Wolf looked up at them both and sighed heavily.

"This could be a trap. We have no idea what he is capable of right now, physically or magically. Sapphire told you herself that he connected with her magic. He could be stronger than all three of us after such a transaction." Fox threw his arms up in frustration and said,

"Fuck!" Bear released his beard, and a small flicker of a smile slipped on to his lips.

"Be calm, my friend. This piece of shit has nothing over us. I will have no problem restraining him if need be." Fox nodded, and flicked his head in the direction of his armoury wall.

"Just in case ... help yourself to whatever weapon you want while I remove the protection spell and wake him up." Wolf nodded and strode to the wall – closely followed by Bear, who grabbed the huge mace and swung it around his head as he readied himself for any surprise attack from Hecta.

Fox stood directly in front of the unconscious gatekeeper and closed his eyes. With his arms stretched out before him, palms up, he began to chant to lift the protection spell. His voice was deep and smooth, and he prayed to the gods and goddess as he chanted that this would not backfire on him.

The magic surrounding Hecta flickered and dissipated as he finished the unbinding process. On stepping closer Fox looked at Hecta one more time before he slapped him hard across the face, which made his head snap back and his body jerk in the chair. Hecta moaned softly and his eyelids flickered.

"Wake up, Hecta, you miserable piece of shit," Fox yelled at him. Just as his hand moved forward to hit him again Hecta opened his eyes and let out a loud gasp, and his body flexed against the chains that held him to the chair he was sitting on. Bear and Wolf stood with their weapons at the ready at either side of Fox. Hecta stared at the three of them, his eyes wide with terror at the realisation that he was trapped.

"Please stop. Don't hit me again," he pleaded. His voice was but a whisper, with an almost pitiful edge to its tone. Fox cocked his head to one side. This was not the man he remembered as his arrogant adversary, a creature who thought nothing of attacking and removing life whenever he felt like it in the past.

"How are you even alive, Gatekeeper? How did you get here? Tell me everything now, before I beat the life out of you again." Hecta blinked. His eyes blurred with what looked like tears.

"I will tell you ... I will. But please don't hurt me again." Bear lowered the mace and looked at Fox with an expression of utter confusion on his face.

"What the hell has happened to him?" Fox shook his head. He moved closer to Hecta, and crouched down a little to face the man who once had no fear.

"I will not harm you, Hecta, if you tell me how this has come to be. How you can be alive after I myself witnessed your death and buried your lifeless body in a hole in the ground on Earth?"

Hecta gulped, sweat forming on his brow.

"Gabriel ... Gabriel brought me back to Shaka. He paid a necromancer to bring me back so that I could spy on Sapphire and tell him everything about her." He scrunched his eyes shut briefly, as if trying to stop a torrent of tears escaping. "He knows she has something very powerful with her and that her magic has grown again ... He wants her, just as Ebony did ... You need to get her away from here. Remove her from Shaka. Take her somewhere safe, where he cannot find her. She is not safe here." Fox shook his head again. Who was this man? Hecta would never have divulged this information to him so quickly and easily in the past.

"If you are trying to trick me, Hecta, I swear to the gods that I will kill you, and it will not be quick or pain-free." Hecta swung his head from side to side in panic.

"No! I am not lying. This is the truth. You are all in danger. Gabriel will kill me anyway, now that you have captured me." A single tear fell across his cheek as he looked down at the floor. His chest was heaving.

"She gave me back my soul, my life. I have never felt anything quite like it ever before ... Such powerful magic I could only ever have dreamt of. She is a creator of life, an angel of rebirth. So very pure and beautiful ... so strong and powerful." His head swung back up. His face was wild, and almost delirious. "My salvation," he concluded. Fox stepped forward and grabbed his chin, forcing his face up so that he was inches from his own.

"Never talk of my wife and her powers again, Hecta. She is mine, only mine, and you will never touch her or her magic again. *Do you understand me?*" The last words were growled in a low, staccato tone. Hecta trembled and nodded. Bear reached out for Fox's arm and squeezed it firmly.

"Fox ... steady, my friend." Fox released Hecta's jaw, making it snap hard as he turned on his heel and paced away. Bear looked at Wolf then back at Hecta.

"If what you are telling us is the truth, Gatekeeper, then you need to explain who this Gabriel is. And do it now." Fox stepped back up to the man, who he no longer recognised as his old nemesis, and stared him in the eye. "You are going to tell us everything, Hecta. Every little detail about what Gabriel really knows before I myself end your miserable life once more." Bear put down the mace and grabbed Fox by the shoulder.

"I think you need to tell us what's going on as well, my friend, for I am totally confused right now."

Kit held Sapphire's hand and stroked her hair gently. They were seated in the lounge together on the love seat. Kit's arm was around her mistress's shoulders as she soothed her.

"How did this happen, Kit? What have I done? None of this makes any sense to me. I killed him. I saw him lying as dead as a doornail on the floor in Foxglove. He was buried in the woods behind the cottage back on Earth, Kit. I must be dreaming. I must be."

Kit smoothed her hair away from her face and stared down at Sapphire with confusion. Sapphire's brow was warm to the touch, and she sensed that she was running a slight fever.

"Sapphire, you are not dreaming. Believe me, this is real, even if neither of us want it to be. But please do not fret. Master Fox is taking care of this and Bear and Wolf are with him, so Hecta cannot and will not harm you. Please try to rest." Sapphire stared at her with glazed eyes that reflected her inner turmoil and the fact that she was close to jumping off the sanity cliff.

"Seriously, Kit how am I supposed to sleep, rest, or even calm down with this happening in my own home again?"

Without warning she jumped up off the seat, making Kit gasp at the speed she moved. Once she was standing again Sapphire paused for a second as she raked her hands through her hair and tried hard to get a grip on the situation. She was very close to losing it.

As she ran up the stairs back into her bedroom she could hear Kit calling her from below as she grabbed some clean clothes and pulled them on. Her hands were shaking and her head spun as if she was drunk, but she could not just sit there waiting for Fox to return. She had to see Hecta again with her own eyes to confirm that she was not going mad, dreaming all this, or just experiencing another premonition.

The magic within her body was beginning to glow like an internal fire, and her skin was lighting up in silver lines that etched themselves across her skin in what looked like hieroglyphics. They were symbols of some kind, which came in and out of focus as if she was a living sarcophagus. Freaky. Kit tried unsuccessfully to stop her at the bedroom door. She was suddenly feeling very strong, and although she did not want to hurt her friend she pushed her to one side as she tried to grab her arms.

"Kit, please let me be. I'll be back." Sapphire moved so fast out of the house that she did not even recall opening the front door until she stood on the lawn and realised that dawn was approaching fast.

The sun was just peeking over the horizon and casting a fiery orange over the sky that spoke of another clear day approaching. It looked like a bush fire in the distance – hot and deadly, and warning her of imminent danger. She hoped this was not the case.

She could feel the energy of her husband and his friends before she even made it to the armoury door. Fox was mad. His anger was as distinct to her now as his other emotions were when they were near each other. Once she had pushed the door open she found the scene before her oddly comforting. Hecta was bound by chains to a chair in the middle of the room and Fox, Bear, and Wolf were surrounding him like a pack of very unfriendly wolves. The gatekeeper had no chance of escape even if he had wanted to.

Fox's head snapped in her direction as he realised she was now inside the room.

"Sapphire. Go back in the house," he barked at her. She stepped forward. Her body was now thrumming crazily with the new magic inside her, which was doing little acrobatics against her skin. She shook her head slowly.

"No, Fox. I need to see him. I need to know that this is real, and I'm not dreaming again." Fox frowned with his hands clutched at his side in frustration. Hecta looked straight at her. His lip was bleeding from where Fox had hit him earlier. His expression changed instantly from despair to delight as he saw Sapphire approaching. His body flexed against the chains again, and Wolf stepped forward quickly and brought a knife up under his chin.

"Steady, Gatekeeper, or you will be feeling the sharpness of my blade." Fox stepped in the path of his advancing wife.

"Sapphire ... Seriously, do as you are told for once. It is not safe for you to be close to him. We do not know what will happen if you connect with him again, or if your magic does."

Her eyes grew wide as she realised that her magic was indeed responding to this crazy little scene before her, and sparks of white were now escaping from her fingertips. After shaking her hands to release this weird effect she placed them on Fox's arms and gripped them tightly. He cocked his head to one side and looked at her with a mixture of confusion and wonder.

"Fox, please let me just speak to him," she pleaded. "I can see that this is real now, but I need to know how he came back from the dead and why my magic is responding like this." Fox looked back over his shoulder at the gatekeeper, who was seemingly hypnotised by his wife's appearance, and then back into her big blue eyes.

"You really are the most stubborn woman I know," he said, and sighed. She released her grip on his forearms and she smiled softly.

"I know," she said. He bent his head down slightly closer to her ear and whispered.

"It was Gabriel, my love. Gabriel brought him back from the dead. We are questioning him now, so there really is no need for you to expose yourself to him any longer." Sapphire looked up at him and nodded as she acknowledged his words with just a slight twitch of her head. She said nothing more but turned away from him, and in the next instant was crouched in front of Hecta. Her new vampire-like speed astonished even her for a second. Hecta stared at her with his mouth open slightly. His body was shaking and making his chains rattle eerily against the chair.

"Hecta, I would like to say it's nice to see you again, but of course it isn't." His eyes grew wide and his bottom lip trembled. Sapphire watched him carefully, while sensing the change in the new magic surrounding him that swirled green and pink. Her fingers were tingling, and she could feel the energy inside her slipping down her palms like tiny electric pulses wanting to be released into the air.

"Fox tells me Gabriel brought you back to life and back to Shaka. Is this true?" He blinked and licked his lips. The trembling in his body was becoming more erratic.

"Yes, it is true," he said.

"What happened to you when my magic connected with you, Hecta? Can you tell me?" He tried to lean forward to get closer to her but Wolf pressed the edge of his knife deeper against his Adam's apple and effectively cut off the movement, as a slither of blood oozed from his skin.

Sapphire flashed Wolf a look that told him to back off. She could feel Fox standing directly behind her. The anger she felt from him earlier was now tenfold. It positively flexed against her back like a pipe about to burst. The room was heavy with testosterone and frustration, and not in a good way. She sighed and waited for Hecta to reply, and closed her eyes momentarily as she tried to rein in the urge to clear the room so that she could talk to the gatekeeper alone.

"I felt your magic hit me in the chest and it threw me back on to the floor. It was like nothing I have ever experienced before, Sapphire ... something unique, something so exquisitely powerful." His voice was soft and gentle, almost a whisper. She narrowed her eyes while trying to see through any deception he may be weaving, but found none evident.

"Your magic removed the spell of the necromancer and brought me back to life for real, Sapphire. I am reborn. You have created a new life within me, and I thank you for that. I promise you that I will never try to harm you again, for you have given me something I have never felt before." Sapphire cocked her head to one side. Even she was curious to hear what he had to say next.

"You have given me love, Sapphire. Unconditional love." Fox pushed his way to stand in front of her. He moved so quickly she felt momentarily dizzy, and then he slapped Hecta hard against the cheek, making his head spring back and then forward again with a loud cracking sound. Sapphire stood up and grabbed her husband to stop him from attacking Hecta further. His anger was beyond restraining now. The language that fell from his mouth in his own tongue made no sense to her, but she had no doubt as to what he was saying.

Bear jumped in and pulled Fox back, and Wolf stood back up to help him. Sapphire remained still staring at Hecta with a strange sensation uncurling within her stomach. She felt pity for this man before her. For the first time in the strange journey she had experienced with the gatekeeper – since she first learnt that she was no ordinary human – she felt an odd connection with him, which was a feeling other than disgust. It was an empathy and an understanding of where he was now. Transformed and humble, Hecta was chained to a chair because she had touched him with her magic and changed everything. She, no one else, had done this. She was Sapphire Whittaker, dream traveller, and now creator of life. Fuck. What was she supposed to do with that?

She spun around and watched Bear and Wolf wrestle with Fox, who had indeed lost it. He was absolutely fuming that Hecta had proclaimed that Sapphire had touched him with anything other than her fist connecting with his jaw. The whole situation was very quickly spinning out of control. She pulled her power from within her chest and threw her hands up in the air which sent it crashing out of her fingertips. It lit up the room and blasted a perfect circle of heat up out of the roof and into the sky.

"Enough of this bullshit!" she screamed, feeling as if her brain was about to explode from frustration. Several pieces of the roof fell down and hit the tiled floor with a hard slapping sound, which made Bear and Wolf duck instinctively. Hecta was just smiling serenely, as if he was Jack Nicholson in *One Flew Over the Cuckoo's Nest*.

Fox stopped his profanity and sagged against the arms that were holding him back.

"Stop making this worse than it already is, Fox, for the love of God ... please." He looked at her – his breathing was heavy – and nodded his head slowly. While turning away from her he shook Bear and Wolf free of his arms and strode out of the armoury. His body was pulsing like a time bomb. Bear looked at her and shrugged.

"He will calm down eventually, Sapphire. His issues with the gatekeeper go back a very, very long way." Sapphire looked up at the hole in the ceiling and cringed inwardly. She had meant to get their attention, not wreck the building.

"Wolf, please go after him and make sure he doesn't do anything stupid. Bear, please can you watch the door for me while I finish my conversation with Hecta?" Both men looked at each other with uncertainty, but nodded at her instruction. After watching both men leave the building Sapphire turned back to face Hecta, who had finally stopped shaking and was watching her with eyes that now sparkled chocolate brown.

"Hecta, I want you to listen carefully to me. And make no mistake: if at any point I think you are lying, tricking, or just humouring me to deceive me or my husband in any way I will kill you again without a thought." He gulped, and the nick on his throat from Wolf's knife moved up and down with the action.

"I am listening, Sapphire." She crouched down once more. With her hands placed on her thighs to steady her she looked him straight in the eye.

"I am going to ask Conloach to take a look at you and see what he thinks with regards to this new lease of life you have. He will take you to his castle and keep you there, away from my rather angry husband and his friends and away from Gabriel." Hecta watched her silently. "Once we have established why this has happened we will make a decision as to what to do with you next." His head lifted to look up at her as she straightened herself to upright and placed her hands on her hips. "Do you understand?" He nodded like an obedient child.

"Yes, Sapphire, I understand."

Chapter Twenty-Four

Fox flung the door to his house open with more exertion than was necessary and made it slam hard against the wall. As he strode through the hallway he swore under his breath while his hands grasped his hair as he tried desperately to control his temper. Wolf followed him like a silent shadow.

"My friend, we should transfer the gatekeeper to the cells at the castle," he said. A deep voice from inside the lounge area replied, making both men jump.

"I believe that decision has already been made by Sapphire. I am here to collect Hecta and take him with me." Conloach was seated on the large chair beside the fire with his arms resting on the wood in a relaxed manner. His fingers curled around the smooth handles.

"Father ... It does not surprise me that you are here. No doubt the whole kingdom has just heard Sapphire screaming at me from inside the armoury." Conloach chuckled softly.

"She is rather zealous at expressing her emotions, my son. We are all well aware of that fact." Fox walked into the lounge towards his father and tipped his head down in a gesture of submission.

"I am glad you are here, Father. I am finding it difficult to control my own emotions in this situation. The reappearance of Hecta has thrown me off balance." Conloach stood up in a quick, almost catlike motion.

"The strain of magic she downloaded is still not completely stable, my son, and you are too close to her to remain unaffected. I will need to teach her how to control it, as presently she is a danger to everyone around her." Fox frowned.

"A danger?" Conloach looked across at Wolf, who was looming in the doorway.

"Her power has revealed itself to be more formidable than I originally thought. Not only can she evidently create new life but she can destroy it just as easily. Without training and restraint she could easily destroy those closest to her." Fox looked up at the ceiling. His eyes closing in exasperation.

"This is just ridiculous. First the seeds, then the essence and the tree on Earth, and now this new strain of magic ..." As he faced his father again he shook his head in frustration. "Will it ever stop, Father?" Conloach regarded him solemnly.

"I sincerely hope so, Fox. For all our sakes." He paused. "And especially Sapphire's." Fox raised his hand to stop him from speaking further.

"I need a drink before this conversation continues," he said. Wolf raised an eyebrow, looked at Conloach with an expression of apology, and said,

"My lord, I will take the prisoner to Calafia if you wish." Conloach shook his head and watched Fox disappear into his kitchen.

His son was clearly struggling with what had transpired. Conloach had felt the shift in energy as soon as Sapphire had unleased her magic on Hecta. He had just woken in his bedchamber when he felt the balance shift. Without any hesitation he had transported himself to his son's house to find out what had happened, and had instantly recognised the energy of Hecta in their presence. He had not needed to be in the armoury to understand what had happened between Sapphire, Fox, and the gatekeeper after that. Despite his cool, calm exterior, even Conloach was fearful of what Gabriel would do now that Hecta had reappeared and been transformed by Sapphire's wild magic.

"Thank you, Wolf. I will indeed be grateful of your help. Please saddle the horses for our return." After bowing deeply Wolf left to attend to the task his king had given him.

Fox returned with a bottle of mead and two glasses. He placed them on the table and filled both glasses. He threw his head back as he downed one glass without hesitation, then he gestured for his father to help himself.

"I will go and retrieve my wife from the armoury, Father, and be back in a moment." Conloach smiled and took the glass of mead.

"Be gentle with her, my son. She is confused right now, and needs you to be strong and calm." Fox grunted in response and disappeared once more. He sensed that this new day would be a particularly difficult one.

As he stood guard at the armoury door Bear watched his friend eat up the ground before him with his long, determined stride. Fox looked calmer than when he had left, but he knew the guardian well enough to know that emotion twisted in his chest and ate at his heart.

"Step aside, Bear," Fox growled. Bear sighed heavily, but stepped aside as commanded. He knew better than to argue at this point. After pushing open the heavy wooden door Fox entered the armoury and stood at the entrance. His eyes pierced through the man who was still chained in the middle of the room. His wife stood to one side looking gloriously powerful, sensuous, and fragile all at once. His heart constricted painfully in his chest.

"My father is here, Sapphire." Her eyes glistened, the pupils wide and dark black. She almost glowed in the soft light of dawn that filtered down from the hole she had blasted through his armoury roof.

"Good. I want him to take Hecta back to the castle and keep him safely locked up there until we know more about his transformation." He nodded and looked back at the gatekeeper. Hecta now hung his head low, and was unable to make eye contact.

"Mmmh ... more than he deserves. But yes, my father will keep him safe for now." Sapphire was suddenly standing before him with her chest pressed against him and her hands on his forearms.

"I love you, Fox," she whispered softly. He sighed deeply as he pulled her closer and pressed his lips against her hair.

"And I you, my love," he whispered in return, suddenly feeling as if his world had returned to the correct position on its axis. "We will need to return to the castle with him." She looked up at him. Her magic was flickering against his skin softly with an insistence that made his head spin.

"I know," she said gently. Fox regarded her solemnly.

"He will also help you control this magic that is consuming you, Sapphire. It is still unstable, and we need to contain it before you hurt yourself." His voice was low, but she felt the urgency within his words. She had come back to Shaka to ask Conloach his opinion of the crystal flower, and now she was faced with several other dilemmas. What should she do with Hecta? And what should she do with this new magic that flowed through her body like a young colt waiting to spring free from its paddock and run wild in the night? Everything was crazy and dreamlike again. Nothing was easy or straightforward any more ... same old, same old.

Fox moved her aside, and walked towards Hecta with purpose to his stride.

"You will be taken to the cells at my father's castle, Hecta. I hope for your sake that you are not leading us into a trap with Gabriel." Hecta looked up and blinked slowly.

"Please take Sapphire away from here, Fox. She is not safe on Shaka any more. I do not care what happens to me now." Fox frowned.

"That I find hard to believe, Gatekeeper. You are suddenly given a new life, and do not care what happens to it? And as for your new-found interest in my wife's safety ... save it for someone who actually believes in your sincerity." Hecta actually looked hurt, but lowered his gaze to the floor again and remained silent.

While raising his arms above his head Fox began to chant once more to surround the man before him with the protection spell that would bind his magic safely behind its magical shield. Sapphire watched him from the doorway. She was feeling uneasy at Hecta's words of caution regarding her safety on Shaka. She was also thinking that the protection shield was a little bit of overkill. Right now Hecta looked as if he would have difficulty hurting a fly – let alone her husband, who could possibly flatten any warrior with his angry expression.

They left the armoury together so that they could gather the seeds and some supplies for the trip to Calafia. Conloach greeted Sapphire in the hallway with a thin smile and a slight nod of his head before disappearing with Wolf to take Hecta away with them.

After stuffing her clothes into a bag as quickly as she could Sapphire found the seeds and the essence and wrapped them inside the bundle to keep them safe. Kit was downstairs with Fox, gathering other supplies that they may need for the time they would spend at the castle. She had intended to only stay on Shaka a short while, and now it looked as if they would be stuck there while Hecta and Gabriel were dealt with.

The thought of having to deal with the master of gatekeepers in any manner at all made Sapphire shiver. She knew nothing of this man, except that he was potentially very dangerous and very powerful. Ebony was gone and had been immediately replaced by another threat – a fact that was not lost on Sapphire.

She longed to go back to the time when she had been just a regular human who worked as a barista in a coffee shop and had fun in the pub with her friends. Being ignorant to the world of magic had been, at that time, a state of bliss. But then, as Pearl had gently reminded her at the beginning of her journey, she would not have met her husband or been fulfilled as a person. She pondered for a moment on the thought before shaking her head in dismissal and running back down the stairs.

Kit hugged her hard before they left. Her face showed all her fraught emotions as plainly as a child who had lost its favourite toy. Fox had already saddled Midnight and Amber and brought them around to the front of the house. They would ride to Calafia rather than transport themselves by magic. Conloach had advised Fox that any more ripples of magic coming from their home would just alert Gabriel to the fact that they were now smuggling his best spy to his prison cells, and that would not be a very good idea at all. Sapphire was surprised he had not just turned up and blasted them all into another dimension already. But then what did she know about his abilities to sense changes within her magic or that of his servant Hecta?

Fox looked decidedly nervous as they mounted the horses and took off at a canter. Bear would follow them shortly, after he had secured the house and made sure Kit was safe.

As the sun rose above the horizon and the new day began Sapphire felt the cold grip of fear as a band across her chest. Would Pearl, Charlie, and Nathan be safe back on Earth now that she had poked the proverbial hornets' nest here on Shaka? Hecta had been able to follow her to Earth and cause harm to her loved ones in his previous life. Would Gabriel choose to do the same?

The dust from the road billowed around her as Midnight cantered ahead of her, which made her eyes water and her mouth dry. Fox had two swords strapped to his back, and his hair was flying behind him like a banner. She remembered the battle with Ebony and the sight of him flying across the landscape with the same two swords on his back.

Déjà vu was a cruel thing sometimes. One thing she knew for sure was that she needed to master the power of her new magic quickly and efficiently so that she could protect them all. This thought alone was the most terrifying.

As he reached for his glass of wine Gabriel smiled. He had sensed a change in the balance of magic this morning which indicated that Sapphire had lost her temper. It amused him that he could now feel her emotions quite easily, as he had been fine-tuning his magic so that he could literally pick up on her unique vibration. Tracking her was also fairly easy although he had found it harder at certain times, when he assumed she had been dream travelling and gone beyond even his reach. She was a magnificent mystery to him, and something he wanted to learn more about.

Conloach had been shielding her when he had at last met her at his castle, and her guardian was linked so strongly to her that the signals had been somewhat distorted. However, with Hecta's help, he now knew that she was more powerful and – more importantly – more dangerous than anything he had ever seen before. When Hecta had told him of Ebony's interest in the dream traveller, and how she had met such an unfortunate end as a result of Sapphire's magic, he had used his wisdom rather than his impulse and stepped back for a while. He did not want to frighten her off and lose her forever. The fact that she held something magical of great importance at her home with Fox made him even more eager to learn more of her existence.

Dream travellers were rare, and his job of controlling the gatekeepers had always been easy in the past. But now this wonderfully new – half human and half magical – creature had emerged, life had quite suddenly become more interesting.

The last time he had been this entertained had been many lifetimes ago. He closed his eyes for a second while savouring the wine and remembered his time with Pearl, when they had lived together there on Shaka as a young couple so consumed with love and fledgling magic that he had lost himself for a while. He could not believe that she had reincarnated on Earth. He had thought she was lost to him, and that the dream he had of ever seeing her again was long gone.

Finding the obsidian necklace tied around Sapphire's neck had thrown him for a moment, as he had recognised Pearl's signature magic immediately. But it had made absolutely no sense to him at all, until Sapphire had confirmed it was indeed from his long-lost love. He had not visited Earth for eons for many reasons. It was a place where the magic had fled deep within its womb again and, as far as he was concerned, the inhabitants were reckless, unworthy, and pathetic. Why Pearl would choose to incarnate there was beyond him. But he would see her again, that was certain ... especially now that Sapphire was part of the equation.

Gabriel thought that Hecta should be back by now, and as he sipped his wine he felt a flicker of annoyance that he had disappeared for so long without sending him word of his whereabouts. It was unfortunate that, now Hecta was without magic and merely a shell that moved around by pure necromancy, he could not track his whereabouts. But he knew the gatekeeper was fearful of him, and that power alone would keep him on a tight leash.

He walked out into his gardens and strolled casually across the grass to his lush herb garden where he breathed in the many strong scents, which held fond memories of his time with Pearl. She had always been the instigator when it came to planting and nurturing the herbs and flowers in his life. Her natural magical ability to grow healing herbs and to create an abundant garden had stayed with him as a memory he had held dear throughout his long life.

She had been the first and only woman who he had ever loved, and the sweetness of her nature had been his undoing. Losing her so young to a fever that he had not been able to cure had destroyed him for a long time. But he had never forgotten her, and had hoped and waited many lifetimes for her return. It had never happened, and he had given up hope until now.

His eyes flashed with excitement at the thought of seeing her again and finding out what her connection was to this strange new dream traveller. Perhaps he could bring her back to Shaka again and find happiness once more. But, as he realised that she was now mostly human and that this would not be possible, his anger returned. He had been cheated of such blessings, and the goddess had withdrawn love from his life when she had taken Pearl from him the first time.

Perhaps the magic Sapphire held within her would be the key to all this. Ebony had coveted its power, and had lost her life in the battle to take it. He would not make the same mistake but would find a way, if he could, to learn more of its unique potential. Conloach and Fox would be unwanted obstacles, of course, but he knew that if he was clever and cautious they would not stand in his way. It was only a matter of time before he understood the nature of Sapphire, and why she was being gifted by the goddess herself with such power.

The sun was high in the sky, indicating that it was close to midday and that he needed to find Hecta. He turned back to the house and shouted for his servant and for food to be brought to him. He would send out his other minions to find the gatekeeper, and would meditate for a while before he made his next step towards attaining his goal. This thought alone was soothing to his cold, hardened soul.

Chapter Twenty-Five

While standing at the bottom of her garden Pearl hummed to herself softly as she tended to her herbs and picked the ones she needed for her latest remedies. It was a bright sunny day, and the cool air was refreshing and a welcome relief after being holed up in her cottage for the last few days. She knew that Sapphire and Fox had returned to Shaka, and that for the time being they did not need her.

Her dreams the night before had been a strange mixture of faces and images that she could not quite place, and it had unsettled her somewhat. She sensed something brewing on the cool air that made her skin tingle and her mind swim with an edge of uncertainty. So much had changed for Sapphire and, after seeing her with the crystal flower and the ring that she had brought to Foxglove, her usual state of trust in the universe that all would be well was a little shaken. She had reassured Sapphire that she should trust her own instincts and step forward with her mission to help awaken their Mother and start the chain reaction of new consciousness for their fellow humans. But at what cost?

Her inner peace was most definitely on a tilt today and despite the normality of collecting her herbs and wandering around her beautiful garden she felt, for the first time in a very long time, a little fearful. As she bent down to tackle a particularly large sprig of rosemary that was growing out of control she felt a shift in the energy outside her stone wall. After standing upright again she looked out across her herb beds and towards the woodland at the back of her land. By straining her eyes she tried to take focus on the shape that was shimmering in the sunlight behind her boundary. It was like a vision in silver. Tall and luminous, it sparkled against the backdrop of the dark green trees.

Her breath caught in her throat as she realised that the vision was actually a person, who was standing perfectly still like an angel in the flesh just outside the perimeter of her land. Her feet began to move of their own accord, and took her closer to the stone wall and to the stranger standing close to its edge.

As she reached the wall her eyes widened in surprise at the figure before her. A man so breathtakingly beautiful, with the longest white-blonde hair that hung almost to the floor in a perfect braid, stood with his eyes closed before her. He shimmered in the light, and his energy was a perfect rainbow of colours that scattered across the grass like a prism of light.

As she reached the wall and placed her hands on the cool stone he opened his eyes and looked directly at her. They were the most brilliant ice blue, with dark black circles surrounding the irises. They flashed at her with sparks of silver, and seemed to cast flickers of what looked like snowflakes within them. He smiled at her peacefully, a serene smile that had an edge of decadent wickedness to its edges.

Her stomach flipped and a gasp escaped her lips. This man was made from magic, and he was standing at the edge of her garden as if he belonged there. Her body suddenly became obstinately stuck in this position, with her hands gripping the stone wall and her heart thumping in her chest. Had she finally gone completely and utterly mad? Or was this actually happening? As if he knew she needed confirmation of this disturbing thought he stepped forward. In fact he seemed to glide across the grass without even moving his legs. With the smile still on his lips he dipped his head at her in acknowledgement.

"Hello, Pearl," he said. Her own legs went a little weak, and she could feel her mouth open in awe. "You are still beautiful, my love ... somewhat changed in your appearance, but your essence has not changed. It is so good to see you again."

A strange sensation, an emotion and a feeling that had been long lost, which she had not felt in a very long time, began to uncurl from within Pearl's belly. The instant recognition of a pure and unbridled passion and love, which could only be one thing ... the sweet and undisputable love of a soulmate. She felt it in her heart and in her mind, and it made her body crave its touch so badly she felt almost faint with the thought that it had returned to her once again after such a long, long time.

Gabriel held the vision strongly as he meditated, and cast his image to Pearl as she was standing in her garden on Earth. While he had been meditating in his garden he had been casting his magic wide and far to find Hecta and Sapphire, and had somehow miraculously stumbled across Pearl instead. She had actually been the last person in his mind before he had sat down to meditate, and he guessed that was how he had found her. Pearl had always told him that he should be careful what he thought about, as "thoughts become things."

He had felt her familiar magic instantly as she had walked towards him, and although his body was firmly planted back on Shaka his energy was projected via his powerful magic to her back on Earth. The expression on her face told him that she now recognised him, and the exquisite sensation of her linking into this memory made his heart swell and his mind spin. He had not realised just how much he had missed her until he had seen her again.

An old woman stood before him now, but she was still the same beautiful creature who he had fallen in love with so long ago. Her magic was much weaker now, but it remained as unique and individual as it had been when she had lived here with him on his magical world. Her eyes were exactly the same, and sparkled with the intensity he remembered when they were young and connected in every way possible. He knew that he could not hold the vision for long, and that in the meditative state he was in the magic would fold very quickly if she wanted it to.

As he pressed further into her world he moved closer to her, desperate to touch her. Her body was trembling now and her mouth opened as if to speak, but no words came forth. His magic made contact with the powerful wards surrounding her property just as he reached out to touch her, and the connection shattered – which left him breathing hard and fast back on Shaka in his own garden. Damn it. He had been so close.

Pearl stepped back from the stone wall. Her legs were almost giving way beneath her. With her hands trembling and her heart fluttering wildly in her chest she felt a gust of air against her cheek as one of the sprites came flying into her hair. It was chattering with fear as it tangled itself in her greying locks. Patting it gently she tried to ground herself again.

"There, there, my friend. All is well. Stop stressing. Everything is OK." She could not quite believe what she had seen, but knew the vision before her had in fact been a projection of someone so strong with magic that it had triggered a memory long forgotten in her mind. This magnificent magical man was someone she knew very well, and someone she had been utterly and profoundly in love with.

She could remember now a time spent in absolute happiness and bliss on a world far away, a world that Sapphire was now connected to and currently on. And this man was, without a doubt, the very same person who Sapphire had quizzed her about when she had showed her the ring. Gabriel, the master of all gatekeepers, had found her at last. The implications of that, despite the happiness that now flooded her heart, could mean only one thing: a complete disaster for her and for her sweet wonderful friend, the dream traveller.

"Oh dear," Pearl said aloud before picking up her herbs and heading back inside the cottage to make herself a calming fruit tea. "This really could be a bother." She smiled to herself as she placed the herbs on her kitchen table. "He still thinks I am beautiful. How wonderful." The sprite clinging to her hair pinched her neck painfully, scolding her for her whimsical statement.

"Ouch! That was unnecessary, my little friend," she said to the sprite. "I am not losing my head over him, silly." The sprite released itself from her hair and flew off, blowing raspberries as it did. They were overly jealous creatures at the best of times. But, sadly, she knew the tiny creature was only trying to protect her and to bring her back to the cold facts of her reality. The love that she had shared with Gabriel had been in another time and on another world and had long gone. The thought that she could ever have that with him again was stupid and dangerous. Very dangerous.

Fox paced the floor in the cell he had now found Hecta to be occupying. Despite his father's insistence that it would be best for him to stay away from the gatekeeper he had felt the uncontrollable urge to track him down and beat him to a pulp, and could not stay away. Sapphire, having said that he was acting like a child again, had given up trying to restrain him from the mission he was on. Once more Hecta had caused them to fight, and that pissed him off even more.

Hecta watched him pace from the stone slab he was sitting on in the corner of the cell. His arms were wrapped around his body protectively, and his eyes were downcast in fear of upsetting the guardian any further than he already had.

"You are lucky that my wife is so forgiving, Gatekeeper," Fox said. "Now that we know you are working with Gabriel and your miserable life has only been given back to you by the good grace of my wife's magic, I really have no reason to keep you alive." Hecta hugged his body tighter. He felt weak and intimidated by the man prowling like a wild animal before him. Another man stood outside the cell with his back to them, the man who was as black as the night and called himself Wolf. He said nothing, but remained utterly still as he stood guard outside the iron gate of the cell.

"I mean no harm to your wife, Fox. Believe me, I am nothing but grateful to her and will do whatever you wish to keep her safe." Fox stopped his pacing and, his face wild with anger, faced Hecta.

"You will do nothing but stay here and rot if I have anything to do with it, Hecta. You abused her time and time again when you took her magic when it was not given freely. I should knock your teeth out right now and shove them in a place where the sun does not shine." He heard Wolf snigger behind him, but his anger was too acute to see the funny side of what he had just said. Hecta shuffled further away from him.

"Please, Fox, just take Sapphire back to Earth and hide her. Gabriel knows she holds something of great importance and that her magic has grown tenfold. He will take it from her just as Ebony wished to, and destroy the amazing gift she now processes." Wolf turned around slowly, opened the cell door, and stepped inside slowly.

"Fox, my friend, I think it would be best for you to keep away from this man. He does nothing but rattle your cage." Fox regarded him angrily.

"I want to smash his skull, Wolf." The huge black man raised a brow and placed his hand on his friend's shoulder.

"As do we all, my friend, but now is not the time and place. Your wife needs you, and you are wasting valuable time in this cell with a man who does not deserve your time or energy." A glimmer of acceptance flashed across Fox's expression, and he nodded and turned away from Hecta with a loud groan of frustration.

Fox left the cell and strode back up the narrow stairway to his father's chamber, where he had left Sapphire. She would not be happy with him, but he had needed to vent his anger at the man who had persistently caused him pain and grief throughout his life as a guardian. But as he ran up the stairs two steps at a time he realised that the man he had left behind was no longer the same. It made him twice as mad. At least the old Hecta would have put up a fight, and they could have had it out man to man. The creature he had left behind in the cell was pitiful and pathetic.

He needed to calm down before he saw Sapphire again. He headed to the kitchens instead of his father's chambers and searched for a bottle of mead to take the edge off his anger. He was turning into a complete wreck, and he knew it was a combination of the wild magic Sapphire had running through her veins – which he was connected to – and his intense frustration at this impossible situation they were now in. He grabbed a bottle, flicked off the lid, and took a large swig straight from the bottle.

"Fuck this," he said, swearing loudly before disappearing out into the courtyard to demolish the rest of the contents.

While standing next to the fireplace Sapphire looked across at her father-in-law with a look of sadness on her face.

"Fox has lost it, Conloach. I cannot control him now Hecta is back again." Conloach was sitting opposite her, a picture of serenity, in his throne-like chair. She envied him for his ability to remain calm no matter what the situation was.

"My son has always had a temper, Sapphire. You have just not known him long enough to see it in its full magnificence." He paused and watched the expression of exasperation cross her features. "Allow him time to release his frustrations and he will come back to you again as the man you know to be strong and sure. His relationship with Hecta has been long and tiresome, and their rivalry has always been turbulent throughout their journey as guardian and gatekeeper from the moment it was bestowed upon them.

"They have always been connected in this way, and it angers Fox that he has no choice in the matter. Such is the path of the gatekeepers and the guardians. They have been linked together for as long as time can remember, playing different roles but often with the same purpose. Sometimes they forget that fact, and it becomes an unnecessary tussle across time and space." Sapphire sighed.

"Mmmh, I'm finally beginning to understand that." Conloach stood up and walked towards her.

"In the meantime, daughter, you and I must work out a way to control your new magic and train you to master its power. If we are to have any chance at holding back Gabriel and helping you on your journey with the seeds back on Earth we must do this." As he stood directly before her Sapphire felt his familiar magic uncurl and embrace her as it sent warm, soothing pulses to her chest, which was painfully tight. She looked down at the floor and shook her head slowly.

"Am I even capable of such control, Conloach?" He reached for her and slowly pulled her into his arms so that she was flat against his chest. His body was warm and his scent was strong with patchouli and sandalwood, just like her husband's. It felt so good and so very safe.

"I have absolutely no doubt of that, Sapphire. I have never underestimated your ability to adapt and embrace the magic that has been gifted to you. You must believe it yourself, however, to truly gain control." While letting her body relax she hugged him back and allowed him to hold her gently, which soothed the troubled, skittering feeling inside her belly. Thank God that at least this man was still thinking straight.

"I came here to talk to you about the crystal flower, and now this has happened. I just wish everything would slow down, Conloach, just for a moment, so I can at least catch my breath." He chuckled softly, and the vibration travelled through her head.

"The goddess sees time and motion differently from us, daughter. She has no understanding of a fast or slow pace. She understands only, with absolute certainty, that we can handle the tasks we are given by her." Sapphire looked up at him into the eyes that were now so familiar to her.

"Well, she must be crazy to think that I can cope with all this at once, Conloach, that's for sure." After releasing her he smiled and gestured for her to sit.

"We are only given the things in this lifetime that we are capable of handling. And you, my dear daughter, are very apt at handling the gravest of situations. You have already proven this time and time again." She laughed and slumped down in the chair.

"Both you and Fox have very high opinions of my capabilities, Conloach. I, on the other hand, still feel like a child floundering around in the dark, and have no clue as to what I'm doing." He shook his head, reached for the wine on his table, and poured them both a glass.

"Look at how far you have come, Sapphire. Just think about how strong you have grown and how much you have taken on board in such a short space of time. Surely by now you trust the fact that you are a very gifted woman ... a dream traveller extraordinaire, who can handle even a king and his son in the most amusing and delightful manner."

Sapphire smiled. He had a point. She did manage to handle them both, and certainly didn't take any shit from either of them. Perhaps she was stronger than she realised, and perhaps Conloach was right. It was time to embrace the wild magic flowing within her veins, stop being afraid of every shadow or magical creature that appeared at her doorstep, and start showing them all who was boss. As he passed her the glass of wine Conloach regarded her with a wry smile.

"You will be more magnificent and powerful than even me, young lady. And that really is quite a feat."

As Fox stumbled across the courtyard he crashed awkwardly into a pile of wooden barrels that were placed against the wall. He cursed loudly and pushed himself upright again – straight into the huge, hulking form of his friend.

"Ah, Fox ... I see you have found some peace in the bottom of this bottle of mead, my friend." Bear steadied his friend who, despite the fact that it was only late morning, was well and truly inebriated. "Let's get you upstairs and into a better state, eh?" Fox narrowed his eyes at the man before him. His head was thumping loudly in protest at the brightness of the sun – which was, most inconveniently, shining directly into his eyes.

"I do not need your help, Bear. Leave me be." Bear grabbed him by the forearms and pulled him upright. Fox's legs had started to buckle like a young foal beneath him, which made him look like a puppet that had just lost its strings.

"I think you do, my friend, and I know just the way to sober you up before we get you back up to your wife and father again." After dragging him across the courtyard (and in front of a small group of curious servants) Bear held his friend by the scruff of his waistcoat with one hand and then scooped a bucket of cold water from the horse trough with another.

Before Fox could react to his imminent soaking Bear tipped the entire contents over his head while holding him at arm's length so that he himself would not get wet. A string of obscene words flew from Fox's mouth as the water drenched him. His hair was dripping wet, and his skin glistened in the sunlight.

The icy cold water brought Fox back to reality and he gasped for air. He shook his head as he realised just how stupid he had been in drowning his sorrows and anger in the two bottles of mead he had found in the kitchen. He had no idea what time it was or how long he had been gone after his visit to Hecta in the cells. Sapphire was no doubt livid by now that he had stormed off and left her with his father. Fuck. How could he lose control so easily over such a pathetic man?

But as he faced Bear, who grinned at him with a knowing look, he knew exactly why he had done such a reckless thing, which was also so out of character. Love. His love for Sapphire and his hatred for Hecta had pushed him over the edge.

Drinking like that was something that he had not done for a very long time. He had naively thought that Hecta had been removed from his life once and for all, and that the threat the guardian had placed over his wife for so long had been eradicated for good. How stupid he had been to let down his guard and not even sense that the gatekeeper had been back on Shaka, his home planet, again. He had become so wrapped up in following Sapphire around with her seeds back on Earth that he had not been astute enough to realise that Gabriel had been manipulating him. He vowed that he would not make this mistake again, and was grateful that his friend had pulled him out of his drunken stupor with the short, sharp shock treatment. Bear regarded him with a patient smile.

"Better, my friend?" Fox slicked his hair back and flicked the water from his fingers with a nod of his head.

"Yes. Thank you, Bear. As always you know me too well, and how to kick my sorry arse back into action." The servants had scuttled off to continue their chores now the show was over. Bear threw his arm around Fox's shoulder and thumped him heartily on the back.

"Come, let's get you back upstairs to your father's chamber. I am sure that he will be waiting for you with Sapphire, and will give you another good kick to bring you back to your senses." Fox sighed heavily. He knew that his momentary slip into an alcohol-induced stupor had done nothing but give him a blinding headache, but at least it had stopped him from ripping someone else's head off and causing even more problems.

"When did you get here?" he asked Bear. As they walked back inside the castle and up the staircase to Conloach's chambers Bear laughed.

"Some time ago, my friend. But Wolf told me you had left Hecta's cell over an hour ago in a foul mood, so I thought it best to leave you for a while until time pressed on ... and I found you in the courtyard, falling about like a fool." Fox shook his head slowly. The action caused his skull to pound even more.

"I haven't lost my temper like that in years, Bear. I needed to switch everything off for a moment." Bear's laughter bounced off the stone walls, which made Fox cringe slightly. The headache was in full swing now.

"And the amber nectar is so good at doing just that, my friend. But the result is somewhat painful, I see." Fox grumbled under his breath.

"Ice-cold water heightened the effect of the comedown somewhat, Bear."

They reached the huge wooden door of Conloach's chamber, and Bear paused and looked at his dishevelled friend with amusement.

"Ah, but it did the trick, didn't it? Are you ready to face the music?" Fox frowned and pushed the door open angrily. As he stepped inside he felt the full force of his wife's mood, which was a mixture of relief and agitation. She was sitting in the chair next to the open fire with her eyes sparkling a brilliant blue. Her magic surrounded her in soft waves of purple and silver, and it filled the room with the added scent of jasmine and roses.

It took his breath away. He stopped dead in his tracks and made Bear bump into him from behind. Conloach stood next to her with his back to the door. It looked as though they had been in a deep conversation. Sapphire licked her bottom lip before speaking, and the action made Fox tremble slightly in response.

"You look like shit, Fox. Where the hell have you been?" Bear laughed loudly and thumped him on the back again as he walked around him and headed towards the long wooden table in the middle of the room.

"I just love your wife, Fox," he said. "She really is priceless." Conloach turned and looked at them both with an expression of disdain. Bear bowed deeply at the waist.

"I found him in the courtyard somewhat the worse for wear, Sapphire. My king, is there anything else I can do for you?" Fox watched his father move towards him waiting for his reprimand.

"No, Bear, thank you. That will be all." Bear winked at Sapphire, who tried to repress her smile as he turned and left the room again. Fox rolled his eyes at his friend as he walked past him. Conloach walked towards him slowly. Fox could tell from the magic surrounding him that he was not amused.

"Now that you have finished behaving like an idiot adolescent, my son, I need you to focus and listen to what I am about to tell you." Fox looked across at Sapphire, who looked undoubtedly entertained and seemed to be repressing a giggle. He felt like a rebuked child, which made his head thump louder and his anger flare hotly in his chest again. After looking up at the ceiling and running both his hands through his wet hair he sucked in a breath and regained control. He faced them both again and straightened his shoulders.

"Yes, Father," he said. Conloach raised a brow and dipped his head in acknowledgement that Fox had at last found his sense again.

"Hecta will remain in my cells and under the guard of Wolf and my garrison while I take Sapphire and you with me to the Oracle. We will ask her opinion of your crystal flower, and the reaction Sapphire's human friend had on having made contact with it." He paused while watching Fox's body language, which had stiffened on reaction to his statement.

"And then I will begin training your wife on how to master this new strain of wild magic she has been gifted with, and help you control the reactions you have to it. Once this has happened we may have some chance of defending ourselves against any action Gabriel chooses to take once he realises we have his gatekeeper and are no longer in the dark with regard to his intentions towards your wife."

Fox looked at Sapphire, who sat calmly in the chair with her lips parted slightly and her cheeks flushed. She looked so very beautiful and so very powerful as she sat like a queen in his father's chair. He realised at that moment, when he saw his father standing all-powerful before him and his wife directly behind him, that he had no other choice. She had stepped so far up in the magical realm that his own power now seemed insignificant, and if he had any chance of remaining her guardian he damn well needed to step up to the mark and stop fucking around.

As he flexed his shoulders he faced them both with a new determination. His headache reminded him just how lucky he was that his father and wife were so forgiving of his weaknesses and were able to overlook his behaviour that morning. He was a guardian and he was a warrior. He needed to prove it to both of them.

"When do we leave?" he asked, his voice deep and dark with emotion. Conloach allowed a thin smile to grace his lips.

"Once you have cleaned yourself up and cleared your head, my son. Now take yourself and your wife to the guest chambers and prepare to leave within the hour." Fox nodded slowly. He needed to find something to stop the persistent pounding in his head before they left, and hoped that Willow was in residence at the castle today.

"Yes, Father." Sapphire stood up slowly and smiled at him.

"Thank you, Conloach. I feel much better now we have had a chat." He regarded her calmly, and his smile grew as she placed her hand on his arm and reached up to place a chaste kiss on his cheek. Fox relaxed slightly. She found the whole thing amusing, he could tell, and for once it was him being chastised and not her.

They left his father's chamber silently and headed up to the guest rooms, with Sapphire taking his hand and interlacing her fingers within his own without saying a word. Her newly acquired scent, which was strong within his nostrils, only added to the sensation of feeling overpowered by her. But he knew that she had accepted his moment of frustration as calmly as he would have done had it been the other way around. The thought soothed his anger and heightened his determination to never let her down again. Hecta would not come between them ever again, and with the help of the Oracle and his father they would become a force to be reckoned with.

This fact he now felt within his bones. Strongly and surely.

Chapter Twenty-Six

"How's the headache now?" Sapphire asked her husband with a grin. Fox had just swallowed the last of the bubbling potion Willow had kindly brought up to the guest chamber, and was grimacing slightly at the obvious bitterness of the tonic. He shook his head and smiled.

"Gone," he replied. She laughed softly and continued to check the contents of her bag, making sure the seeds and other items they had brought with them to the castle earlier were still safely inside.

"That stuff would make a serious killing back on Earth if it worked that quickly there," she said. Fox stretched his arms above his head and leant back slightly, allowing his body to stretch out the last remaining knots of tension he had collected back in the cells when he had lost his temper with Hecta. Sapphire watched him with her lips parted slightly. The bottom of his shirt had lifted slightly as he stretched, revealing his flat stomach and happy trail ... always a pleasure to see.

"Thankfully Willow keeps a large supply of the potion here at the castle, as it is often needed by the soldiers. I doubt very much that she would be keen for me to expose its content to the people of Earth, for fear it would blow their heads off." Sapphire laughed.

"That strong, eh?" she remarked. Fox kicked his boots off and began to unbutton his trousers. Sapphire watched him with her eyes narrowing with confusion. "What are you doing?" she asked. After lifting his shirt off and stepping out of his trousers he stood naked before her, which created a warm flush to spread like a feather's touch across her neck.

"I need to bathe, Sapphire ... clean myself up, as Father requested." He smiled mischievously. "Would you care to join me?" Despite the insistent sexual tension – that seemed to be a permanent fixture when they were around each other – which was now pushing at her buttons she shook her head.

"I don't think that would be a good idea right now, Fox. We will never get to see the Oracle if I join you, and I doubt that your father would be willing to wait much longer for us than he already has."

While walking towards her slowly, with a crooked smile on his lips, Fox tipped his head to one side as he reached for her cheek. He ran a finger across her skin down to the pulse that was flickering – because of his touch – on her neck, and leant in closer.

"Are you sure?" Her magic began to ignite, and again created the strange symbols that she had noticed earlier – which started flashing under her skin again. Fox looked down at her arm and licked his lips, suddenly aware that she was pulsing like a neon bulb again.

The heat being generated between them became overwhelming, and Sapphire gasped as Fox's body responded quickly and urgently before her. He closed his eyes, stepped back slightly, and groaned.

"Actually you are probably right, my love. I will take a cold shower, and we can be on our way." She could feel the tension, tight and coiled, in his body. It looked painful. They really needed to get this under control. It would be totally unfair, and a little embarrassing, if Fox kept standing to attention every time he was near her.

She stifled a giggle as he turned around and headed for the bathroom. His gait was awkward, and he walked with a slight limp. She slumped down on the bed and breathed out heavily. The heat of the new magic in her veins was starting to make her feel uncomfortable, and she wished she could jump under the shower with Fox to cool herself down.

As she closed her eyes she heard the water running in the room next door and visualised that she was standing under the cool water with her husband. Her body temperature began to drop instantly. She could also sense Fox regaining his balance once more, and smiled. Perhaps it wouldn't be as hard as she thought to control this wild magic, and perhaps it just required a certain degree of concentration and thought on her part to create her own sense of equilibrium again.

Pearl had taught her how to control the magic she had when she had first come into her power through meditation, and Fox had helped her to visualise and create when they had come back to Shaka the first time. Conloach's suggestion, that with his help and that of the Oracle she could master this wild and as yet unknown strain of new magic, was most definitely the best plan of all.

Her mind wandered to Hecta, and how at this very moment he was sitting broken and fearful in the cells below them. She could see him, in her head, looking at her with sad, deep brown eyes. All remnants of the man he once was had been removed. What would become of him now? How quickly would Gabriel realise that he was no longer under his control and was a creature who had been reborn and changed by the power of her own magic?

She shivered and opened her eyes again to find Fox standing before her, dressed once more. His hair was wet and glistening with water droplets that sparkled against the gems threaded through his dreadlocks and braids. He was smiling at her again. His energy was calm once more. The spangled edges had been removed and his passion, for now, was well and truly restrained in his leather trousers.

"Let's go, my love," he said. "The sooner we see the Oracle and learn how to control your new magic the better."

They left the castle with Conloach on their horses shortly after, leaving Wolf, Bear, and a large number of the guard on the watch for any signs of Gabriel. As they cantered off towards the Oracle's residence Sapphire could not help but feel that the master of gatekeepers already knew Hecta was being kept prisoner within the castle walls, and that he was just biding his time before making a move.

She was desperate to get back to Earth and check that Pearl, Charlie, and Nathan were all still safe, but knew that this next part of her journey needed to be completed. The seeds and the crystal flower, along with the essence and the dirt she had received back on Earth, were all inside the bag strapped across her back. She could hear them singing to her softly, like small children happy to be connected to her energy and alive with mischief and playfulness.

As they grew closer to the beautiful crystal building that housed the Oracle and her priestesses Sapphire could feel them grow more persistent as they clamoured for her attention. Their song was louder, and their thrum of power stronger. It was if they knew they were going to meet someone they recognised as one of their own. She wished she could hand them all over to her guardian angel and ask her to take care of the job she had begun.

On reaching the boundary of the Oracle's home Sapphire felt the magic surrounding the land swell and pulse against her, which made her heart jump in her chest. She had no doubt whatsoever that the

Oracle knew they had arrived, and that what she was carrying with her was something unique and possibly very dangerous. It was highly unlikely, therefore, that she could give Sapphire her wish and take the burden from her. That was wishful thinking on her part.

Fox pulled Midnight to a sharp halt before her and swung him around quickly.

"We dismount here, my love. The guards may see us as a threat if we come charging in on our horses." Conloach had already begun to dismount his huge white horse, which stamped and snorted with impatience to keep moving.

"I think she knows we are here, Fox. But, if it makes you feel better, of course," Sapphire said. Fox jumped from his horse with animal-like grace and grabbed Amber's reins as she pulled her to a stop.

"It is just a precaution. I do not like to antagonise her guards," Fox replied. Conloach stood silently next to them, looking at the beautiful crystal building in the near distance with a thoughtful expression.

"You are right, Sapphire. She is waiting for us. But it is wise to walk from here, as Fox suggests, as her guards will no doubt be wary that all three of us are here at the same time." Sapphire nodded as she slipped down into her husband's arms.

"OK. Let's go and get this over with," she said. As they walked with the horses towards the flickering light of the crystal building Sapphire could feel the energy building between the three of them and wondered just how they must look to anyone watching them approach. They were three intensely powerful creatures moving across the landscape in a wave of new magic that was calling loudly now to the woman sheltered within the protection of her home. No wonder Fox was being cautious. She, for one, would be terrified at the sight of them if she knew no better.

There were at least ten warriors standing guard at the entrance of the crystal building when they reached the gates that allowed them access to the Oracle's home. Sapphire held her breath as the warriors stepped forward in unison with their swords held at the ready and their armour glistening in the sunlight. She could feel the energy, strong and powerful, surrounding them in a defensive stance that pushed back against her own magic.

Conloach motioned for her and Fox to remain back as he moved forward slowly.

"Warriors of the Oracle," he said, "we come in peace, and ask for audience with our most beloved priestess. I, Conloach, king of Calafia, my son, and his wife wish for safe passage into her home."

One of the warriors stepped forward. Sapphire noticed that he was at least a foot taller than the others, and the sword he carried was twice as large as those of the others.

"The Oracle is expecting you, my lord, but we ask that you leave any weapons you may be carrying with us before you enter." Sapphire raised a brow. She wasn't aware that Fox or his father were hiding any weapons. Fox looked at his father, who nodded slowly. Without saying a word Fox began to remove a couple of knives that he had on his person. One was hidden in his boot and the other was hidden up his sleeve.

Sapphire had not realised that her husband had been concealing the blades, and was a little surprised that he had even doubted his safety on this journey. It was obvious to her now that Fox was taking his role as guardian very seriously again, and the threat of Gabriel and Hecta were still clearly first and foremost on his mind. After handing the blades to the guard Fox took her hand and squeezed it reassuringly.

"You may enter, Conloach," the guard said. "The Oracle will see you in her personal chamber."

After leaving the horses with the warriors they entered the crystal building. The familiar shiver of magic touched Sapphire's skin like a soft breeze as the shield was dropped to allow them inside. Fox gripped her hand tightly. His own magic skittered again as it made contact with the intense energy that seemed to permeate the air around them.

A young girl dressed in white with long black hair waited for them at the end of the corridor. Her hands, which were clasped gently before her, gave her the appearance of a sweet and serene choirgirl. She smiled at them and dipped her head as they approached.

"Welcome, friends. The Oracle awaits you in her chambers. Please follow me." Sapphire stared at her surroundings. Although she and Fox had been to visit the Oracle before they had been presented to her in a room filled with many women, and at the time her mind had been overwhelmed by the strength of the magic within its walls. Now she could see things a little differently, and with her newly trained magical eyes the walls and ceiling seemed to move slightly as if they were breathing. It was slightly unnerving, but comforting at the same time.

The whole building was alive with something quite beautiful: a life force of its own that vibrated at a pitch so high that any creature of lesser magic would not see it. Conloach smiled at her knowingly and she smiled back. This was truly awesome. Fox, it seemed, was also aware of the high tuning of his surroundings, and was vibrating like a singing bowl. His aura was flashing with sparks of silver.

The young girl paused before a huge door which was covered in symbols that looked like writing interlaced with flowers. There was also a huge tree at the centre that covered both door frames, and its branches were heavy with fruit. Sapphire looked up in awe. It reminded her of the crystal tree she had created back in Egypt, and it gave her a sense of relief that the Oracle would understand exactly what had happened when she had planted the seed and started the new magic back on Earth.

As the door was opened and sunlight poured through the glass ceiling in the room before them Sapphire felt a massive pull within her chest and a ringing in her ears that made her gasp out loud. Blinded for a second by the light of the room, Sapphire felt disorientated for a second before she realised that they were now standing before the Oracle and the room they had entered was filled with the thick and heady scent of lush tropical flowers. The air around them was practically pulsating with magic.

Conloach knelt slowly. Fox pulled her down to her knees with him and bowed his head. She had no idea what she was supposed to do, and so followed suit. Conloach said,

"Oracle, our most beloved priestess, we come to ask for your guidance and help once more, and hope that you can help us understand the wild magic that my daughter now holds within her veins." Sapphire peeped out from under her eyelashes to see the

Oracle stretched out like a cat on a chaise longue. She was dressed in a sumptuous cloak that looked like a peacock's tail feathers, and she grinned at Sapphire with an expression of absolute excitement.

"Ah, Sapphire! How wonderful to see you again, and transformed so magnificently." She gestured with a flicker of her hand for them to stand.

"Conloach ... Fox. As always it is a pleasure to receive you in my home. Come and sit. You must be tired after your journey." Sapphire stood slowly. Her ears were still ringing and she realised with horror that the symbols under her skin were flashing again, making her look as if she was about to combust.

The Oracle tilted her head and smiled. By raising her hand she sent a shimmer of light to Sapphire and it settled against her skin like the kiss of a butterfly, gentle and sweet. The symbols retreated and her magic calmed immediately. Fox released her hand and licked his lips slowly. His eyes were dark and filled with lust again, and he was clearly having a hard time (literally) controlling himself.

Conloach coughed softly, clearly aware of his son's internal struggle. He walked towards the Oracle and sat down gracefully in one of the chairs to the side of her. He closed his eyes for a moment before speaking.

"My son is finding it difficult to be close to his wife with this new magic running wild within her body. He will need your guidance, as will Sapphire, on how they can control it." Sapphire could feel a blush spreading up her neck into her cheeks. The Oracle laughed, and the sound vibrated like birdsong around the room.

"Such strong emotion – such powerful lust – can be difficult at the best of times to control, Conloach. But I can help them, do not fear. They are merely reflecting their love for each other in the rawest form. Wild magic has this effect at the beginning, as you well know, but it is easily tamed." Fox looked across at Sapphire and a wry smile appeared on his lips.

"Thank the gods," he said. Sapphire wanted to giggle again but refrained from doing so. They stood silently in front of Conloach and the Oracle and waited for her to address them.

"And I sense that you have some items you wish to show me with you, Sapphire. I would very much like to see them." She stood up suddenly, the peacock cloak fluttering around her like a living thing and flashing blue and green as if the bird had actually materialised before them. "But for now I will bring you some refreshment and let you ground yourselves as the connecting of our energies together in this room is a little …" She paused, and the grin spread wider on her lush lips. "Overwhelming." Fox seemed to breathe a sigh of relief. Conloach nodded in agreement.

"As you wish, Oracle," Conloach said. And just like that she disappeared, and the room became still and less heady. The pulse of magic withdrew, and Sapphire felt her body reconnect with her head once more. This was going to be extremely challenging for them all. There was no doubt about that.

Sapphire looked around the room. Her eyes were gradually becoming accustomed to the brightness of the sun, which reflected off the glass and the crystals that hung from the ceiling on what looked like tiny droplets of water.

"Sit and rest for a while, Sapphire. The Oracle will call us when she wishes to see us again."

Conloach gestured to the chaise longue that the priestess had been sitting on when they had stepped into the room. Fox fidgeted beside Sapphire. It was obvious that he was trying to recover from the burst of energy they had all felt when they had entered her chamber.

"I may need to step outside for a moment, Father," he said. Conloach looked at him with amusement.

"As you wish, Fox. Try and ground yourself before you come back." Fox looked almost embarrassed, and his cheeks were slightly flushed. Sapphire actually felt sorry for him. It just wasn't fair that she was the cause of his permanent arousal. The wild magic in her was flicking him on and off like a light switch. Women could hide the fact that they were turned on. Men could not. Fox smiled at her with an apologetic shrug.

"I won't be long, my love." Sapphire, suddenly feeling weary, slumped down on to the chaise longue.

"Take your time, Fox," she said. He was gone before she could even slip off her boots.

Conloach turned slowly to face the huge doors that opened up into the gardens outside. They too were made from glass that rose from the ground up to the ceiling towering above them.

"The effect of your new magic is stronger here, Sapphire. Overwhelming, in fact. The Oracle can see this, and is no doubt adjusting her own magic before she comes near you again. Fox will need to ground properly before he can join us once more." Sapphire lifted her legs up on to the chaise longue and leant back as she stretched her body out with a sigh.

"I feel like a freak, Conloach," she said. "Even my own husband can't be near me any longer." He chuckled softly.

"Do not be hard on yourself, Sapphire. We are in the best place to adjust the vibration levels, and to do it safely." After throwing her arms over her head she tipped her head to the side and watched him walk towards the glass doors. His energy was pulsing strongly and the colours – bright blue and dark purple – swirled around him like a mini tornado. He looked suitably impressive.

"I'm not a microwave, Conloach. I don't have a power switch." He stopped at the door and placed his hands against the glass. This made it shimmer for a second before it literally dissolved beneath his fingers, and allowed the fresh air from outside to sweep into the room and fill it with the scent of apple and lemon.

"I have no idea what a microwave is, Sapphire, but let me assure you that you most certainly have a power switch." He paused and looked over his shoulder at her with a wry smile on his lips. "We just have to find it." Sapphire blushed, looked back up at the ceiling, and watched the crystals spin on the light breeze that had blown into the room. They glittered and shone as they cast mini rainbows across the floor ... dazzling.

The chamber door was opened suddenly by two women dressed in the same white attire as the young woman who had welcomed them had been. They were carrying trays of food and drink. With their faces serene and their eyes downcast they placed the trays on the table to one side of Sapphire and dipped their heads without saying a word. They left just as quickly as they had arrived, and the chamber door closed behind them with a soft thud.

Sapphire eyed the plates of food with a renewed hunger. She was indeed famished, and very thirsty. She jumped back off the chaise longue and padded to the table as she licked her lips. The food looked amazing. It was of the brightest colours and the strangest shapes and it resembled fruit and perhaps vegetables, but it was nothing like the food she had sampled so far on Shaka.

Conloach joined her at the table and began to pour water from the jug into some crystal glasses. Everything seemed to be made from glass and crystal here. Sapphire laughed as she wondered who had the immensely difficult job of washing and cleaning it all. Conloach handed her a glass.

"Take small sips, Sapphire. The water here is very special and, to some, extremely intoxicating." She laughed as she picked up what looked like an apple with her other hand.

"Oh, great. I really need something else that is going to push me into a magical orbit." As she bit a huge chunk from the apple she let out a groan as the sweetness and pure deliciousness of the fruit hit her taste buds. It was almost orgasmic. Her eyes grew wide as she savoured the fruit. It literally melted on her tongue. Conloach regarded her with a smile on his lips before taking a piece of fruit himself.

"Holy shit," she groaned again as she sipped the water. The coolness of the liquid ignited like a trail of silken vodka down her throat into her belly. Conloach laughed.

"I remember the first time I sampled food in the temple here. I too had a rather intense reaction to it." Sapphire took another bite of the apple. She closed her eyes and licked her lips while her feet tapped a happy dance on the floor.

"Intense reaction … I think that's an understatement, Conloach. I have never tasted anything like this in my life. It should have a warning label on it." Conloach laughed again, and walked back to the open doorway into the garden with his own food and drink in his hands.

"Your magic responds well here and heightens the experience, Sapphire. This is obvious. At least we know from your reaction to just the food that part of your magic gives you the ability to experience even the simple pleasures in life at a much higher state of consciousness than your average magical creature." Sapphire was feeling like a kid in a candy store. She did not know what to try next, and her body was responding in the strangest way to the fruit and water that she had just taken the smallest taste of. It scared her and thrilled her at the same time.

"With this knowledge we can work on adjusting the levels of your own magic and the way that you respond to the surroundings you are in. That way we can fine-tune your abilities." Sapphire took another piece of food. Bright green in colour, it was small and round like a tiny shell but soft and squidgy to the touch. As she popped it into her mouth she sighed heavily as her taste buds exploded again with a mixture of sweet and sour sensations that made her body tingle all over. It was like tasting chocolate for the first time and then mixing it with champagne, heroin, and sex all at once. It would be seriously addictive and quite clearly dangerous in the wrong hands, and even she was having trouble with not grabbing the entire plate and gorging on its contents like a pig.

"Sapphire, are you listening to me?" Conloach said. He was standing at the edge of the garden sipping his water, and his face was now glowing gold in the sunlight.

Sapphire felt guilty and jumped back from the table. She grabbed her water and followed him outside, away from the table of decadent, orgasmic food. She looked up at him with her face a little flushed as she swallowed the last of the piece of green fruit. Her body was shivering with tiny aftershocks as the last of the taste sensation slid down into her belly. She smiled apologetically.

"Sorry ... Yes, I'm listening." He raised a brow and continued to gaze out at the lush lawns and vegetation before them.

"Tell me how you are feeling right now," Conloach said. She sipped the water again and almost choked at the question.

"What?" He looked down at her coolly, like a disgruntled schoolteacher waiting for her to answer.

"Tell me how your body is responding right now, Sapphire. I need to know what is happening inside you so that I can help you." She could feel the flush of embarrassment spread across her chest as she realised that she was feeling extremely turned on, and the sensation was much stronger than ever before. It was indeed as if someone had turned on her power switch. Conloach waited with his eyes fixed on her own like two laser beams. She fidgeted under his stare.

"Well?" Sapphire looked down at her feet.

"I feel as if I'm on fire but as cold as ice. Every single nerve cell in my body is screaming at me that it might explode at any second.

And my skin feels almost tender, as if I have a fever." His pupils grew wider and darker, and his chest rose and fell deeply as he took in a deep breath.

"OK," he said. She could feel her cheeks getting even hotter under his scrutiny. What she had just described to him was actually not 100 per cent true. She felt as if she was going to self-combust at any moment. It felt as if she was on the edge of a climax ... not something she wanted to admit to her father-in-law, of all people.

"I want you to take this sensation, Sapphire, and grasp it in your mind, feel it in your chest, picture it as a ball of energy and take control of it, reduce it in size, and surround it with a ball of soft gold light, gentle and sweet. Hold the image in your mind and know that you alone have the power to control the intensity of its effect on you. Take this energy and savour it for a moment. Really feel it." He paused and sipped his water again. She watched his Adam's apple bob up and down as he drank. She felt almost giddy.

"Then take its power and release it slowly through your chest out into your arms and into the palms of your hands. Hold it there, Sapphire. Do not let it go." He waited for her patiently to respond. Her body was pulsing now. She did not know if it was the effect of the strange fruit and water, Conloach himself, or the place she was in, but it unnerved her and excited her all at once.

She placed the crystal glass on the floor and wiped her hands on her thighs. They were shaking suddenly, and had become slightly clammy. He watched her. His eyes were dark and still like two cat's eyes. After closing her own eyes she did as he had asked and began to focus on the sensations skittering around her body, the intenseness of it all, and the power and hum of this wild, untamed feeling that threatened to overwhelm her.

He was pushing her to test her control. Could she control this? Did she want to? It felt utterly delicious, like hot honey and cinnamon being dripped through her veins with a mixture of Fox's tongue licking across her skin. Oh, God.

Conloach coughed.

"Concentrate, Sapphire," he said. She took a deep breath. There was no way she was going to make a fool of herself in front of this man. She was not going to self-combust in front of him.

As she drew the mixture of sensations into her chest she began to visualise – as Conloach had suggested – a ball of energy, and she formed it into something that she could in fact control rather than a mess of spangled sensations running across her skin. As she did her body began to cool slightly, the feeling of giddiness calmed, and her hands stopped shaking. Now she was feeling a little more confident she surrounded the ball of energy in her mind with the soft, gold light and felt her body regain its previous control. The feeling of imminent climax subsided, and she let out a sigh of relief.

"Good, Sapphire. Now you have control of the magic hold it for a moment so that you can recognise it again if you need to. And know that *you* own it, and not the other way around. You have control." She did as he asked and held the image in her mind. It spun and sparkled like a beautiful gem in her head.

"Recognise its signature, its essence, Sapphire. This magic is yours and yours alone. The way you are responding to the fruit, the water, this room, and my own magic is just a mirror image of the powerful magic you have inside you." He paused. She could almost hear the wavering in his tone as he too tried to control what was happening beside him.

"Now take this energy and move it slowly down your body, into your chest, out through your arms, and into your hands. Do not release it just yet. Just hold it there and open your eyes." Sapphire felt the thrum of the energy ball as it passed down her body and into her chest, across her solar plexus into her arms, and finally into her hands. They pulsed suddenly and she gasped.

"Keep control of the energy ball, Sapphire. It will try to overpower you, but you are the master of this magic. You control it. Do not forget this. Own it. Believe that you are the stronger of the two. You must remember this." While steadying herself by widening her stance she did as he said and breathed in deeply, and then she took the energy ball into her palms and saw it now as a small, contained power source. She felt a deep sense of peace envelop her, and her body went completely still as a wave of extreme calm washed over her.

"Now open your eyes, Sapphire." She did. Conloach was now standing directly in front of her with his own hands – palms flat – facing her as if he was pushing against an invisible wall. She could see that he had created a wall of protection around himself as if he was ready for an impact, ready for an explosion that might just blow him apart. He was, however, smiling at her broadly.

On looking down into her hands she could see two beautiful flames of violet light within her palms. They flickered and wavered like tiny serpents, innocent but deadly at the same time. Conloach remained completely still before her.

"Take the energy you have in your hands, Sapphire, and push it down into the ground beneath your feet. Ground the energy and extinguish it, so that it will not harm you or anyone around you." She looked at him with confusion for a second. How could these tiny violet flames hurt anyone? His eyes widened slightly as he watched her process his command.

"Do not doubt the power of the energy you have in your hands, Sapphire. Trust me when I tell you that right now you hold something extremely powerful in your grasp." She nodded her head then turned her palms down to the grass below her and pushed softly, which sent the flames flickering downwards into the earth beneath her feet. She watched with fascination as the energy licked at the grass for a second like actual fire ... before disappearing and leaving tiny wisps of white smoke as the only evidence it had even existed. Conloach sighed, dropped his shield, and stepped forward slowly. He smiled at her in what looked like relief.

"Good, Sapphire, very good. And how do you feel now?" She shook her head and smiled back at him as she suddenly realised that her body, for the first time since she had downloaded the new strain of wild magic, was calm and still ... normal ... relaxed. Thank God.

"I feel OK ... I feel good ... really good, as if I am in control again." Conloach nodded slowly. The smile was still on his lips, his pupils were back to normal again, and she noticed that his muscles had relaxed slightly. Had he been nervous?

"Well done, Sapphire. You have taken the first step in managing your new magic." He chuckled softly. "And, thankfully, you did not kill anyone."

Fox wandered along the narrow pathway that wound around the side of the crystal palace. His legs moved with fluid, graceful strides. Leaving the building had helped his head clear instantly, and the guards had acknowledged him silently with a tip of their heads as he moved away from the doorway to follow the brick path that led to the gardens behind them.

He knew that coming here with his father and Sapphire would be difficult, as the combining of their magic under this very powerful roof would obviously ignite their magic tenfold. He had not expected it to be quite so spectacular. The Oracle had clearly sensed that Sapphire was now something quite extraordinary, and her magic alone was intensely powerful even without the priestess standing close by. He wondered if they could ever learn how to control it together. He had never seen or experienced anything like it. Even his own father's magic seemed weak in comparison. It worried him and excited him at the same time.

The fact that he was walking around with a constant erection was also becoming very uncomfortable and extremely inconvenient. Every time he thought he had control of his body it jumped up (quite literally) and surprised him again. He sensed that his father and Sapphire were working on her energy as he left the building, and that Conloach was wasting no time in his role as teacher to his wife. He hoped that between them and the Oracle they could tone down the sheer power of this wild magic she now owned.

As he walked slowly down the pathway he noticed that the gardens opened up into various different sections. There were some that looked like herb and vegetable gardens, and others that gave the impression of a maze. Each section was filled with the most exotic and wonderful plants and flowers, all giving off strong scents and sensations. It reminded him of Pearl's garden but on a much bigger and more magnificent magical scale. Pearl would have loved this.

A smile slipped on to his lips as his thoughts turned to his wife's teacher and friend back on Earth. She had been a constant rock from the beginning, and his instinct told him that she would be playing a much bigger role in the future for Sapphire if her journey with planting the seeds was to continue back on her home planet.

As he headed towards a clearing that opened up before him he allowed his own magic to open up and reach out. It was almost like flexing his muscles, so that he could at last relax his body without it flipping him into sexual overdrive. He understood what the Oracle had said regarding his own energy and Sapphire's reflecting their emotional and lustful connection to each other. It had been this way since the very first time they had met, and it powered their magic and created something quite magnificent. They just needed to learn how to control it and use it to their own advantage. To keep her safe and to hold the gatekeepers at bay Fox needed to learn this fast. He knew this deep within his bones.

The clearing before him led out to a beautiful lake that stretched out across the landscape. The sun reflected off the water in flashes of silver that shimmered and glistened like tiny mirrors. He stopped for a second and removed his boots and sunk his bare feet into the grass. As he closed his eyes for a moment as he savoured the extreme coolness of the earth beneath him. He sighed deeply and remained still, allowing the soft pulse of the ground beneath his feet to steady him and to pull his energy deep and low within his root chakra. The sensation of being completely grounded once more made his body breathe a sigh of relief. He was constantly flying around his wife. Her scent and her vibration were like a siren to him right now, and he was unable to function normally without this clarity of complete grounding.

"Feeling better now, young guardian?" A soft, musical voice interrupted his concentration, and his eyes jumped open again to find the Oracle standing before him. She was still wearing the peacock cloak. Her hair flowed freely around her shoulders and her face was alight with the brightest smile, like a mischievous child. Fox tipped his head and dropped his eyes to the floor.

"Priestess," he said softly. She moved closer to him and he held his breath as she placed a finger delicately under his chin and lifted his face so that he could look at her again. She was small – not as small as his wife – but he found the fact that she was standing so close to him slightly unnerving, and the urge to kneel before her was strong. She laughed softly, and placed her hand into the crook of his arm and tugged him gently. He felt the whisper of her magic envelop him like the softest of touches, so light but so powerful it made his skin ignite in goosebumps.

"Walk with me, Fox," she said. Her command was gently spoken, but the power behind her words made Fox walk with her as if he was hypnotised. He had never been this close to the Oracle before, let alone been touched by her in such a familiar way. It was comforting but overwhelming. She was silent as they walked but he could feel her magic flowing freely around him strongly and surely, like a constant blanket that touched his own power like rain falling from a summer sky. It was soft, warm, soothing, and wonderfully intoxicating. His eyes widened as he realised suddenly that it was very similar to his wife's energy.

"I know that it has been a difficult time for you lately, Fox. But do not fear. You are well on the way to stabilising the wild magic that flows freely between you and your wife. The discomfort you have been experiencing around her will become much less intense now Conloach has taught her how to restrain and control her power." He turned his head to look down at her. His feet seemed to glide across the grass now, as they walked as if they were walking on air. The Oracle looked up at him and smiled again, a sweet innocent smile.

"You have done well to keep her safe so far, Fox. She shines so brightly on this world and her own that it has not been an easy task for one as young as you." He blinked, a little confused.

"I have been a guardian to the dream travellers for many lifetimes, Oracle. There was no doubt I could keep my wife safe." She laughed again, and her hand squeezed his arm as she did.

"Oh, Fox, I do not criticise you in your role as guardian. It is merely an observation that you have been up against several formidable foes along this journey." He sighed deeply.

"Apologies, Oracle. I am always a little defensive when it comes to my abilities to keep my wife safe. She is my world, my love, my life, and my ego is often wounded to think I am not able to save her from the people who covet her magic." The Oracle patted his arm, sending a shower of silver sparks into the air as she did.

"I understand, Fox … I do. But I must warn you that the greatest test of all will be coming soon, and it will cost you both dearly in a way that will be hard to bear." She paused and watched him intently. "But the wild magic that Sapphire now possesses will be a powerful weapon for you both, as well as your link to her, and it will keep you safe on the next stage of your journey together." Fox frowned.

"Are you referring to Gabriel?" She pulled his arm, which indicated for him to stop. They stood a few feet from the edge of the lake. The gentle lap of water at its edge was the only sound in the air.

"The master of the gatekeepers is the most powerful of us all, Fox. He is more than just interested in Sapphire. He wants the gifts she has with her. He wants the key to creation, and the missing parts of his heart that were lost long ago. I fear that the visions I have had lately will most definitely come true, and unfortunately they tell me of a great loss to you both." Fox felt his body stiffen. The energy around them changed again, from soft and calm to eerily foreboding.

"What do you mean?" She smiled. Her eyes were soft and dreamy, and there was a sadness to the edge of her lips.

"I cannot tell you more than this, guardian, for that could possibly change the path of your future. At present it is just a dreamlike possibility that is not set in stone. You may be able to change the outcome of the vision I have seen. You may not. But, if I tell you what I have seen in detail, it could alter your decisions and create a path that is not destined to be.

"Know that you and Sapphire have the power between you to create the most amazing and magnificent magic for our planet and her homeland. Any sacrifice that needs to be made along the way will need to be a decision made by both of you, and as I know your heart will always belong to Sapphire it is best that you do not know this before it happens." Fox shook his head slowly.

"You talk in riddles, Oracle. I understand that destiny needs to unfold in its own way, but can you at least give me some idea as to what danger I need to look for? Apart from the obvious, that is." She smiled again, and released his arm.

"All I can tell you is that the person you have always seen as the most dangerous is not, and may just come to your aid when least expected. Keep your wits about you, Fox. You will need them when you return to Earth. And you will as soon as Sapphire has finished her training here with me. I will always be with her along this path. Sometimes I can intervene. Sometimes I cannot. But you are her sword, her master at arms, and you will be the man who fights for her when she cannot. Trust your instincts, young guardian, and allow the love and lust you have between you to empower the wild magic and give you protection. I will see you again soon."

And with a soft kiss blown from her lips to his she disappeared, leaving him bewildered and confused as he stood at the edge of the lake.

Chapter Twenty-Seven

Sapphire stared up at the glass ceiling above her and looked out in awe at the night sky. The stars seemed to shine so much more brightly here on Shaka than on Earth, and with the two moons gazing down at her – both a shimmering slither of silver blue – she felt almost overwhelmed by their magnificence. It was as if she was floating in the dark sky itself with no roof to stop her drifting off on the astral trail that was scattered above her.

Fox lay beside her in the bed they had been given for the night at the crystal palace. He slept soundly. His breath was a soft whisper in the air, and his energy was a flickering gold and green that glowed like a lantern in the darkness. He had returned to Sapphire after some time spent alone in the gardens. He had seemed more grounded and calm, but Sapphire had sensed a subtle change in his manner and she knew that he had spoken to the Oracle again. The conversation had obviously troubled him but he would not speak of it and reassured her that all was well, and that she should continue with her training as planned.

Conloach had left shortly after, and had headed back to Calafia to check on Hecta and make sure that Gabriel had not approached his castle in search of him. They had been given food and water by the priestesses once more. And then dusk crept upon them, and with silken arms, it wrapped the stillness of the night around the crystal building where they were now residing.

Sapphire had felt proud of what she had achieved with Conloach earlier that day, but being there in such a powerful place as guests of the Oracle was making her own magic jittery and excited again. She could not sleep. Fox had tried to calm her in his usual manner by taking her into his arms and kissing her in a slow, almost tantric-like manner, which soothed her body but did nothing to dampen the pulsing of her magic. They had made love slowly and passionately with the night sky as a witness, but it had not given her the usual release into a state of blissful sleep.

After untangling her body from Fox's arm, which was resting against her hip, she slipped away from him as quietly as she could. He sighed heavily, and whispered her name before turning over and facing in the opposite direction. She paused and waited for him to wake up. When he remained in the same position, with his breathing steady and slow, she placed her feet on the floor and pushed herself up and away from the bed.

She padded silently across the room, gathered her clothes, and dressed, while watching him for any movement and willing him to stay asleep. She needed some time to think, and she needed some air. After heading out of the bedchamber she walked down the long corridor that linked their room to the rest of the crystal palace. The building itself was like a Tardis, and seemed to be like a maze of corridors and rooms that she quickly realised could be easily confusing if you did not know where you were going.

As she realised that she was in fact quite lost she felt a quickening in her chest, a flicker of energy that pushed and tickled inside her solar plexus. It began to tug her forward as if an invisible string were attached to her sternum ... and it was being gently pulled, urging her to move with it through the corridors to an unknown destination. She closed her eyes and smiled, for it seemed that someone or something was guiding her out of the building. Her magic began to hum softly, and the hieroglyphics that she had seen after the initial download of her new magic were lighting up eerily under her skin once more.

She could sense that it was absolutely no coincidence that she was wide awake and Fox was not. Although she was not asleep or dreaming her body moved as if she was, and it was clear that her vibration had changed and she was walking through a film of magic that seemed to be bending and shifting as she did.

Quite suddenly, and with a sharp jolt of pain into her chest, she found herself sitting on a rock in the middle of what seemed to be a lake. As she faced the crystal building that glittered and shone before her like a vision in the darkness she realised that she was now in the palace grounds, and that she was not alone. She felt the person standing behind her before she saw her. A strong, steady pulse of magic, which engulfed her in the sweet scent of hyacinth and honeysuckle (it was so thick and heavy that it was almost too overpowering) began to vibrate against her skin. She knew at that instant that the Oracle was about to address her.

"Welcome, Sapphire. It is time that you and I had a talk." Before she could answer Sapphire found herself looking up at the Oracle, who stood in an almost translucent robe that fell to her feet and swirled around her like grey-white wisps of fog on a summer's morning. The Oracle smiled, her eyes sparkling like they always did with the mischief of a young child who was about to play a naughty prank on you.

"Your magic has grown to its full strength now, my child, and you are more than ready to embrace the next step of your journey." Sapphire blinked, unable to speak at that moment. "I have watched you closely on this journey, Sapphire, and am very happy to say that I feel confident that the goddess has gifted you wisely – for not all who are given such powerful gifts can use them with the love and compassion they are intended for." She paused, looked down at her feet for a second, then up again. Her smile changed into a grin.

"You are a unique and interesting creature, and I am very excited to work with you on this part of your training." Sapphire nodded.

"I am honoured, Oracle, that you feel that way," she said. The Oracle laughed and clapped her hands playfully.

"I am the one who is honoured, Sapphire. Never, in all my time as one of the chosen, have I been so close to one of the goddess's vessels." Sapphire frowned.

"Vessel?" The Oracle nodded, and clasped her hands together as if she was holding in her excitement.

"Yes, my child. You are a vessel. You have the ability to create new life, and you will help us be reborn in her vision of love and light. Such power is magnificent on its own, without the added benefit of human emotion." Sapphire shook her head in confusion.

"I really don't understand, Oracle," she said. The Oracle turned around slowly so that she now had her back to her and spread her arms out before her. Her long robe was fluttering around her like a wave of silken feathers.

"This place you see before you was once created long ago with the same magic as you hold within you, Sapphire ... pure magic that is so very powerful and strong it can create or destroy in the blink of an eye." Sapphire stood up slowly and tried to digest the words that the ethereal woman before her was saying.

"Are you talking about the seeds?" The Oracle turned again to face her.

"Not just the seeds, Sapphire. You are the creator of new life, the bringer of hope for all of us." She paused. Her eyes were flicking from the sky above and back to Sapphire again as if she was listening to someone from high above them. Perhaps she was.

"From the very beginning of time, Sapphire, there have been certain beings who have been chosen to help create this vast and wonderful universe that we have around us. Its vastness is incomprehensible, and the possibilities endless ... such a huge task for just one being to endure. And so the god and goddess choose the strongest and the most pure of heart for the most difficult tasks.

"You were chosen not only as a dream traveller but as a vessel for this magic. You have been given the tools to complete this task, and the magic to make it possible. I have been given the gift of clairvoyance – and the magic of the angelic realm, which helps those given such difficult tasks. This is the reason why I have been able to help you on your path so far. I am one of your many guides, and it is my job to help you now to open the first doorway from our world to yours and start the process of consciousness."

Sapphire swallowed the lump that had suddenly appeared in her throat. This was some seriously heavy shit, and it was making her feel totally and utterly out of her depth. As if sensing these very thoughts the Oracle stepped towards her and placed her hand on her arm.

"I would like to see the seeds now, Sapphire, and the essence you were given back on Earth." Sapphire shrugged apologetically.

"They are in our room, Oracle. I will have to go and get them for you." The Oracle raised a delicate brow and tutted.

"Oh, my dear Sapphire. Really? You can do better than that. How did you get here on this island tonight without even trying?" Sapphire frowned again.

"I'm not actually sure." The Oracle pursed her lips.

"You now have the ability to move very quickly across time and through dimensions through thought alone, Sapphire, without your magic of dream travel. If you ask for something it will happen. Ask for the seeds and the essence and they will come to you. It is as simple as that."

Sapphire felt her eyes grow wider at just the thought. She knew that she could manifest now, and she knew that she could visualise and create, but she had not realised it would be a simple command now for her every whim.

She closed her eyes and did just that. She pictured the seeds safely tucked in their pouch and the essence and the dirt sitting next to them, and called them to her. With a pop in her ears she felt them land at her feet with a gentle thud.

"Wonderful. Now let us have a look at them," the Oracle said. Sapphire picked up the bags and lifted them up slowly as she watched the Oracle to see her response. The crystal flower was also wrapped securely in the same pouch as the essence. It was folded within some tissue paper that she had found back at Fox's house.

The Oracle indicated that Sapphire should place them all on the rock before them. Sapphire laid them out like offerings on an altar. They slipped from the magical pouches with a sparkle and a sigh. Each one seemed to vibrate and hum at a different level. Even to her eyes they looked remarkably beautiful and deadly all at the same time. The Oracle crouched down and stared at them in silence. Her hair lifted around her head as if it was dancing to a silent tune.

"So very powerful, so very beautiful," she said. She turned and faced Sapphire, her expression now deadly serious. "Tell me what happened when you planted the first seed on Earth."

Sapphire remembered the moment ... Well, it had nearly killed her. Without Fox creating and holding a circle of protection around them she would have most likely blasted the whole of Egypt into the ocean.

"It was a little overwhelming," she confessed. The Oracle nodded.

"And are you ready to try this again, here on Shaka?" she asked. Sapphire shivered.

"What, right now?" A slight twitch on the Oracle's lips made Sapphire realise that she was either teasing her or testing her. "Do you think I should?" The Oracle smiled.

"I was asking you a question, Sapphire. Are you ready to take the next step in your training?"

This was it. This was the moment Sapphire needed to embrace her power and believe that she had the strength to jump off the magical cliff and dive straight into the deep ocean of the unknown. She searched her mind for an answer. She listened to her breathing become quicker and her magic become excited. Her body began to tremble. It was now or never.

"Yes. I'm ready," she said.

Like a bolt of forked lightning that hit the ground simultaneously at four different points of the ground, a surge of wild magic so strong and powerful ripped through the bodies of four different magical beings on Shaka. Each one of them felt it at the same time in a different way throughout their energy field, and it trembled and groaned like a tempest raging across the seas as it bucked and dipped up and down their bodies.

They all felt it, and they all knew that something absolutely incredible had just happened. They did not know exactly what it was or how it had been created, but it made them all sit up to attention. Their skin crackled and their magic spun as the surge filled them inside and out. As it spun and swirled around them it grasped at their own magic, while teasing and snapping at the edges of it.

One of them knew exactly where the magic had come from and he shot out of the bed that moments ago he had been sleeping in and jumped up, his hair crackling with static. With his eyes wide and his muscles taut he grabbed his clothes and dressed quickly, almost stumbling as he pulled up his trousers in haste. After heading out of the bedchamber he ran down the corridor with his bare feet slapping on the marble tiles. His solar plexus was buzzing as if a hornets' nest had taken up residence inside it and had been poked with a very large stick.

He had felt this wild magic before and tasted its power. It had almost blown him to pieces when he had tried to contain it the first time. His body shook with the need to move faster, and his breathing was heavy and fast. On reaching the corridor that led to the gardens he pushed his weight against the glass doors that led outside. He opened them with a loud thud and rushed out into the cool night air. The grass, which was damp beneath his feet, seemed warm, and even softer than he remembered from earlier that day.

And then he saw it before him ... a sight that he would never be able to erase from his memory. A beam of light so bright and pure rose up in a direct line from the island in the middle of the lake and pierced the dark sky like a laser beam. It pulsed so strongly that he had to turn his head and shield his eyes before he could look back again and face the breath taking spectacle before him. As he panted for air as the wild magic continued to press against his body in wave after wave of incredible power he pushed forward and reached out in his mind for his wife.

"Sapphire! What have you done?" he shouted.

Fox ran to the edge of the lake while still shielding his eyes, and pushed his magic back against the wave of intense power that radiated like the blast of a nuclear bomb into his body. His own shield of protective magic began to wrap around him instinctively like a cloak of silk. It clung to him, though it was wavering under the pressure.

He could just make out the silhouette of his wife standing in the middle of the beam of light. Her hair was flying around her head and her arms were above her in a perfect V shape as if she were indeed channelling this wild magic from the universe above her. It lit her up like an apparition, pure white, and beautiful, as if she was an angel from the heavens.

Fear ran up his spine in dark, sharp prickles and made his skin break out in sweat. He was not there to help her, and this magic was stronger than when they had been on Earth in Egypt. The magic of Shaka was amplifying the power tenfold. It could kill her.

He closed his eyes and pushed again to transport himself across the water to Sapphire, who stood perfectly still, like a statue, with her back to him. The pressure built in his chest and he felt a sharp stabbing in the back of his head as he whipped across the lake to the island. He felt the ground, hard earth this time, beneath his feet again. It was hot, almost unbearably so, and the smell of sulphur filled the air.

As he opened his eyes he raised his arms and threw his protection shield far and wide to envelop Sapphire and close the circle she had opened. He chanted loudly the spell his father had taught him that would contain the magic and stop it from exploding across the landscape and destroy them all. As he called out to Sapphire in his mind he felt a hand on his shoulder. It clasped his bare skin with a tenderness that made him falter in his chanting and turn his head in surprise. The Oracle faced him, a smile on her beautiful lips.

"Do not be afraid, Fox. Your wife is safe, and she is in control. You can stand down now, my brave guardian. Stand down."

Hecta gripped tightly on to the cold steel bars of the cell he was inside as he shouted out desperately into the dark corridor.

"Guard, let me out of here. I need to speak to Conloach immediately." His voice echoed off the stone walls and reverberated in his head like a frustrated child wailing with impatience. He shook the bars for extra effect and heard the heavy steps of the guard move towards him. The dark face of the fierce guard he had seen earlier appeared before him. His expression was not amused.

"Stop making such a racket, Hecta. The day has not yet broken, and my lord will not be impressed if I wake him at this hour." Hecta pressed his face against the steel and breathed heavily. The wild magic he had felt just moments ago was still tingling within his veins and creating a surge of heat that travelled throughout his limbs. It was the most exquisite and agonising feeling he had ever had, and he knew that it had come from Sapphire. She was possibly in danger, and he needed to alert Conloach to the fact despite the magician's dislike of him.

"Listen to me, warrior. Sapphire is in danger, and I need to speak with your master before something bad happens to her. Do you want to be the one who stops him from protecting her?" The guard lifted a brow, clearly contemplating whether Hecta was just looking for attention or if his claim that Sapphire was in trouble was true.

"Step away from the bars, Hecta. You are delusional if you think I am going to wake Conloach at this hour just because you have a bad feeling about Sapphire. Your obsession with her is beyond sick." Hecta felt his stomach clench in anger. His connection to the dream traveller had given him the ability to sense when her magic was being used, and the jolt of power he had just received was something that could not be ignored. His lips curled into a snarl and he felt a low growl rumble in his chest. The huge guard on the other side of the bars tipped his head to one side as if he were merely observing a wild beast that was acting crazy.

"You will regret this, you imbecile," Hecta retorted. Clearly this was the wrong thing to say, as the huge black man turned on his heels and disappeared without another word.

Hecta pushed himself away from the bars with frustration and, his breathing heavy, began pacing the floor. How was he going to get Conloach to even listen to him and take action when everything he did was seen as a threat or a trick? His body trembled as he thought about Sapphire and the fact that he was useless to her because he was trapped within this cell.

The overwhelming urge to protect her was so strong within his chest that he wanted to smash and break things in rage. He had never felt this out of control in his life. The new life that she had given him was a mixture of unknown sensations, and it made him dizzy with confusion. He grabbed his hair between his hands and pulled on its strands as he tried desperately to control the emotions filling his head. The magic was settling again now, and he knew that whatever magic Sapphire had used was slowly diminishing. But the fact remained that he needed to alert someone that she may be in danger. He did not want to speak to Fox for fear that her guardian would smash his head to a pulp. The last time he had seen him it had not gone well.

As he paced the cell he felt a swell of new magic envelop him. It was Gabriel.

"Hecta, exactly how long have you been in this godforsaken place? Was it your intention to cause me such distress by disappearing without a trace and making me so very angry again, or are you just plain stupid?"

Hecta spun around to face his master, who stood in all his fiery glory before him with his hands on his hips and his eyes swirling as if a grey thunderstorm was about to erupt behind them. His face was like a mask of pure calm but the energy pulsating around him painted another picture, one of extreme agitation and rage. Hecta swallowed hard. He knew that he was in serious trouble unless the guard came back and saved him from the wrath of his clearly less than happy master. He lowered his eyes and fell to his knees with his head bowed low.

"My lord, you found me," he said. He sensed Gabriel step forward, and grimaced as he waited for the pain that he was most likely to feel any second at the hand of the powerful man before him. It did not come. Instead he felt the gentle pressure of Gabriel's fingers as they slid into his hair and gripped it as he just slightly held him down.

"Yes, I found you, Hecta. You are glowing like a beacon right now. It seems that our favourite dream traveller has gifted you with a new life, eh? And the surge of power that ripped right through me a moment ago seems to be lingering on you like a second skin. How did you get so lucky, my obedient servant? What did you do to deserve such a gift?" The grip he held on Hecta's hair tightened just a fraction more, and made him lift his head so that he stared directly up into Gabriel's eyes once more. This time they were the most perfect ice blue, and the coldness reflected in them actually made Hecta shiver uncontrollably.

"You disobeyed me, Hecta. I asked you to carry out a simple task for me – nothing more – and you stepped over the line, took advantage of my good nature, and then threw it back in my face." Hecta felt his jaw open slightly as Gabriel literally lifted him to his feet by the roots of his hair.

"I should dispose of you right now. You have disappointed me greatly. However, I think that you will serve me better in this position and, seeing as you are already behind the walls of Conloach's stronghold, I will grant you some more time in this realm." He paused and watched Hecta's expression of disbelief and discomfort as he squeezed his fingers even tighter against his scalp.

"I have other things to attend to, but I want you to remember that you work for me, Hecta ... no one else, regardless of what you think of the dream traveller now that she has clearly taken any sanity you had and replaced it with the thoughts of a lovesick puppy.

"I heard your conversation with the guard, and can see quite clearly now that she has some hold over you. More than she ever did before. She is dangerous, Hecta. A powerful temptress filled with magic that she has no right to. You have been bewitched by her, as have all the other males who seem to spend time around her. The fact that her own guardian claimed her as his wife and brought her to this world is ridiculous."

He released his hold on Hecta's hair and allowed him to slump back down to the floor again on his knees. Hecta looked up at him with dark coffee-coloured eyes that glistened with moisture. He was pathetic. She had rendered his best man spineless. It almost made him want to spit with disgust. But this was not the time to take unnecessary action against the dream traveller, as it would ultimately spoil his intended plans.

"I will leave you now, Hecta. I want you to take this time in this cell to really think about what is happening here. Your connection to Sapphire is nothing more than a mistake on her part, of that I am sure, and I want you to get it into your thick skull that you mean nothing to her and never will. The magic she holds is far more important than your life or of the lives she holds so dear to her."

Hecta watched him, unable to speak. His mouth had become uncomfortably dry, and his head felt as if it was about to explode. His master's words hit him hard in his heart, as he knew they were true. The emotions he felt – these alien feelings – were all an illusion, and no matter how much he wanted to change this fact he knew Gabriel was speaking the truth. He would never be anything but an inconvenience to Sapphire – and an unwanted one, at that.

"You will tell no one of my visit to you here in this cell, and you will not whisper a word of the fact that you and I both felt the shift in energy that was clearly of her doing tonight. I want you to be my eyes and ears here and do as you are told, for once." Hecta, his heart heavy in his chest, nodded his head slowly. He felt utterly defeated and broken once more.

Gabriel raised his right hand, swirled his wrist, and sent a shimmer of magic across to Hecta that hit him in the centre of his forehead and made him cry out in pain.

"You will be unable to speak of me again to those closest to Sapphire – nor, of course, to Sapphire herself. Do you understand?" Hecta once again nodded like an obedient dog that had been kicked into submission. He could feel the spell Gabriel had just cast settle within his brain. It was a restraining spell, and he would indeed have no way of alerting anyone now that his master was using him once more as a pawn in the game of entrapment. He now knew without a shadow of a doubt that Gabriel was taking his time in stalking his prey. Eventually he would make his move on Sapphire and Fox, and there was absolutely nothing he could do about it.

A loud knock on the door of his chamber made Conloach pause as he dressed quickly in his robe. He had been woken quite unexpectedly by a bolt of pure, powerful energy that he knew was quite clearly coming from his daughter-in-law. He had intended to reach out for his son just as his door was knocked.

"Enter," he said impatiently. Wolf appeared, looking decidedly awkward as he entered the chamber.

"My lord, I apologise for disturbing you at this early hour, but I am a little concerned that our prisoner is becoming delusional again. I think you should perhaps speak with him." Conloach regarded his captain thoughtfully.

"What seems to be his problem?" Wolf looked to the floor and then back up again, clearly anxious that he might be causing a fuss for nothing.

"He seems to think something may have happened to Sapphire, and is growing more and more agitated." Conloach sighed deeply and nodded.

"You did the right thing, Wolf. I will speak to Hecta and settle him down. I want you to make sure that the guards are on full alert today, just in case." Wolf tipped his head in acknowledgement and left the chamber silently.

Conloach fastened his robe around himself and reached out in his mind for his son. He requested reassurance that he and Sapphire were still safe at the Oracle's residence. If the jolt of power had been felt by Hecta and him then he knew that his son would most likely also be dealing with something quite demanding. He only hoped that Sapphire had not just blasted a hole in the Oracle's roof while she had been dreaming. It was quite possible, even though he had been confident when he had left them both the day before that she had the upper hand with her new magic.

He headed down to the dungeons and placed a shield around himself just in case. Hecta had always been a tricky character at the best of times, and he wasn't about to be deceived by the gatekeeper with his plea of help. Now was not the time to be complacent.

Chapter Twenty-Eight

Charlie stared at the plastic strip in her hand and blinked. It was impossible to say exactly how she felt as she digested the piece of information sitting innocently in her palm. Excitement, shock, disbelief, fear ... all the above, plus a slight feeling of nausea that threatened to spill out at any second as she sat on the toilet seat.

How the hell could she be pregnant? She was on the pill, and had not forgotten to take it each day at the correct time. The only reason she had done the stupid test in the first place was at the suggestion of her doctor when she had made a call to speak to him about the fact that she had been feeling sick for a few weeks, and did she need to come in for an appointment?

Nathan had been the one to push her to make the call after she had thrown up a few times lately. The sickness bug that she had been fighting was clearly lingering longer than it should. She hated doctors, and had placated him by phoning instead. After she had described her symptoms the doctor had made the absurd suggestion that she should do a pregnancy test and come in for some bloods to be done.

Her legs had started to go numb and her backside was definitely getting cold as she put the offending pregnancy test down on the edge of the sink and wiped herself. She had been sitting there for some time just staring at it. A small smile began to grow on her lips as she realised that she was about to become a mum. The smile dissolved when she realised that she had never even discussed the possibility of a child with Nathan in the future. They had been dating for quite some time now and she knew he was most definitely the one, but kids ...?

Was he even ready for such a responsibility? He was like a big kid himself, and how would she even cope with a baby with such a crazy life? Her face paled even more when she thought about the lifestyle she had and how much she smoked and drank, plus the occasional drug taking. That would all have to stop immediately if she was to bring a healthy child into this world.

Her mind started filling with visions of health visitors telling her what a bad mother she was, and how her baby may have something wrong with it due to all her naughty habits when she had conceived. She turned around and crouched down just in time to throw up one more time. Her stomach dry-heaved after it had emptied what little she had in her stomach. With tears in her eyes she wiped her mouth with some toilet paper and flushed it, then pushed herself up on unsteady feet.

"Well, shit happens, doesn't it, Charlie? Deal with it, bitch." She laughed shakily. Time to face the music.

As she placed her hands against the warm bark of the beautiful tree before her Pearl closed her eyes and sighed deeply. She opened her chakras and felt the soothing magic of the tree fill her completely. It surged and stroked at her body like a wildcat, soft and fierce all at the same time.

She had felt an overwhelming urge to come into the woods that morning and find her tree. It had been as if it was calling to her today, and she had been more than happy to pay it a visit. As she opened her brow chakra fully to meditate she felt a shift in the energy of the tree and, quite unexpectedly, also felt a wave of fresh power so strong it knocked her back on to her well-padded backside into a pile of leaves.

The tree shimmered and glistened like a chandelier reflecting in the sunlight. Every branch was lit up beautifully. Pearl gasped as she watched the tree transform into something much more powerful than ever before. The gateway that she had always suspected was held deep within its roots began to unfold before her. A doorway to something as yet unknown, and quite possibly very dangerous if used by the wrong people, opened up before her. Small creatures began to gather closer to the tree, scurrying and rustling in the undergrowth as if they too were drawn to this new power source and could not resist its pull.

"Oh, my," Pearl whispered as she watched the energy shift and grow before her with wide eyes. The gateway was glowing as clear as day against the huge trunk in a rainbow of colours. It was the most beautiful thing she had ever seen, and she had no idea why it had just opened. A deer appeared by her side and grunted at her. She smiled, and used its sturdy frame to help pull herself up off the woodland floor.

"Thank you, my friend," she said softly. They both faced the tree with a silence that seemed to permeate the air. The animal was breathing softly, as if it too was in awe of the magic glowing brightly before it. Pearl reached down and petted its head gently.

"Do not fear, my friend," she said. "It will not hurt you." Pearl continued to stroke the deer soothingly, while praying to the god and goddess that she was right.

This was most definitely an unexpected turn of events. She quickly realised that she would need to strengthen the wards around the tree that Fox had created some time ago, and craft a stronger repellent to deter the average human walking in the woods. This was no longer a place for people to wander into and it would need to be carefully watched, as something this powerful most definitely had a purpose. She had absolutely no idea what purpose it had at this precise moment. Unless, of course, this new doorway had something to do with the fact that Gabriel had popped up on the other side of her garden wall recently.

Sapphire had returned to Shaka with Fox, and they had yet to return. She knew that time was different from place to place, and that for them time may have not moved on so far. It had been several weeks since she had seen them. Perhaps something had happened again, and Sapphire had opened a door without knowing. It was a definite possibility, as she knew of no other magical being in her vicinity that could do such a thing.

The sculptured, beautiful face of a man with white-blonde hair and ice-cold blue eyes entered her head again, and she shivered with both excitement and a touch of trepidation. Perhaps it was him. Gabriel had pushed through to this world recently and spoken to her. His magic had always been very strong when she had known him in their previous life. She had no idea what he had matured into as a fully grown man, or even how old he was now. Had he opened the doorway so that he could step through and visit her again? She shook her head and frowned. No, of course not. If he was as strong in magic as Fox and Hecta were he would have been standing outside her gate a long time ago.

The deer snorted and stamped its foot impatiently, as if sensing her troubled mind.

"I am fine, my friend. You can go now," she said. "Thank you again." The deer looked up at her with soft brown eyes. Before running off into the undergrowth its eyes reflected a peaceful soul that was concerned that the witch beside it was acting strangely.

After brushing herself down Pearl picked up the cloth bag she always carried with her and rummaged inside for a few tools that she would need to strengthen the wards. Luckily she always carried a witchy toolkit, which consisted of a small bag of salt, an athame, some runes, various herbs (sage and rosemary), and a slightly crushed candle. She could use some of the stones scattered around to cast a visual circle, which would hold more strongly due to the physical connection with the earth.

As she softly hummed an old song her mother had taught her she began to work on the wards while watching the tree flicker and shine before her. The magic was dimming slightly now, but she knew that the power held within the tree was not to be underestimated. After collecting some flint and stones from the ground around her she placed them at equal distances around the great tree trunk, and her song grew louder and more powerful as she slipped pieces of sage and salt along the edges to increase the protective element of her spell.

She felt the air around her grow warmer and thicker as she worked and could sense the energy held within the boundary of her spell push against it softly, as if it were testing its effectiveness. She did not want strange creatures wandering into her woods now this door was open, and it would certainly not be a good idea for a human to accidentally find the gateway. There was some truth in the fairy stories, and she knew all too well the dangers of stepping inside the fairy ring.

After she had finished she stood and looked up once more at her tree and smiled. It was safe for now, and she would come back again tomorrow just to check that nothing had disturbed her boundary around the tree. While heading back to Foxglove she wondered if Sapphire and Fox would return soon, and if they would know why the gateway had opened. She herself had been tempted to take a peek inside, just to see where it would take her. But, to be quite honest, the idea of being hurtled across time and space was just a little too exciting for her old heart nowadays. She would leave that kind of adventure to the younger folk.

The sun shone brightly today, and it seemed the worst of the cold weather was now over. Spring would soon be on its way, and a welcome relief that would be. She walked a little faster. The vision of a hot cup of spiced tea and a freshly baked muffin gave her the extra boost of energy she needed to get home quickly.

As Pearl stepped out of the woods into her lane she noticed that someone was standing at her gate. At this distance it was difficult to see who it was exactly. Her eyesight was not at its best these days but as she walked towards the person she realised that she was most definitely female, and her aura was glowing so brightly there was absolutely no doubt she was with child. The woman turned around, and Pearl smiled broadly as she realised who it was.

"Pearl! Oh, thank God you are home. I really need to talk to you." Charlie did not wait for her to reach the gate, but ran towards her and wrapped her arms around her in a huge bear hug. Pearl laughed softly and patted her back comfortingly, as she sensed the young woman's obvious distress.

"Well, it's nice to see you too, Charlie. Let's go inside, and I will make us a nice cup of tea." Charlie released her and looked at her with an almost perplexed expression. She worried her bottom lip like a little girl about to own up to some naughty deed.

"Mmmh, that would be awesome. I'd have something stronger, but I don't think I can right now." Pearl smiled and nodded.

"I can see that," she said. They walked through the wooden gate and into Pearl's garden towards the house. Charlie was holding on to the crook of Pearl's arm as if her life depended on it. Pearl chuckled.

"You seem a little out of sorts, young lady." Charlie snorted as Pearl pushed the door open and they entered the cottage, where a warm burst of air filled her lungs along with the smell of fresh bread and herbs.

"That's an understatement," she said. Pearl took off her coat and indicated for Charlie to do the same. Then she headed into the kitchen to prepare some tea.

"Have a seat, Charlie, before you fall down." Charlie did as she was told. Her face was flushed but she looked decidedly peaky, and the obvious signs of shock, worry, and fear were drawn clearly across her features. Pearl busied herself with filling the kettle with water and putting it on the stove. She collected the cups and the teapot. She rummaged through her herbs to find something suitable for a woman who was quite obviously in shock with the news that she was now with child.

"How far along are you, my dear?" Pearl asked. She had her back to Charlie, but could hear the gasp she let out at her keen witchy observation.

"How do you know?" Pearl turned around and smiled as she raised an eyebrow. Charlie sighed heavily, and a small smile graced her lips.

"Well, of course you know. You know everything. I actually have no idea, Pearl. I literally just found out this morning, and I haven't even told Nathan yet. He went out early into town, and I can't get hold of him on his phone. He never switches the bloody thing on, and then he never listens to any messages, so there was no point even leaving him one." She was babbling, and Pearl watched her with amusement. The poor thing was clearly in a state of shock and did not know what to think.

"I am sure he will be home very soon, Charlie, and then you can sit down with him and tell him the news. It is wonderful news, isn't it? A new baby is always such a joyous occasion." Charlie looked at her as if she thought otherwise, but smiled weakly.

"I don't even know how it happened, Pearl." She paused and laughed. "Well, you know … I know how it happens, but I have been taking precautions and haven't been stupid. I've always been careful. You just can't take risks with these things, you know." Pearl nodded as she mixed some of the herbs she had found (which would calm her friend down) into some water. She handed it to Charlie, who took it without question and sipped it. She screwed up her face as she tasted the bitter liquid.

"What the hell is that, Pearl? Christ, it tastes like cat piss." Pearl laughed.

"Just drink it, Charlie. It will help you to digest this new piece of information in a much calmer way." Charlie sniffed the water in disgust but continued to sip, regardless of the taste.

"I just can't get my head around it, Pearl. I mean – really – me with a baby? It's just a ridiculous notion. Sapphire and Fox? Yes, I can see that, and am quite frankly amazed that she doesn't have a bun in the oven already. But this seriously changes my game plan, you know. It's a lifetime commitment, and how will I ever be a responsible parent? I can barely look after myself, and as for Nathan … Well, he's amazing, and I love him with all my heart, but he's the biggest kid of them all."

The kettle began to whistle on the stove, and Pearl turned. She lifted it with an oven mitten so that she could pour the hot water into the teapot. Charlie gulped down the rest of the potion Pearl had given her and then sat back in the chair. Her face changed almost instantly to a much calmer expression. She smiled at Pearl.

"Fuck, that stuff's good. I feel much better." Pearl placed the teapot in the centre of the table and left it to brew. She had decided that some ginger and apple spice would be just the thing in this situation.

"You really should stop cussing, Charlie. It may be a good habit to start practising in view of your impending motherhood." Charlie grinned.

"My child will probably say 'fuck' as its very first word. How funny would that be?" Pearl pursed her lips and tried not to smile.

"Not very funny at all, Charlie, but I am sure this will not be the case." Charlie placed her chin in her hands and propped her elbows on the kitchen table.

"How the hell did this happen, Pearl? And why now?" Pearl regarded her for a moment as she used her magical senses to probe into Charlie's aura for any further clues as to why this had indeed happened at such an unexpected time.

"New souls come into our world when they are ready, Charlie. And this new little soul was quite obviously ready, regardless of what precautions you were taking. It has chosen you to take this wonderful journey with, and the hows and the whys will not be made known until much later along the path of parenthood. I sense that this soul is going to be very different from your average human. In fact it seems that a touch of magic may have been involved in this little one's creation." Charlie sniggered. She was quite possibly a little too relaxed from the potion.

"Saf's zapped me, then. It's all her fault. I knew it." She watched Pearl begin to pour the tea and then sat up straighter as her face grew redder. "Oh, God, do you think it's because of that flower thing she gave me? I bombed it, thinking it would be funny, and at the time I thought nothing had happened ... It was disappointing, actually. But Saf did tell me the next day that I flipped out on them both and had acted like a looney."

Pearl passed her a cup of the ginger tea and frowned. She had felt the power of the crystal flower, and it had been like nothing she had ever experienced before. She had no idea that Sapphire and Charlie had even attempted such an experiment with it. She would have strong words with Sapphire on her return. Such an irresponsible action should not be repeated, even if it seemed that Charlie may just be right and the effect of the magic within the flower had helped her conceive.

"I cannot say for sure, Charlie, but I do sense that it is a distinct possibility you could be correct in assuming that this helped you fall pregnant." Charlie sipped her tea and smiled.

"Well, that's just bloody marvellous. I'm now going to get fat and grumpy, thanks to Saf and her magical flower. That's the last time I take anything remotely drug-like – or anything out of this world, for that matter." She looked at Pearl again with laughter in her eyes. "Please tell me there's only one in there, and I'm not about to gestate a brood of weird fairy creatures." Pearl laughed loudly.

"I can assure you, Charlie, that you have only one baby in your belly and it will most definitely be human. And I think you are only just pregnant ... probably about three weeks." Charlie looked up at the ceiling as if calculating in her head the timescales involved.

"Yep, that's about the time I took the flower bomb. Crap. It's my own fault for being adventurous, but I will be giving Saf some serious shit over the fact that she has now changed my entire life plan." Pearl smiled and said,

"You will be absolutely fine, Charlie, and I know without a doubt that you and Nathan will make exceptionally fun and caring parents." Charlie sighed. A silly grin came over her face.

"I hope it's a boy. It will be so cute and gorgeous, just like Nathan." Pearl was about to reply, but thought better of it. Best that she kept that little surprise a secret, and allowed Charlie and Nathan to enjoy the moment they actually found out exactly which sex their child was.

"Are you feeling a little better about this news now, my dear?" Pearl enquired. Charlie sipped her tea and shrugged her shoulders.

"Yeah, I suppose so. I am kinda excited, now that I've talked it over with you. I hope Nathan takes the news OK. He's so young at heart … I don't want to cramp his style." Pearl reached across and patted her hand kindly.

"He will be over the moon. You are both very happy together, and perhaps it was just the right time for you to take a step forward in your relationship together." Charlie laughed.

"Well, there's no doubt that being parents will push us much further forward together. He's stuck with me for life now, isn't he?" Pearl nodded.

"I am very happy for you, Charlie. If there is anything you need in the next few months you just let me know." Charlie grimaced.

"Well, the first thing you can do for me, Pearl, is make something up for this awful puking that's been going on. I just can't keep anything down at the moment." Pearl smiled.

"Now that I can do with absolutely no problem at all," she said.

Chapter Twenty-Nine

Fox stared up at the magnificent crystal tree before him in disbelief and awe. His very powerful wife had yet again created something so amazing and incredible it made his jaw drop.

The Oracle stood beside him humming softly, with a childlike grin on her face. Her aura pulsed gently with a mixture of silver and pink that reflected the tree's own energy in the grey-blue light of the approaching dawn. Sapphire was no longer a beacon of light, alien-like and scarily powerful, but had returned to an almost painfully human state once more. Although she still had her back to him he could see that her chest was heaving deeply, and her breathing was ragged in his ears as if she were struggling to catch her breath. It looked as if she would fall to her knees any second.

As he regained his senses he stepped forward to catch her. Before he could do so his wife turned around so quickly that her image flickered eerily and made his head spin. She was suddenly standing directly in front of him with her eyes wide. Her lips were open and dark red, and they invited him to claim them with his own.

Time stood still for a second as he devoured her features greedily. At that moment she was the most beautiful thing he had ever seen. Her hair, wet from perspiration, was plastered to her skin, and her skin glistened like dewdrops. She looked so ripe and soft it took all his control not to rip her clothes off and take her right there and then on the floor, with the Oracle standing next to them. She smiled up at him. Her breathing was gradually slowing to a more natural rhythm.

"Fox, you look as if someone just pressed all your buttons," she said, her voice husky and low. He laughed, threw his head back, and looked up at the sky as he shook his head at the comment. She really had no idea what effect she had on him.

"You scared me, my love," he said. She lifted her hands to his face and touched him gently on the cheeks. She stroked his skin softly, which sent shivers down his spine.

"I'm fine … more than fine. I feel amazing." He leant down into her and kissed her, while feeling the softness of her lips against his own and moaning into her mouth as she opened for him and allowed him to pull her into his arms. They were lost for a time in each other. The energy of the tree and what Sapphire had just done rippled around them, adding to their excitement. The amused laugh from the Oracle stopped them from disappearing further down the lust path. As he pulled back reluctantly Fox looked into the fathomless blue of his wife's eyes and smiled broadly.

"I see that you have been busy without me," he said wryly. Sapphire looked over her shoulder at the crystal tree and shrugged nonchalantly.

"It was the right time, and the Oracle helped me hold the energy. This tree will anchor the others on Earth and stabilise them. It will open the gateway between the magic here on Shaka to the tree in Egypt and to any others that are formed back on Earth."

Her voice was calm and even. Fox found it mind-boggling that she was taking all this so well. It seemed that her training was coming along better than they had anticipated, and she was at last embracing her new-found power. Her fingers drug into his biceps slightly, and she looked back at him with a coy expression on her face.

"I thought it was best not to wake you while I played with fire." The Oracle clapped her hands joyfully.

"You have done so very well, Sapphire. This tree of life will not only enhance the magic of Shaka but bring great joy and wisdom to your own people." She paused as she watched them both with a distinct twinkle in her eye. "I am very excited for you all." Fox raised a brow.

"I fear that 'excited' is perhaps the wrong emotion to be feeling at the prospect of humankind being exposed to such a gift, Priestess," he said. Sapphire pouted at him.

"You are always the party pooper, Fox. Everything is as it should be. No one can reach this tree without the Oracle's consent. It will be perfectly safe here." Fox licked his top lip hesitantly.

"I am glad you are so confident, my love, and I trust your judgement. But for now I will remain cautious as to what this will actually mean for us all. There is absolutely no doubt you have just caused the biggest magical ripple through our planet that any of us have ever felt." Sapphire's happy face fell suddenly forlorn at the thought she had just put them all in further danger.

The Oracle stepped towards the tree with her arms outstretched and reached up to touch the energy shimmering around the trunk.

"Only those with the strongest magic will have felt any disturbance within the magic surrounding our world, Fox. Have no fear," she said reassuringly. Fox pulled Sapphire once more into his chest and hugged her tightly as he allowed the warmth of her body to soothe his jittering heartbeat.

"That is exactly what I am fearful of, Oracle." She clicked her tongue, as if she disapproved of his pessimistic opinion.

"Your wife will no longer walk in fear from such things, Fox. You have witnessed yourself just how strong she has become. Your connection to her has also increased your own power, guardian. Enjoy this gift for what it is." Fox blinked slowly as he tried to digest her words.

"And what is that exactly?" The Oracle ran her fingers through the air and touched the vibrating energy of the tree as if it was a pet that she was stroking lovingly. On turning around to face them both she smiled sweetly.

"The chance to transform from the chrysalis into the butterfly, my young guardian ... to be something stronger and wiser. That will make quite a formidable team, I think." She laughed again as if she were punch-drunk on the essence surrounding her, which was something that seemed utterly ironic. The most powerful priestess on Shaka was behaving as if she was as high as a kite. Fox closed his eyes briefly and calmed his body. The goddess help them all. Sapphire tugged his arm.

"I think I need a bath, Fox, and then I need to sleep for about a year." Fox nodded and smiled.

"Let's do just that, then," he said. The Oracle spun around in circles. Her hair was flying around her head and scattering silver shards of light into the air.

"Yes, my children. Go and rest now, and I will see you soon." Sapphire looked up at him and bit her lip. She looked a little guilty at turning her guardian angel into an intoxicated naughty fairy.

"Will she be OK?" she asked. Fox shrugged and bent down so that he could whisper into her ear.

"I have no doubt of that, my love. Let's go before anything else happens." He transported them back to the crystal palace in the blink of an eye with Sapphire wrapped in his arms safe and sound. He could still hear the tinkle of the Oracle's laughter in his ears as he ran them a bath in their bedchamber. It made him smile even more.

Conloach approached the cell holding Hecta with silent footsteps. His mind was spinning with all the possibilities of what he had felt in the moments before Wolf had entered his chamber. If Hecta had felt the disturbance in magic as he had it meant that his connection with Sapphire was as strong as the bond he and Fox had with her. This would not be good news to his son. In fact he would be positively enraged by the prospect that Hecta was now linked to his wife again.

Hecta was pacing the cell as he reached the door, and Conloach flicked his hand to open it with his magic. The gatekeeper looked positively distraught, and snapped his head up with fright as Conloach entered. His eyes looked dark and apprehensive. He stepped away from the king as if he were about to receive a beating – not that Conloach had ever touched the man before, despite the urge on several occasions.

"You need not fear me, Hecta. I am not here to harm you." Hecta retreated to the safety of the bench at the back of the cell, regardless of his words. He sat down with his hands on his thighs as if he needed to calm himself. His head dropped and his breathing slowly calmed down.

"I am grateful of that, Conloach," Hecta said. He remained staring at the floor, and Conloach realised that something was alarmingly different about the gatekeeper since he had last seen him. A whisper of magic that he could not quite recognise hung in the air around him, as if someone had altered his very essence.

"Wolf tells me that you were quite agitated, and wanted to talk to me about Sapphire. Tell me why you feel she is in danger." Hecta gripped his thighs. His legs were now shaking as he tried to restrain them to keep still.

"I had a bad dream, nothing more. It was foolish to disturb you at this hour. I apologise."

Conloach moved closer to him. He removed his protection shield and reached out with his magic to test Hecta's aura. Someone had placed a restraining spell around him. It was clearly a very powerful spell, and would have gone undetected by any one with less powerful magic. He tilted his head to one side as he watched the man before him and analysed his reactions. Hecta was clearly torn between speaking the truth and making up some fabricated rubbish.

"Your presence here creates a problem, Gatekeeper. I know that you have experienced some rather radical changes recently, but I must warn you now that I cannot trust you and the words you speak. I know you felt the shift in magic, as did I. It indicates something of immense importance within our world, and Sapphire is most likely the cause." He paused, wondering whether he should try to remove the spell hanging around Hecta or not. "I fear we may need to remove you after all." Hecta stood up so fast that Conloach stepped back, ready to react if he tried to lash out.

"No! I promise you I mean no harm to you or Sapphire. I will be no trouble. You can leave me here in the cells for as long as you wish." Conloach shook his head slowly as he realised that the old Hecta, who would have schemed and fought his way out of this cell, was well and truly gone.

He was definitely no threat, but for some strange reason Conloach realised his link to them all was now a bigger hindrance than ever before. He made the decision there and then that Hecta would be removed from the castle and taken to a place so far away from them that he could be kept under surveillance and out of the way of Fox's wrath – which would most surely follow once he discovered that Hecta was able to feel Sapphire's magic as he did.

"When I say 'remove you', Hecta, I mean that I need to get you away from this place. You are a danger to us here. Your link to Gabriel is too strong, and he will use you to his advantage.

"I can see that you are a changed man, Hecta. The magic Sapphire used to bring you back to life has created a new path for you. I will allow you to live your new life as you see fit, but it will be as far away from my son and his wife as possible. The risk is too great to allow you to stay here with us. I am satisfied that you mean us no harm, but I cannot be complacent and think that your master will have no hold over you." Hecta opened his mouth as if to speak, but the words did not come. He made a strangled, choking sound that resulted in him coughing loudly. The restraining spell was clearly working on its victim all too well.

Conloach reached forward and placed his hand on Hecta's shoulder, which sent a flicker of magic into the gatekeeper that stopped him choking further. Hecta looked at him with an expression of helplessness.

"Thank you," he whispered as he regained his voice. After dipping his head in acknowledgement of the gratitude Hecta was showing him Conloach turned to leave.

"I will arrange transportation to the mountains on the outer edge of the next kingdom, Hecta," Conloach said. "You will be safe there, and far enough away from us to give me some peace of mind. I do not care what you do when you are there, but understand that you will be watched ... and if at any time I find out you are acting in a way that could be dangerous I will have you permanently removed."

Hecta nodded slowly, as if he had already resigned himself to his fate of banishment. It was better than he deserved. After all, if Gabriel had his way he would be spying and causing destruction at the next possible moment. Or he would be dead.

His dream of staying close to Sapphire was now long gone, and he needed to grieve the loss of his impossible dream. He wished that he could see her one last time before Conloach sent him off to the mountains to start his life as an outcast. His days of being a gatekeeper were over. He hoped that his days as a spy were also over. Conloach closed the cell door with a loud clang behind him and concluded by saying,

"I can see the spell around you, Hecta. I know that your master is just watching and waiting for his time. Despite all the sins you have committed in your role as gatekeeper I do not have the heart to throw you back into Gabriel's den just to be used, abused, and destroyed again. I believe that Sapphire brought you back to this world for a reason, and I hope that I am right in thinking that it will be for a good reason." Hecta swallowed hard. He knew that he had no other options and that, despite Gabriel's best efforts, Conloach had taken the upper hand.

"I am grateful for your kindness, Conloach," he said wearily. His voice was low and gravel-like. He felt his heart drop like a cold stone into the bottom of his chest as he watched the great magician walk away down the corridor. He knew Gabriel would not give up on his quest to gain Sapphire's magic, just as Ebony had not given up until she had died trying. He was no good to any of them any longer, and the thought crushed him more than ever before.

He also knew that, despite Conloach's gesture of releasing him to start a new life far away, Gabriel would find him and kill him once he knew he was no longer of any use to him. He would need to be quick and clever, resourceful and ruthless, if he were to indeed stay alive on this world – or any other, for that matter.

It was time for him to test his magic once again and to see if he could travel, as he once did, across the universe to wherever he pleased. It was time for him to reach into his past and pull out some of the old skills and strengths that had allowed him to survive for so long as a gatekeeper. He just hoped that he could remember them, and that his new-found life would not just be a waste of everyone's time.

The warmth of thick, wire-like hair between her fingers made Sapphire jolt within her sleep state. She had travelled again without even realising that she had slipped away from her bed with Fox and taken off into the ethereal realm once more. On opening her eyes fully she felt the heat of the animal beneath her, and grasped even more tightly to the mane of white hair she was holding.

The horse she was riding was pure white and magnificent, and its strong muscles glided and rippled beneath her as they thundered across a landscape filled with golden corn. The fact that the horse carried her so effortlessly and without a single sound was not strange to her in this dream world that she now found herself in. What did strike her as strange was the long ivory-coloured twisted horn that sprang out from its forehead. It bobbed up and down as the horse moved gracefully and silently across the terrain, with just the whisper of breath escaping its flared nostrils. She watched it, mesmerised for a moment, as she gripped the mane for balance.

"I'm riding a unicorn," Sapphire whispered in her head. "Holy crap."

After some time the beast began to slow down, and the rhythm of its legs gradually turned from a canter into a trot. Sapphire realised that they were neither on Shaka nor Earth as they approached a wall of crystal that rose so high into the sky she could not see where it ended.

The sense of familiarity began to pull at her chest. She had been here before, and the crystals glittering like a sheet of ice before her were calling to her as if they were welcoming her return. The unicorn slowed down and came to a stop, then stamped its foreleg to indicate that she should get off.

As she looked around Sapphire hesitated for just a moment before jumping down on to the ground. The earth beneath her feet was almost spongy, like nothing she had felt before. The soft grass with a myriad of flowers that glistened like tiny gems scattered through the green made her gasp. The scent of jasmine and roses filled her mind and soothed her soul.

This place was powerful and beautiful, and it was like coming home. She immediately relaxed, and patted the magnificent beast beside her with thanks. He had brought her here, and she was grateful for it.

Creating the tree on Shaka had been the most terrifying and exhilarating experience of her magical life to date, but it had drained her immensely. After bathing with Fox – who, basically, had washed her and tended to her while she floated pathetically in the hot water – she had eaten very little and retired to bed with Fox, who had agreed she needed to recharge. And, if it did take a year of sleep, then so be it.

She wondered if the taint from the essence she had used was draining her again, as it had on Egypt. It had taken a heavy dose of Willow and Conloach's potion to remove it the last time, and a great deal of rest. Sleeping for a very long time had seemed a good way to start the healing process. She was utterly exhausted, and was filled with the remnants of the magic from the tree and adrenalin surges that – despite her body's state of tiredness – insisted on spiking through her veins.

Fox had soothed her into a state of sleep by stroking her back gently and whispering a lullaby into her ear as he lay beside her. But now she was travelling again – and luckily for her, in this dream state, she had travelled to a place that she knew would recharge her fully.

She had found the crystal cave where she had been when the new strain of magic (that had been mischievously playing with her life recently) had been downloaded into her. It was, without a doubt, the source of her magic and it had called her back again, hopefully to give her some respite and a much-needed boost.

As she walked slowly towards the sheet of crystal she felt a shift in the air beside her.

"Now that really is a most beautiful sight, my love," Fox said. Sapphire smiled and wrapped her fingers around Fox's open hand as he stepped up beside her. She turned to look up at him and found the expression on his face was filled with joy.

"You followed me?" He nodded and returned her smile.

"As always, my love. I sensed you travelling, and decided that it may be wise to join you." She returned her gaze to the wall before them and sighed.

"I'm glad you did," she replied. They walked forward together, holding hands as if this was just another walk in the park and something they did often just for the fun of it. Dream travelling was a big part of who she was and it was becoming the norm lately, and Sapphire realised that she was at last embracing the weirdness of her life with open arms.

"I have been here before, Fox. The magic in this place is very strong," she said. He squeezed her hand gently.

"I can feel it, Sapphire. But this place is new to me. I have never been here before." He paused and looked around at the fields of gold and the lush, green grass of the pathway before them. He smiled as he noticed the unicorn that stood grazing quietly beside them.

"I have absolutely no idea where we are right now. I literally pictured you in my mind and then found myself standing here with you in this amazing place." He smiled. "It seems the Oracle was right, and my magic has also been updated recently." He laughed softly, and shook his head as if amused by this new ability to travel so far away from their usual destinations.

Sapphire placed her free hand against the sheet of crystal before them, closed her eyes, and reached out in her mind as she looked for a way inside. The wall shimmered for a second and then disappeared, then opened up like an invisible doorway for them to enter. Walking through the wall of crystal was like standing in the summer rain with the sun on your face ... pure bliss. She felt Fox shiver beside her as he too felt the magic around them draw them inside and embrace them fully within its heart.

The cavern inside was pure and clear crystal quartz, and the light reflecting around them created a rainbow of colours that spun and flickered against their skin. Fox released her hand and stepped back his breath leaving his lips in a soft hiss.

"Such immense power, Sapphire ... I have never seen a place like this before. It is even more incredible than the crystal caves we visited together when we first met." As she raised her hands above her head Sapphire spun around slowly in a circle and laughed out loud. The sound echoed like a wind chime against the crystals.

"It's wonderful to be back here. I never thought I would see this place again." Fox caught her around the waist and pulled her into his chest as she laughed.

"You needed the energy again, my love. It seems that the goddess is helping you once again." She looked up at him and smiled widely, her eyes sparkling with happiness.

"I need all the help I can get in that department. I'm grateful for it." As he pulled her in closer to kiss her she felt the energy around her lift her up higher and higher, filling her body with a surge of clean, fresh magic. The taste of Fox on her tongue as he kissed her made her head spin. She knew that if it was not for the man holding her right now she would have spun off into a place far away, such was the power of this place. A woman's voice whispered in her mind as she kissed Fox and drifted on the wave of magic.

"Remember this place, my child. You will need to return here from time to time. Your gifts are strong, but will drain you utterly if you use them too much. Remember to use them wisely. You will need all your strength for the tasks ahead of you. Blessed be." The voice was new to Sapphire and she did not know who it belonged to, but as she kissed her husband and recharged her magic in this beautiful hidden place she had no doubt whatsoever that it was a voice of great wisdom and that she needed to take notice of what it had said.

Time itself had spun and flown around them as they had stood wrapped in each other's arms, lost in the kiss that had begun softly and grown into something much more intense.

Fox could feel his own energy lifting higher as they clung to each other in this strange, magical place. Voices – words in languages even he did not understand – flickered inside his head like whispers that teased him softly. It was as if they had landed in a place that had been visited by many other magical beings, and the residual energy from each of them was being played back inside his mind like a never-ending tape recording.

Sapphire gripped his arms and pressed her body against him with an urgency that he recognised as her need to get much closer. Her leg had lifted and was wrapping itself around him in an effort to climb him further. He grabbed her behind the knee and steadied her body against him, and pushed his groin forward so that she could do just that.

The soft whimpers coming from her mouth as she tangled her tongue around his made him groan. The energy here was quite literally mind-blowing and pushing them together in a fiercely primeval way. It was connecting them in a wave of deep sexual energy that was growing stronger and stronger by the second.

Fox released his mouth from Sapphire and threw his head back and moaned loudly as she literally pulled herself up his body. Both her legs were wrapped around his waist and her hands were now gripping the back of his neck. The heat from her groin pulsed madly against him, sending shock waves of pleasure throughout his body. His hands moved to her buttocks and gripped them hard so that he could steady her body, which began to move on its own accord against him.

She had turned into a wildcat and, at the speed of a fast sports car, had gone from nought to sixty in a few seconds. Without warning she clamped on to his neck and bit him hard. His cock hardened instantly and pushed against her. He wanted release and he wanted it now. This strange journey of magical healing was quickly spinning out of control – of which, it seemed, they had none at that moment.

Both of them were wrapped up in the need to find release, and Sapphire was attacking him now like a nymphomaniac. He tried to regain some clarity and shook his head, as he was staggering a little at the heady energy that had suddenly smothered them both.

The voices in his head became louder, and he tried somewhat desperately to stay upright as the energy surrounding them hit him like a sucker punch straight to the chest. It felt as if they were both being zapped by something much more ancient than he had ever felt back on Shaka – or in any other world he had visited, for that matter.

Despite the intense pleasure it created within his veins he had the distinct impression that they were being watched, and it created an uneasy sensation within his chest as he held Sapphire in his arms. Was this a test of will? Had Sapphire really been brought here for cleansing and recharging or was this something else altogether? She was grappling with his clothing now and almost growling at him as he staggered again, his knees almost buckling beneath him.

"Sapphire," he panted against her lips as she tried to kiss him again. "Sapphire ... stop. Stop for a second."

She continued her onslaught, lost in the power of the energy that surrounded them. Her whole body seemed to be lit up now, and the symbols he had seen under her skin when the wild magic had first been downloaded into her flickered eerily like neon blue lights.

Something felt wrong. This was far too intense for just a recharge, and it was pushing their buttons to such an extreme that it was almost painful. Fox dropped slowly to the floor on to his knees and began to prise Sapphire's fingers away from his shirt, which she was trying to rip away from his chest. Her eyes were closed and her mouth was open slightly.

She shuddered and took a deep breath as he pushed her away. She was lost in the magic surrounding them, and it made him shake with both excitement and trepidation at how it had transformed her so quickly. This wild magic was something different altogether.

And then suddenly he realised why he was the one gaining back his control and not Sapphire. This was her dream state, and she was creating this scene. It was her manifestation, and she was thoroughly enjoying herself. He almost laughed in relief. He had been so caught up for a moment in the power of it all that he had forgotten why they were here in the first place. The voices in his head were just a whisper again, and he listened for a second to see if he could in fact translate what they were saying.

"Fox, please, what are you doing? Don't stop," Sapphire whimpered as she opened her eyes and grasped for the button on his trousers. She was fumbling now in her eagerness to release him from the confines of his clothing. Her legs were still around his waist and her backside was on the floor as he knelt down on his haunches before her. He grabbed her chin and pulled her face up to look at him.

"Sapphire, stop. Stop now. You are out of control. Slow down, my love. This amount of sexual energy is too intense even for me." She blinked up at him as if not understanding a single word he had just spoken. He smiled at her as a voice in his head spoke quite clearly to him in his own language,

"The power your wife holds is truly magnificent, guardian, but she needs you to ground her now, my servant, or it will consume you both. You are her balance, her protector, in times that she needs you. Do your job, Fox, for she needs you now." He nodded and released her chin and, after grabbing both her wrists to stop her from unbuttoning his trousers, he sent a pulse of his own magic through his body into hers that grounded them both at the same time.

She moaned and tipped her head back and revealed her neck to him, with her hair flowing down to the ground in a stream of white-blonde locks. It took all his restraint not to let her continue and fuck her into oblivion because the sight of her submission made him shiver.

The energy around them began to dissipate and the intensity of it gradually subsided and floated away like a cloud on a breeze. His cock remained rock-hard, however, and he laughed as Sapphire sighed heavily lifting her head back up to stare at him in bewilderment.

"What just happened?" Sapphire asked. Fox pulled her into his chest and rested her head against him as he stroked her hair gently.

"You became a little overexcited, my love. No harm done, but I think it would be best if we return to our world now. I think we are both very much recharged, and that it would be best to continue this moment in our bedchamber back on Shaka." Sapphire pushed her face into his shirt and breathed in his scent deeply, like a wild animal recognising its mate.

"Am I still dreaming?" He laughed.

"Most definitely, and I think it is time you woke up."

Sapphire did just that, as she gasped for air and sat bolt upright in the bed they were sharing in the crystal palace back on Shaka. She looked beside her, and found Fox staring at her with eyes that glowed like two gold coins sparkling in the sunlight. He smiled at her and chuckled.

"Fuck, that was trippy," she said and laughed. They were both naked, and the sunlight streamed in from the beautiful day outside and reflected from their skin like fireflies. They were shining like two beacons and sending rainbow colours across the room that spun and danced against the bed sheets. Fox sat next to her with his chest rising and falling quickly, as if the trip had indeed been far more exciting than even he had anticipated when he had joined her.

"Indeed it was, my love." She looked down and smiled coyly, as she noticed he was still standing to attention.

"Did I do that?" she asked. He nodded slowly.

"Mmmh." As she looked up from under her dark eyelashes she tilted her head to one side.

"It looks uncomfortable." He continued to smile at her, his chest still moving quickly.

"Mmmh hmmm." She had rendered him speechless, it seemed.

"I think I should help you with that." His hand lifted to her face and he ran a long, nimble finger across her cheek that sent a shiver of magic across her skin.

"I think that would be a very good idea," he said.

They stayed at the Oracle's home for another three days to continue Sapphire's training. This consisted of her working with Fox and the Oracle alternately, using both her magic and her physical skills to help her gain control once more.

Fox left briefly on the second day to visit his father again. He did not tell her the reason why, but she knew it had something to do with Hecta. She no longer wished her head to be filled with thoughts of the gatekeeper, and so she left the details of what would happen to him now up to her husband and father-in-law. Her main focus was on fine-tuning her abilities and learning how to control her dreaming after what had happened to them the last time she had travelled.

The Oracle explained to her that the place they had visited was the source of her power, but it was a place that needed to be treated with great caution as it magnified her power so much it could be very destructive if not handled properly. She had almost raped poor Fox the last time he had blindly followed her there when she had needed to recharge. They agreed that as and when she needed to return to this place she should go alone, and only if she really needed to.

Sapphire was still trying to get her head around it all and desperately wanted to return to Earth and her real home, where she knew her friends would help knock her back to reality. The threat of Gabriel was still lingering in the back of her mind, but she knew that with her new-found abilities and the training she had received she no longer had to feel so afraid of him. Her time there at the palace had certainly been enlightening in more ways than one.

As she stood beneath the branches of the crystal tree, with the Oracle standing beside her, Sapphire felt a wave of sadness spread through her body. The tree had begun to flourish with the same crystal flowers that had appeared on the tree back in Egypt. They looked the same, but Sapphire knew instinctively that these would be much more powerful.

"Why are you so sad, my child?" the Oracle asked as she reached for Sapphire's hand and linked her fingers within her own. Sapphire had grown accustomed to the Oracle touching her now in such an intimate way, and it comforted her immensely.

"I feel unsure, Oracle … unsure of what will happen now that I have created the bridge between our two worlds." The Oracle laughed softly.

"Doubt is a very human concept, my child, and one that may just be useful for you as you move forward on this journey … as to be too confident can sometimes create its own problems." Sapphire smiled.

"You mean the human ego." The Oracle swung their joined hands back and forth between them like a child would.

"Perhaps. Doubt, confusion, and fear … they all have a purpose, as well as the opposite emotions: clarity, certainty, and confidence. Everything needs its balance. You will always retain your human emotions and instincts, Sapphire, and they will serve you well. What you see before you is a very powerful creation, and it must be respected and guarded well. Never forget this." Sapphire snorted.

"How could I forget it? Fox constantly reminds me of these things as he has less faith in my fellow humans than, it seems, you do." She laughed loudly, and the sound travelled across the lake before them like beautiful birdsong.

"He is not of your world, Sapphire, and will always be a little cautious when it comes to the evolution of your species." Sapphire sighed.

"Sometimes I wish I could just be totally human again, Oracle. Life would be so much easier." The Oracle pulled her closer to the tree and, as she smiled, pressed her hand against the trunk.

"But much less exciting, I believe." The tree shimmered in response to the Oracle's own magic, and Sapphire shivered as the energy travelled between them.

"I would be happy to do 'less exciting' for a while." The Oracle stroked the tree trunk lovingly.

"Be careful what you wish for, young Sapphire." She turned to face her and released her hand. As she looked down at her with mischief in her eyes she placed both her palms on to her cheeks softly. The Oracle dipped down and kissed her softly on the lips.

"Now go, Sapphire, to your homeland, and be 'less excited' for a while. Rest and enjoy your time with your guardian and your friends before the next step of your journey begins." Sapphire closed her eyes and revelled in the touch of the Oracle's lips – so soft and sweet, like ripe cherries, on her own. "I will take care of your tree, my child. Go now. Blessed be."

Sapphire and Fox left that afternoon and went back to Calafia to say goodbye to Conloach, Kit, and Bear before they returned to Earth once more. Sapphire felt infinitely stronger and calmer, and was looking forward to seeing Pearl, Charlie, and Nathan again. Because she was now armed with her new insight of magic and the power that she could wield she no longer felt afraid of the small bundle of magical tools that she carried with her containing the seeds, the essence, and the means to plant them.

She was looking forward to having a pint at The Swan and eating some junk food in front of the TV. At last she was feeling more at ease with her ability to move across time and space using her dream travelling skills and magic. As she hugged Kit and kissed Bear goodbye on the cheek she felt a new sense of calm envelop her. This was at last becoming more familiar to her. Effectively she had two lives now: one on Shaka, and the other on Earth with her extended family.

Conloach stood beside them like a pillar of strength – always calm, always wise. She was grateful to have him as her father now, for that is what he had become. As she reached up to kiss him on the cheek she felt his magic, soft and soothing, against her skin. He whispered quietly into her ear as she touched her lips to his skin.

"Hecta has been dealt with, Sapphire. You no longer have to worry about him. He is far away now, and no threat to you or Fox. I will be watching him and Gabriel." She nodded and grasped his hand, and squeezed it briefly in acknowledgement.

"Thank you," she whispered back. Fox stepped forward and claimed her free hand.

"It is time we left, Sapphire," he said. They stepped back and away from the people they loved, who were standing before them, and Sapphire felt a twist of emotion in her chest as she faced them all as they stood waiting for her and Fox to disappear once again on a wave of magic. She loved these people now with all her heart, and she knew that they would always be there for her when she returned once more. At that moment she had absolutely no idea when that would be.

She gripped Fox's hand tightly and smiled at them with as much joy as she could at such a difficult moment. It was always so hard to leave the people she loved. They smiled back, and Fox pulled her closer as his magic enveloped her like a soft cloak of silk. As he pulled her away from Shaka and back down the wormhole she wondered whether she would ever get used to this constant tug back and forth between her two worlds. She sincerely hoped she would.

Chapter Thirty

Charlie walked down the corridor towards the main doors of the maternity ward at the local hospital with a mixture of excitement and nerves spinning around inside her stomach. She was holding Nathan's hand tightly. It was time for her first scan, and she was feeling a little anxious about the whole thing. Nathan gripped her hand when he sensed her apprehension of seeing their 'little bean' for the first time.

"Stop stressing, babe. Everything will be fine. Our baby will be strong and healthy, just like us." Charlie looked up at him. His smile lit up his cute face in a way that made her heart flip. He was always so happy and cheerful, always looking on the bright side of life, and she was thankful for it.

Right now she was stressing that due to all her reckless drug taking, alcohol consumption, and general craziness her baby might just be glowing a nuclear green colour in her belly. Nathan had taken the news of her pregnancy like he did everything else in life: with extreme excitement and a great deal of enthusiasm. He couldn't wait to be a father. In fact it had taken a large number of threats on her part to stop him from telling the whole world that they were soon to be parents. Charlie wanted to wait and make sure everything was healthy and OK before she launched this news on to the world of social media – and of course on to her parents, who were (at present) in the dark, and who would most likely faint at the thought of their daughter actually settling down and being responsible for once in her life. He tugged her arm again as they opened the door into the waiting area.

"I promise you, Charlie, nothing bad is going to happen. Everything will be hunky-dory. You wait and see." She smiled at him weakly as she approached the desk. At least the remedy Pearl had been giving her had helped with the morning, evening, and every-minute-of-the-day sickness she had experienced at the beginning of her pregnancy. She was guessing that she was now around twelve weeks pregnant. There had been no sign of Sapphire or Fox for a while, and she hoped that her friends would return home soon as not being able to share the news with them was killing her.

The receptionist smiled and, when Charlie gave her name, indicated that they should take a seat. While sitting on the plastic chairs with all the other big-bellied and hormonal women in the waiting area Charlie began to fidget.

"Babe ... seriously ... calm down. You are starting to make me nervous," Nathan said. He leant across, placed his forehead on her own, and took her hands into his to steady them. "Just breathe, babe. Breathe." His warm skin and the subtle scent of his aftershave soothed her and made her feel a little nauseous both at the same time. Her hormones were doing some seriously weird shit at the moment. Everything smelt stronger and tasted strange. She had gone off coffee immediately, and couldn't stand the smell of wine. What a fuckin' bore. He kissed her softly and moved his hand to the back of her neck and held her gently. His lips tasted of peppermint and, thankfully, this helped with the impending 'I'm going to puke' sensation that threatened to pop up again.

"Miss Daines, if you could go to Room Four please," the receptionist called after five minutes of Nathan trying to calm her with his very kissable lips. He grinned at her and pulled her up from the chair, which squeaked loudly as she stood up.

As they walked towards the door of Room Four Charlie noticed a man leaning against the wall of the opposite corridor. He looked oddly out of place, and was staring straight at them. He was dressed in a long coat that looked as if it belonged in *The Matrix* and he had the most striking blue eyes and white-blonde hair, which was pulled back and braided down his back like a rope. She shivered as he watched her. There was a slither of a smile on his perfect lips that made him appear almost catlike. He appeared beautiful and deadly all at the same time. She caught her breath and paused when his image seemed to flicker suddenly. And then he just disappeared. Just like that.

"You OK, babe?" Nathan asked her. She shook her head and frowned. Had she just seen that? Was she at last going completely fucking mad?

"Yeah, I'm OK," she said. Nathan looked over her head to see what she was staring at in the opposite corridor. It was completely empty of anything except for a wall of pregnancy pictures advertising all sorts of baby-related information – that he, quite frankly, did not understand.

"OK ..." he said with amusement. Charlie took a deep breath and smiled back up at him.

"Let's get this done," she said. Nathan laughed, pushed the door open, and pulled her inside. She knew he must think that she had just had another moment of nerves and was acting like a crazy woman full of baby hormones. Charlie, on the other hand, had the distinct feeling that something very weird was most likely about to happen. And that was not a pleasant thought at all.

"So everything is fine and healthy. No problems at all?" Charlie asked once more, as the nurse beside her wiped her belly clean from the gel she had used to carry out the ultrasound. The nurse smiled at her and nodded.

"Yes, everything is absolutely fine, and from the measurements we have taken today I would say that your due date will be 31 October." Nathan laughed out loud, which made Charlie jump.

"Trust us to have a baby due to be born on Halloween. That's so fucking funny." Charlie slapped him and frowned.

"Stop swearing in front of the nice nurse, Nat. And it's not funny." The nurse watched them with amusement.

"No problem with the swearing. I have to stop myself in front of the patients all the time. I blame it on my Irish blood for giving me the tendency to want to swear at everyone and everything." Nathan laughed loudly again. Charlie continued to frown, although a little less, as she knew the nurse was just trying to be kind and break the tension in the air.

"When do I need to come back again?" she asked the nurse. Nathan was stroking her stomach absently as the nurse tidied up. He was clearly in love with his child, even in its early embryonic state.

"Your next scan will be between eighteen and twenty-one weeks. We can book that in nearer the time." Charlie stopped Nathan's hand from slipping under her top by gripping it firmly and scowling at him again. He grinned back at her.

"So what do I do now?" The nurse turned to face her after tidying the tray, which was covered in scary-looking objects.

"Put your feet up, enjoy having the ability to paint your toenails for a while longer, and prepare for your new arrival." Nathan nodded enthusiastically. Charlie almost growled.

"So I don't have to do anything else then to make sure this little one is OK?" The nurse smiled again.

"There are lots of classes you can attend and information available for you at your doctor's surgery. But, to be honest, as long as you are feeling well and eating well … no, nothing else." Nathan helped Charlie off the couch and raised his hand as if he were a child in class.

"Actually, I have a question." The nurse regarded him with the never-ending smile that was still on her lips.

"Yes, of course," she said. Charlie waited for whatever daft question was about to come out of his mouth with bated breath.

"What about sex? Is it still OK for us to have lots of sex?" Charlie felt her mouth pop open.

"Yes, of course. Lots of sex is always a good thing, and perfectly safe." She paused and looked at Charlie, who had started to turn nicely pink in the cheeks. "But always check with your lovely lady that she is in the mood first, young man. Pregnancy can make you one way or the other, you know. She will either want lots or none at all." Nathan nodded seriously.

"Well, I hope it's the first option," he said. Charlie grabbed him by the arm.

"Come on, you sex fiend. Let's go home."

As they left the hospital to head back to the cottage Charlie looked around for the strange man she had seen earlier, just in case he had been real. Nathan literally bounded to the car. He was beaming like a madman carrying the picture of their little 'alien' baby (who, luckily, wasn't glowing green) in his hand as if it was the most precious object in the world.

Charlie wanted to see Pearl and check that everything was OK on her witchy radar, and that she wasn't going crazy. As much as she believed in the good old-fashioned methods of the NHS for checking your baby's health she now trusted her witchy friend more when it came to her life, and what might lay ahead for her. After everything that had happened with Sapphire and Fox and the nutcase Hecta she wanted to double-check that there were no other weird and wonderful magical creatures out there hunting her down. Especially now ... especially with this extra little person inside her, who she was now solely responsible for – for growing into a fully developed and functional person without any defects whatsoever.

"Oh, God, I think I'm gonna puke again, Nat," Charlie said as the realisation of it all swept over her muddled brain.

"OK, babe. Don't panic. Just bend over here by the bush. No one will mind." As she dry-heaved a bit, and processed the fact that suddenly she was going to have to be sensible for once in her life and actually eat properly and not take any risks, she was very, very thankful that she had the most amazing man in her life to help her. Nathan was the perfect man to coddle her, care for her, and protect her for the next seven or so months, but she wished with all her heart that Saf would come home. She needed her friend now more than ever.

Pearl smiled at the shopkeeper sweetly as she took her bag of groceries from the counter and pocketed her change.

"Thank you, Debbie. Have a nice evening." She had stopped at the small village shop to collect a few items that she had run low on in her pantry, and was keen to get home again before the evening drew in. The days were growing much warmer now, and the evenings drawing out just that little bit more. Spring was most definitely peeking over the horizon. After the cold winter they had just had it was a welcoming balm to see the seasons turn once more.

The bell clanged over her head as she pushed the door open and stepped outside into the high street. It was Saturday afternoon, and the high street was fairly busy with local people going about their business. The familiarity of this place was soothing to her soul. She had lived here all her life, and its gentle rhythm suited her even more now that she was growing older.

Pearl knew instinctively that her life path would most likely be coming to its end fairly soon. She could feel it in her bones and in her soul, and she welcomed it. She was not afraid of leaving this world and passing on to the next. For a witch this journey from one world to the next was celebrated rather than feared.

She did hope, however, that Sapphire would return soon, as Charlie needed her support now and it would be good to tie up the loose ends with her dream traveller friend. Pearl had the distinct feeling that this special woman would be much changed again on her return and that she may need just a few more pieces of wisdom and insight from her before she did finally move on.

As Pearl left the high street and took a turn towards her part of the village she felt a brush of magic move across her senses that made her sniff the air like a dog picking up an interesting scent. The area itself was highly energetic – and now that her tree, with its spectacular doorway, had blossomed into something quite unique she could feel the change in the air and in the ground beneath her feet. The magical breeze followed her as she walked home. As she drew closer to her lane the scent changed and became stronger. It was a mixture of citrus and base notes that reminded her of orange and ginger blended with the musky scent of cedarwood.

As she reached her lane she stopped for a moment and closed her eyes after placing her shopping bag on the floor. Dusk was approaching quickly now, and she could feel the temperature drop a little around her. The sky was turning a warm orange as the sun began to slip further down over the horizon. Someone was approaching her. Someone magical.

As she opened her eyes again she sighed deeply at the sight before her. Standing a few feet in front of her was the man she had been trying not to think about since his appearance at the bottom of her garden some time ago. He smiled at her. His face was serene and glowing with magic, which pulsed and danced around him in glorious Technicolor.

"Gabriel ... Is it really you?" He stepped forward and his hands moved to clasp her own. As his fingers touched her she let out a small whimper, not from fright or pain but from pure, exquisite pleasure. His magic filtered into her tired old bones and filled her completely, making her body shiver involuntarily. The sensation was quite unexpected, and something she had not felt for a very very long time.

"My love, I have come to take you home." She looked up into his crystal blue eyes that flickered with white flakes of snow and was lost for a moment in the storm that lay behind them, lost in the blizzard of emotions that filled her as she stared into them. She was totally hypnotised – mesmerised – by them. He pulled her gently into his arms and wrapped himself around her, and pulled her closer so that he could press his face into her hair and breathe in her scent. She felt her entire body melt into his – dissolve, almost like sugar in hot coffee. So delicious was his warmth and presence that she felt as if her body would literally liquefy into a puddle on the pathway.

"You belong with me, my beloved, and I am at last able to claim you once more. The gateway is now open, and I am taking you home with me so that we can be together again ... forever." Pearl felt her heart flutter in her chest as if it wanted to take flight and break free from her body at any moment. While lifting her face from the broad expanse of his chest she looked up at him and blinked slowly.

"But I am an old woman now, Gabriel, and much changed from the young woman you fell in love with so many lifetimes ago. I cannot be with you now. It is not possible." His eyes flashed at her again, this time with a touch of anger.

"Nothing is impossible, my love. Not now, not with the help of your young friend and the wonderful magic she now possesses. The gateway is open between your world and mine, and it will return you to your former glory as the woman who I have always loved in the physical and magical way that you deserve." He paused and smiled once again, and his lips curled up slowly. "We can be happy again, as we once were."

Pearl felt the pull of his magic. Her body responded to it as it had all those years and lifetimes before, as did her energy. She had loved him with every fibre of her being then, and it was clear that the love they had shared was still there. He was beautiful and magnificently powerful, more powerful than she had remembered, and the allure of it all was tempting her to take him up on his offer and jump over the rainbow for the chance of a new life with him once more.

But at what price? The magic he spoke of belonged to Sapphire and it was for another purpose, not to restore her to her former youth and beauty. It was not a gift to be stolen and used for vanity or lost love. She knew that the man holding her right now had become lost somewhere along his pathway, and only wanted her to fill the void that he had clearly been suffering in during her absence. She could see it quite clearly now in his expression, which verged on the edge of madness.

It would be wrong to change the path of her destiny in this way, and karma would not allow it or like it. The price to Sapphire would be too high to pay, and could change everything the young dream traveller was trying to achieve. The higher purpose of the gateway in her woods and the magic Sapphire had been gifted with was not to be used on the whim of a magical man who had lost his only love. It was for Mother Earth herself to reawaken and help her children to rise to a new level of consciousness that would, in time, allow them all to heal and grow. Pearl shook her head slowly.

"Gabriel, I cannot take this path you offer me. My time is coming to an end, and although it saddens me that you have only just found me again we cannot do this together." She paused and gripped his arms tightly. "You have to let me go," she said. He drew in a deep breath. The air around him seemed to expand for a moment and swelled like a balloon about to explode.

"No, Pearl. You are coming with me, and Sapphire will help me take you."

Sapphire, with Fox by her side, stepped up to the doorway to the cottage that would always have a special place in her heart. He smiled at her as she raised her hand to knock loudly on the shining new door knocker. They waited silently. Their magic was flowing freely between them in excitement as they heard the footsteps inside come closer.

"I'll get it, Charlie," Nathan hollered loudly on the other side of the door. Sapphire shifted on her feet. She was anxious to get inside and see her friends once again in the flesh. She had realised on her return to Earth that time had moved on again here, and the season had changed from the cold winter from their last visit to the warmer promise of spring. She wondered what changes had taken place in her absence.

The door was pulled open and Nathan stood before them with a piece of toast in his mouth. His face was a picture of surprise as he took in the couple before him. He spluttered out the piece of bread and stumbled forward as he reached out for Sapphire.

"Saf! Holy fuck, you're back." He grabbed her with one arm and pulled her into his chest while still trying to keep a hold of his breakfast. Fox chuckled as the young man swung his wife around on the doorstep. He couldn't stop laughing.

"Charlie! Get your beautiful arse out here. Saf's home." The thunder of feet from further inside the house clattered down the hallway. Charlie appeared in her pink onesie looking flushed and flustered with her hair piled on top of her head as if she had literally just woken up. Nathan was pulling her inside now as Charlie launched herself at her friend. Fox stepped aside as the two friends collided in the landing. Nathan smirked and raised a brow at him.

"Ah, the magical man returns with his beautiful wife. Good to see you, Fox. You're looking as fabulous as ever, the pair of ya." Fox dipped his head and smiled.

"It is always good to see you, my friend," he said. They greeted each other with a bear hug. Nathan gripped him a tad longer than necessary, as if he was about to burst into tears. Charlie had done just that, and was holding Sapphire to her as if her life depended on it. She was sobbing into her shoulder and jumping up and down at the same time. Sapphire laughed. She was trying to remain upright as her friend hugged her tightly.

"Oh, Saf, thank fuck you are back. Where the hell have you two been this time? It's been ages. So much has happened. I thought you were never gonna get your arses back here." Fox tipped his head to one side as he watched them for a moment. His eyes flicked back to Nathan, who grinned like a Cheshire cat and nodded his head with that 'Oh, yes!' look. Fox smiled widely.

"Well, it seems congratulations are in order for you both. You have been busy, my friends." Sapphire pulled back from the weeping Charlie and held her at arm's length as she surveyed her friend and noticed the change in her aura, which shone the most beautiful brilliant pink and lilac.

She was pregnant. It was as clear as day, and the slight bump in the front of her onesie confirmed it. Charlie had always been as slim and as trim as a willow tree, and it was almost odd to see the tiny protrusion from her stomach. Charlie wiped her nose with the sleeve of her onesie and laughed.

"Yep, I'm up the duff. Bun in the oven … totally impregnated – thanks to you, young lady, and your trippy magic flower thingy." Sapphire shook her head slowly and beamed at her friend, who seemed to shine so vibrantly now in a glow of love and light.

"I think Nathan is the one to blame, honey, not me. But wow! That's amazing news. I'm so happy for you both." Nathan closed the door behind them and bustled them into the cottage. The familiar smell and feel of the place hit Sapphire hard in the chest, and made her want to cry along with her clearly hormonal friend.

"Oh, no … Pearl confirmed that it was all down to your magic, Saf. I blame you entirely for my current predicament." Nathan had a pretend frown on his face.

"Hey! It was my supersonic sperm, babe. You can't let Sapphire take all the credit." Fox laughed.

"I have no doubt that you can take all the credit, Nathan. Don't let Sapphire steal your moment of glory." Charlie sniffed, clearly having trouble in containing her joy at seeing her friend again.

"It's so good to see you both. Come in and I'll make us some tea. Do you realise how fucking early it is? Seriously, you guys just pop up at the most inconvenient times, you know." Sapphire laughed and took her friend's hand, revelling in the feeling of actually touching her overly warm skin again for real.

"We could always leave again if it's not a good time, Charlie," Sapphire said. Charlie gawped at her.

"Oh, shut up. Now is not the time to start joking. Come into the kitchen. I want to know everything, and I mean *everything*," she said, emphasising the last word as if it were mightily important.

Sapphire looked at her husband and grinned widely. This was most unexpected, but there could not have been a better reason to return home after everything that had been happening back on Shaka.

"I think you two need to update us on what's been happening here in our absence. In the places where we have been, Charlie, time passes differently, and it has literally only been a couple of weeks since I saw you last." Nathan, clearly confused, screwed his face up.

"What the fuck? That's just trippy, guys." Fox followed them to the kitchen smiling at them both.

"Believe me, Nathan, that is not the only thing that has been trippy for us since we left." Charlie slumped down into one of the kitchen chairs.

"Nat, sweetie, put the kettle on. We need more tea, and make it snappy." He saluted at her with a grin and pulled a couple of chairs out for Sapphire and Fox.

"She's become so much more bossy since I impregnated her, Saf," Nathan said. Sapphire raised a brow.

"Is that even possible?" Nathan laughed loudly as he gathered more cups and flicked the kettle switch down to boil. Charlie frowned as she grabbed her mug and took a loud slurp of her tea.

"Hey, I am not bossy. It's just my hormones. They make me cranky sometimes." Fox regarded her with an amused twist to his smile.

"How far along are you, Charlie?" She smiled now, and her face became soft and gooey.

"Almost three months now. Little bean is due on 31 October." Fox nodded. His elbows were on the kitchen table and his fingers were steepled in thought.

"Samhain is one of the greater pagan sabbats. It marks the beginning of both the Celtic and the Wiccan new year, and is a very powerful and fortuitous time to have your baby come into this world." Charlie, wide-eyed in confusion, looked at him.

"Halloween, Charlie. You know: All Hallows' Eve," Fox explained. Nathan opened the fridge to grab the milk as he looked over his shoulder and grinned.

"Yeah, our babe's going to be a spooky little fucker." Fox laughed. Charlie rolled her eyes.

"I will not be dressing our baby in a pumpkin suit when it is born, Nathan, or calling it a 'spooky fucker' under any circumstances." Sapphire closed her eyes. She smiled and breathed out heavily as she lifted her arms above her head to stretch them out. After the long, magical journey down the wormhole to Earth she needed this familiar banter. It was quite refreshing.

"Oh, God, it's so good to be back," she said. Charlie smiled wistfully.

"I'm so glad you are back, Saf. I need you to help me organise my life now that it is going to involve another little person. I have no clue, despite all the books Nathan has insisted on buying, what I am supposed to do or how to organise the cottage. I mean ... I have been keeping your room for you guys, but we might have to start thinking about turning it into the nursery ... and I didn't want to start on the painting until you came back. That would have just been rude, and I really didn't want to do that without you being here." Sapphire reached across the table, took her hands within her own, and squeezed them gently.

"Charlie, honey, this is your home. You go ahead and make it into the wonderful little nest that you need to help make your baby welcome. Fox and I can always find another place to stay when that happens. I'm buzzing for the pair of you right now. It's wonderful news to return to. Quite honestly, I needed something normal to return home for ... and this is a most welcome distraction to what I've been up to back on Shaka." Fox took the mug of tea Nathan had made him, and nodded in thanks.

"It is indeed the most blessed news. We are both more than happy to help you with your nursery and anything else you may need," he said. Nathan grabbed the biscuits and Sapphire's mug and handed it to her with a smile.

"I could do with a night off, Fox. Fancy coming up the pub tonight? We can leave these two to catch up on the last few months – I mean weeks." Charlie huffed.

"You went out with Simon on Wednesday," she said. Sapphire smiled widely and said,

"Ah, and so it begins." Charlie frowned.

"What's that supposed to mean?" Sapphire shook her head and chuckled softly. Fox was also amused, and was biting his lip to stop himself from laughing.

"Nothing, honey. It's just great to see you two getting along like an old married couple, all settled and with a baby on the way. It's just so wonderfully human." Charlie allowed a small smile to grace her lips.

"Well, we are most definitely human, Saf. I'm not sure what the baby will be like, however, seeing as *you* helped get me pregnant." They all laughed at that. It was such a beautiful sound on such a beautiful day.

They spent the time in the kitchen that Sunday morning catching up on what they had respectively been doing in their different worlds. Sapphire left out all the more scary details of her new magical abilities and the fact that Hecta was now alive and living in some faraway place on Shaka again. But she did fill them in on how she had been in training with her new magical skills, and that she was feeling much more confident with her abilities now. In fact she left out a great many of the finer details.

Fox looked at her over the edge of his second cup of tea with a knowing glint in his eyes. He, for one, knew that all that information would be far too much for Charlie – who was now in a much more sensitive state – to take in. Nathan was always clearly a little confused but nodded, smiled, and looked concerned in all the right places of the conversation.

It seemed that Pearl had been her usual amazing self, helping Charlie out with remedies for her morning sickness and generally reassuring her that everything was just as it should be. Nathan had beamed with happiness as he had shown Sapphire and Fox the picture of the baby scan they had taken recently. Sapphire stared at it and narrowed her eyes as she tried to make out what was what.

"That's the baby's head, Saf. And look: that's his massive cock," Nathan said with pride. Charlie thumped him hard on the arm.

"Nathan, stop doing that. It's the baby's arm, you stupid idiot." Fox laughed loudly.

"I think he may just be right, Charlie." Sapphire looked at him with a raised brow. He was very good at sensing things, and may have been able to detect the baby's sex after all. Charlie also regarded him with interest.

"So it is a boy, then?" Fox leant back in his chair and smiled slyly.

"Surprises are always much more exciting; don't you think?" he said. Nathan slapped him on the back heartily.

"Yep, it's a boy. I can tell by the look in your eye, Fox. Thank God for that. I don't really mind whatever the baby is as long as it's healthy, but raising a girl … well, that would be a challenge, I think. I would probably be a nightmare. She wouldn't be allowed to date until she was at least twenty-one. I know what men are like."

Charlie smiled at him with that gooey look again. Sapphire could see that a lot had changed in her absence but, although it was clear that her friend's emotions and hormones were flipping up and down like a roller coaster ride, one thing was certain. This unexpected pregnancy had certainly brought her two friends even closer together, and they were now even more in love than they had ever been before.

"Ah, someone pass me a bucket," she thought to herself as the pair of them continued to stare at each other in lovesick wonder. Fox coughed to break the moment.

"Do you want to visit Pearl today, Sapphire? It may be good to check up on her now that we are back." He looked at Charlie with serious eyes. "Have you seen her recently, Charlie?"

Sapphire nodded. Yes, she did want to see Pearl, and now that Fox had mentioned her she felt the urge to do so push insistently in her mind.

"I saw her on Friday," Charlie replied. "She was fine. She popped by with some more of that awful-tasting stuff that is keeping my puking at bay. She will be absolutely psyched to see you both. She has been missing you guys as much as we have. I think she has been spending a lot of time in the woods again lately." Sapphire looked across at Fox, who returned her gaze with a flicker of concern.

"Then we will leave you two wonderful people to finish your morning and return later, after we have stopped by to see Pearl. I look forward to going to the pub with you later, Nathan." Nathan grinned at him.

"It's a date, Fox," he said. Charlie insisted on giving Sapphire another overly zealous bear hug before they left and told her not to be too long, as she needed to show her some pictures of the possible nursery decorating themes. Deep joy.

Chapter Thirty-One

Fox wrapped his arm around her shoulder as they walked down the lane towards the woods.

"Are you glad to be back, my love?" he asked. Sapphire sighed deeply as she breathed in the clean air, which had a tang of spring rain at the edges.

"Definitely. I needed a break from magic for a while. This place brings me back to Earth – literally." He chuckled and kissed the top of her head, and then moved his hand to the back of her neck and pushed his fingers under her hair so that he could hold her loosely at the nape. His warm and nimble fingers massaged and stroked her absently as they walked. They caressed her, sending the tiniest flickers of magic into her veins. He always had an air of dominance when it came to holding her, with just that slight twist of indifference that set her skin on fire. It was always oddly arousing to be held in such a way, as if at any minute he could pull her into his arms and restrain her without any means of escape.

They walked slowly as they took in the scenery. The English countryside was beginning to awaken once more, and nature was stretching its arms up again in the form of the tiny green buds and delicate flowers that threatened to break free any second from their long winter sleep. It was one of Sapphire's favourite seasons here on her home planet. Shaka seemed to be in a permanent state of summer. It was almost tropical, and the air was different – thicker, with the dense magic that permeated the land there. She had not really noticed it so much before on her previous visits but today, on coming back to her real home, she could feel the immense difference between the two worlds she now coexisted in.

As they reached the end of the lane and stepped on to the gravel driveway that led to Pearl's cottage she felt another shift in the air. The distinct scent of magic ... magic that she was now beginning to easily identify. It seemed that her training had been more than useful.

Fox gripped her neck a little more tightly, as if he too sensed the change in the air at exactly the same time she had. His breathing shifted slightly, and she could have sworn that she heard him literally sniff the air into his nostrils like a dog would. She hoped he wouldn't shift suddenly into his animal form and take off into the woods with a yelp. That would be just too damn freaky.

"The magic is stronger than normal here, Sapphire. I can smell it and feel it in all my senses," he said. Sapphire frowned.

"Do you think something is wrong?" He shook his head and released his hand from her neck after stepping forward so quickly his image flickered for a second as he moved up a gear into vampire speed again.

"I don't think so, but wait here just a moment, my love," he said as he disappeared up the lane, leaving her standing alone like an abandoned child.

"Fox, really ... wait for me," Sapphire said. She pushed forward, using her magic, and found herself standing at Pearl's gate with Fox, who was actually scratching his head and looking puzzled.

"Her wards are up as usual, but they are stronger than normal. Something feels a little off."

Sapphire, eager to see her old friend now, shook her head. She was, quite frankly, fed up with feeling as if she was in a permanent state of trepidation. She placed her hand on the frame of the wooden gate but as she went to push it open she felt a cold, hard slap of pain kick up into her arm. It literally knocked her back and made her stumble.

"Ouch. That hurt," she yelped. Fox smiled as he tried not to laugh out loud.

"Your magic is too strong now, my love. Even you will need permission to enter now."

Sapphire had not even thought about that. She had always come and gone from this second home as she wished in the past. Things had certainly changed. As she rubbed her hand a little defensively she growled softly at Fox.

"Mmmh ... OK, I get it." Fox stepped up to the gate but did not touch it.

"Pearl! Pearl, we are back. Can you let us in, please? We would love to pay you a visit."

Everything seemed eerily quiet for a moment. Even the usual birdsong seemed to be absent today. Sapphire turned to her husband and frowned. He shrugged in response.

"Perhaps she is out in the woods again. Let's go and take a look." Just as they were about to retreat Sapphire felt another sharp sting to her cheek as if someone or something had slapped her.

"Ouch!" she yelled as she slapped her face, expecting a mosquito of the size of one from the Jurassic period to be squashed against her skin. She felt Fox switch into warrior mode. His energy rippled around him as he spun around in a defensive stance.

"What the hell was that?" she asked. Fox suddenly laughed loudly as he stepped back and raised his hand up into the air. He gradually began to refocus the shimmer of light that settled on his finger into a tiny sprite – complete with opaque wings and hair that stuck up at all angles in a bright red colour, which made him look like a matchstick. Sapphire watched the little creature do a virtual dance on Fox's finger, shaking its tiny fist and flapping its wings so fast that they blurred in and out of focus.

"OK, OK my friend, slow down. I cannot understand you if you speak so fast." Sapphire suddenly had a very bad feeling settle like a stone in the pit of her stomach. If one of Pearl's little helpers was outside the gate and attacking them in a fury, then something was most definitely amiss.

Fox was frowning now. His eyes started to widen, and his irises were glowing dark amber as if a furnace had just been lit within them. He nodded and released the sprite up into the air. It whizzed off in the direction of the woods at the back of Foxglove and made his hair lift up and away from his face as if a strong wind had hit him.

"What's going on, Fox? Tell me. I'm starting to freak out a little now." Fox regarded her solemnly.

"A gateway has opened in the tree in the woods, Sapphire. It is very powerful, and the sprite is worried that something has happened to Pearl. She has not been home since yesterday."

Sapphire did not hesitate. She literally transported herself by thought and will across the woodland to stand in front of the beautiful beech tree that had started her journey at the very beginning of it all. Fox appeared beside her. He too had used magic to reach the place the sprite had wanted them to go to. Sapphire stared up in awe at the tree before her. It was completely transformed and, quite clearly, something entirely magical now. It was surrounded by sprites that whizzed and spun around it, creating the illusion of a mini whirlwind that dipped and flowed around and around in a frenzy. It looked as if they were trying to get inside it. Fox placed his arm in front of Sapphire and pushed her back slightly, despite her need to get closer.

"Sapphire, you need to step away for a moment. This gateway is not stable. It is surrounded by an energy that I do not recognise. Someone is shielding it with magic that is not secure." Sapphire stared at him with her mouth open slightly.

"Is Pearl inside?" He shook his head in bewilderment.

"I don't know, but this is not right. The energy coming from the gateway feels strange, like a mixture of Pearl's magic intertwined with something else."

Sapphire walked away from him. She stepped back but turned to the side so that she could walk around to the other side of the trunk. Fox followed her, his magic spreading out around them both in a protective shield. The sprites were forming into a cluster now, spinning up and down like swallows riding on the thermals in a summer sky.

A buzzing in her ears began to make her skin tingle, and she felt her energy open up without her permission. Someone was trying to tap into her magic. Fox literally growled. He placed his hand against her chest and pushed her back again.

"Sapphire, get back. Step away now." She felt her energy flare deep within her chest, and her eyes flickered and rolled back for a moment as if a pressure so great was being forced upon her that she could not keep them open. She pressed the heels of her boots into the earth and pulled down deep into the ground with her magic as she looked for a way to anchor her energy before it spun out of her body and hit something. Fox was glowing brightly now. His face was alive with a fierceness she knew would only mean trouble for anyone who approached them.

The buzzing grew louder and louder and Sapphire pushed back against it, using all her new-found skills to stop her wild magic bursting free from her chest and exploding into the air around them.

She closed her eyes and focused, and imagined her energy as she had when Conloach had taught her how to create the energy ball and diffuse it into the ground.

Her body began to shake, and the ground beneath her began to tremble. Tiny clusters of earth shook free and rose up around her as if the whole woodland floor had been turned upside down. Leaves and stones rose before her in the air, as if they were on invisible strings being pulled up and over her head. Fox raised his arms and began to chant. He was desperate to help contain the situation, which was quickly escalating out of control. The tree before them glowed silver white, and the gateway the sprite had told them of appeared like an apparition that wavered against the trunk. Fox pushed against the magic that was surrounding them and roared loudly.

"Run, Sapphire, run," he shouted. Without hesitation Sapphire did just that, before she could harm him and the woodland around her. She took off at lightning speed, with her heels kicking up the dirt around her and the vegetation whizzing past her as she used her magic to propel her forward. She could hear a great roaring in her ears, as if the person trying to grab her magic was angered by her retreat. She did not look back, but focused on getting the hell out of there. She knew that Fox would not be far behind her.

The loud crack of a tree falling behind her made her hesitate for a second. It was followed by the sound of something snapping that sounded like metal on bone. Her chest felt as if it had been punctured by a knife, and she felt a drawing deep within her body that was pulling her backwards. It pulled hard and greedily against her as she ran. Her vision wavered, and she felt her chest constrict again as her body tried to fold in on itself. She fought against it by trying to move further away from this terrifying, unknown energy that was literally trying to eat her up. She could vaguely hear Fox yelling out behind her. His voice was breaking against the sound of the trees and the branches snapping around her as it pulled and pulled at her magic and her body.

Suddenly she felt a cold snap inside her head and the whisper of a voice in her mind. It was Pearl and she was crying out her name, over and over. Sapphire gave up the fight and turned around. She was damned if she was going to run away from this thing and leave her friend and her husband to battle it alone. After taking a deep lungful of air she screwed her face up. While narrowing her eyes and putting her head down she dug deep inside for her strongest ally. Her anger.

Sapphire held her hands before her and pushed her wild magic out into a blaze of flame. It turned purple and gold like a dragon's breath before her as she moved back towards the tree. Her eyes were wild with anger. She felt as if her feet were no longer on the ground, and she was floating above the grass like a ghost. Her anger fuelled her and steadied her all at the same time. She was prepared to meet this perpetrator head on and fuck him the hell up. How dare he harm her friend and her husband? She was not about to be pushed around, whoever or whatever this was.

What she was not prepared for as she moved back to the tree was the sight of her husband trapped on the floor in a bubble of light that was clearly causing him extreme pain. His body convulsed and twisted as if he was being blasted with bolts of electricity.

Her anger grew like a beast in her chest in response. She threw her magic at it, intending to break the magical cell he had been placed within. It flashed against the edges and scattered like fire across the ground, and sent another ripple through the earth beneath her feet. She heard Fox groan loudly, as if what she had done had only made things worse. Her eyes glowed and her hair, full of static and power, began to rise around her head.

Just as she was about to throw another bolt of energy at the shield she felt a shift in the magic pulsing around her. Pearl appeared out of nowhere to the side of Fox, who was still struggling on the floor. Her face was pale and she was clearly distraught. She looked at Sapphire with fear in her eyes and her hand raised, as if to stop her from moving closer. Sapphire stopped a few feet from them both and shook her head. She blinked her eyes and tried to regain some form of clarity as to what exactly was happening.

"Sapphire, stop. Please turn around leave this place. You are in great danger. Please, my child, leave us," Pearl begged. Sapphire frowned. Why would Pearl tell her to go and leave them when they were clearly in trouble?

The answer to all her confusion stepped out from behind the tree in all his magnificence. Gabriel, master of all gatekeepers, revealed himself in all his glory. He looked as if he was suddenly ten feet tall and built like a Greek god, and he strode forward with a satisfied smile on his lips. He raised his hand. With a flick of his wrist he removed the shield from around Fox, and threw a bolt of pure energy so powerful at him that it picked him up off the ground and tipped him up and over into the air so that he landed with a heavy crash and thud on the floor at her feet. He was out cold. Not even a whimper or groan left his lips as he lay at her feet. Pearl fell to her knees and flung her hands to her face as she cried out in fear.

"No! Please, Gabriel. Stop this. Stop this now." As she too dropped to her knees, grabbed Fox, and pulled him into her arms, Sapphire felt as if her heart had been crushed and pulled from her body. He was still alive, at least. His chest was rising and falling quickly, as if he had indeed just received the heaviest possible bolt of lightning to his heart. She trembled with rage.

"What are you doing, Gabriel, you fucking idiot? How dare you violate me and my husband, take my friend hostage, and try to steal my magic?" Her eyes stung with tears of her own. She could feel herself losing it now and, despite all the help she had received recently from Conloach and the Oracle, she knew that at any moment her magic could explode out from within her – and, quite frankly, obliterate them all. Nuclear was not even close to how she felt right now. It would be messy and it would be final. End of.

Gabriel smirked ... actually *smirked* at her.

"Sapphire ... my dear, dear Sapphire. You are so utterly fabulous in your most basic and raw form. Mesmerising in, fact." Sapphire held Fox within her arms and tried to push some of her magic into him to help him heal without burning his head off.

"Oh, shut up, Gabriel. Shut the fuck up. What have you done to Pearl? And why, for God's sake? What do you think you are going to achieve by opening up this gateway and scaring the hell out of my friend? Do you think I am going to just let you get away with this? I am not your little servant like Hecta, who you can push around and plug into for an energy boost whenever you feel like it."

He laughed. Gabriel threw his head back and laughed. He reached for Pearl and pulled her up and gathered her into his arms as if she was his most beloved object. Sapphire felt Fox stir beneath her. His breathing changed slightly and his muscles twitched back to life.

"Oh ... But, Sapphire, you have already given me more than enough to serve my purpose today. Your anger really does amplify your magic beautifully, doesn't it? Hecta did tell me just how magnificent you could become when your emotional buttons were pushed." Sapphire took a deep breath and flicked her eyes to Fox quickly before looking up again. He was waking up. Thank the gods.

"What do you want, Gabriel?" Fox opened his eyes. A look of confusion and then anger flashed across them. Sapphire twitched her head at him to remain still. His hand gripped her sleeve tightly in response.

"I am taking Pearl with me through the gateway. But I could not do it without you, Sapphire, and now you have very kindly opened up your glorious magic and given me what I needed to complete the process." Fox shook his head.

"It will kill her, Sapphire," he said. "Do not let him take her. Her magic is not strong enough to take her across the dimensions," he whispered. Gabriel tipped his head to one side as if sizing them both up.

"Ah, and there is the choice, young dream traveller. Do you allow me to take her, with a generous gift of your magic? Or do you kill her by being totally selfish and making me drag her through unwillingly, just to see if I can do it on my own? Eh? The decision is yours." He paused, and stroked the back of Pearl's head lovingly.

"Or I could always just take her and then come back for your other friend ... the young woman carrying the child in her womb who has the distinct signature scent of your magic, Sapphire. Would you like that instead?"

Sapphire stood up so quickly that Fox dropped to the floor again and groaned as his head hit the ground. She strode forward until she was merely a few feet from Gabriel. Her body was trembling and her eyes were fiery. Pearl turned her head and looked at her with sad but suddenly calm eyes. She smiled at her and pushed away from Gabriel slightly so that she could face her friend. Gabriel held her to him and took a small step back.

"Sapphire, do not let him take your magic, my dear," Pearl said. "It is not for this purpose. Let me go now if he wants to take me, and I will either find my way across or move on to the next life. I am not afraid, child." Sapphire staggered backwards slightly. Her heart was thumping in her chest.

"No. No, Pearl, I will not let you go like this. He has no right to do this to you." Her bottom lip began to tremble as she watched her frail but powerful friend before her become helpless within the arms of her old lover. Fox was suddenly by her side with his hand on her arm.

"Sapphire, my love, have a care as to what you do next," he said.

Gabriel's eyes turned stormy. The icy blue of his irises had been replaced by white snow that swirled and spun as if a great cloud was rising within them and was about to smash through like an avalanche. Pearl smiled softly.

"It is my time, child. I am ready. Go back to Foxglove and take care of my sprites. They will need you now, for it will be your home once I am gone." Sapphire felt as if her whole world was collapsing around her. Everything was slowly turning in on itself in some strange, mad nightmare that could not be real.

"No. No, Pearl," she sobbed. Fox grabbed her, and pulled her back suddenly as Gabriel opened up his magic to its full force. She watched in horror as he moved back towards the gateway within the trunk of the tree. His smile grew wider and his eyes lit up.

"So be it, Sapphire. I feel I have enough of your magic to take the risk. Be it on your head if she does not survive. But I thank you if she does. For I love this woman, and will not give her up. Not again. Not ever."

And with that he stepped back into the doorway that had opened behind them with Pearl wrapped within his arms. They disappeared in a flash of pure white brilliant light that lit up the woodland like sheet lightning.

The only sound that Sapphire could hear at that moment was of her own voice screaming out into the air in pure terror, in realisation that she had just unwittingly and most likely killed her most beloved friend, and there was nothing she could do about it.

Epilogue

Mother Earth shuddered at the great shift in magic that trembled throughout her body. The transition had begun, and at last her body was beginning to awaken again. A great sacrifice had taken place to allow this most wonderful process to begin. She smiled and felt a wave of both pure love and great sadness fill her body once more as the balance of both light and dark flexed and filled her to the core. The first stages of enlightenment for her people had now begun, and the gateways were opening.

She knew that the magical creature she had sensed some time ago would aid her well, and continue this process across her beautiful world. It was only a matter of time now before the magic she held deep within her was released once more, and life would blossom and flourish in a way it had not done in a very long time.

The blend of two types of magic coming together at the same time within one of the gateways had started the process, and she knew it had come at a heavy price. She could feel the ripple of energy travel down deep into her womb and ignite in an explosion of light. It had been such a unique blend of two souls from two different worlds, who were interlaced with a love so great that it had created a new spark within her.

Sometimes a great sacrifice had to be made to create something new. The fire deep inside her flickered and grew, slowly at first, like the smallest ember in a fire that had just been lit.

But it was the beginning. The beginning of something wonderful.

Printed in Great Britain
by Amazon